FEB **17** 2018

Also by Marie Harte

THE MCCAULEY BROTHERS
The Troublemaker Next Door
How to Handle a Heartbreaker
Ruining Mr. Perfect
What to Do with a Bad Boy

BODY SHOP BAD BOYS
Test Drive
Roadside Assistance
Zero to Sixty
Collision Course

THE DONNIGANS
A Sure Thing
Just the Thing

All I Want for Halloween

D0972086

FEB 17 2018

COLLISION COURSE

MARIE HARTE

sourcebooks
casablanca

Copyright © 2018 by Marie Harte
Cover and internal design © 2018 by Sourcebooks, Inc.
Cover art by Craig White

Sourcebooks and the colophon are registered trademarks of Sourcebooks, Inc.

All rights reserved. No part of this book may be reproduced in any form or by any electronic or mechanical means including information storage and retrieval systems—except in the case of brief quotations embodied in critical articles or reviews—without permission in writing from its publisher, Sourcebooks, Inc.

The characters and events portrayed in this book are fictitious or are used fictitiously. Any similarity to real persons, living or dead, is purely coincidental and not intended by the author.

All brand names and product names used in this book are trademarks, registered trademarks, or trade names of their respective holders. Sourcebooks, Inc., is not associated with any product or vendor in this book.

Published by Sourcebooks Casablanca, an imprint of Sourcebooks, Inc.
P.O. Box 4410, Naperville, Illinois 60567-4410
(630) 961-3900
Fax: (630) 961-2168
sourcebooks.com

Printed and bound in Canada.
MBP 10 9 8 7 6 5 4 3 2 1

To D&R, I love you.

Chapter 1

"TWO DOZEN RED ROSES AND I'M SORRY I SCREWED your sister?" Josephine "Joey" Reeves stared at the thirtysomething guy in front of her counter, thinking she must have misheard him.

"Yeah, that doesn't sound so good." He sighed, finger-combed back his trendy bangs, and frowned. "I was going to go with 'Sorry I fucked your sister,' but that's a little crude. Probably just 'I slept with your sister,' right? That's better."

She blinked, wondering at his level of stupidity. "Um, well, how about ending at just 'I'm sorry'?"

He considered that and nodded. "Hey, yeah. That'll work. Do I need to sign the card? Maybe you could write that for me. My handwriting sucks."

So does your ability to be in a committed relationship. Joey shrugged. "It's your call. But if it were me, I'd prefer a note from the person who's sorry, not from the woman selling him flowers."

Her customer brightened and chose a note card from the stack on the counter. "Good call. Hey, add another dozen while you're at it. She loves roses."

Joey tallied up the order while he signed the card, then took it from him. The guy really did have crappy handwriting. After he paid and left, she tucked the note into the folder of orders due to go out in another hour. For a Monday afternoon, the day had gone as expected and then some. The store hadn't been chock-full of customers, but it hadn't been empty either. Late spring in Seattle had most people out and about working on their gardens, not inside shopping for hothouse blooms.

Still, enough anniversaries, birthdays, and relationship disasters had brought a consistent flow of customers into S&J Floral to make Stef, Joey's boss, more than happy.

Joey hummed as she organized, thrilled that she'd gotten the hoped-for promotion to manager that morning. She'd worked her butt off for it, and that diligence had paid off. She wanted to sing and dance, proclaim her triumph to the masses.

Except it was just her, Tonya in the back putting together floral arrangements, and a random half-dozen shoppers perusing the store. It had been Joey's idea to add some upscale gifts to their merchandise. Buying teddy bears, pretty glass ornaments, and knickknacks went hand in hand with buying flowers. S&J had seen a boost in revenue since last December when they'd implemented the big change.

Thank God it had worked. Joey appreciated Stef taking a risk by believing in her. And now…a promotion to manager and a $50K salary! With this money, she and Brandon could finally move out of her parents' place and start fresh, away from the history of mistakes her family never let her forget. She couldn't wait to tell her best friend Becky the good news.

Determined to start over again, Joey dug into her orders and updated delivery times, getting in touch with their new delivery guy, a cute twenty-year-old who'd no doubt soon be rolling in tips.

"Well, hello there."

She glanced up from the counter and froze.

"You work here?" A large grin creased a face she'd tried hard to forget.

The man who'd been haunting her sleep, who'd dogged her through a wedding and sizzled her already-frazzled nerves, looked even better in the hard light of day.

"H-hello." She coughed, trying to hide the fact that her voice shook. When she could breathe without hyperventilating, she said, "Sorry. What can I do for you today?"

The look he shot her had her ovaries doing somersaults and her brain shutting clean off.

The first time she'd seen him had been on a visit to her first wedding client ever, and she'd been *floored*. The guys who worked at Webster's Garage all looked larger than life, covered in tattoos, muscles, and that indefinable sense of danger they wore like a second skin. But it had been this guy. Webster's paint specialist. The tall Latin lover with dark-brown eyes and lips made for kissing, who had snared her.

He had a way of raising one brow in question or command that turned her entire body into his personal cheering section.

"…for some flowers. I dunno. Something that looks like I put thought into it?"

Focus, Joey. Be professional. This isn't personal. Don't get all gooey on the man. "Ah, budget?"

He sighed. "For Stella, it has to be decent. Girl is like a human calculator when it comes to anything with value. If I skimp, she'll know," he said, still grinning. He took the binder she slid to him and leafed through the floral selections. "I'm Lou Cortez, by the way."

"I remember." He'd only introduced himself once, months ago in the garage while she'd been going over flower choices with his boss. But Joey had never forgotten those broad shoulders, chiseled chin, or bright white smile. Wow, was he too hot to handle.

She'd kept her distance—or at least tried to. She'd been invited to the wedding, having become friends with the bride. Of course, all the woman's employees had been invited as well. Joey had done her best to steer clear of the man women seemed to drool over. Talk about trouble she didn't need.

She realized he'd stopped looking through the binder and was staring straight at her. More like through her. Wow. How did he do that? Bring so much concentration and intensity, she felt as if his gaze reached out and wrapped around her, holding her still?

And why, when confronted with all that masculinity, did she want to stammer and obey any darn thing he said? She had to force herself to be strong, to speak. But she just stared, mute, at so much male prettiness.

His smile deepened. "And *your* name would be…?" God, a dimple appeared on his left cheek.

A dimple. Kill me now. Breathe, dummy. You can handle this. It's business. "Oh, right. I'm Joey."

"You don't look like a Joey," he murmured.

Her heart raced, and she forced herself to maintain eye contact. "Short for Josephine. So the flowers. Did you find anything you like?"

A loaded question, because his slow grin widened as he looked her over. Then he turned back to the binder and shook his head. "Nah. I need something original. Do you design bouquets?"

"Yes." More comfortable on a professional level, she nodded. "We have some amazing florists and—"

"No. *You*. Do you put flowers together?"

"Yes."

"Good. I want you to do it." He shrugged. "Del, my boss at Webster's, you remember her?"

She nodded. How could she forget the woman with such cold gray eyes, tattoo sleeves, and funky ash-blond hair braided in twists? The same woman she'd made friends with not long after meeting. Heck, she'd attended Del's wedding.

"She said you were amazing. My sister needs something amazing right now."

The flowers were for his sister. *Oh man. He's sexy as sin, he has a body to die for, and now he's buying flowers for* his sister?

She softened toward him. "Do you know her favorite flower or color? A scent maybe? Did you want sophisticated or simple? How old is she?"

"Ah, something cool. I don't know. She's gonna be twenty-three." He rattled off a few ideas, and she made quick notes.

"I can have this for you by…" She paused to check the computer. "Tomorrow. Would that work?"

"Hell. I really need them today. Her birthday isn't until Friday, but she got some shitty news, so I wanted to give them to her when I see her later. I'm willing to pay extra, no problem."

Adding *charming* and *thoughtful* to the Lou List, Joey did her best not to moon over the man and kept a straight face. "Well, if you can wait until the end of the day, I'll try to fit them in. We close at seven. Is that okay?"

His face broke out into a relieved smile. "*Gracias*, Joey. You're doing me a huge favor."

Ignoring his smile, she called on her inner manager. "Well, you're doing something nice for your sister. And I know all about crappy days."

"Yeah?" He leaned closer, and she caught a waft of motor oil and crisp cologne, an odd blend of manly and sexy that nearly knocked her on her ass. "Who tried to ruin your day, sweetheart? I can fix that."

She blew out a shaky breath and gave a nervous laugh. "Ah, I just meant I've had those kinds of days before. Not now. It's just a regular Monday for me." A great Monday, considering her promotion.

He didn't blink, and she felt positively hunted.

"Well, if anyone gives you any trouble, you let me know, and I can talk to them for you. Nobody should mess with a woman as pretty and nice as you." He stroked her cheek with a rough finger before she could unglue herself from the floor and move away.

Then he glanced at the clock behind her, straightened, and said something in Spanish. "Sorry, Joey." Her name on his lips sounded like a caress. "Gotta go. I'll be back at seven to pick them up, okay? Thanks. I owe you."

"You don't owe me anything. I mean, I'll probably have to charge you extra for the sudden notice. It's a rush order," she blurted, not wanting him to think she was giving him special favors.

"I'll pay, no problem." He slid a card toward her. "My number in case something comes up with the flowers. Or a customer bothers you." He nodded to it. "You're a sweetheart. I'll see you soon."

He left, and she could breathe again. Still processing

the overwhelming presence that had been Lou Cortez—mechanic, paint expert, and all-around heartthrob—Joey tried to calm her racing heart.

One of their regulars plunked a few items on the counter, her blue eyes twinkling, her white hair artfully arranged around her face. "Don't know how you let that one get away. If I was a few years younger, I'd have been all over him." She waggled her brows. "Then again, he looked like he might be open to an octogenarian with loads of experience. Think he'd mind if you gave me his number?"

They both laughed, even as Joey tucked the card into her pocket and rang up Mrs. Packard's items. The thing burned in her pocket, a link to a man she knew better than to step a foot near. She'd throw it away after he picked up his flowers. Joey had made mistakes with a charmer a long time ago, and she had no intention of ever going down that road again.

~~~

"Aw. Come on, baby. Don't be like that." Silence, then the groveling of a man who'd done wrong echoed through the garage bay, adding a jolt of much-needed humor to Lou's late Monday misery. Sam continued to apologize into his cell phone. "Okay, okay. I swear I'll take you to that stupid party. Ivy…" Sam sighed. "Yeah, I know. I'm sorry."

Lou snorted. Some men didn't know a thing about women. Like the dickhead who'd just dumped his younger sister. Lou wanted to bend the guy into a pretzel, and he hadn't liked the SOB to begin with. Good riddance. Then take his buddy Sam, still groveling into the phone. Before the guy had hooked up with his girlfriend,

he couldn't talk to, compliment, or even look at a woman
without sounding like a Neanderthal. Thank God Ivy had
managed to kick his ass into gear. Now the giant with a
jaw like granite was apologizing—with sincerity.

Lou glanced out from under the hood of his current
project, wishing they weren't down two mechanics this
afternoon. But with one guy helping his mother with
something and the other at the dentist, it was up to Lou
and Sam to take care of the afternoon schedule. Three
rush jobs didn't help either, but at least oil changes
didn't take as much time as this shitty Chrysler he'd
swear was possessed. And, lucky him, its owner had
asked for Lou by name.

Sam finished his phone call and disconnected, tossing
his cell on his cluttered workbench. He glanced around,
saw that Lou had been listening to every pathetic word
he'd uttered, and flushed.

"Yo, jackass. Get the lead out," Sam barked. "Del
said we have to finish the LeBaron and Grand Am by
the end of the day if we want to stick Foley on Blue
Altima tomorrow."

Blue Altima—a car he loathed like nobody's business. The damn thing had been in and out of the shop
three times in the past six months, and no one liked
working on it or dealing with the pain-in-the-ass owner.
An old woman who ate bitch pills for breakfast.

"I'm all over it," he muttered.

Lou had been raised by his mother, his grandmother,
and five aunts. He had five sisters and thirteen female
cousins—who lived *way* too close by—and he'd been
working for Delilah McCauley since her father had all
but retired.

Lou respected women. He *loved* women.

Yet Patsy Sidel did nothing but bitch about her car, no matter how many times the crew and Del had begged her to trade it in for one that worked.

No, he had no urge to deal with Mrs. Sidel. Not when he had his mind full of another woman with no time for him or his charming ways, which frankly baffled him.

He swore as he busted his knuckles against a stubborn bolt, the pain right up there with the headache brewing anytime he thought about Josephine—Joey—Reeves.

It continued to confuse the hell out of him that the one woman he'd had his eye on for months still refused to respond to his obvious appeal, handsome good looks, and killer grin.

He swore some more as he fought with the spark plugs on his current project, his thoughts on a sexy brunette who spooked if he so much as took a step in her direction.

What the hell had happened? It was like he'd fallen into an alternate reality. His badass boss had snagged a decent guy, complete with a kid and a dog. His fellow mechanics, all gruff, tatted, and coarse, had scored sweethearts. Even the boss's dad had a fine woman who thought he hung the moon. And Liam was an all-around bruiser.

But Lou—the best-looking and smartest of the bunch—could barely get a smile from the chick he'd been digging?

He'd first seen her when she'd timidly stepped into the garage, months ago, asking for Del. His entire world had centered on that one moment, and it was like the fucking sun had spotlighted the petite brunette, showcasing the perfect woman in the center of his world.

Then she'd scurried by him, not looking much at any of the guys, as a matter of fact, and disappeared into Del's office. Joey had come by a few times after that to deal with Del and flowers for her wedding. But somehow she managed to avoid being anywhere near Lou.

The guys thought it hilarious, since he'd made his interest clear. Even Del questioned what had happened to Lou's famous ability to charm women. What made it even worse? Del liked the chick, and she'd invited Joey to hang at the wedding as a guest.

Again, he'd been denied. He'd tried talking to her only to have her stammer and light out as if her hair had caught fire. Then she'd disappeared when he'd tried to ask if she was okay.

Sheer luck had brought him into her shop today, inspired by the idea of getting his sister flowers to celebrate her breakup with a major asshole. Of course, Stella wouldn't see it that way. But he did.

He sighed. Josephine Reeves. Demure. Sleek and pretty. *Joey* had a tiny frame, gently curved in all the right places though. Her mink-brown hair curled around her shoulders, long and thick. She had pretty features, nothing too remarkable. Lou had been with knockouts. Women with huge breasts and round asses, thick thighs, muscular frames, blonds, redheads, you name it.

But for some reason, Joey Reeves and her tiny hands, less-than-a-handful breasts, and slender figure got him harder than steel. Just thinking about her brought out all the dominant instincts he'd made good use of since he'd first taken a woman to bed.

Man, the thought of all he wanted to do to her...
Touching her in the store hadn't been smart, but he hadn't
been able to stop himself. Finally, they'd had a face-to-
face conversation. More than the physical attraction, just
being around her made his heart do weird somersaults.
He'd felt happy just being near all that sweetness.

And he had another couple of hours until he'd get to
see her again.

He smiled and chuckled, wondering if she'd try to
pawn him off on another employee. Not that it mattered.
He planned to seduce the woman into a date if it was the
last thing he ever—

"Shoot, Lou." A husky female voice jarred him from
his fantasies. "My father works faster than you anymore."

He jolted, scraping across that damn bolt again and
bleeding over the engine. "You need to wear a bell."

"No kidding." Liam, Del's father, didn't sound happy.
No doubt insulted that his daughter had compared him
to Lou. "For the record, I'm still a better mechanic than
any of the dickheads in here." He flashed a satisfied
smile. "No offense, Lou, Sam."

Sam grunted.

"What he said." Lou swore under his breath, cra-
dling his stinging hand.

Like the rest of the guys who worked in the shop,
Liam Webster wore his brawn well. Six-two and
built like a brick, the guy looked and acted a decade
younger than his sixty years. Hell, Lou was no push-
over, but he had no intention of ever going up against
Liam. The old man looked like the type to fight dirty.
With a daughter like Del, he no doubt knew how to
handle conflict.

On a regular basis.

Del *McCauley*, now that she'd married Mr. White Picket Fence, looked good wearing a gold band on her finger. Other than the ring, going home daily at five, and smiling all the damn time, his boss hadn't much changed. Then again, it had only been a week since she'd officially become a Mrs.

Lou realized Liam had used the word *dickhead* and Del hadn't laid into him. "So we can swear again?"

"Yeah." Liam blew out a breath. "Now that my princess snagged herself a man and is living in wedded bliss, the rest of us are free to talk like normal people."

Prior to her wedding, Del had pronounced the garage "swear-free" for months in an effort not to swear at her own wedding.

"It worked, Dad." Del grinned. "I didn't say one fucking thing wrong."

"Ah, there's my girl." Liam hefted a beefy arm over her shoulder and squeezed until she squeaked.

Lou grinned. Del really was a cute Amazon. "You two taking off?" The time had reached five already.

Only two more hours until he got to visit his own *princesa*.

"Yep. Time for this old man and his daughter to go home. I'm eating at the McCauleys' tonight." Liam beamed.

Must be a great thing to see his daughter married to a decent guy and into a hella nice family. Lou constantly struggled to keep his sisters in line and his cousins from going off the deep end when it came to men and bad choices.

"Oh?" Lou wiped his hands on a dirty rag to stanch the bleeding.

"God, Lou. Stop." Del marched off and returned with a clean rag and bandage. "Use these."

Lou used the rag to take care of the excess blood, then slapped the bandage on his throbbing knuckle. "Check that, Liam. Your baby girl is all domesticated. Want to kiss it and make it better, Del?"

She flipped him off, and they laughed. "Don't work too hard, Lou." Del shook her head and darted a sly look his way. "Wouldn't want to be too late when you pick up those flowers for your sister."

"How the hell do you know that?"

She shrugged. "I know all and see all, Cortez. Remember that." She huffed. "And make sure to tell Heller to stop hogging all your time when you see him tomorrow. I need you in here too, you know."

"Yeah, yeah." Lou worked for Del mostly, but his paint work he did through Heller's shop. Heller's Paint and Body—which had read Heller's Paint and Auto Body before the *Auto* fell off the sign—specialized in high-end paint jobs, and Lou got a real kick out of creating works of art with wheels.

"I'm not kidding. I don't care how big or mean Heller thinks he is. You belong to me." She scowled, then turned on her heel and stalked back to the office.

Liam shook his head. "Be nice when you tell him that."

"Oh, I will." Only a man courting death mouthed off to Heller.

Liam followed his daughter out of the garage.

"Tell Heller what to do? I don't think so." Lou snorted, heard Sam's mumble of agreement, and got back to work.

Heller had first been his boss, but now Lou considered

the guy a friend. A lot like the jack-holes working in Webster's, Heller had size, muscles, and a toughness brought about by a hard life. He also had a stare that could shrivel a guy in seconds. In addition to his fierce physique, the guy had a brain like a computer. Heller didn't say much, but when he did, people listened. He was fucking smart *and* lethal.

He also looked like an angry Nordic god, and his scowls sent most people running in the opposite direction. Lou didn't mind and liked the guy just fine.

"Del said you're working at Heller's tomorrow?" Sam asked.

"Yeah." Lou went back to finishing the Chrysler. He had to get started on that next oil change. They didn't make any money off the routine jobs, but they kept clients happy and coming back because they did everything for the car. Easy stuff, but Lou also had another to finish before he could leave to get to Joey's flower shop on time.

"He's not a bad guy." Sam didn't say any more.

Done with his project, Lou drove the Chrysler outside, took the Grand Am into the bay, and readied it for an oil change.

"Helped me out with Senior a while back," Sam continued, his deep voice like the growl of an angry bear. And that was Sam in a good mood. The guy had huge arms tatted from his wrists to his shoulders and up his neck. His scruffy cheeks showed him regrowing a beard and 'stache. Sam didn't laugh much, but he smiled more since dating Ivy than he had in the three years Lou had known him.

Sam didn't like many people. The gang at the garage,

Ivy, and J.T.—Del's brother. And now…Heller? "Heller helped you out?"

Like Sam, Heller could be particular about those he called friend. Lou drained the oil, waiting for Sam to continue.

Sam told him about a fight at a popular bar they frequented and about how Heller had stepped in to keep things mostly fair. Meaning Sam kicked the asses of four douchebags while Heller made sure no one brought a gun to the fight.

Sam looked away from the engine he was working on. "Make sure to tell him the next beer at Ray's is on me. The plan is to head there Friday night."

"Nobody told me." Lou scowled.

"I'm telling you now, Romeo. Try to get a life and show up. Or is your mom still keeping you in on curfew?"

Lou cursed him in Spanish, getting an honest-to-God laugh out of Sam. Freaky. "Are you on drugs? What's with all the cheer, man?"

"It's called love, Lou. You ought to give it a try. With just one woman, I mean."

"Funny." Lou changed out the filter, then took the oil pan and dumped it in the drum in the back. He returned, put on the new filter, cleaned up the undercarriage, then finished refilling the oil and putting the vehicle to rights.

Sam, being Sam, refused to let it go. "Of course, since you're still panting after Del's flower chick, maybe you're actually gonna follow my advice, huh? Doing your best to find some love, Casanova? Except the chick is smart and sees right through all that charming shit that normally works." Sam smiled. Again.

"You got a point to make, Mr. Mouth?"

"Nope. I'm done. Heading home to Ivy for dinner." Sam sounded more than satisfied, and Lou couldn't blame him. He liked Ivy, the sweet thing. Though he still had no idea what a cutie like her was doing with a thug like Sam.

Sam left the bay to hang up his coveralls and grab his jacket. He returned to the bay, then parted with, "Hey, Lou, you ever find a date, we'll double. How about that?"

"Fuck off, Hamilton."

"Eat shit and die, Cortez." Sam left, whistling.

The bastard.

Noting the time, Lou hustled to finish his last oil change. He cleaned then locked up after himself. Nothing he could do about the bloody bandage or smell of oil coating him like cheap cologne.

He raced to the flower shop, praying she'd waited an extra ten minutes past closing.

Not that it mattered. He'd still give Stella a shoulder to cry on, even without the flowers. If Joey had gone home, he'd have to swing by the next day. Or the next. It wasn't that Lou would resort to harassing the woman. But if she'd just give him a chance to show her how much fun he could be, he knew he'd have a shot at seeing the real Joey Reeves.

Preferably in just the skin God gave her.

He groaned, now aroused again, and did his best to think clean thoughts as he motored through traffic to win a certain *princesa* needing a white knight. Or, at least, a slightly tarnished one.

Chapter 2

JOEY GLARED AT HER PHONE, NOT PLEASED TO STILL BE stuck hanging around the shop fifteen minutes past closing. She'd already texted her mother, but since Brandon had been invited to dinner with a friend, she didn't have to pick him up until eight anyway. She would have texted Lou to see what had held him up, but if she did that, he'd have her personal number.

What to do, what to do... Oh, screw it. Lou Cortez could just—

A car zoomed into the parking lot in front of the store. A sleek, highly polished, dark-purple muscle car. A Camaro maybe? She had no idea. But the thing had been custom designed for sure. She stared in wonder at the lifelike cobra subtly shimmering on the back side panel before the car turned to park and she couldn't see the image anymore. Artwork like that had to cost a fortune. No amateur spray painting. Lou's car would look totally at home at a car show.

He stepped out in the same jeans and gray tee he'd been wearing earlier, complete with black boots and a black denim jacket. What would look casual on anyone else looked spectacular on Lou. All he needed to turn himself into an advertisement for the ideal man's man would be a woman on each arm, a beer in hand, and that amazing smile he'd turned on her earlier.

He hustled up to the front door and knocked,

peering inside past the closed sign and tugging at the locked door.

She sighed, went to the front, and opened the door. "You're late." Oh yeah. Manager Joey was sticking to her guns. Joey had no time for those who didn't stick to her schedule, sexy smile or not.

He held up his hands in surrender, and she noticed a big bandage on one that hadn't been there before. "*Lo siento*. I'm so sorry. Totally my fault, but the sludge in Johnson's car made the oil take forever to come out. And my boss is a total hardass. If I hadn't gotten that last oil job done, I'd be working on Blue Altima tomorrow, and that car is straight-up cursed." He spoke fast, his accent thick.

"Blue Altima?"

He shivered. "You have no idea how many fingers, wrists, and arms I've busted with that thing." He held up his bandaged hand. "This is nothing. I'm really, really sorry I'm late. I swear. I broke a few speeding records to get here."

Familiar with the city traffic, she well knew it could take twenty minutes to go a mile in this town, even after rush hour on a Monday. She tried to hold onto her mad, but he'd talked so fast and looked so earnest, she couldn't. "Come on. I'll get you the flowers." *And then you can leave and not come back.*

Behind her, he seemed to loom. Joey was on the short side, and Lou had to stand a few inches over six feet. He made her feel downright tiny. When she reached the counter, he started to follow her behind it.

She turned and automatically put a hand out before she could think about it.

He took an extra step before stopping, so that his warm, broad chest pressed against her palm. He glanced from the contact to her face, his expression impossible to read. But *intense* seemed to describe it well enough.

She blew out a breath and quickly lowered her hand. "Nobody goes behind the counter unless Stef says it's okay." Stef's orders, and Joey was nothing if not a stickler for the rules.

He took a step back and crossed his massive arms over his chest. "Stef?"

"My boss." And friend. The woman had taken a chance on a teenager, and unlike Joey's parents, Stef had never judged her for her choices. "There you go." She pointed to the flowers she'd put together in a square glass vase, sitting on the back counter.

"Oh man. Are those for Stella? They're perfect."

Seeing that he made no move to follow her back and that he seemed thrilled with her arrangement, she relaxed. "Purples, whites, and a few sprigs of pink to mix it up. It's lightly scented, a hint of lavender. You said she'd like that."

"Yeah." He whistled. "This should help ease the sting from the jackass who dumped her."

She cringed. "Ouch."

He looked back at her and smiled. "Nah. He was a jerk. She'll be much better off with someone else." He dug in his back pocket, pulled out his wallet, and slapped a card down. "Whatever it costs, it's worth it."

Joey rang him up, making no mention of the fact she hadn't charged him extra. As much as he bothered her, she couldn't hold being a good brother against him. She handed his card back, then waited for him to sign and *leave*.

He signed, then handed her back the slip.

But he didn't move, didn't even reach for the bouquet. "So, Joey."

Those eyes mesmerized her, and she quickly looked down and fiddled with his ticket. He had that bedroom stare she'd seen before, the one that invited a girl to take all her clothes off, lie back, and wait for the good times to roll. How sad that anytime she saw this man she barely knew, she thought of sex. Talk about needing to get back into the dating scene to cool her jets. Desperation did not a pretty girl make.

She wanted to look him back in the eye, to mouth something smart. She'd say, "So, Lou," and just pause the way he had. Except Manager Joey had left the building, and girlie, stupid, shy Joey took her place. She felt tongue-tied. *Crap*.

A regular customer, a person she talked to without fear of complication, and she had no problem conversing. The moment she felt that something intimate, that spark of desire for a man or a relationship, she turned shy. It was so weird and totally unlike the real Joey. And also a telling sign of whom she should steer clear of.

She blew out a breath, grabbed his flowers, then held them out to him, looking at him from under her lashes. Determined to be pleasant and get him out of the shop before she made a fool of herself, she forced a polite smile. "Here you go."

He took the flowers, his thumb grazing hers before she pulled away. "Hmm."

The heat from his hand sparked. She'd swear she felt the tingle in her toes. "Wh-what?"

"You're shy, aren't you?" He sounded amused.

"You have your flowers. Can you please just go?" Great. And now she was rude.

He laughed. "Not that shy. Easy, Joey. I'm leaving. I just wanted to thank you again for this." He nodded to the bouquet. "And for not charging me extra."

Oh man. He'd noticed.

She glanced at his face again and saw his satisfied smile. And something deep inside her woke, responding to the warmth in his expression.

In that deep voice that made her want to step out of her panties without being asked, he said, "Let me ask you something, then I'll go."

"What?" How to tell him no to a date and sound like she meant it…

"Do I scare you?"

She hadn't expected that. She stared up at him. "Huh?"

"Do you think I might hurt you?" he asked softly.

"No. I mean, I don't know. I don't think so, but I don't know you."

He cocked his head in study. "So if it's not that you're scared of me, maybe it's that I came on too strong?"

"You did?"

"Not that either. Hmm." He glanced at her hands on the countertop. "You married? Seeing someone?"

"No." Shoot. The smart thing would have been to say yes. "You know, technically we're closed. Don't you have somewhere else to be?"

"Tell you what. I'll go. But how about we meet for a cup of coffee tomorrow at noon? I'll even throw in something to eat if you want. Just as a way to say thank you for being so nice."

"It's no trouble. Don't worry about it." Her palms felt

sweaty. Sudden images flooded her mind's eye of them doing things she had no business thinking about. She felt her cheeks heat and looked down again. Man, she had gone too long without a date if she could get that hot and bothered off a few fantasies.

"I do worry about it. A Cortez always pays his debts," he said quietly, serious. "Joey, I'm not into harassing women. I've never had a problem getting a date." She could well believe that. "I just want a chance to get to know you and for you to get to know me. It's that simple."

She looked up again, only to see that dimple back in play, those eyes so liquid, so pretty. "If I say yes, will you stop bugging me and go home?"

From shy to too blunt. It was like she had a mental deficiency that only appeared around good-looking men, and this one in particular.

Lou laughed. "Yeah. Sure."

"Fine. Okay." *What? No.* Yet her mouth didn't seem to be conferring with her brain before spouting random words.

"Perfect. How about Nichols Caffè Bar next to the garage? Will NCB work?"

"Oh. I love their bear claws." *Stop talking!*

"I'll make sure to grab one for you."

Unable to say anything else without coming across as a complete fool, she looked beyond him to the door.

He chuckled, took his flowers, and paused at the doorway, not looking back at her. Over his shoulder, he said, "You have my number if you want to back out. I only want a chance to get to know you, but I'm okay with the word 'no.' You don't show for coffee, I won't bug you again. But I hope I see you tomorrow, *princesa.*"

She watched him leave, her gaze drawn to that amazing ass until the door closed behind him. Food and a handsome man to watch while she ate.

What the hell was she thinking?

No. No. No.

After closing up the shop, she drove home in a daze. Joey hadn't been on a date in months, the last guy a two-dinner wonder before she couldn't take his small talk and überpoliteness anymore. Though she hadn't been shy with Jim, she hadn't been that attracted to him either. And before him, Adam had been the same. Predictably boring. What was wrong with her that only assholey, strong men flipped her switch? With them, she turned shy, flirty, lusty.

God, lusty. She missed sex so much—but only with a powerful man.

She was smart enough to steer clear of abusive jerks. Intelligent, savvy, worldly at the young age of twenty-four because she'd had to be, Joey had a brain she used daily. Well, maybe not tonight, saying yes to Lou Cortez.

Desiring a man so far out of her league, one who was clearly older and who might as well have *trouble* tattooed on his forehead, should have warned her off. God, he'd had her feeling nervous, excited, and aroused in the same breath. That turbulent feeling she got when in the presence of a man she knew would be bad for her. Oh, so *bad*.

She shivered. Apparently she hadn't learned that much after all. Because she'd said yes to coffee. He'd even given her an out, told her she had only to call and beg off and he wouldn't bother her again. A man who made her want, who made her feel things—not just physically but emotionally as well—and, yes, scared her, would go away if she asked him to.

Go away? That she didn't want. Not yet.

Oh hell. He's F-I-N-E fine, and I want to spend a little more time with him. It's not like I'm doing anything more than coffee and a bear claw. The pastry made everything worth it. Because, of course, it was all about the bear claw.

She neared the house before remembering she had to pick up Brandon at his friend Kyle's. She drove by, thanked Kyle's family for having Brandon for dinner, then took her boy home.

"So then he spilled the milk, and his mom called him an asshole."

Joey gaped at her third grader before turning her gaze back to the road. "Brandon!"

"Sorry, but that's what she said. Under her breath, kind of. But I heard it, Mom."

"Carly called Kyle a bad word?" Funny, PTA secretary Carly hadn't seemed the type.

"No, she said that to Bob, Kyle's dad."

"You mean Mr. Sorenson."

"No, they said to call them Carly and Bob." Brandon grinned. "But Carly called him an asshole for daring Kyle to snort milk out his nose."

She stifled a laugh. "Brandon, watch your mouth."

"Sorry." Under his breath he added, "Not sorry."

She rolled her eyes. "So what did you do after school?"

As her son launched into a fascinating tale involving Kyle's tadpoles and an epic experiment with a dirty dog, she couldn't help thinking about how her life might have gone differently if she'd done everything her parents wanted. In Andrew and Amy Reeves's imagined world, she'd have graduated college with a fancy degree, been making six figures, and made rounds with Ivy Leaguers before settling down with a millionaire CEO.

Instead, she had the best kid in the world, a management gig at S&J, and no Mr. Right in sight. And that suited her just fine. She didn't count coffee with Lou as anything more than a thank-you. She wouldn't *let it* be anything more.

After they returned home and Brandon finally stopped talking, she had him wash his face and brush his teeth to get ready for bed. Lots to do before he could sleep in their one-bedroom apartment above her parents' garage.

"I'll be right back," she told him. "I just need to talk to Grandma about something."

"Okay, Mom," he said through toothpaste. She managed to translate a bunch of grunting and slurred words to "I'll get a story and wait in bed."

Joey walked down the side stairs then around the garage to the back door to the house. Just as soon as she could, she'd find them their own place. She'd been living at home forever. As a single mom on her salary in Seattle, Joey knew owning a home was nothing more than a distant dream. And renting something in a decent area? Nearly impossible. Having her mother watch Brandon after school had been a blessing she never took for granted.

Joey did her best to be mindful of how much she relied on her mother. She hated feeling like a charity case. Not that her mother seemed to mind. Now. Amy Reeves loved Brandon more than anything. *Heck, more than me,* Joey thought with a snort.

She found her parents in the kitchen, having dessert.

Her father was addicted to chocolate chip cookie dough ice cream. And yep, he was wolfing down a bowl and lecturing her mother about something, no doubt. Andrew Reeves had definite opinions on just about everything, yet twenty-five years after saying their I do's, the pair was still in love. Yeah, because those who judged together stayed together.

Feeling bad about mentally dissing her parents, Joey cleared her throat and smiled at them.

They turned to her when she entered.

"Hi, guys. Brandon is brushing his teeth before heading to bed. I just wanted to say thanks for taking him to Carly's, Mom. He had fun."

"Good." Amy smiled. "Want some ice cream, honey?"

"No thanks." She paused. "I have some good news."

"Oh?" Her father put his spoon down and gave her his undivided attention. A head supervisor at a medical clinic in town, he lived and breathed responsibility. The man had been supporting his family, always paying his bills, and working hard forever. She doubted he knew the meaning of the word *vacation*. She sure couldn't recall ever taking one with the whole family.

"Yeah." She felt nervous. "Today Stef told me I got the promotion. I'm the new manager, and that comes with a pay raise."

"Why, honey, that's wonderful." Her mother gave her a hug and a kiss, beaming.

Joey felt calm then nervous, as if she stood on a tight wire waiting to fall off. Her father remained quiet as he studied her.

"Manager, hmm? After seven years, I'd hope so." Then he added, "Congrats, honey. We're proud of you."

She blinked to keep her eyes dry. Her father so rarely said anything positive that she treasured the backhanded compliment. After a bit of chatter about her day, then her mother's morning spent doing medical transcription from home and her father's new doctors on staff, she left to go back to her place. She'd opened the back door when she realized she'd forgotten to mention an upcoming field trip to her mother. She shut the door and walked back toward the kitchen. When she heard her name mentioned, she slowed, still in the hallway out of sight.

"Manager." Her father grunted. "Jesus, she's been working in that dump since high school. She should be a full-out partner in the place."

"Andrew, Joey's done a terrific thing. Like you, she set a goal and met it. Before you know it, she'll be running her own set of flower shops. And be reasonable. She hadn't even been full-time until three years ago."

"Girl should have a master's and a decent job by now. Hell, we should be able to rent that unit out to help with the bills. Instead it's losing value."

A familiar grumble, but this time it hurt Joey. A lot.

"You know that's not true."

"We're not hurting for money, I know." He sighed. "I'm sorry. I just can't help wondering what would have happened if she'd kept her damn legs closed nine years ago."

"Andrew, take that back," her mother snapped. "I love my grandson, and I can't imagine a world without him."

"I didn't mean it like that," he said, his voice gruff. "I love Brandon too. I just meant I can't stand how she's screwed up her life. Her choices are so—"

Joey didn't wait around to hear any more. Wiping

tears from her cheeks, she eased her way out of the house, careful not to make a sound as she returned to her son.

It never went away. A mistake at fifteen continued to haunt her, nine years later. She'd made her peace with being a young single mother, and though she regretted giving her virginity to Brandon's father, she'd never regretted having her son since she'd first held him. Not once.

But her father couldn't see it that way. To him, Brandon was a sign of his daughter's massive screwup. She'd spent the past nine years playing by his rules, living on the straight and narrow, having maybe a dozen dates and hardly any sex. And still she could never do right by her father. Never work hard enough, succeed enough, unless she could go back and undo that one night with Felix.

The only thing her dad approved of had been her decision to have Felix sign away his rights to his son. Her then-boyfriend had wanted her to get an abortion, but she had never considered that a possibility. There were some days, early on in her pregnancy, when she'd wished she had. The straight-A honor student working toward a full ride to the University of Washington had instead given birth to a baby boy, gotten her GED, and taken multiple classes from community colleges ever since to earn a degree in business while also working and mothering full-time.

But none of that meant anything to her father. And never would.

She didn't know why she was surprised. She'd followed the rules her entire life. The one time she'd made an error in judgment, she'd paid for it and continued to pay for it with Andrew Reeves.

But she'd done something right. She entered her tiny unit and found Brandon in his twin bed across from hers, his Lego night-light on, his book open as he read and smiled at Brownie Bear's antics. Love swelled for her baby, who wasn't so little anymore.

No matter what her father said, Brandon was the best thing she'd ever done. And no amount of rule following or breaking would alter that.

She read to him before closing the book for bedtime.

"Good night, Brandon." She kissed his forehead.

He surprised her with a hug as he pulled her down and squeezed. "Love you, Mommy."

More tears, but these were happy, coming from a very warm place. "You too, baby."

He smelled of toothpaste and soap and little boy. She pulled back and stared into brown eyes just like hers. If not for his blond hair, there would be no trace of Felix in the child. But it didn't matter. Brandon held her heart as surely as if he remained a part of her, body and soul.

She left the single bedroom, closed the door, then entered the other room in her parents' unit. A small kitchenette, complete with a tiny sink, mini-fridge, and counter, lay along one wall. A table and chairs separated the kitchen area from the living space. In the compact living room, she sat on the dark-red couch, which made out into a bed, and propped her feet up on the barn-wood coffee table. The place had charm despite its small size, filled with decent appliances and a nice TV and stereo.

But as Joey put on some mellow music and stared at the blank television, she thought about choices. About what following the rules had ever done for her. She pulled out Lou's card from her back pocket and sent him a text before she could think herself out of it.

See you tomorrow at noon. Joey.

Mistake or not, Joey would live her own life. No more trying to please her father because, as she well knew, nothing she did short of turning back time would ever be good enough for Andrew Reeves.

Chapter 3

LOU CONSIDERED HIMSELF A MAN WHO COULD MOVE IN many worlds. He worked with a great bunch of guys at Webster's Garage, tough mechanics who talked a big game but would go to the mat for those they considered friends. He dealt with women day in and day out, his family chock-full of estrogen and issues. But he loved them like crazy, as much as they threatened to erode his sanity.

And then there was life at Heller's Paint and Auto Body, a vastly different environment than Webster's. With Del and the guys, Lou could talk smack, shoot the shit, and bitch about whatever he wanted. At Heller's, the vibe was all professional all the time. No chaotic stations, not a speck of dust or disorder in the main office. And their coveralls were dark blue and free of holes. Clean of any extraneous substance but paint and/or sanding dust. No personal complaints, no chitchat about who was beating whose ass at darts, woman problems, man problems, nothing. No bullshit.

When Lou worked at Heller's, he created, he painted, and like the other guys in Heller's shop, he kept his personal crap to himself.

Or at least that's the way Heller *used* to run the place. Lately, the guy had started to change. Lou wasn't sure he liked this new, softer version of the taciturn giant with attitude, who now sometimes *smiled*.

"So. Have you been to Ray's lately?" Heller asked, his German accent always present. He leaned over Lou's shoulder as Lou sketched out what their newest client wanted to see on the hood of his '72 Corvette. Allowing for the molding and width of the hood and side panels, Lou was trying to make sure he wrapped flames over the edge while keeping the grim reaper to scale.

"Sorry. What?" He glanced up and blinked, envisioning a horned helmet atop Heller's blond head. Heller's Paint and Auto Body, owned by a Viking born a few centuries after his time.

Heller had emigrated from Germany a few years after his birth. Then his parents had moved back to Stuttgart for some work, traveled around Bavaria, and managed to come back to the States seventeen years ago. Teenage Heller had been so in love with all things German, he'd refused to speak English for months.

Until his father had beaten sense into him. The elder Heller wasn't a nice guy. But he'd created a man in his own image, if not sensibility.

Six-foot-six, built like a tank, and with the chiseled jaw and blond features of an Aryan poster child, Heller looked every bit as dangerous as he was. When Lou had first come to work for the guy, he'd worried he was being jerked around by a white power gangbanger. Turned out Heller had just had a bad haircut. Having grown his hair back, he kept it slightly long, so as not to be confused with a skinhead.

The guy said little, but over the years spent working with him, Lou had come to appreciate Heller's dry sense of humor—buried way deep beneath muscles that made even Sam jealous.

None of the guys at Webster's were small. Like Lou, they all worked out, mostly because they knew what it was like to be on the wrong end of a fist. But Heller put them all to shame.

"We're going to Ray's this Friday, actually," Lou said, conscious of the dark-blue eyes regarding him without malice or pleasure. Predatory wolf eyes—something Heller and Del had in common. "Sam said to invite you and that the first beer was on him."

Shockingly, Heller's lips curled into a grin. It transformed the guy's face from serial-killer savage to almost handsome. "*Ja?* I'll be there." He paused, coughed, and glanced down at Lou's drawing, trying to act casual. "So who else is coming?"

Lou totally knew where Heller was going with the question, but he'd make the guy work for answers. Just because. "Well, me and Sam. Johnny and Foley too, but not the girls unless Lara is working." Johnny and Foley were the other two mouthy mechanics he worked with at Webster's. Lara and Johnny were dating, and she still pulled shifts at the bar to support her nursing school tuition. Sam's and Foley's girls were too sweet for a dive bar like Ray's. Lou didn't think either would be there.

But that wasn't who Heller wanted to know about.

"That's good. The gang." Heller grunted but didn't move. He slowly looked back at Lou.

Damn impressive how the guy could look so intimidating without trying.

Heller waited.

Lou waited.

"And?" Heller growled.

"Oh, well, I think Sue might be working. Maybe Earl, Big J…" Lou laughed. "Oh relax, man. Rena will be on shift, I'm sure." Rena was Del's cousin and a sweetheart everyone loved. Some—he gave Heller a look—more than others.

Heller smiled. *Again*. Twice in one day. "Good. Now get to work. After the death painting"—he pointed to Lou's sketch—"you have two jobs needing your attention. See if they'll work, *ja?*"

"Yes, yes. Now leave me alone. Your big-ass body is scaring away all my creativity."

Heller muttered something in German that Lou just knew wasn't complimentary, so he responded in Spanish about Heller's inability to reason and small dick size.

The big German just laughed as he walked away, a study in black. The guy wore yet another black T-shirt and jeans and those steel-toed tanks he called boots. Hallmark Heller.

Lou glanced at himself in comparison. Jeans, black boots, and a white tee. *Maybe I need to start expanding my wardrobe*. He leaned over the table, studying his drawing, and felt his phone vibrate in his back pocket. Which reminded him of a certain text.

Yeah, I need to look good. Especially because I have a hot date at noon.

Lou didn't understand this sense of excitement, but he hadn't felt it for a woman in so long, he knew Joey was special in a way he didn't yet comprehend. Why else would he pressure the girl so hard into a date?

He should have felt bad about it. Though he had given her an out, after all, telling her she could always cancel if something came up. But she hadn't. Now if she just didn't change her mind until he had her in his clutches. Er, at a table with him while he subtly worked to put her under his spell.

He shifted in his seat, dismayed to find himself aroused at thoughts of her. To a man who prized control, lived and breathed it, this situation with Joey demanded exploration.

Fuck, that smile. Those full lips and big brown eyes that warmed when she was happy. When he thought about her, her eyes and smile were the first things to come to mind. Then his dick took over, and he imagined her nipples in his mouth, her breasts weighting his hands, her taut belly beckoning a kiss before he turned her over and took a bite out of her ass...

He lowered his forehead to the table and groaned.

Once he stopped daydreaming, he finished sketching, then ran some timelines on prep and workability for the next two projects they hoped to secure. He dropped the sketches at Heller's desk before heading out.

At Webster's, he'd have walked next door. But from Heller's place, he had to drive a few blocks. No biggie, but he wanted to be there so he could grab a seat and wait for his lovely lady to join him.

To his bemusement, he felt nervous.

He walked in and saw Cyn, Foley's woman, behind the counter. Smart, stacked, and a freakin' hot-as-hell redhead, Cyn Nichols co-owned Nichols Caffè Bar with her brother and sister-in-law.

When she saw him, she beamed. "Hey there, handsome. *¿Qué pasa?*"

She'd been learning small bits of Spanish, so he said back in the same language, "Ah, Cyn. The things I would do to you if Foley hadn't found you first."

She frowned. "I haven't gotten that far yet, but knowing you, whatever you said would not make Foley happy."

He chuckled. "Probably not." He looked at the pastry case. "I need two coffees and a bear claw."

"I thought you were Mr. Clean Living. You have a sweet tooth now?" She grabbed him two coffees and the treat and tried to push them at him without charge.

He sighed and handed her a twenty. Then he gave her two bucks out of his change as a tip.

"Lou."

"Cyn." He looked down his nose at her. "So feisty. You sure Foley is making you happy? Somehow I think you're too much woman for him."

She grinned. "I am."

He really liked her, especially for his buddy.

"So stop changing the subject. What's up with the bear claw and *two* coffees?"

The bell jingled, and he turned to see Joey heading his way. When she saw him, her cheeks turned pink. Man, fucking adorable. She wore dark-brown pants and a pale-pink top under a light jacket. Scuffed sneakers fit her tiny feet. So petite, so pretty. All woman.

He groaned to himself.

"Joey!" Cyn smiled. Figured Cyn would know her. Cyn knew everyone. "What can I get you? Bear claw…" The woman glanced from his bear claw to Joey and smiled so wide, he feared she'd crack her jaw. "Ah. Right. Hold on, Lou. Joey likes a hazelnut latte." She grabbed back one of his coffees and fixed a latte instead.

"Hi." Joey smiled shyly up at him, and his heart did a funky misstep.

He cleared his throat and put on his game face. "Hey.

Nice to see you. Thought maybe you'd changed your mind." Just to needle her, he added, "You know, since I scare you."

She snorted. Again, so damn cute. "Please. You're not that intimidating." Yet her cheeks remained pink, and she looked everywhere but at his eyes.

He grinned, saw her focus on his mouth and lick her lips, and swore he was in hell. His body reacted as if he'd been shot up with Viagra. Terrific. With any luck, she wouldn't look below his belt and think him a huge pervert.

"How about that table back there?" He motioned with his head and carried the coffee, latte, and pastry on a tray Cyn handed him.

Joey led, and he tried to look where he was going and not just at her ass.

"Okay?" She sat, and he joined her, planting himself across from her at the tiny table.

"Great. Thanks for coming."

"Sure. I love Cyn's bear claws." Joey's brown eyes sparkled, and Lou had to do his best to get it together and not look like some starry-eyed fool. Lou Cortez didn't gape at pretty women. He was *the man*. Women gaped at him.

Except Joey wasn't just any woman, and he couldn't seem to stop staring at her smile that brightened everything around her.

—⁓—

Joey wondered what she should do. Lou kept looking at her in a weird way that made her threaten to break into an all-over-body sweat.

"So, um, are you having a good day?" Lame, but she had no idea what else to say. The guy had yet to blink. One move and she feared he'd pounce.

He smiled. "Yeah. You?"

"It's good. Really good." She sipped her latte, pleased Cyn had remembered. Then again, Joey had been Cyn's go-to for flowers since before Del's wedding. Cyn had recommended her, in fact, and the entrepreneurial woman had put a bug in Joey's ear about convincing the owner to expand the flower biz, maybe just focusing on weddings.

For that, Joey would be eternally grateful.

"What's really good about it?" Lou asked.

For a moment, she had no idea to what he referred, her head lost in flower dreams and financial independence. "Uh, I got to work on time."

"Always a good thing," he said, the smart-ass.

"And I'm the new manager of my store."

He smiled and held his cup to hers for a toast. "Outstanding. Pretty *and* smart."

She blushed. "Stop."

"What? Truth is truth, right?"

"What about you?" she hurried to ask, not comfortable with his flattery. Or the subtle once-over and smile of approval. Because knowing he liked the look of her did nothing but overheat her.

"What about me?"

She put the drink down and picked at her bear claw, her appetite fluctuating from starving to absent and back again. Talk about the jitters. "Well, what's good about your day?"

"I finally got this really sexy woman to go out with me."

"Lou."

"And she said my name." He sighed.

She chuckled. "Cut it out."

The sight of his pleasure made her feel good for having caused it…and gave her dirty thoughts. Totally inappropriate, rated-R kind of thoughts, which had no place in a coffee shop, for God's sake. She really needed to get back out in the dating world if a smile got her so hot and bothered. She glanced back down at her latte.

Lou sipped his own drink, then answered, "Today I got to sketch an amazing hood for a sweet Corvette this car collector brought in for a job."

"Huh?"

"I work at Webster's Garage fixing cars. On the mechanics of them. But I work at Heller's Paint and Auto Body doing custom artwork. You know, like custom paint jobs?"

"Really?" She studied him, wondering about him. "So you're an artist."

"Yep."

"So if my car gets a ding and needs paint to cover it…"

"You hit Maaco. Or you go to Heller's, and his body shop dudes fix you up. You want a bitchin' barbarian queen on your VW van, you call me." He grinned. "Although somehow I don't see you driving an old van."

"More like a crappy little Toyota, but hey, it runs."

"So does mine."

She nodded, oddly at ease talking with the man. She watched his face, saw his genuine interest in the conversation, and warmed. "You did the work on your car. The snake along the side that disappears in the back. That's your drawing."

"Yeah."

"It's amazing. Were you always into art?"

Lou shrugged. "I was kind of forced into it." He nudged her pastry. "You going to eat that or pull it apart?"

She took a bite, chewed, and asked, "What can you draw? Anything? Or just snakes and skeletons and half-naked barbarian queens?" As soon as she said it, she heard herself sounding so flirty, she wanted to bury her head under the table.

Lou laughed. "That's what my mother thinks I do. Draw naked people all day. I did it once when I was in high school, and she never let me forget it."

Joey smiled. "Caught you, huh?"

"Yeah. But that was okay, because if I was at home drawing late into the night, I wasn't out robbing a liquor store or rolling some rich jerks for money." At her look of shock, he sighed. "What can I say? I grew up under the influence of some not-so-nice people. A few smaller-scale gangs. I was a rebellious kid living in a houseful of women, so you can see why I wanted some guys to hang out with. Fortunately, my mother doesn't play."

She stared, wide-eyed.

"A short stint in corrections when I was ten helped change my mind-set. Well, that and my mother slapping me upside the head, sticking me on babysitting duty for my younger sisters, then having my aunts sit on me. I had nowhere to go but crazy. So when she offered to let me try art lessons to get away from all the women in the house, I went. Turned out I had a knack for drawing, and it stuck."

"I'll say." His car was amazing.

"Enough about me. What about you? Have you always wanted to work with flowers? That's a pretty creative profession."

Surprisingly pleased to have something in common with the man, she nodded. "I always liked creating things, and I love the outdoors. Gardening especially. When I was younger, my parents kept pushing me to be a doctor, a lawyer, an engineer." She sighed, aware she'd fallen way below the mark in their estimation. "But I ended up falling into the flower shop right out of high school. I needed a job, wasn't ready for college." Not with a baby in hand. She didn't plan to mention Brandon to Lou, mostly because she didn't share her boy with strangers. Even good-looking ones. Her baby never got to know her dates, rare though they were. Not unless she planned to get serious, and it had been nine long years since she'd considered a real relationship with anyone other than her son.

"Well, you're great at it, I have to say." Lou nodded. "My sister's eyes about fell out of her head. She forgot all about the asswipe who dumped her. Thanks for that."

She blushed. "Sure. I love flowers. They're bright and cheerful."

"And dead. Sorry, but I had to point that out."

She frowned. "Yeah, but even in death, they bring joy."

"Good point. Open your mouth."

She parted her lips to ask why and got a bite of bear claw for her trouble. Her lips brushed his finger, and her heart seemed to stop. The sugar in her mouth broke her paralysis, and she chewed for all she was worth.

"Eat. It's killing me you're not enjoying this." He broke a piece off and tried it, feeding himself with the same fingers that fed her. "Oh man. This *is* good."

She swallowed before saying, "I know. Why do you think I get one whenever I come in here?"

"You come here a lot?"

"When I was helping Del with her wedding, I went to the garage a few times. This was a great place to get my morning coffee."

"A caffeine addict, huh? Me too." He nodded. "I typically stay away from the sweets though." He eased out of his jacket, and she nearly choked on her drink.

She stared at his conditioned torso, seeing the volume of muscle. "I can tell." *Good God.* The man was seriously ripped. He leaned to drape the jacket fully over the chairback, and she noted the hint of a tattoo on his left arm, just under the T-shirt.

"Eat up." He held another bite out to her, but this time she took it from his fingers, not wanting them near her lips. The last time had nearly shot her into cardiac arrest, and it felt way too intimate for a first just-getting-to-know-you kind of date.

They chewed, watching each other. For the life of her, Joey didn't understand why Lou had such an impact on her, a woman who'd sworn off men. A guy like him, so much bigger than life, handsome, and, yes, charming, was after *her*? A pretty but not spectacular woman who worked in a flower store?

"What's that look?" he asked, his voice deep, smooth. Velvety.

"Why are we here?"

"We're talking. Becoming friends." He shrugged. "I thought we settled that yesterday."

"But why? What do you want from this?"

He sipped his coffee, watching her over the brim of his cup. "You're a suspicious little thing."

She frowned.

"That's not bad, Joey," he said, amused. "I like you."

"You don't know me."

"I know you're a hard worker. That you soften when you look at flowers, and you like being creative. You made Del super happy at her wedding, and she liked you enough to invite you. My boss is not easygoing. If she liked you, you have to be okay on some level."

Joey flushed, not needing the praise but lapping it up all the same. "But that's not—"

"And you're kind." Lou smiled, the expression sincere and heartfelt and absolutely beautiful on the man. "You worked extra hard yesterday for my sister, a person you don't even know, because she had a hard time. She loved those flowers, Joey. A lot. You did that."

She shrugged. "It was my job."

"Not charging me for the time? Staying open later than closing for some dumbass mechanic who was late? No, you're a good person. You're beautiful, and I'd like to spend more time with you."

"You mean have sex."

He didn't miss a beat. "Yeah, I'm attracted to you. I'd like to *make love* to you." God, when he said it like that, it didn't sound like sex at all but an out-of-body experience. "But I'm into mutual enjoyment, the dance of getting to know someone. Feeling good about being together, not feeling rushed or pressured."

She huffed and fiddled with her cup, annoyed he was saying all the right things. Even worse, he seemed to mean them.

"Joey, look at me, *princesa*." He waited until she looked into his eyes. "I like you, and I think you might like me back." When she gave a little nod, his eyes crinkled with pleasure. "How about we go out to dinner this week? My treat. Not for sex or so that you'll sit across from me and ooh and ah in amazement—because, I mean, come on." He gestured to himself.

She had to smile.

His expression warmed even more. "But so I can see your smile and feel good. We can share a meal; we can laugh. I'll tell you stories about the guys at work, and you can tell me about the people at your store who annoy you. It'll be fun."

"Well…" She tried to think if she could find a sitter for Brandon, because no way did she want her parents knowing about her social life. Though her mother treated her much better than her father did, Joey always caught the worry Amy couldn't hide, that her dumb daughter would get knocked up again.

"I swear. You have nothing to worry about from me. I'll be the perfect gentleman. I have sisters, you know. I'll treat you the way I'd expect any man to treat them."

She wanted to ask more about his family, but then he'd expect the same from her. "Okay, on one condition."

"What's that?"

"We keep things light between us. Talk about work, what we like or don't like. No deep, meaningful stuff. No family talk, no relationship drama. I can't handle that in my life right now. I have too much riding on my promotion and need to focus on work."

"*Bueno*. It's a deal." He held out a hand to shake, and she tentatively gave him hers.

But Lou didn't shake. He watched her as he brought her hand to his lips and gave her the gentlest kiss.

She couldn't hide a tremble of need, unexpected and strong.

His eyes seemed to darken. Or was that her imagination? He released her and said something about the boss he'd just left, a giant of a man with a crush on a certain waitress he knew. Changing the subject and easing the tension between them, Lou became the perfect lunch partner.

He ordered them both another coffee, and before Joey knew it, an entire hour had passed.

"Oh no. I have to get back." She scrambled to her feet.

Lou grabbed his coat and the tray of trash and dumped it before she could offer to.

"Thanks for coffee, Lou." She felt shy again all of a sudden, and it bothered her. Why now, like this, with him? She'd been this way with Felix way back when, and look at where that had gotten her. Talk about life changes.

"Anytime, Joey. I mean that." He took her by the elbow and escorted her outside. Then he waited while she opened the door of her car. She got in, started the car, and lowered the window.

He crouched by the side of the car. "Man, you weren't kidding. This is a piece of crap."

Jolted into a laugh, she stared at him, unnerved to see him so focused on her mouth. He raised his glance and smiled into her eyes. Maybe he was just an intense kind of guy.

"It runs," she said of the car.

"Yeah, that's always a good thing." Then he brightened. "And hey, just think, now that we're becoming good friends, if you ever have a problem with your car, you can bring it to me and I'll fix it, no charge."

"Lou—"

"But then you have to promise to throw together more flowers for me at the last minute. I have a lot of sisters, and at least two of them at any time are dating idiots." He sighed. "God save me from the Cortez women."

She chuckled. "Oh please. More like God save the world from the Cortez men."

He laughed. "I'll text you about dinner. Thanks for coffee, *princesa*." He moved away to his car, and she backed out of the lot, determined to concentrate on work when she returned.

Not on the sexy man starting to star in all of her dreams. Or would that be sex-filled nightmares? Only time would tell.

Chapter 4

LOU SPENT THE REST OF THE DAY WITH A SMILE ON HIS face. Joey had been so much better than he'd imagined. At turns shy then funny, vibrant and soft. A real woman he wanted to get to know, to understand what made her smile or cry, and to see why she acted so guarded. She'd been hurt before, that much was obvious. But she seemed too young to be so cautious. She had to be in her early to midtwenties.

Would she be bothered by their age difference? He was close to thirty-five. Did it matter? He'd never dated a woman based on age, only on interest. Not to say he wouldn't dismiss a nineteen-year-old for being too young. But Joey seemed worlds older than what had to be her age. Her eyes spoke of experience, loss, acceptance.

Man, knowing even that much about her made him crave to know more.

"Come on, Lou. Wake up." Heller smacked him on the shoulder. "Give me what else you have."

Lou swallowed the curse that came to mind and showed Heller what he'd been planning once he cleared the grim reaper. The two classic car projects would take some time. The owners wanting them had been referred by other clients. They only wanted Lou to do the paint work, and they were willing to pay.

Lou worked on commission for Heller and Del. And he made a pretty penny when creating designer stuff for the rich guys who dealt with Heller. But he'd have to pull some real overtime to get his shit done at both places.

"Oh, and Heller, I can't be here during the day too much. Del might cry. What can I say? She's missing me."

Heller grunted. "Your boss is a pain in my ass. But I like her." He paused. "Don't tell her I said that."

"My lips are sealed. So let's schedule my hours at night a few days next week and the weekend, so I can get this done." It figured that Del and Heller would get along. Both were perfectionists and hard workers, and both liked to make their own rules. Talk about controlling.

Lou wondered if that's why he got on so well with them both. He appreciated a dominant personality and didn't chafe at taking instruction from those who knew the score. Del and Heller had worked hard to earn their places in life, and he respected them both. Truth to tell, he wasn't sure who scared him more: Heller with his huge fists or Del with her smart mouth.

At the thought, he wondered who would win in a smackdown between the pair.

Heller raised a brow. "What's that look?"

"Nothing, man. I need to go. Mama's making her famous posole for dinner. She even puts the radishes and lettuce on top." Lou loved the hominy-based soup. "If I'm late, she'll swing by my place with the girls. Then I'll never get them out."

Heller shook his head. "I don't know how you do it. Go to your mom's. And maybe bring in some leftovers tomorrow, eh?"

"You know Mama loves you. I'll have some."

A ghost of a smile, then Heller left to bark orders at

Mateo, who hadn't yet finished sanding a troubled Viper with a truly awful paint job.

On the drive to Renton to see his mother, Lou wondered what she might think of Joey. Not an odd thought to have, because Lou loved his mother without question. Had she always made the right choices in life? Hell no. He had five sisters. One by his father, that scum-sucking loser. Three others by a guy just like his dad, but at least his mom had been married to the guy during his shitty behavior, so she'd had some financial support. Then the youngest's father, who'd been a stand-up guy. Unfortunately, he'd passed away five years ago.

Renata Cortez Hernando had made mistakes. Sure. But she'd never squandered her love. She had too much to spare, in Lou's opinion, but she loved the hell out of her kids. Problem was she hadn't understood the best way to care for them when they'd needed it most; hence Lou and his oldest sister, Lucia, had stepped in when Abuela wasn't around. Now he spent his time containing the youngest of them, Rosie and Stella, when they went wild.

He hoped Stella would get over her ex soon. Because she was the one he worried about the most. She'd had a massive crush on Sam for a time, but Sam had never returned her affections, thank God. Lou would have had to work to kick Sam's ass. But at least Sam would have treated her right. Stella had a tendency to choose dickheads.

He sighed and pulled into his mother's drive. She had purchased the house more than twenty years ago with two of her sisters, raised ten kids between them, then helped her younger sisters move close. More

Cortez women lived on Oakesdale Avenue than any-where else in the Pacific Northwest.

He still got queasy thinking about moving back in. Hell no. Life in Rainier Valley suited him just fine. Close enough to help if family needed it, but far enough away his mother wasn't barging in to check on him every freakin' day. That she still did on occasion he'd take to his grave. God forbid the guys or Heller found out his mother really did try to keep an eye on him.

He took a hard look at the house and made a mental note to take another pass at the screen door. Rosie had no doubt been slamming in and out again. Only Rosie, Stella, and his mom still lived in the place, unless Tía Adelita and her girls had moved back in. Last he'd heard, his aunt and two of her four girls had been living in an apartment a few minutes away.

He noted the cars lined up in the driveway and in front of the house and saw that Lucia, Carla, and Maria were here. But none of his aunts. Maybe, just maybe, he'd be saved from Tía Alma tonight. Man, could that woman nag. If he had to hear one more time how he was hurting the family by not procreating…

Fuck. There were twenty-six of them, including all his cousins, sisters, aunts, and grandmother. And she wanted *more*?

When he entered the house, Rosie ran up to him, and he lifted her into a hug.

"*Guapo!* You're here!" Rosie had been calling him *handsome* since she'd learned to talk. Repeating too much of what her older sisters said. Except they'd called him handsome with snark, whereas she meant it.

"Hey, Rosita. Where's everybody?"

He took a huge whiff and sighed. The scent of food made his stomach rumble, and he realized he hadn't eaten anything all day but a few bites of bear claw... and Joey.

"In the basement. Mama wanted us to have the party down there."

"Party?" He set her down and managed not to trip over the high heels and sandals littering the hallway. He added his boots, knowing he'd never hear the end of it if his mother saw him tramping around her house wearing shoes.

He stopped in the kitchen to grab a beer and shoved a twenty under the magnet on the side of the refrigerator, where he typically gave his mother something for her trouble. Before he left for the evening, she would walk to the fridge and demand he take his money back, protesting that she didn't need it. He'd insist she take it, add another ten for her stubbornness, then leave after she grudgingly relented.

Rosie opened the door to the basement, and he heard chatter in a mixture of Spanish and English over muted music. Something not Latin, for once, but an alternative band. Most likely Stella's choice. He followed Rosie and ended up hugging the girls, oldest to youngest. Lucia, almost five years younger than Lou. Then Carla, twenty-seven, Maria, twenty-six, Stella, now twenty-three, and again back to Rosie, eight. They all looked alike, sounded alike, yet couldn't be more different.

"About time you got here," Lucia muttered. The oldest of the girls and the most rational. She worked as a paralegal and loved being single, dating sporadically, much to their mother's consternation. Carla and

Maria owned a cleaning business together, just like their mother and aunts. They'd become even more successful than Mama, the little brainiacs. Both were dating guys he wasn't quite sure of, but since the guys treated his sisters right—so far—he'd been leaving them mostly alone.

Stella, no longer dating the dickhead, started mouthing off about how Mama had found her a nice boy from down the street. A boring guy who'd just graduated college and cared for his grandmother.

Lou thought he sounded pretty damn good.

Rosie abandoned him for Abuela, their grandmother. Shit. He'd forgotten to return her call yesterday; he'd been so wrapped up in thoughts of Joey.

Doing his penance, he gave Abuela a kiss, a hug, and an apology. In Spanish, because Abuela didn't speak English, though she could understand some of it, he said, "I'm so sorry, Grandma. I meant to call but got caught up in a project. You should see the new paint jobs I'm scheduled to do." He told her all about the grim reaper on the Corvette.

She nodded, smiled, showing a gap where she was missing a tooth, and punched him in the arm.

"Ow."

"Liar. You got a woman on the brain. I know." Behind her, his mother brightened.

Hell.

"But that's okay, Guapo. She'll make pretty babies for your mama to care for. I'll let it go."

"Is that true, Luis?"

Lou sighed. "No. Not exactly." He didn't like lying to his mother. Plus the woman read him as well as his grandmother did. He sometimes feared Abuela had a touch of the sight, because she could know things about him even he found out later. And of course she always shared with Mama.

"Well, what then, exactly?" Renata sparkled, the love for her family showing in everything she did. When they all came together, she practically glowed. And her good mood infected everyone.

Even Stella laughed when only yesterday she'd cried on his shoulder over douchey Paul.

"Okay, you want the truth? A pretty girl called me last night, and I was so surprised to hear from her, I forgot to call you back."

"What girl makes you forget your grandmother?" His mother narrowed her eyes on him. So did his grandma.

Then Rosie did it, and he couldn't help laughing. "You're all very scary, you know that?"

"Bah. Nothing scares you, Guapo." Rosie shrugged the notion aside. "But I don't know... You talk to girls all the time. What's the big deal?"

"I, ah..." He saw too many of his sisters listening in and changed the subject. "What I want to know is how Miguel and Doug are treating my sisters. Do I need to pound anyone this week or what? And Mama, where's dinner? I'm starving."

"Hold on, boy." She and Abuela went with Lucia to grab the food from the small kitchenette in the corner. His mother had so many people coming and going from her house, or at least she used to, that she and her sisters had turned the basement into its own little living quarters. Now, for parties, they cooked downstairs and opened up the double doors leading to the backyard. Or, like today, they made a meal everyone could enjoy either in the basement or outside. He noticed the doors open and a few tables with tablecloths outside on the patio.

Considering the weather felt just on the warm side of cool, they'd do well to take advantage of Seattle's spring.

"Maria, Carla?" Lou asked, his voice overly loud. "I'm still not sure about these bozos you're dating. Want me to talk to them for you?"

"The way you talked Doug into nearly peeing himself the last time you mentioned 'talking' to him? You had him convinced you were a homicidal ex-con who liked pretty boys."

Carla said, "Juvenile detention is not real jail, moron. Leave Miguel alone too."

"Well, Doug is pretty." Lou grinned at the girls. "And juvie wasn't a cakewalk. I could have been in real trouble if Mama hadn't flirted outrageously with the judge to get me less time."

"Luis Cortez!" His mother glared.

"Kidding." He wasn't, actually.

Maria fumed. "Doug's a good man. And he wasn't flirting the last time we went out. He knew the waitress from work."

"Uh-huh." Lou didn't give a shit. Nobody messed with his sisters.

Maria rolled her eyes. "Doug is great, business is fine, and I'm not planning to get married anytime soon. Happy?"

"He proposed?" Wow. Lou hadn't thought the little guy had it in him.

She frowned. "Not yet. But when he does, I'll think it over before saying yes."

"Good. And you?" he asked Carla.

"Miguel and I are just having fun. I'll leave babies and marriage to my older sister and brother." She gave him a fake smile. "How's that going, by the way? Anyone you're interested in proposing to, *hermano*? Like your little phone friend?"

She only called him "brother" in that tone when annoyed. Mission accomplished on that front.

He spent the rest of the night filling his belly, laughing at his sisters, fending off his grandmother's demands to meet his "phone girl," and talking his mother into cooking something special for Heller next time. The man was half in love with her anyway, and it couldn't hurt to kiss his ass so that Lou could take some longer lunches to flirt with Joey.

After helping to clean up, because all the Cortez children cleaned after themselves, he cornered Stella. "You doing okay?"

"Fine." She sighed. She wore dark makeup around her eyes, a bright red on her lips, and her hair straight and long down her back. Demurely dressed in jeans and a baggy sweatshirt, Stella looked like a young Salma Hayek, and she had the admirers to prove it.

"How are you really doing?" he asked.

"I miss Paul." She sniffed. "He was an asshole, and he cheated on me, but I think I might have pushed him into it."

Yeah, right. "How's that?"

"He and I were only together a few months, but he was so nice to me. And it was so cool seeing him up on stage."

Paul, the drummer for an alt-rock band, seemed to

think he was on the rise. A hot girlfriend had certainly helped his cred.

"And?"

"He was always playing at night, but I couldn't stay out so late. I mean, I have work, you know?" Stella cleaned for Maria and Carla's company while also working on her cosmetology classes. "And we were, well, I know everybody does it, but I wanted to take it slow while dating. You know, to really get to know him first."

Even better. They hadn't had sex. "Good. So what's the problem? His balls turn so blue he had to go fuck a girl so he wouldn't die?"

"Lou." She blushed. "He said it was hard."

"I'll bet."

"That we weren't doing anything," she said through gritted teeth. "And they were throwing themselves at him, but I wasn't there to help." Her anger melted, and she sniffed. "He said if I would have stopped acting like a little girl and given him what he needed, he never would have gone to the others."

"Others? With an *S*? What a prick." He pulled her in for a hug. "You can bet your ass a real man wouldn't cheat. It sucks, yeah, but if you like and respect your girl, you wait until she's ready. And you sure as shit don't go to other girls because she said no." Maybe he would go pound the little shit after all. "You are so much better than him, Stella. You know that, right?"

She shrugged, her tears burning his shoulder. He pushed her away so she could see him telling the truth.

"No. Let me tell you something. Sam would never treat a woman like that. Ever." He knew she still idolized the guy, even though he'd found Ivy. "You think he'd go hounding after some other woman if Ivy couldn't 'take care of him'?" At the small shake of her head, he added, "Do you think I would do that to someone I cared about?"

"No."

"So why is it okay that some douchebag can screw around on you? Just because you said no? Would you go out and see some other guy if he was busy some night? Because I know you get hit on all the time."

"Of course I wouldn't."

He grew angrier. "So why are you acting like he's God's gift to women? Jesus, Stella. Grow a pair. Get mad. Get even—be happy. Know that you're better off without him."

"I do, okay?" she shouted.

There. He liked her rage much better than her tears.

"But he slept with Missy Bonekker, and she's a complete bitch."

"Stella," their mother cautioned, hearing the language.

"Well, she is, Mama. She's in my classes at school, and she was bragging about how she stole him away. She's such—oh. I *hate* her."

Now understanding the issue a lot more clearly, Lou shared a glance with Lucia.

Lucia came over and took Stella aside. "You want to get even with this witch, let me tell you how…"

Leaving Stella in good hands, Lou crossed to his grandmother and kissed her on the forehead. "I have to go, Grandma."

"Bring your girl for dinner, and we'll see."

He rolled his eyes. "She's not my girl, and we only had coffee. It's nothing serious." Yet.

"Bring her. You have two boys and a girl, I think. Next year, a baby for me to hold, okay, sweetie?"

"Oh my God. Grandma, no."

She laughed at him before joining Stella and Lucia.

After finishing his goodbyes, he and his mother walked upstairs, where they haggled by the twenty he'd left on the fridge. He gave her the ten he'd been saving, promising to take Rosie to the park on Saturday.

"I'll pick her up at noon. So you good, Mama?"

She smiled. "Yes. I'm seeing a new man."

He swallowed a groan of disappointment and forced a smile. "Great." Life would have been much easier if his mother hadn't been so easy on the eyes.

"I know you don't like me with other men, but *hijo*, that's normal. It's not natural for a woman to be alone. Or for a young man to stop dating." She gave him the look. "It's past time you got married."

Like you? Two marriages and three baby daddies? All those boyfriends we were forced to share a dinner with, wondering if they'd be moving in or moving on? No thanks. He loved his mother, but he didn't understand how she could so easily fall in and out of love. Or how she could think that hadn't affected her children. "Yeah, great. Just be careful, okay? No more sisters. I can't handle it."

She laughed. "I know about safe sex, Luis."

He cringed. "I have to go."

"Rosie still wants a little brother, you know."

He lit out of her driveway and didn't look back.

———

Thursday morning at work, Joey rubbed her gritty eyes. For the past two nights, she'd done nothing but dream about Lou. Naked.

He pranced, he danced, he stripped her down and

went wild. She'd woken sweaty and frustrated, and this morning she'd been joined by an equally angry little boy. Apparently Brandon didn't want to take a lunch box anymore. He wanted a hot lunch, which, one, wasn't in the budget and, two, would only guarantee he got a slice of pizza and tater tots. Starch plus starch in addition to the apple the school would plunk on his tray but he wouldn't eat.

And when Brandon didn't get enough to eat, the boy could rival Oscar the Grouch for grumpiness. Please. Been there, done that.

Then the hot water had given them fits. So with cold showers, the last of the dino-egg oatmeal, and an argument over hot versus cold lunch, she'd shipped her boy to school then went to work on three hours of sleep.

Miserable, to say the least. To make matters worse, she had dinner scheduled with Lou later that night. Her boss had been almost more excited than Joey that Joey had a date, so she'd volunteered to take Brandon out for burgers. He loved Stef, so at least that had gone Joey's way.

But now Joey had too much time on her hands to think about sexy Lou and what he had planned—or not planned—for this starter relationship.

While there was no reason to take him too seriously, she didn't think she'd be able to handle him in the long run. In her fantasies, they made love, and he was magnificent. Then he'd bowl over any objections she had to keeping her heart safe. She'd fall in lust, then in love… and he'd break her heart after giving her an STD. Best case. Or she'd get pregnant while on multiple forms of birth control. The other best case.

She sighed. Even in her dream world, reality reared its ugly head.

Still not sure why she'd gone out with him in the first place, she wanted badly to regret it. But she couldn't. She'd felt special Tuesday. For all of an hour over coffee and a bear claw, Joey had felt not like someone's mom or disappointing daughter, but like a real, desirable woman.

Lou didn't know her as a screwup. She attracted him, and he'd laughed with, not at, her. Big difference.

She'd enjoyed herself enough to want another date. And now she had one in eight and a half hours. *Oh man, today is going to drag.*

Except it didn't. A last-minute beauty pageant fill-in had them making a dozen corsages and large bouquets for the winning age classes. Between her and Tonya, they'd worked hard. Manning the front and taking calls in between creating grand-prize arrangements, they also had their regular deliveries as well as the new guy to handle.

To her surprise, she'd recognized him from Del's wedding. Apparently Theo Donnigan was Del's new cousin by marriage. Talk about a small world.

She figured she'd need to take time out to show him around, but he'd been more than happy to help out where needed.

"Theo, can you hand me the gyp? I mean, the baby's breath?" she asked.

"Uh, that one?" He pointed to the bucket of delicate white flowers.

"Yep. Gyp. It's actually common gypsophila. The delicate little white-and-pink flowers are great as filler, but they get overused that way a lot. We're just going to use a smaller branch of it here"—she tied it to the floral wires sticking through the base of the purple spray rose—"in addition to a larger frond and two white carnations. Simple but effective." Then she wrapped floral tape around the wires and managed the tiny arrangements.

Next to her, Tonya had already finished her fourth corsage and was starting on a fifth. "So how do you like S&J, Theo?" The older woman smiled at him, probably seeing her own teenager in the young man.

He'd come by looking for part-time work two weeks ago. Stef had been so impressed with his work ethic and stellar references, of which he had many, that she'd hired him on the spot. Apparently his current job at a coffee shop was hitting a few bumps due to a girlfriend who'd recently been promoted to manager. His hours had gone down, and he thought he might need to quit sooner than later.

In any case, Theo would soon be twenty-one and joining the Marines. In the meantime, he needed gainful employment.

"Can I make one?" he asked, watching intently.

Joey nodded, and they worked in companionable silence for a while.

"You guys need music in here," he said.

"Good point." Tonya turned to Joey. "Well, Ms. Manager?"

As pleased as Joey that she'd gotten the job, Tonya had been glad to see the last of their old manager. Not that Georgette had been a bad sort, but she'd been too rigid, afraid to try anything new. Her move away had come as a blessing. Especially because it had opened up the possibility of Joey taking over.

"Manager? Sweet." Theo grinned. A good-looking

guy with dark hair and a tall if skinny frame, he'd be a definite lady-killer in a few years. Despite only being a few years older, Joey felt worlds apart from the younger man. She had a son and responsibilities while he was just getting started with life.

"Joey worked hard for the promotion, let me tell you." Then Tonya did just that, regaling Theo with stories about Joey staying late and butting heads with Georgette.

The buzzer signaled new customers in the store, letting Joey know to wait by the counter. And the day went steadily onward from there, busy then slow, with arrangements to put together in the back. Theo spent much of the day working with Tonya. By four, Joey told him to go home.

"You did great today, Theo. We'll get you going on deliveries soon enough. Get familiar with the city traffic and road closures."

He sighed. "No kidding. It takes forever to get around here anymore."

"I know."

He looked down at her from his impressive height. "Man, you're short. Boss."

"Hey, not nice." She grinned. "How tall are you?"

"Six three." He flexed a skinny arm. "But I have a lot of filling out to do to catch up to my brothers. They're home now, but they used to be in the Marine Corps."

She nodded. "Is that why you're going to join up?"

"Partly. And partly because I always wanted to." He shrugged. "It just feels right."

"That's great."

He smiled. "What about you? Did you always want to do this?"

"Not exactly. I was never really sure what I wanted to do. My parents always pushed me to get straight A's and excel in everything, so I never had a chance to just breathe and figure things out."

"Yeah. My parents kind of pushed me too. Until I pushed back." He snorted. "My mom, I love her, but she's hard to please sometimes. Not as bad as my dad, though. And everyone thinks he's the easygoing one."

Do I know what that feels like. "Funny how that works, isn't it? But at least we have a good thing going here. The flower shop is an awesome place to work. Stef is great. You met her." At his nod, she continued. "It's not too snooty, the people are nice, and we don't worry about getting robbed or mugged in the parking lot. Plus we're always busy. This is a great location. Wait until you start making deliveries. Everyone loves to get flowers. And you're cute, so you'll make big tips."

He flushed. "Thanks."

She stifled a laugh. "Sorry. Didn't mean to embarrass you. But we deliver to a lot of women, and that's what our last delivery guy told me, and he was kicking thirty. An old man," she teased.

Theo nodded, apparently not getting the joke. "So why did he leave?"

"He and his wife moved to Tacoma to be near family, and he started working for his father-in-law."

"Makes sense."

"You did great today. Go home, Theo. Rest up for tomorrow."

"Yes, boss." He saluted, grinned, and left through the back with a shout to Tonya.

Tonya soon joined her out front, pushed her glasses

higher on her nose, and combed her dark-blond hair behind her ears. "I like him. He works hard. Reminds me of Billy." Her son.

"Me too. I think he'll make a nice addition to the team, for as long as he's here anyway. I figure we'll have him a few months before he leaves for basic training, right?"

"I guess." She looked at Joey. "He's pretty cute, don't you think?"

"Billy? Sure. He looks like you."

"I meant Theo."

"Oh. *Oh*." Joey flushed. "Come on, Tonya. That kid makes me feel ancient."

Tonya laughed. "Honey, 'that kid' is maybe four years younger than you. That's not too old."

"It is to me." She felt nothing but manager-ly toward their newest employee.

Tonya laughed. "Sorry I asked. But you know, Stef and I talk. We think you need to start dating again. Don't let that Adam and, who was the other one?"

"Jim." From nine months ago. Adam had been a year past. Oh boy. She did need to get out more.

"That's right. Jim. Don't let them put you off men, honey. You're young, smart, and pretty. You deserve some fun in your life."

"I have a date tonight" slipped out.

Tonya gaped. "Well, no kidding." She grinned. "Good for you! How did that happen?"

"He came in the other day to get flowers for his sister. Then he asked me out. We're just doing dinner tonight. No biggie."

"I want details tomorrow. Don't hold back."

Joey rolled her eyes. "Yes, Mom."

Tonya cracked up. "Is he coming to pick you up?"

"I'm meeting him at six-thirty. Stef is watching Brandon for me. And no one but you, me, and Stef know about this."

Tonya twisted an invisible key over her lips. "Mum's the word."

Chapter 5

LOU HAD BEEN LOOKING FORWARD TO HIS DINNER WITH Joey all damn day long. In fact, he'd had a difficult time thinking about anything else. Fortunately, the Corvette's owner had come in to talk about what he envisioned for the car, a welcome distraction Lou more than needed. Even better, the guy loved Lou's concept.

They'd discussed some color options as well as a higher grade of paint and finish, and the client was all too happy to fork over his money. It was all about the car—a notion Lou had no problem understanding. He understood devotion to something that drew him. A car, the Seahawks, a certain dark-haired beauty.

How long had it been since he'd been this excited about the prospect of spending time with a woman? Oh, he loved the ladies he'd dated. Many he'd enjoyed in bed, making sure they had no complaints. And he couldn't say he'd just sexed them up then left either. Lou wasn't a one-nighter kind of guy. He liked to wine and dine women, to linger over the seduction and part ways as friends. He always left them wanting more while happy to distance himself.

But with Joey, it was different. He couldn't understand why, and he'd thought about it a lot. Perhaps her initial rejection had put the spark of challenge in his belly. Or maybe her shyness had intrigued him to see if she'd be that compliant in bed; he had every hope of eventually finding out the answer to *that* question. Then he'd remember her warm brown eyes, her smile, and he'd get a pang in his chest that had nothing to do with sex and everything to do with emotion.

Christ. If he was already feeling this for a woman he hadn't yet fucked, he was pretty much screwed. And not in a good way. He had no intention of ever getting married, and Joey seemed like the hearts and—no pun intended—flowers type. Having a steady girlfriend didn't bother him, but he didn't feel ready for that either. So why all the lovey bullshit?

Had to come from watching all his friends couple up. They'd turned him soft…so to speak.

He glanced down at himself, aware this constant hard-on when thinking of Joey had to stop.

Heller walked out of his office and glanced around. "I don't like it this quiet." To Lou he said, "We go to Ray's soon, I buy you a beer. You need it. Now quit mooning over whatever woman crawled up your ass and get to work." Lou caught a few unflattering comments in German he'd heard before just as Heller disappeared back into his office and shut the door. The phone rang, and Lou returned to work. Seconds later, Heller erupted in some harsh German. And man, the big dude had a booming voice that carried, even through a closed door.

The guys who'd been hand sanding a Camry stopped and stared at the office. Mateo and Smith shared a glance, then shook their heads.

"I'm not asking him now."

"Me neither."

As one, they turned to Kelly.

Kelly, Heller's newest hire and a damn fine paint

guy, sighed. "Why is it always me? You know predators always go for the weakest prey—and I'm like a hundred pounds less than the boss. At least make Lou ask to give the rest of us a fighting chance."

Lou chuckled. "Yeah, right. No way in hell am I going in there after hearing that." He paused. They heard more shouting, then something slammed into the wall with a crack. Dead silence. "You think he's talking to his old man?" Lou had met the bastard once and had no urge to repeat the experience.

Kelly swallowed. "Um, that'd be my guess. I've only been here four months, but no one else gets him that pissy that fast. You know he's slow to boil."

"But when he does, he's friggin' insane," Mateo added. "No way in hell I'm asking."

"For fuck's sake." Lou sighed. "What do you guys want?"

They all looked at each other before Kelly, the group's sacrificial lamb, said, "We want a vending machine. For drinks. It gets dry in here, you know?"

Lou blinked. "A soda machine?"

"Hey, the customers could use it too."

"What customers?" Lou snorted. "People come in here to drop off their cars. They don't wait around for you guys to sand and paint. That takes days. Weeks."

"No shit." Mateo scowled. "We're not stupid, Lou. I've been asking for one for two years. We're just saying we want stuff to drink. And a coffeepot would be nice. We're not lucky enough to walk a few doors down for coffee and donuts like you Webster pussies."

Lou chuckled, remembering the bear claw. "NCB does serve donuts sometimes. The homemade, old-fashioned kind. But the other day, man, I had the best coffee. And I remember Foley eating some sweet cheese tarts. An apple fritter too, come to think of it."

Smith groaned. "You're a mean bastard."

The door banging against the wall interrupted the conversation, and they froze.

"Why is no one working?" Heller growled.

Man, the guy was almost worse than Del on a tear. Lou decided to take one for the team and stood. "The guys want a soda machine."

Heller scowled. "What? Why?"

"They've earned it, dealing with your moods." Probably not the smartest thing he could have said. He swore he could see ice forming in Heller's eyes—ice that *burned*. "Think about it. It's something your old man would never go for. He'd throw a fit before getting his people anything to boost morale."

Heller opened then closed his mouth, his stare down-right frightening as he gazed at Lou before shifting to look at the others. "*Ja*. Okay. I'll get one."

"And a coffeepot or machine. Come on, man. Have a heart. Even I like the idea of a coffee machine. And it would be nice for clients too. Besides, the guys are weak. You know they're more effective when they're less whiny and slowly dying off a caffeine high."

"Well, that's not so nice," Mateo muttered.

"Okay. Fine. But you." Heller pointed at Kelly, who flinched. "You'll figure out the cheapest and best product. Then we'll see. Come use my computer."

"Sure, sure. Bury the new guy where no one will find the body, why don't you," Kelly said under his breath as he passed Lou and slunk by Heller into the office.

Laughing at the kid's melodrama, Lou finished doing his estimates before suiting up. Time to disassemble the Corvette so they could start sanding. He glanced at the clock. He'd give it two and a half more hours, then bail. And if Heller didn't like it, too bad. Not that Lou would put it to the guy exactly that way.

Three hours later, Lou swore. He'd gotten so wrapped up in his work that he'd lost track of time. That's all he needed, to be late again with Joey. He had a feeling if he blew it tonight, he wouldn't get another chance.

He hustled out of the bay housing the Vette and yelled a goodbye before racing home. After quickly showering, shaving, and dressing in nice jeans, a loose red V-neck sweater, and his favorite Frye boots, he found a parking spot and hustled to the front of one of his favorite places to eat. Casual but perfect for a date.

He entered and snagged a table near yet not too close to the bar. The noise was loud enough to ensure privacy but allowed for ease of conversation. The scent of home-cooked Italian food and pizza made his mouth water.

"Yo, Lou." His favorite waitress, Barb, gave him a smile. She glanced at the empty seat across from him and brightened. "What? You're here alone?"

"Funny, Barb. My date should be arriving…ah. There she is." He took in Joey's petite build, bundled up in a rose-colored jacket. She wore her hair down, and more than one guy checked her out as she made her way toward him.

She looked young, sexy, and vulnerable all at the same time. He felt a strange urge to both muss her and protect her. Yep, weird.

Barb sighed. "I'll be back with waters for you." Then she left.

Joey gave him a shy smile that had his heart racing.

When she neared the table, he stood. "Hi."

"Hi." She looked taken aback when he helped her out of her coat and seated her at the table, hanging the coat on the back of her chair. The button-up lavender blouse emphasized her slender frame and delicate neck.

When he leaned close, he got a whiff of a light perfume. It went straight to his head—and other places—so he hurried to sit across from her.

"Have you been here before?" he asked.

She shook her head.

"It's a favorite place of mine. They make amazing pizzas. They also have salads and smaller dishes. It's all Italian. I hope that's okay."

"Great." She busied herself with the menu, which gave Lou a chance to calm the fuck down.

He cleared his throat after a minute and was about to start conversation when Barb returned with waters. She took their orders, gave him a subtle wink, then left.

"No beer or wine for you?" he asked.

"I'm driving."

"Me too."

She eyed him up and down. "Yeah, but you could probably drink a six-pack and not feel anything. It only takes a few sips to do me in." She made a face. "I'm a lightweight when it comes to alcohol."

"Good to know." He waggled his brows.

She gave a good-natured grin. The girl had a sense of humor. Thank God.

"I'm surprised you're here."

She took a sip of water. "Why?"

"Because going out with me once was pushing it. I

thought for sure you'd wise up and ditch me for something better. Like *Sharknado 5*."

"Tempting, but I already saw it." She grinned, and he swallowed a sigh. Damn she was pretty. "You did mention dinner. I put in a full day."

"Me too."

They spoke about her many floral orders, the new young guy they'd hired at the flower shop, who knew Del, surprisingly enough. Or not. His boss seemed to know everybody, especially since marrying into the nosy McCauley clan. Barb brought their food, and the conversation continued. It wasn't forced either, despite Joey not being as talkative as many of the women he'd been with.

He'd just told her about the Corvette he'd started working on, about the artwork he couldn't wait to get into. But he had to know. "Look, I'm just gonna ask."

She paused in the act of forking more salad. "Yes?"

"Why did you ignore me for so long?"

Her cheeks turned pink. "What do you mean?"

"You know what I mean. I think I made my interest pretty clear months ago when you first came by the shop. But you avoided me."

She shrugged and put down her fork. "You're intimidating."

"Yeah, right."

"Lou, that whole garage is full of giants. You included. So there's that. Then there was the fact that Del's wedding was my first solo job. I didn't want to mess it up. And you guys were all distracting." She paused then dug back into her salad. "You especially," she muttered.

Well now, that was okay. "I'm distracting? So are you. The guys were all making fun of me because you wouldn't give me the time of day. Barely even looked at me."

"I was working."

"Man, your cheeks are really pink."

She choked on a laugh. "Stop."

Pleased she had noticed him back then, he relaxed into the date. But as much as he tried to get to know her, she made it difficult.

"So you're not married?" he asked.

"You're asking that now?"

He shrugged. "Doesn't hurt. Besides, all we've done is share dinner and coffee."

"And a bear claw," she reminded him.

"True." He savored his pizza, knowing he'd need to lift a lot more tomorrow to make up for his carb loading today. "So no husband. No boyfriend?"

"No." She frowned and speared a tomato. "I'm single, okay? I don't date a guy while seeing someone else behind his back."

"Good to know. Me neither. Not the guy thing, but about women."

"I figured that."

"Do you have family around?"

"I'd rather not talk about my family, if you don't mind. My parents are usually unhappy with me about one thing or another. And I was hoping to have a good time." She sighed. "That sounds awful. I love my parents. But sometimes I need a break."

"Sure, I get that. Joey, I come from a big family. A grandmother, single mom, five sisters, five aunts, and thirteen cousins—and only one of them is a boy. I'm only telling you this because I believe in being fair. You're at a disadvantage."

"How's that?"

"I've grown up surrounded by women. I know how you people think. You're a little harder to read than what I'm used to. But I'll crack you."

"I'm not a nut," she said drily.

"You sure? You did agree to dinner with me, after all."

She laughed and dug back into her salad. He'd devoured his in minutes, though his had been a smaller portion. Still, no wonder she was so small.

"Hey, you want a slice?" He pointed to his romana pizza.

"No, that's yours."

Considering he'd already had his salad and split an appetizer of suppli al telefono, an amazing combo of fried risotto and mozzarella, he had no problem sharing his remaining two slices with her. Even if he was half-starved, he'd give her whatever she wanted. Call him a sucker, but for Joey, he'd part with a lot.

"Come on. Succumb to peer pressure. Everybody's doing it."

She rolled her eyes.

"Just have a slice."

"Oh my gosh. You're pushy."

"And you're just learning this now?"

"True. Okay, I'll bite."

He lifted the food to her plate then watched her nibble like a rabbit.

"It's good." She chewed, intent. "What are these olives?"

"They're Castelvetrano on that slice. My favorite."

"Wow." She ended up eating the whole piece of pizza.

"There you go. Want another?"

"No thanks. That was perfect."

"Great. Now you'll have enough energy for what I planned next." The suspicion he'd expected flashed in her dark-brown eyes. "A walk, to get rid of my beer gut."

She eased back into a smile. "Yeah, right. If that's a beer gut, I'm seven foot three."

"Which we both know is ridiculous. What are you? Five one?"

"I'm five three," she said with pride. And hostility. "Just because you're huge doesn't mean I'm short."

"A little testy, are we?"

Barb swung by and asked if they wanted anything else. When they said no, she handed them the bill. Before Joey could grab it, Lou deftly slid it to his side of the table.

"It's on me. And don't argue. I'm old-fashioned. Besides, my mama would slap me upside the head if I let a woman pay for my food on a date."

"Are you sure?"

"Yes."

"I could leave the tip."

He just stared at her.

"Uh, thank you."

"You're welcome." He held out his credit card for Barb when she swung by. "Now tonight wasn't so bad, was it?"

"No." She chewed her lower lip. "I'm sorry if I seemed mean or snobby before. When I was working Del's wedding, I mean. Or even at the flower shop. I didn't mean to act—"

"Standoffish? Aloof? Untouchable? Hey, don't look so surprised at my vocabulary. I read."

She glanced at him from under thick, sooty lashes. Her big brown eyes like pools of dark wine. Rich, vibrant, exotic. He wanted to think of more words to describe her, but his mind went blank, and all he could do was stare.

"All that," she said. "I'm sorry."

He blinked, trying to break free from her spell. "You have nothing to apologize for. You were fine. Hell, *I'm* sorry if I seemed like I was stalking you. I just wanted to get to know you better." He fixated on her ripe mouth, noting the rosy color of her lips, wondering if she wore lipstick or her lips were naturally that color red.

Joey gave him a sweet smile. "This was nice."

"Yeah." Nice was a good start. "Now how about that walk?"

"If I can get up from the table. I'm stuffed."

Barb returned his card. "See you next time, Lou."

"Bye, Barb." At Joey's questioning look, he explained, "I come here a lot. I love their pizza."

"That bite I took of yours sold me." Joey stood with him and seemed startled when he helped her into her coat. "Thanks."

"Sure." They left the restaurant, and Lou wanted to hold her hand. *Badly*. So he shoved his hands in his pockets instead. "This is a nice neighborhood. How about we just walk down the side streets? It's residential."

She nodded. They strolled a bit in companionable silence, checking out the established neighborhood, the well-tended lawns and blooming flowers. The sun started to set, and the wind picked up. Yet the evening couldn't have been more perfect, especially when the moon played hide-and-seek with the fluffy lavender clouds overhead.

Concerned with her comfort despite being comfortable in his sweater, Lou asked, "You okay? It's getting chilly out."

"I'm good." The moon drifted out from behind some clouds, and the glow settled over Joey's features, bathing her in moonlight. "So you can't cook?"

It took him a moment to realize the question, so lost in her features. "Where'd you get that idea?"

"You said you go there a lot to eat."

"Oh. That's just because I'm lazy." He shrugged. "Between my mother and grandmother, I usually have plenty to eat. I learned how to cook a long time ago. I just choose not to if I don't have to."

"I get tired of cooking too. I don't like to ask my mom to cook for me too much because then I'll feel like more of a burden than I normally do." There was a story there for sure. "And my grandparents still living are out in Montana, so Grandma's famous chicken-and-rice soup is out. Gosh, I haven't seen them in years."

He nodded, not wanting to stop her. She hadn't said all that much about her personal life, so he'd take anything about her he could get.

"I love my parents, but I need to get some space from them too. You know?" she reiterated.

"Seriously? I told you I have a million relatives in town. All girls—mostly. Of course I understand."

She smiled, stumbled on a rock, and bumped into him. He whipped out a hand to steady her.

"Thanks."

"Anytime." He let his hand drift to his side. Their fingers brushed, and she whipped her head up to study him.

He watched her as he slowly curled his much larger hand around hers.

Her eyes widened. "You're hot."

"Thanks, I hear that a lot."

She blushed, as he'd meant her to. "I mean, your hand is really warm."

"Warm hands, warm heart."

"I thought that was cold hands, warm heart."

Yet she hadn't tried to tug free.

He gave her a gentle squeeze. "Nah. My people have a different saying. It's all about heat. And I'm hot. So you should stick by me. Really close, I think."

Her lips twitched. "Yeah?" Her gaze skittered from his face to their hands then shot to the street.

"I'll keep you warm, Joey." *All night long if you let me.* He cleared his throat. "So where do you live?" He felt her tense and knew he still had a long way to go with the wary woman. "I'm not asking for exact directions. I'm making conversation. Like, north of town? South? I'm in Rainier Valley. It's not great, but there I can afford to live in a house bigger than a shoebox."

She blew out a quiet breath, but he heard. Why was it he found her caution so endearing? Lou normally went for a woman who knew the score. Adventurous, lusty, confident. Proud of her desire. He liked a woman who enjoyed a man and had no problem saying so.

Yet he found Joey's awkwardness oddly appealing. She was a mixture of cute and sexy, and the dichotomy of wanting to protect her and fuck the breath out of her baffled him.

"I live with my parents," she mumbled.

"Okay."

"I hate it. But I can't afford to move out yet. That's why my promotion is such a big deal. It's going to give me a lot more freedom than I have now."

"Good for you." They stopped in front of a house exploding with color. Flowers and shrubs landscaped to perfection. Very unlike his humble home. He could account for a mowed lawn outside but not much else, having poured all his efforts into the interior of the place.

Joey pulled her hand from his and rested it on the wooden fence bordering the property. "Wow. This place is gorgeous."

"It's small." A tiny cottage of a house, though quaint.

"Look at all the flowers." She sighed. "That's what I'm going to have someday."

"You will if you want it bad enough. You're the driven type. I can tell."

She smiled. "Thanks."

"See? I know women. Telling you you're smart, successful, driven. That's totally better than letting you know I love the color of your eyes. Or that your size is perfect for me. Or that you are so incredibly beautiful."

She stared, blinked. "Oh, er. Yes." She coughed. "I'd take driven over pretty any day."

"Me too." He grinned. "I know I'm beautiful, but I'd much rather be loved for my brain than my amazing body and to-die-for biceps."

"Lou." She chuckled.

They started walking again. He reached for her hand, and she didn't protest.

But the best part of the walk was when he saw her subtly checking out his ass.

Chapter 6

"STEF LET ME EAT CAKE FOR DINNER." BRANDON baited Joey, gauging for a response.

They were nearly late for his first-period class Friday morning, but she didn't dare speed through a school zone. "That's great, Brandon."

If she hadn't tossed and turned, caught in a weird, extreme bout of sexual frustration, not helped in the least by her lurid dreams of Lou Cortez, she might have heard her alarm this morning.

"Stef told me she's getting married."

"Uh-huh." Last night had been magical. Special. And he hadn't done more than hold her hand and talk to her. Not *at* her, but *to* her.

"To a lady, a man, and a goat."

"Good for her."

"I'll be her ring bearer, even though I'm eight and three-quarters."

"Right."

"Mom, where do babies come from?"

She sighed. "Yes, Brandon, I'm listening to you. No, Stef didn't give you cake for dinner. No, she's not getting married, so you won't be bearing any rings. She and I talk, you know." Joey turned into the parking lot and found a space easily since she wasn't dropping off.

"Yeah? So what did you do without me last night, Mom?" He was dogging her something fierce. "Stef wouldn't say. Did you go out with a boy? Did you?" His expression grew crafty. "Because that would be okay if we got a dog too. Then an extra boy would be fun."

"You want to know what I did? Fine. I sold your next tooth for a foot rub, so we have to keep wiggling that front one. Oh, and I met the aliens who sold you to me in the first place. Yeah, they're green and ugly. Just like you."

"Ha-ha." Brandon rolled his eyes. "You're a riot, Mom. Trolled me good."

"What?"

"You know. You trolled me? Like, you pranked me?"

"Ah, trolled. Got it."

"Actually, Stef took me out for hamburgers. But I got a chocolate milk shake too."

"Wow. I had a salad for dinner." *With the most amazing man. I could so easily fall down a rabbit hole I'll never climb out of with this guy. Why is that such a bad thing again?*

"Lettuce. Yum. Not." He chuckled.

She ruffled his spiky blond hair. "Funny guy. I'm glad you had fun with Stef. She missed you, you know."

"Because I'm awesome."

"And so shy and unsure of yourself," she said wryly.

"Nope. I'm great. You're supposed to believe in yourself, Mom. Because if you do, the world will believe with you. Ha. Yeah right."

"Where'd you hear that?" Her father? No way. The man was not a firm believer in extolling the virtues of confidence to the only son of his daughter, who'd had a child at sixteen. In Andrew's eyes, there was no coming back from that. Even his grandson shared the taint of her "mistake."

"At school. We have 'positivity lectures,'" Brandon ended in air quotes. Her kid, "eight and three-quarters" going on forty. "It's actually kind of lame."

"Brandon." She had to stifle a laugh. "Thinking good thoughts makes you stronger, mentally. In a way, they're showing you that if you think positively, you'll be a better person."

"I'm already amazing."

"Yes, yes you are." She sighed. She prodded him to get out, locked up behind them, then signed him in. She got her kiss on the cheek and watched him skip and whistle on his way to class.

Time to bite the bullet and see *the counselor* about him. Hopefully, this meeting wouldn't take too long and Brandon hadn't been acting out again. Then she could talk to her best friend instead.

She knocked on the counselor's door. "Ms. Oliver?"

"Oh, Ms. Reeves. Come in."

Joey walked in and carefully shut the door behind her. Then she dragged herself to the chair in front of Becky Oliver's desk and sat. "It's been the morning from hell. Please tell me Brandon is behaving."

Her best friend laughed and pushed a cup of coffee she'd been holding for her. "Here. It's a little cool since you're…fifteen minutes late."

"I'm sorry." Joey chugged the caffeine. "My life is getting so weird."

"Tell me about it. No, really. Tell me about it. You texted me about your promotion, and we have yet to celebrate! That is so awesome. What I have to tell you about your gifted son will fit into a five-minute bubble."

"Gifted? Not heading toward a youth detention center?"

Becky laughed. "Not yet. I think he was acting out before because he was bored. We're going to challenge him and keep him nice and busy. He'll love it. Now, while you have the time, talk to me, woman. I can't believe how long it's been since we've gone out."

At least four months, sadly. And that last time had been to celebrate Becky's birthday. She loved Becky. Could tell her anything. They talked almost daily on the phone. But Joey was all too aware of their differences.

While Becky had partied in college and after, Joey had been raising her son. Last year, when Becky had started working at Brandon's elementary school, the two friends had reconnected. A great thing, because now Joey had a friend her own age to hang with. Not that Stef and Tonya weren't great, but they had a motherly feel to them that Becky didn't. And she couldn't see hitting the bars with the ladies, not that she did with Becky all that much either.

"I don't know that I ever thanked you for standing by me in high school," Joey admitted, missing those young and carefree years.

"Why wouldn't I? Unlike most of our class, I knew I couldn't get pregnant just by standing too close." She laughed. "Our 'friends.' What a joke. They were like rabid sharks in a feeding frenzy to take as many people down as they could. Consider yourself lucky you didn't graduate with us. But listen, that's not why I called you in here today."

"No, you wanted to talk about Brandon."

"In a nutshell, we want to put him in the advanced program. You good with that?"

"Well, I don't know, I—"

"Think about it. He's a great kid." Becky rubbed her hands together. "Now, for the big news. Did you know Miranda Layton just got divorced?"

Joey sipped the lukewarm coffee, needing the jolt. "Miranda? No way."

"Yep. From prom queen to drag queen, apparently."

"*What?*"

"Her husband. He's gay. She found out when she saw a video of him online. He was wearing a Cher getup, singing at that place downtown in drag. He ended his performance by making out with a drag Madonna. Is that awesome, or what?"

"Holy crap. Seriously?" She drank more coffee.

"Seriously. And Mandy Hue is still engaged to Dave Applebaum. He doesn't care what she spends his money on, and she doesn't care who he sleeps with when he's not with her."

"Get out. Dave Applebaum is cheating on her?" She'd really missed out on the good gossip by not going to that mini-reunion, it seemed. "Dave. The guy with the buzz cut and big ears?"

"Yep. Same Dave. Except now he's a big tech player and worth millions. I heard all this from Amelia Bladt, by the way. She's back in town. She was in Portland for years. I pretended I forgot all about her calling me a beached whale during that football game. You remember the one."

Joey cringed. "Oh yeah."

"So now I have a new 'friend' and we caught up. Oh man, the stories I now have to tell you."

Becky had always been a cute, perky blond. Back in high school, she'd worn an extra ten pounds of baby fat.

But it had since worn off. Good for her for schmoozing Amelia, that mouthy skank of a hypocrite.

"Who else?" Joey checked her phone. She had a good hour before she needed to get into the shop.

Becky ran down the list of half a dozen more names. Some good news, some bad, but all of it interesting. Times like these made Joey realize she wasn't the only one who'd had to grow up.

Becky gave her a strange look. "One more thing."

"My head is spinning as it is. But hey, at least Autumn is still with Jeff. I always liked them as a couple."

"Me too. Now shut up and listen." Becky grew more animated, her hazel eyes flashing with impatience as she waved her arms around. "This is big, big news."

"And?"

"Felix is back in Seattle. He moved back last month."

Felix Rogers. Brandon's father. A burst of…something…filled Joey. Then nothing. "So?"

"When's the last time you two talked?"

"That would be a week after they admitted me to the hospital for Brandon's birth. When Felix signed away his rights to be a father while his mother stood over his shoulder calling me a whore."

"Oh, wow." Becky's eyes widened. "That's something you never forget."

Joey snorted.

"Now you know he's back. Mitch ran into Jesse, who knows Felix, and get this." Becky paused.

"Get what?" Just a faint curiosity about the father of her child.

"He asked about you."

"Huh." How should she feel about that? "Interesting."

Becky looked disappointed. "That's it?"

"What do you want me to say? Felix and I dated. He knocked me up, then tried to act like he didn't. He wanted nothing to do with me after that. While he finished high school and went on to college, I had a baby and did my best to deal with everyone's disappointment." Whoa. Apparently she'd been festering some hostility for Felix after all. And she thought she'd gotten past that. "But now, nine years later, it's all done. Felix and I are over. It's normal he'd ask about me. If I knew he was around, I'd probably ask about him, just out of a sense of morbid curiosity."

"Good point. But I got the impression he was interested in seeing if you and he had that same spark you used to."

"That was no spark. That was me not understanding how bad my first time would be. Or how awful he would be at sex."

"Ouch." Becky grinned.

"As a matter of fact, I could care less about Felix."

"Actually, it's 'couldn't' care less," Becky corrected.

Joey frowned. "Whatever. There's a new guy I'm kind of seeing." *See? I'm no longer the queen of lametown. I too can have a social life.*

Becky leaned over the desk, scattering a few folders. "Tell me." She pushed one of the folders at Joey. "Before I forget, here are the details for the gifted program. Enroll Brandon. We good? Great. Now who's this guy?"

Joey described Lou a little too well, because Becky started panting after him. "Does he have single friends? Are you into him? Because if not, I'll check him out for you. You know, just to help a friend out."

"How generous of you."

They both laughed.

"I'm kidding, Joey. I'm kind of crushing on this guy who lives in my apartment complex. Don't worry. He's far enough away that it won't be awkward if we break up but close enough I can easily dance back to my place in socks on my walk of shame." Becky waggled her brows up and down. She'd always been more open and candid about her liaisons. Not like Joey.

Dating stories Joey had no problem swapping. But adding sex to the mix was adding an intimacy she didn't share. Her time with Lou was fun and uncomplicated. On his part at least. She didn't know how she felt about him other than she really liked him, she dreamed about having sex with him, and she didn't like the thought of Becky thinking too hard about him.

Time to change the subject. "So tell me more about…?"

Becky grinned. "His name is Trent. And he's hot."

"But does he have tattoos?" Joey teased.

"Not that I've seen yet. I mean, we haven't been totally naked with each other. Not even half-naked. I've seen him a few times without his shirt on when he's come back from a run." Her expression turned sly. "But I dream about hand- and blow jobs while our clothes are mostly on. You know, for when we're first dating. Later we'll be naked and doing it."

Joey sputtered on her coffee. "Ah, right."

Becky laughed. "Still a prude, I see."

"Not true." Joey didn't mind dirty talk in bed. She liked being bossed around and handled a little more roughly than the normal girl, as a matter of fact. Two

things that rarely happened in her safe little world. The
few guys she'd had sex with had never pushed all her
buttons, probably because she still held herself back, her
first experience with intimacy ending in a life-changing
baby. Then too, she seemed to choose guys who weren't
a challenge.

"I think maybe it's a little true. But that's okay, Joey."
Becky squeezed Joey's hand resting on the desk. "You
should never change who you are. I like you, and isn't
that what's really important?"

"Ha." Joey grinned.

"Plus, being you seems to have nabbed a hot
mechanic, am I right?"

"Maybe. We just did coffee and dinner. That's it.
I mean, he's sexy, and I like him. A lot. But Brandon
complicates things."

"Because you're a good mom. You want to keep
your baby boy safe. But are you really going to live in
a vacuum until he's eighteen? How healthy is that for
your son to see, that Mom's always alone, living under
Grandma and Grandpa's roof, with no boyfriend but her
son for company? Oedipal much?"

"Ew. Okay. Stop. I get it."

Becky nodded, her hair brushing over her eyes until
she blew it aside. "You and this Lou. Have fun. Bang his
brains out. You don't have to make him Brandon's new
daddy or anything."

"You have such a way with words."

"I know. That's why they pay me the big money and
give me a huge office."

They both stared at the tiny closet she called her
home away from home.

"Anyhow," Becky continued, "if it were me, I'd have fun with Lou. Do all the neat stuff, the dating, the kissing, the sex." She sighed. "Oh, the sex. He doesn't need to know Brandon even exists. Not if the relationship is just between you two. Now if it got serious, then sure. But you don't even really know this guy, right? So why is he entitled to your life story after two dates?"

"You make some good points."

"You don't have to sound so surprised by it," Becky grumbled.

Joey laughed, feeling better about things. "You're a good counselor, Counselor. Let me see this gifted program."

"So we're shifting to talking about work now. Fine." Becky leaned farther forward. "But don't think we're not going to discuss Lou again. I want to meet this tattooed paragon who wooed my bestie out of her moth-eaten, oppressive, dusty old virginity cloak. Such a wretched amalgam of desperation and seclusion."

"You have got to stop taking those writing classes. You're killing me, Mrs. Merriam-Webster." Joey pretended to hang herself.

"Don't be obstreperous."

Lou figured it wouldn't hurt if he swung by the flower shop at closing. He just wanted to say hi to Joey before hitting Ray's with the guys. Plus he wanted to make sure she closed up okay. The girl worked harder than most people he knew. And since they'd texted a few times since last night, he knew her schedule.

All that small talk. It was…nice.

Not clingy or too demanding. He liked their dialogue.

Lucia would say he'd finally matured. Though he'd taken on the role of the family patriarch, she'd always been their pseudo-mother. While Renata had fallen in and out of love, introducing the kids to "this new daddy" or "that new daddy," Lou and Lucia had kept the household on an even keel.

They'd been old enough to remember the awful years with their father. They'd all been better off without him around. But those memories made it difficult for adult Lou to accept just one special person in his life, knowing she could turn into a wreck. Lou didn't want permanence. He also didn't drag a new woman around his sisters every other week.

He could count on one hand the number of women he'd ever introduced to his family. Hell, or even his guy friends, for that matter. His family only knew his friends from Webster's because he considered them honorary brothers. Men he would trust with his sisters, with his life. Tight, another kind of family.

And damn, but I am thinking way too deep for a Friday night. He parked and saw the hour had reached seven thirty. He didn't see another car in the lot, but he assumed Joey typically parked in the back.

Lou arrived at the front door just as she did but from the inside.

She blinked and stepped back as he walked through *the unlocked door.*

"Hi, Joey." He glanced around. "You alone?"

"Yes. I was just locking up."

He frowned. "It's after seven. Past closing time. You need to lock up and close the shop once you're alone. It's not secure."

"Are you lecturing me on safety?"

He sighed. "Sorry. But you don't want to be alone with some douche after hours." At her look, he scowled. "I'm not talking about me, damn it. Don't even." Her chuckle made him smile. "Smart-ass."

"Okay. You made a good point. I promise I'll be more careful."

"Good." She smelled like flowers. Trite but true. Except the floral scent mixed with that unique feminine essence that was all Josephine Reeves. And like that, he wanted to do her. *Bad*. He bit back a groan. "So, ah, why are you still here?"

"Want to see?"

He nodded.

"Follow me."

He walked deeper into the shop and toward the front counter. "Wait. I'm not allowed back there, remember?"

She nodded. "Good point. I'll check with the manager." She paused. "Oh right. That's me. Come on back."

He grinned and followed her into the back, where they housed their cuttings and did their arranging and cutting on the worktables. Several bunches of flowers sat in vases or in Styrofoam-balled contraptions propped up by wire.

"Oh, those aren't done yet. I'm just keeping them in place until we finish fitting the rest of the greenery and filler in them." She motioned to the grand centerpieces, two of them, filled with bold color and big flowers. "These are what took so long. Aren't they beautiful?" She sighed.

He wanted to sigh with her. Because the sight of her satisfaction did something to him.

He had to clear his throat. "Yeah, great."

She spotted a rose that had come loose and tried to grab it from the center of the wide table. She rose on tiptoe to reach it. "I love these. They're fragrant."

"Let me smell." He moved behind her and tried to catch a whiff as she held it up. "I can't smell it."

She held it closer at the same time as he leaned into her, pressing his front to her back.

They both froze. The scent of soft rose petals hit him at the same time as his body woke to full arousal. Joey must have felt it as well because she let out a shuddery breath.

Lou tingled everywhere they touched. He sniffed her neck then nuzzled the side of her smooth skin. "You smell good too. Like the rose and something else." Something uniquely her.

"Lavender," she whispered, then groaned and leaned back, effectively pressing him fully against her. "It's floral."

Lou couldn't mistake that signal, especially when she sighed and arched her neck to the side, giving him more access. He felt light-headed, all the blood pooling in his lower body.

He lightly kissed her neck, needing more.

"Lou," she breathed.

"Fuck," he whispered, totally done in. A few grinds against her and he'd come, which was crazy. He had stamina, patience, seduction down to a science. But not with Joey apparently. Rushing but unable to stop himself, he ran his hands up her sides and around to her front, cupping her breasts.

He bit back a curse when she moaned and ground her ass against him. Her breasts easily fit into his large palms, and the stiff nipples begged him to touch. To squeeze.

He pinched one, and her hand moved behind his head, pulling his lips closer to her throat.

"Turn your head," he managed, barely able to speak past the roaring in his ears.

She did, and they kissed. An explosion of heat and electricity that filled him from head to toe. She tasted like chocolate, a sweet lust that glided over his tongue and stayed there. So much smaller than he was, she stood, pliant, while he kissed her.

She responded beautifully, and he didn't think. He acted.

Pinching her breasts then molding them in his hand, he continued to play with her, loving the way her body moved against his. With his other hand, he reached down her front and eased beneath the waistband of her pants, moving slowly, giving her every chance to stop him.

Half hoping she'd put an end to this sweet torment, half praying she'd let him go as deep as he could.

The kiss ended so they could breathe, and she whispered his name like a prayer.

"Yes, *cariña*. Let me inside. God, let me in." He sucked her throat and reached between her folds, stroking through her silky hair to the slick cream of her arousal. "So hot." He moaned and slid a finger inside her, nearly coming at the feel of her extremely tight flesh sucking his digit deep.

The knowledge that she'd be that tight around his cock nearly set him off.

"Oh, yes. Yes." She writhed in his arms, and he was lost. Unable to stop. He removed his hand and unbuttoned her blouse, keeping her pinned between the table and him, her back still to him. Then he parted the blouse before moving to the front clasp—*thank you, Jesus*—of her bra. He unfastened it and waited.

She moaned and reached for his hand.

"No. Stay there, just like that. Let those tits feel the bite of the air." He nipped her neck, and she cried out but didn't move.

Lou had to free himself from the pressure building on his dick. "Put your hands over your nipples and pinch them," he ordered while unzipping his jeans. With real speed, he withdrew the condom from his wallet and ripped it free. He had it rolled over himself in seconds and returned to her hot little body, shoving her hands aside while he took over fondling her breasts.

"Fuck me, you're sexy."

"So are you." She turned her head, and slumberous eyes met his. He'd never seen anything more erotic in his life. And yeah, he was a total head case for thinking it, but he loved her smaller size, feeling like he could do whatever he wanted to her, and she'd be helpless to stop him. Macho and non-PC and sexy as fuck.

He groaned and kissed her again, letting go of her breasts so he could make short work of her pants.

She kicked her shoes off.

He pushed her pants down her legs and followed with her panties, then nudged them off her feet. He tore from her kiss, only to feel her awkwardly trying to kiss his cheek and what she could reach of his neck.

On fire to have her, to put an end to this unquench-able lust, he ordered, "Bend over," but didn't give her a chance to obey. As he pulled her hips back and shoved her legs wider, he positioned himself between her legs, right at the wet entrance to her sex.

"You ready for a fast fuck, baby? I'm hard and wearing a rubber. And I'm two seconds from coming in that hot pussy."

As wet as she was, her body knew what she needed. He hoped she did as well.

"Please, Lou. I'm so—"

He shoved inside, thrusting without cease as her body gloved him as if made for him. He was two pumps from coming but refused to go off without her. Reaching around, he rubbed her tight little clit and withdrew, then slammed home again.

She cried out and clamped down on him. And the pressure, the heat, the clear arousal she felt for him… He lost it.

Lou grabbed her hips and thrust twice more before coming so hard, he saw stars.

Joey continued to whisper his name, shivering under him, those narrow hips still moving, her body milking him so hard.

After what felt like forever, he trembled, overwhelmed with sensation. The orgasm had short-fused his brain. And hers too, apparently, because she remained bent over the cutting table while he stroked her ass, unmoving while she caught her breath.

To his shock, he hadn't done more than get semisoft. As if his dick knew he might never get another chance at this, he remained hard enough to go again if he went right away.

"Let me, baby." He knew he'd filled the condom and didn't care. He needed one more go.

"Lou?" She sounded sleepy. So satisfied.

He grinned as he pumped inside her, and it didn't take him long to go from semi-erect to full-out hard again.

"Again," he said.

"But—"

He slapped her ass then ran a hand up her front to grip her breast. "Again," he growled, needing to show her he could… No, wait. He didn't want to scare her off. This kind of play would only scare—

"*Oh, yes*." She melted before him, tilting her ass up to allow for better penetration. "Yes, again."

"Play with yourself. Get off when I do," he rasped.

He didn't give her a chance to change her mind and rode her into another orgasm while her clever fingers found a rhythm she clearly liked. When he found his release not long after, the feel of her body taking him to new heights made him weak at the knees.

Finally withdrawing from her, he nearly spilled out of the condom. Not wanting to jar her, he stepped back, zipped back up, and found a nearby trash can to dispose of the rubber.

Turning back to her, he saw her shaky as she reached for her pants and underwear.

"Let me." He was quiet as he knelt, holding her panties for her as he faced her near-naked body. The small triangle of dark hair covering her sex was soft, so pretty. He would have leaned in for a kiss but wanted to show her comfort, not act like the raging sex fiend she probably now thought him.

She placed a hand on his shoulder while she stepped into the clothing. Her pants followed, and he slowly rose to fasten them for her. Which put him in line with her gorgeous breasts.

She hadn't spoken yet. A glance at her face showed uncertainty. Which he couldn't have.

"You are fucking beautiful," he murmured and gently sucked each nipple into a little bead.

Her indrawn breath, the tentative cupping of his head before she threaded her fingers through his hair. She turned him on so simply with her acceptance. In Spanish, he said, "I want to suck you until you scream. To fuck you into a pile of warm woman. Again and again. God, I want you even more now, honey." He kissed each nipple once more, then fastened her bra and buttoned up her shirt.

She just watched him, so small, so vulnerable.

"Ah, Joey. *Bella*, you get to me." He drew her in for a hug, and she relaxed and hugged him back.

"I needed that," she mumbled against his chest.

He laughed. "No more than I did. Damn, Joey, I really filled up that condom."

He thought she might have laughed before she pushed at his chest.

When he let her get some space between them, she sighed. "That was, ah, unexpected."

"No kidding." He blew out a breath. "You made my knees weak. I'm not kidding."

Her shy smile made his stomach drop. "Good. Because you made me feel so good. So fast." Her blush amused him. "I don't normally… I mean, I don't have a lot to compare it to. But that was unusual for me."

"Coming?"

She dropped her gaze to his chest and nodded.

"Yeah? Well, it normally takes me more than a few thrusts before I come too. And it's really a big deal if I can go twice in a row like that. You got me so hard, baby." *And I'll be ready to go again if you say the word.*

But her shy smile and uneasy stance settled the

matter. He'd pushed too fast already. Time to slow things down and not scare her away for good.

"So if you're not busy this weekend, maybe we could hang out again?" he asked. "And not just for sex, though I wouldn't say no to that. But I had a great time last night. Being with you."

She glanced into his eyes, her face so full of expression, of freakin' joy, that he wondered if she could hear how fast she made his heart beat.

"I have to see if I can make it. But I'd like to," she added softly. "Can I text you?"

"*Princesa*, you can do any fucking thing you want with me." He normally didn't swear so much, but with his heart so full of...something...he was at a loss to maintain a cool dignity. "Tonight, tomorrow, Sunday. You name it, I'll be there."

She smiled. "I think I need to go home and let my jelly legs relax."

They both laughed.

"But I'll text you later about this weekend, okay?"

"Sure." He leaned in and kissed her, a soft press of his mouth to hers, and hoped he conveyed how much tonight had meant. "Thanks, sweetie. I'll talk to you soon, I hope."

He walked her out to her car after she locked up. "Man. I am going to be dreaming about you again tonight," he said as she got into her vehicle. *Shit*. Hadn't meant to let that slip.

Her shy smile warmed him. "Again, hmm? Glad I'm not the only one." Then she started up the car and drove away after promising to text him.

Lou whistled, pleased with life and knowing his evening could not be more perfect.

Hot sex—twice—with the girl of his dreams. A beer with the guys and a chance to screw with Heller again.

"Finally. Life is back to normal." He grinned, feeling loopy, and walked to his car. Once inside, he leaned his head back and closed his eyes. He could still taste her nipples in his mouth, could feel the heat of her body gloving his finger, his cock.

His dick stirred to life again, and he blinked his eyes open and stared down at himself, wondering if being with Joey would be this enervating again or if tonight had been a fluke. He had been in a dry spell since first seeing her, after all. Because for some weird reason, no other woman but Joey would do.

And even after having had her, he still felt the same way.

Only time would tell.

Chapter 7

LOU STARED AROUND THE TABLE, PLEASED TO SEE THAT Johnny, at least, had made it. He'd said he'd come, but now that everyone at the garage had girlfriends, the guys occasionally did couples shit instead of hanging out. Like Sam and Foley having to bail due to some chick thing their women had previously planned. But he didn't blame them. Having had a taste of Joey, he'd have thrown the bastards over in a heartbeat if she'd suggested continuing their evening together.

"Hey, Casanova. What's with the dopey smile?" Johnny asked. "Did the bear claw finally get the flower chick to that pity date you've been after?"

Lou cracked a smile. "Yes, it did. Foley's better half did me a solid."

Johnny laughed harder. "Better half, no kidding. I can't believe Cyn hasn't booted him out yet. I'm still thinking she's into heavy drugs or something," he teased.

"That one is a mystery," Lou agreed. "But then, look at your woman. Lara is so sweet. How is it you two are a couple again?"

"I groveled like a pathetic moron," Johnny confessed.

"Yeah, it took you a while to get your head out of your ass. But she's worth it, right?"

Johnny gave a goofy smile. "Yeah. She's the best."

Lou held up his glass, and they toasted the lovely Lara. "Don't fuck it up."

Lara swung by with a fresh pitcher and leaned in to give Johnny a kiss. "Hey, sweetie. This is for you guys."

"Thanks, baby."

Lou grinned. "Gee, Lara. You bartending tonight?" Since she wore a black shirt with white letters that read "Bartender," they knew the score.

"Funny, Lou. But with this crowd, it helps to be clear." Lara took the money Johnny slid her and winked before walking away.

"She's got a point." Johnny nodded. "Look at what just walked in."

Heller entered, and a path instantly cleared for him as he made his way to their table. A surprising addition trailed behind him.

"Well, well. Look who else decided to show." Lou raised a glass and drained half of it. "Looks like the other half of the gang's all here."

"Except for Del," J.T. Webster, Heller's shadow, said as the pair joined their table. "But she's married now."

"So sad." Lou commiserated with Del's brother, who looked right at home sitting with her crew and Heller.

Interesting that Del and J.T. could act so alike yet look so different.

For one thing, J.T. was obviously African American. Light-skinned and with a resemblance to a popular wrestler-turned-actor, according to Del's stepson, J.T. took after his father only in size and temperament. Technically he was Del's half brother, since they biologically shared a father.

But Del and J.T. possessed such snarky senses of humor, it was easy to see that they were siblings.

Like the rest of the guys at the table, J.T. had a large

build, huge arms, and an ability to get under Del's skin. So, a natural fit for the group. Plus he owned an amazing tattoo studio and had done most of the ink in the place, including a few of the tats on Lou's chest and upper arm.

"Nice to see you again, J.T." Lou nodded at his fellow artist then at Heller.

Johnny nudged a beer glass at Heller. "Heller."

"Johnny." Heller glanced around the table, nodding at Lou, then not so casually looked at the bar.

Lou caught Johnny's gaze and grinned.

They all knew the deal. Heller had it bad for Rena, everyone's favorite *single* bartender.

Rena had cocoa-brown skin, tight golden curls framing a pixie face, and a trim figure just about everyone at the table had fantasized about at one time or another. Lou was no saint. Rena was fine, no two ways about it. He'd thought about asking her out when he'd first come to Ray's years ago. But knowing she was a cousin to the Websters and understanding her kind heart and joyous personality probably couldn't handle a nonpermanent relationship, he'd steered clear.

As had the rest of the guys. The Websters were protective about those they called family. And since he felt a reciprocal affection for the domineering clan, he had no problem watching out for Rena too. Heller surely had his hands full trying to win her over.

Though he'd made headway a while back, he'd since busted a few heads at Ray's, and Rena had avoided him ever since.

"Should I get us more beer?" Heller asked, drank his down in one swallow, then rose for the bar before anyone could stop him.

"He's toast," Johnny predicted, pouring a glass for J.T. from their still-full pitcher. "Rena's mad at some dickhead she dated for about two seconds. No way Heller gets anything more than a beer for his trouble tonight. Poor bastard."

The guys talked about their latest projects in the garage and bet on how long it would take Foley and Sam to finally propose to their ladies.

Heller returned looking grim and slammed a new pitcher on the table. No one cautioned him about spilling beer.

"No good?" J.T. asked.

Heller slumped in his seat, sighed, and drank.

J.T. patted Heller on the back. Considered by the big guy to be a true artist, like Lou, J.T. often had a pass when it came to dealing with Heller. "It's all good, man. Just give her time to realize you only pound bad guys. Last week just got a little messy is all."

At Lou's arched brow, J.T. explained, "The last time we came in, Fletcher mouthed off. You know Fletcher? That racist asshole with the stringy blond hair?"

"Oh, that guy. Good riddance."

Heller grunted.

"He said something about Rena that Heller took exception to. Except Rena didn't hear the mouthy part. She only saw Heller take out Fletcher and his cousins." J.T. turned back to his buddy. "And speaking of which, you'd better watch your back, man. Fletcher has an in with some of the gangs running guns in town."

"Whatever." Heller muttered in German and poured another beer.

Lou and Johnny eyed him with caution before Johnny

said, "He's not going to go apeshit in here, is he? The last time he downed beer that fast, he wiped the floor with Argess and Monroe."

J.T. laughed. "That was a fun night. No. He'd never drink that much," he directed to Heller, emphasizing each word. "Not when Rena's still watching him from her safe spot behind the bar."

Heller sighed, took another sip, then pushed his glass away. "I'm hungry."

Lou tried not to laugh but couldn't help it. Another powerful man brought down by a woman with dimples.

Heller cursed in German, Lou answered in Spanish, and then the big German chuckled. "You're such an asshole, Lou."

"You got that right." Johnny and J.T. clinked glasses, then Johnny said, "So if we're not going to bug Rena or make fun of Heller, I think we should skip the trash talk and go straight to darts."

"Which is all about trash talk, dumbass," Lou said.

"Darts?" Heller sat up and blinked, then gave a slow smile. "I like darts."

Lou grinned. "He might look like a bear, but he's a softy at heart."

Then Fletcher and his cronies moved toward their table. *Shit.*

"A softy, my ass," J.T. muttered.

"Hey, Adolf." Fletcher sneered. "Let's play."

"Oh boy. Heller really doesn't like being called that," J.T. muttered to the group as they proceeded to watch Heller beat the crap out of Fletcher before turning to Fletcher's friends. Bets were placed, beer flowed, and the night got steadily more entertaining.

Lou had seen Sam fight, and Sam was amazing with his fists. But Heller made the Terminator look like a pussy. He never flinched when hit. He just got mad.

Lou wondered what Joey would think of the place, of Heller, of his friends. He could see her tolerating the guys if not the atmosphere. Not with a heart that fragile.

He sighed and drank more beer, not surprised he couldn't stop waiting for her to text him about this weekend. In the mood to treat Heller to something to eat, because watching the man fight was a thing of beauty, Lou excused himself to the bar.

"Rena, honey, we need food," he said loudly to be heard over the rowdy crowd. A Friday night at Ray's usually brought out the scumsuckers. Tonight was no exception. The place normally smelled of stale beer and burgers. Some smoke, because despite the no smoking signs, Ray didn't actually enforce too much. A scarred wooden floor covered with chairs and tables, then some booths that weren't too much the worse for wear lined the walls. A half-decent jukebox played a mixture of hard rock, alternative, and grunge music. The waitresses had threatened to quit if Ray put country on the machine.

A rowdy crowd of bikers, blue-collar stiffs like him and the guys, and other lower life-forms frequented Ray's. It was Lou's favorite place to hang out. Especially on a night like tonight. It felt good to be free from rules sometimes. Even better if he could watch the chaos from the outskirts, his hands safely protected from impacting some jackass's jaw.

Rena scooted past her fellow waitresses, slid a beer to one beefed-up biker, took a bill, then sidled to Lou's spot by the bar. "Whew. Are we busy or what?" She gave him her bright wattage of a smile, and he couldn't help but smile back. "So what can I get you, handsome?"

"A plate of nachos, burgers and fries for eight." There were four of them, after all. He paused. "And some water for Heller. He's not drinking."

She frowned. "Why does he keep fighting Fletcher and those jerks? He's going to get himself shot or stabbed. Or worse."

How to tell her Heller had been defending her honor? But then Heller could have explained but hadn't, so he'd stay out of the guy's business. "I don't know. But Fletcher's an ass. It wouldn't hurt to convince him to go elsewhere for a good time. Before he starts dragging his friends from the triple-K club here."

She sighed. "There's that. Okay, food for the He-Man table, coming up."

Before she could leave, he leaned over the bar and grabbed her by the arm. "He's a good guy, Rena. You could do worse." He nodded back at Heller, who held one whimpering cretin by the collar while he glared at Lou and Rena. More particularly, at Lou *holding* Rena.

"I have done worse," she said with a huff. Then she kissed Lou on the cheek and smirked. "Ha. That's what you get for defending him. Now you're in big trouble." She laughed and flounced away.

And Lou had to go back to deal with the nightmare that was Heller while J.T. and Johnny laughed at him. Yet the possibility of the big guy's rage couldn't wash away his pleasure when Joey texted her agreement to meet him the following night.

Man, he had it bad, all right.

Heller dropped the creep he'd been holding, and the

bouncers dragged Fletcher and his thugs away, since several of them had trouble standing.

Lou returned to the table and held up his hands in surrender. "Not the face or the hands. I need to be pretty for my girl when I see her tomorrow." At Heller's barely concealed rage and J.T.'s narrow-eyed stare, he hastily amended, "For Joey. Not Rena. Jesus, Heller, get a grip."

Mis-take. Because now everyone focused on him.

Heller grunted and eased back.

Johnny and J.T. exchanged money.

"Hey."

"All's fair in love and rejection," Johnny said. "Though I'm still surprised it took you this long to win over the flower chick."

"Her name is Joey."

"*Her* name?" J.T. kicked back in his chair. "Hey man, be who you gotta be. We just want you to be happy. And if it takes 'Joe-y' to get you there, so be it."

Heller barked a laugh. "This I want to hear." But he still shot a fist to Lou's gut that made him blow out a breath. "But no more flirting with the bartenders."

"She was flirting with me! Okay, right, gotcha." He wheezed. "And Joey is a her, asshole," he said to J.T.

"Yeah, the flower chick." Johnny nudged J.T. "You remember. The woman who straight-up ignored him for how long?"

"Four months," J.T. answered without missing a beat.

Heller laughed.

"Shut up, Webster," Lou growled. "Or I start talking about you and a blond I remember you mooning over at your sister's wedding."

"Time for a refill." J.T. darted away. Smart guy.

Everyone turned back to Lou, waiting.

He sighed. "I had coffee with Joey at NCB. And then we went out to dinner the other night."

Johnny sighed. "I'm always the last to know. Well, Lou? We want details. Because we need to figure out how long you'll last before she gives you the boot. I'm down for a month. Foley and Sam will want in on the action too."

Heller shook his head. "And these you call friends?"

"Sad, I know." Yet Lou wanted to know the answer to his drop-dead date as well. With any luck, he'd ensnare the woman before she could think to tell him no. Not until he'd gotten his fill of her. Which wouldn't be anytime soon; he knew that for a fact.

Joey spent her Saturday morning doing chores. That afternoon, she took Brandon to a matinee, a cartoon about ninja fighting snakes he'd wanted to see, then they walked downtown through the crowds. She liked making sure her little boy felt comfortable in the city. Fear had never been a good instructor in her opinion. Better to know the good and bad about a thing before making up one's mind.

Words to live by, because every time she thought about Lou, her girlie parts tingled and she wanted to throw up from nerves. No way that amazing time with him could happen again. Or could it?

And there went the butterflies of nausea again.

"I want a bowl of soup, Mom."

Since she'd budgeted for the day with her little boy, she

had no problem loading him up with a cup of stellar clam chowder. They ate and walked, enjoying the crisp spring weather. The sun shone over Seattle for once, and after petting Rachel the Piggy Bank at Pike Place Market— Brandon's favorite thing to do—they walked around downtown before heading to a park closer to home.

She watched him run and play with some other children on the playground, swing to his heart's content, then slide a few more times. "Brandon, we need to go."

To her pleased surprise, her boy had made his own plans for the evening before she'd had to make them for him. A sleepover with a buddy. She now had no good excuse not to go out with Lou. Time to court her fear and learn what it was about the mechanic that affected her so.

Lou Cortez was just a man…with kissable lips and strong, firm hands. A man who'd actually given her an honest-to-God orgasm, her first with a partner in, well, forever.

Oh my God. I am pathetic.

She had to laugh, because she didn't want to cry. Twenty-four years old and never been kissed…down there. Never had a partner given her a roaring O before "big" Lou. And never felt such honest-to-goodness lust in her life. Not even with Felix, and then she'd been drowning in nervous excitement and wonder. A sentiment quickly overridden by fear, regret, and guilt.

No wonder she had issues with sex. She'd never gotten it right until Lou.

She hadn't been able to stop thinking about him since leaving the shop last night. Nor had she been able to forget so many sensations. Feeling him buried inside her while she found pleasure she'd never known existed.

Typically Joey hoped for a slim connection, a physical tie to another person for a short time. The pleasure of just being close to a man had been all she'd expected. But she'd never anticipated it could be so intense, so out-of-this-world amazing. No way it could be that good again. *No*. Better to not set herself up for disappointment. She should set her expectations low.

Yeah, she could do that.

She calmed herself while Brandon finished his last slide.

"If we don't get going, you'll be late for Todd's party."

A soccer buddy. Brandon played soccer on the weekends with a few friends from school, and he'd been dying for a sleepover with Todd for a while. It just so happened Todd had a birthday to celebrate. Tonight.

While she hung out with Lou. Would they go out, have a date? Or would they have more sex? Facing each other, maybe. Or not. That would be way more intimate than she'd be able to handle so soon. Maybe she should cancel the date and slow everything down.

But what about not succumbing to fear? Live what you preach, hypocrite.

She'd had sex on the third date. Well, technically, it hadn't even been a date. More like a spontaneous sexual explosion.

Her cheeks heated, and she forced herself not to think about sex while spending time with her son. He was so excited to be with his friend at a sleepover party. She'd had qualms about him being gone before because he was so young, because he needed her to care for him. She was all he had. Yeah, and he needed to have friends and spend time apart from Mommy.

To her dismay, the idea of him leaving, even for

the night, made her feel left behind. So stupid. Her son had to grow up sometime. It was good he felt confident enough to stay away from his mom, away from home. Besides, this wouldn't be his first stay at a friend's house overnight. Yet his eagerness to attend after giving her the third degree the other night when they'd been apart didn't make sense.

If she hadn't been so frazzled at the thought of seeing Lou again, she might have tried to figure the boy out. Instead, she put one foot in front of the other and managed to live in the now.

She took Brandon home, had him gather his things, then drove them to Todd's. "Use your manners, be polite, and you call me if you need me. I can come pick you up. You don't have to stay over tonight if you don't want." *Yeah, call me and I'll cancel with Lou. No problem.*

"Yes, Mom." Brandon rolled his eyes.

"I saw that."

He giggled and rolled them again, then crossed them.

She kept glancing at him out of the corner of her eye so as not to cause an accident while driving. "If you keep doing that, they might stay that way."

"That would be epic."

She sighed. "*Trolled, epic, a-hole.* Your vocabulary is hard to keep up with."

At that, her boy laughed uproariously, and she couldn't help joining him.

Dropping him off, she thanked Todd's parents and handed the boy's mother his present. "When should I pick him up? The invite said noon, right?"

The dad smiled and turned to address the gaggle of boys grouping behind him at the doorway. Once he'd ushered them back in the house, Todd's mother ruffled Brandon's hair.

Joey gave Brandon a kiss, tucked his arms in his overnight backpack, and shooed him toward Todd, who jumped up and down with excitement. "Have fun, Brandon."

"I will. Bye, Mom." He darted inside the house, not even a glance over his shoulder to see her leave.

"Noon? Hmm." Todd's mother looked ten years older than Joey. Her house had to cost a pretty penny. Joey had gotten so used to feeling inferior to the other kids' parents that apparent wealth no longer threw her.

"Or sooner if you want. I'm flexible." *I'm also poor, but I'm getting there, one step at a time.* Joey straightened and firmed her smile.

"Oh no. Please, let him stay at least until noon." She glanced behind her then turned back to Joey and in a lower voice said, "We were actually hoping he could stay to play a little longer after the others leave. Todd loves Brandon. I was going to take them and maybe one other boy to the indoor soccer place for a while. Can he stay until three?"

Joey did the math. Twenty hours of alone time? "Seriously? How much do I owe you for my mini-vacation?" Realizing how terrible that sounded, she started to stammer a retraction when Todd's mother laughed.

"I know exactly what you mean. We love 'em, but sometimes we just need a break."

Joey relaxed. "Um, yeah. It's fine if he stays. But I can always come get him if he changes his mind."

"We'll ask him tomorrow then, so he doesn't slip and tell the other boys. Don't want them to feel slighted." The woman smiled. "I'm Janice, by the way."

Joey blushed. "Sorry. I'm Joey. It's a pleasure to meet you."

"Likewise." Janice nodded. "We'll have a blast tonight. You go enjoy the break." Janice winked. "I plan to take a long, hot bath while my husband watches the kids. He owes me since I volunteered to be this season's soccer mom."

Joey grinned. "Have a great bath. I'll just go sit at home and think about not having to nag anyone to brush their teeth tonight." She felt giddy just thinking about it.

"Have at it. You have our number if you need anything."

Joey left wearing a huge grin, pleased to know she could sleep in. A glance at her phone showed she had another two hours until she planned to meet Lou. She wondered where he'd want to meet. The location would surely tell her about his intentions.

Yes, she should wait to make up her mind about throwing up until after he told her where they should meet. In the meantime, she'd see if Becky was free.

Ten minutes and a text later, she drove to Becky's house and planned to indulge in some girl time. Maybe Becky could help her understand her fascination for Lou.

She arrived at Becky's soon enough. Her friend shared a condo with a fellow teacher. As Joey entered, said teacher left with a smile.

"She's got a date tonight." Becky motioned to the coffee table, laden with wine, crackers, and cheese. "And apparently now so do I. Dig in." Becky lowered her voice and said, suggestively, "Welcome to my pad, sweetness. *Boom chicka bow bow*."

Joey laughed. "Stop. That only works when I'm the plumber or the delivery guy."

Becky sighed. "Guess I'll have to save that for

Trent, who's out of town this weekend. How the hell am I supposed to seduce him when he's helping his grandmother move?"

"Aw, that's so nice."

"Nice ain't sexy. Gah." Becky munched on a cracker. "But I'm excited to hang with you. I can't believe you finally got paroled. So Brandon the criminal is hanging with the other hooligans, eh? Way to dodge that bullet, Joey."

"Funny." Joey paused. "Ah, there's one thing. I can't stay past eight. I have a...date."

Becky stared. "Not with sexy Lou again."

Joey's silence answered for her.

"Oh my God. Dinner must have gone well the other night. Tell me."

Joey swallowed. "He was polite, charming. He looked amazing. He's really built." She flushed, feeling that "built" inside her all over again. "We talked then walked after dinner. He paid too. And he was so nice, so sweet. We held hands."

"Romantic." Becky sighed.

And then last night he bent me over the flower table and made me see stars. Yeah, romantic.

Becky hugged a pillow to her chest, her expression dreamy until her eyes narrowed on Joey's face. "Why are you blushing so hard? I mean, your face is really pink." Her eyes widened. "Holy crap. You had sex with him, didn't you?"

"N-no." She cleared her throat. "That's a little personal, don't you think?"

"Oh my God, you did. You did! Joey Reeves got some lovin'. Hot damn. It's about friggin' time!"

Still feeling overheated, Joey glanced up at her friend. "You can't tell anyone." She swore. "I can't believe it happened. It just…I'm still trying to process it."

"What's to process? You fell for the magic in his man-wand." Becky shrugged, as if it was no big thing. "Happens to the best of us. Well, except for me and Trent the Boy Scout," she grumbled.

Joey was stuck on *man-wand*. "What did you call it?"

Becky burst out laughing. "If you could see your face. Hey, you should hear half the things they call it. *Fuckstick*, *staff of life*, *lady's lollipop*. I could go on."

"Please, don't." Joey grimaced.

"I know, right? *Man-wand* is so much better." Becky paused. "Is it, Joey? Is it *better*? Or did you lollipop him? You know, like what we in the know call it—the hand and blow."

Joey's face threatened to melt clean off. She had a feeling she could fry eggs on her cheeks. "I can't believe I'm having this conversation."

"Me neither." Becky grinned. "You're like beet red right now. Or fire-engine red, maybe. Hey, did you guys remember to wear a 'raincoat'?" Becky snickered.

"Stop talking, please."

"Just tell me this. Do you want to do it again? As in, was it any good? Tell me, and I'll shut up."

"It was amazing, okay?" Joey growled. "So great I can't stop thinking about doing it again. And I don't tend to do well with men and sex."

"That's because you live like a nun in the Church of Reeves, presided over by Father Andrew and Sister Amy. God, it's a wonder you have a kid with all the guilt your parents keep throwing on you. And after eight—"

"Nine."

"—years, you'd think they'd let it go."

"So maybe I was just desperate. It was a one-shot deal, right?" *So why am I thinking of being with him again when I know it's a mistake?*

Becky shrugged and ate more crackers and cheese. "I think you should be desperate again. If you want him, have him. You have a right to be happy. Take joy in his man parts. Go forth, just don't prosper."

Joey choked on a laugh. "Yes, Mom."

"Ouch."

"Don't worry. We were safe." Rather, *he* was safe. She'd been so far gone, she hadn't thought about protection until it was almost too late, which was just stupid. Granted, she wouldn't have babies with Lou while on birth control. But she could always chance a disease with an unknown. She'd been so wrapped up in the moment, lost to her body's needs.

But Lou had thought ahead.

Which put his actions in a different light. Had he expected to have sex with her?

"What's that look?" Becky asked.

"He was ready for it. Us, I mean."

Becky looked confused.

"He was *prepared*."

"Jesus, Joey. You can say *condom* and not burn in hell. So he was prepared. Good for him."

"You think?"

"Who cares why he had the condom? He had it, you had fun. And if you're lucky, you'll have more fun tonight." Becky poured herself some wine. "Have some for me, would you? Because I'm clearly not getting any." She cocked her head, considering something. "Unless Will's home."

"Becky."

Becky laughed. "Nah. Will's in Italy this month." She chuckled. "Kidding, kidding. I'm wanting Trent. I am. Really."

They laughed some more, and when Joey excused herself for the bathroom, a new text popped up. Lou had decided on the place. An address in Rainier Valley, where he'd mentioned he lived.

She didn't know what to think, so she took care of business and blanked her mind.

She returned to the living room. "He invited me to his place."

Becky blinked. "You were gone maybe five minutes."

"He just texted me."

"So go."

"To his place?"

"Why not? Is he rapey or something?"

"No." He'd been a perfect gentleman since she'd known him. And even after sending her to heaven, *twice*, he'd ended their impromptu session at the flower shop with a hug and by walking her to her car. "No. He's nice. Sexy. Too—"

"He's exactly what you need." Becky nodded. "Give me your phone."

Joey handed it over and bit her thumbnail, a nervous habit she thought she'd broken.

"There. You'll see him in half an hour. Well? Get moving." Becky nudged her to the door. "I want a full report tomorrow."

Then she shoved Joey through, slammed the door after her, and laughed.

"I can hear you," Joey said.

"I know," came back, muffled through the door. "Now go get laid."

Joey raced down the hallway so no one would associate her with Becky's comments. Back inside her car, she laid her forehead on the wheel and tried to figure out what she wanted.

Live in the moment for once, the daring part of her insisted. *You don't know what he wants. He might just want to hang out, be friends without sex on the table.* She laughed hysterically when she realized "sex on the table" applied, literally, to her.

Joey lifted her head, trying to talk herself out of going the entire way to Lou's house. But the tough woman under all the wussiness, the girl who knew it was time to stop trying to please her father by being a born-again virgin, who wanted to be a role model for her son by facing her fears, knew she had to go.

After parking in Lou's drive, she let herself out, locked the car, and took two steps up the driveway.

"Who the hell are you?" came an angry woman's voice from behind her.

And this is why we should never listen to imaginary voices in our head, common sense told her before she turned to face the proof that she'd made a huge mistake.

Chapter 8

Stella stared at the pretty brunette, taking in her wide eyes, petite frame, and wary tension. So not Lou's type. But she'd bet hard cash this was the reason Lou had kicked his own sister out of his house. A grieving, needy, lovely younger sister needing his attention outed over some petite bimbo with big brown eyes and tiny boobs.

Gimme a break.

"I'm sorry. What?"

Mierda. Even her voice sounded pleasant, kind. Stella pursed her lips, deciding not to make it easy. Lou might be hung up on her, because yeah, even Stella had noticed how evasive he'd been discussing the "phone chick." Frankly, after dealing with Paul, she was soured on relationships. Her brother was the best guy she knew. Smart, loving, handsome, and worth ten of any number of the weak women constantly panting after him.

"I said, 'Who the hell are you?'"

Phone Chick couldn't be much older than Stella. She had a bright-eyed, wholesome appearance. Not some slutty female out to get a piece of her brother, which Stella knew should be a good thing. Lou could do with a little more substance to his women. But not too much substance. With Lou, family always came first. Not kicking out his poor, vulnerable sister for a piece of ass.

Stella grunted. This woman looked scared of her own

shadow. Oh yeah. She'd last maybe a minute in Lou's bed. Stella grinned and in Spanish said, "You think you can handle my brother? His last girlfriend had tits bigger than yours and a better ass, too." Insulted, yet the *puta* had no idea.

Phone Chick stared at her with intensity, then gave a surprising smile. "You must be one of Lou's sisters. You look like him, only a heck of a lot prettier. Which one are you?"

Stella unwillingly answered, "I'm Stella."

"Oh. It's so nice to meet you." Phone Chick seemed to soften, then had the nerve to get right up in Stella's personal space and…stick out a hand.

Stella grudgingly took it, surprised to feel calluses on the woman's palms. Obviously no stranger to hard work. For some reason, she reminded Stella of Ivy, Sam's girlfriend. She had the same wholesomeness, the same kindness in her eyes. The same way of making Stella want to rip her hair out by the roots while feeling bad for disliking her.

"Lou said you liked the flowers."

"Huh?"

"The bouquet of flowers Lou gave you."

"Oh. Those were nice." Beautiful, actually.

Phone Chick nodded. "Good. You deserve nice."

She did. Hmm. Stella was starting to understand what her brother saw in the woman. The warm compassion in her tone, the clear intelligence, the ability to recognize beauty when she saw it. "Why did Lou tell you about my flowers?"

"He bought them from me. I work at S&J Floral." Phone Chick glanced at Lou's front door, then back at

Stella. "When he said his sister had had a hard day and needed something special, I knew just what to make. Men can be such assholes."

Stella blinked, not having expected those words from such an innocent-looking face. "Ah, *sí*. I know."

"You're better off without him," she said, a fierceness to her tone. "I'd be surprised if you don't already have a dozen guys drooling at the thought of you being single."

"You get the same thing, eh? Men all over you." Stella could well understand it, even if she still didn't all the way like the girl.

"Not me. I can't tell you the last time I went out. Before your brother, I mean." Phone Chick blushed. "But don't tell Lou."

"Yeah, *mi hermano* has a big head already. You should make him work for you." Wait, what? She hadn't meant to say that, but somehow the woman with the kind eyes had Stella blurting things she didn't mean. "What's your name, anyway?"

"Oh, sorry. I'm Joey."

"I'm Stella. But you know that."

"Yeah." Joey smiled.

And somehow Stella smiled back.

The door opened. "Hey, get lost, little sister. I have important company." Lou's dopey face looked different. Caring, almost gooey-eyed affectionate. *What the hell?* Hadn't he just met this woman? "Hey, Joey." His voice was deep, soft, gentle. So sweet, and so unlike the suave charmer with seduction tattooed to his tongue.

To Stella's bemusement, Joey turned even more pink. She glanced from Stella to Lou. "Hi." So shy, so quiet yet glowing under her brother's appraisal.

Stella needed to get back to her sisters pronto. They had to hear about this. "Oh, hey, I have to go. See you later, Guapo."

He barely waved, intent on greeting Joey and escorting her up the walk into the house. As if the woman couldn't manage on her own two feet without macho badass Lou to help her carefully up four steps.

Stella didn't know whether to be proud, worried, or ecstatic. Because she'd never, ever, seen her brother act so gone for a woman before. And the fact he'd been keeping this one secret? Hmm. Time to call in the big guns.

She drove away. "Lucia? It's me. You would not believe what I just saw…"

―⁓―

Lou couldn't look away from Joey's smile. She'd worn her hair down in a soft brown wave over her shoulders. Her lips again looked rosy, and he leaned down to kiss her, absorbing the knowledge that the vibrant red was indeed all natural.

She blinked at him when he pulled back, looking as dazed as he felt. "Ah, hi."

He grinned. "Come on in."

The small white house had a lot more space than it seemed from the outside. Though the grass had been cut, the shrubs looked a bit untended, and he knew he needed some flowers. But once inside, many a guest had been pleasantly surprised to find it homey.

Old wooden floors lay between whitewashed walls decorated with art. Different kinds from portraits to abstracts to photographs decorated the space. He'd remodeled the older house to reflect an open floor plan, and his simple furnishings spoke more of comfort than class yet still complemented the decor.

"You want something to drink?" he asked and eased her jacket off her shoulders, concerned when she tensed. As if realizing it, she relaxed, and he took her coat and hung it over the back of a nearby chair.

"To drink? Oh. Yes, please."

Lou drew her with him to the kitchen, which flowed directly from the living room. Bright and airy, the space was inviting. The lower cabinets had a dark finish, the top cabinets a lighter color. The counters were done in speckled black and looked cleaner than his mother's, which gave him much pride. Even Abuela preferred his kitchen to his mama's.

"Wow. Are you always this clean?"

"Sadly, yes." He kissed the top of her head, and he swore she tensed again, so he subtly backed away, paying attention to her signals. He stepped to the fridge. "I have beer, lemonade, or water. Oh, and milk if you want some."

"Lemonade is great, thanks."

He fixed her a cup and took a beer for himself, then leaned against the V of the counter, watching her. "You look nervous, *princesa*. Don't be."

She shrugged. "I don't know what I'm doing here. I mean, I do. But I don't know where we go from...you know. Before."

"You can be so direct one minute and shy the next. You want to talk about what happened?"

Talk about turning pink. She was so cute in her nerves. Her gaze darted everywhere but at him as she nursed her lemonade. "No. Yes. We probably should, but not right now, okay?"

"No problem." He'd play it cool, not seduce her or anything. Instead, he'd ease her into trusting him, like a skittish colt needing a firm but gentle hand. The thought had him grinning, because he knew being compared to a horse would turn the shy woman before him into an ass-kicking florist who knew how to use shears.

"What's so funny?" Her eyes narrowed.

"Nothing. Just glad to see you again."

She bit her lip then gave a slow smile that turned him inside out. To his chagrin, he had to wipe his sweating palms on his jeans, surreptitiously, one a time.

"I thought we could"—*fuck through to tomorrow*—"hang out and watch TV or play some cards. Just chill out together."

Her shoulders relaxed. "Oh, sure. But I can't stay too late."

"Your carriage going to turn back into a pumpkin?"

"Something like that."

"So then, you know how to play gin?"

She grinned. "I'm actually pretty good."

And so Lou, once a sought-after bachelor and all-around ladies' man, spent his Saturday evening playing cards with a woman he wanted with his next breath. Every hand she won, every spark of merriment in her eyes, the husky joy in her laugh, shot him further into no-man's land, a bad place where he had no leverage and she held all the cards.

Or rather he did, because she just went out again. The cardsharp.

"I win." She grinned.

"Do you play darts?"

"No, why?"

"That's what we're playing next time." A man could only handle so much humiliation.

"Darts, huh? Sure, why not?"

"And no more sugar for you," he groused. "You're downright perky."

She snickered. "Oh? I was going to get another glass."

"Go ahead." He sighed then couldn't help smiling at her chipper dance from the dining room. He followed her into the kitchen to grab some water. Beer was all well and good, but a guy needed to hydrate with the real stuff.

He saw her leaning over, her ass out as she rummaged in the refrigerator.

His throat went dry, recalling another time when she'd been bent over. "It's in the back."

She bumped her head and said something he couldn't make out. Then she straightened with the jug of lemonade in hand and closed the fridge. She refilled her glass and moved to put the jug away, but he took it from her and set it aside.

"Lou?"

He crowded her until he'd backed her against the counter. This time he had her chest to chest. Damn, she was fine.

"I've been wanting to do this all day." He leaned close and gave her a barely there peck on the lips, pulled back, then waited.

Just the touch of her shocked his body into being fully alive and ready for her.

He watched the confusion, the lust darken her eyes.

Joey didn't hide much, her expressive face telling him all he needed to know.

Filled with tenderness for the woman he was by all accounts coming to care for, deeply, he leaned in and kissed her again. This time he cupped her cheeks, stroking her soft skin, the line of her jaw, as he showed her how he felt. Taking his time, drawing back to look in her eyes, he dove back in when she tugged him by the shoulder.

The heat in that small palm did him in.

He continued to touch her with care, molding his hands to her slight shoulders, her thin arms and hands. He put her hands on his hips then grabbed her narrow waist as well and plastered them together, pelvis to pelvis.

She had to feel what she did to him, but he couldn't stop from wanting that connection. To let her see how she affected him.

So attuned to their shared attraction, he needed a moment to realize her responses had cooled. The kiss went from hot to awkward, her lips trembling under his.

He immediately pulled back and stroked her hair, so as not to spook her. "I'm sorry. I went too fast, didn't I?"

A glance into her tear-filled eyes struck him to the quick. He ached at the thought of causing her harm. But from a kiss she'd more than been a part of? "Joey, it's okay."

"No. It's not." She pushed at his chest, but her pathetic attempt at distance didn't move him. Her tears did.

He stepped back and crossed his arms over his chest to keep from reaching for her and offering the comfort she clearly didn't want.

"I'm so sorry. I knew this was a mistake." Her breath hitched, and she wiped away a stray tear.

"Fuck, Joey. What's wrong, baby? Did I push you into something you didn't want? I swear I didn't mean to."

"The kiss, I…" She stopped speaking.

"Talk to me."

More tears spilled, and she shook her head.

He could do nothing but follow her as she hurried back into the living room, grabbed her jacket, and tore out of his house.

"Joey, wait."

"I have to go," she mumbled and raced away.

Leaving him still hard, confused, and terrified he'd lost her before he'd had a chance to love her.

—∞—

Joey spent Sunday morning awake and miserable, staring at her ceiling when she should have been sleeping in. Last night could not have been more humiliating.

She'd been wrong to think she could have a normal relationship when she was anything but normal.

Once again, she'd kissed a man and felt nothing. Oh, at first Lou had been warm and sexy, his entire body smelling so good and feeling the way a man ought to feel. But the gentle way he'd touched her, treating her like a fragile creature unable to handle a little passion, had thrown her. He'd been so unlike the out-of-control sexual dynamo from the flower shop.

She had to write off Friday night as a fluke. Great sex would apparently never be in the cards for her again. If she couldn't get hot over a guy like Lou, she was doomed. Crap. She could never go to NCB or the garage again or hang out with Del.

Joey sighed. So much potential. Then she'd thought

too hard, allowed her worries about her possible performance to ruin it all, and left in tears.

In tears. How much more non-sexy could she be? God. A real woman would have either taken Lou up on his generous offer or said no thanks and left. Not run away crying. She continued to behave like the irresponsible little girl her parents thought her to be. No wonder she got no respect from her father. She wasn't worthy of it.

Bad enough she'd had sex with Lou once. She'd thought about doing it again. And then her father's face had entered her mind's eye, that sad look of disappointment. Her mother's frown of worry, then the disillusioned sigh and quiet acceptance that her daughter had screwed up yet again.

A normal woman didn't think about her father when with a sexy man. Joey typically did nothing but obsess over making the wrong choices and dealing with unintended consequences. She'd have thought that nearly a decade of repentance should have cured her of any need to please her father.

Yet whenever it came to sex, she had a difficult time dealing. Dating was one thing. Playing cards, having dinner, enjoying time with Lou had been wonderful. And the sex before—fast and hot and out of this world. But tonight, instead of getting turned on again, she'd turned cold.

She should see someone to talk about her issues. Maybe she was frigid. Unable to get past disappointing lovers, inured to bad sex when she had it. But Reeveses didn't do therapy, and she didn't have the money for it anyway.

She shoved a pillow over her face and screamed.

Then she did what she always did. Joey soldiered on. She got up, made her bed, cleaned her tiny apartment, and did her laundry, keeping well away from her parents unless putting in or changing a load.

Once she'd finished everything, she called to check on Brandon while avoiding texts and calls from Lou. By ten, after she'd been up for four hours, she knew she had to put an end to it to be fair to them both, and she texted him back.

> Lou. You were so sweet to me. I'm sorry I left the way I did. But we're too different anyway. Thanks for the cards and the kiss. I hope we can still be friends. Joey.

There. That said "broken up" better than anything could, if they'd even been going out in the first place. A coffee date, dinner, and sexy encounter did not make a relationship. Heck. For all she knew, Lou had another date on standby and two more in the wings.

By three, she'd resolved herself to going back to being Andrew and Amy's daughter. Brandon's mother.

A woman with little hope for a future with a man and even less desire to have one.

Or so she kept telling herself.

Chapter 9

BY WEDNESDAY, LOU HAD HAD ENOUGH. AND SO HAD the guys at Webster's.

"That's it. Take off, Lou. Get drunk, get laid, get out. Man, it hurts just to look at that face." Foley stood over him, shaking his head. So of course Sam joined him.

Lou glared at up at the twin busybodies. "I can't see, assholes. You're blocking my light." He'd been trying to work J.T.'s sketch of a busty mermaid into something that wouldn't get their new client arrested for indecency. Damn. Did J.T. know any real women, the kind that didn't have breasts larger than cannonballs and a waist the size of a pencil? At those dimensions, she should break in half.

"Hey, moron, we're talking to you," Johnny said, having joined the crowd. When Lou glared up at him, he backed away. "Kidding, kidding. Just saying what Sam is thinking."

"You got that right." Sam sighed. "Lou, call her."

"I'm giving her space," Lou muttered. Due to all the frowning and swearing Lou had been doing since Monday, the guys thought Joey had dumped him. That she'd finally seen reason and left their buddy behind.

What they didn't know was that Lou had no intention of being left anywhere, especially when he had no idea what he'd done wrong.

Joey's head was all fucked up, and he needed to be calm and collected before he went fishing for answers.

"Look," he said to the brood now staring at him like a two-headed zebra in a fishbowl. "Joey and I aren't over. We're just taking things slow."

"Like the work on the Charger over there," Liam boomed, then laughed. "Saw you flinch, Johnny. Thought I was Del for a minute, didn't you?"

"Maybe for a second. But your voice is higher."

Foley chuckled, and even Lou had to smile at that.

"Ass." Liam snorted. "Now, everyone, back to work. Don't worry about our boy here. Lou knows women."

Sam frowned. "How is it that you're up everyone else's ass when it comes to our personal lives, but Lou, who's obviously messed up, gets a pass?"

Liam shrugged. "I've met his family. He knows women."

Johnny agreed. "With that many female relatives, he should."

"Any man who can live with that many women and not go crazy? A genuine Svengali." Liam nodded.

"A what?"

"Never mind," Lou muttered to Foley. "Thanks, Liam."

"Don't mention it." The bastard had the nerve to chuckle. "Though I have to admit I'm entertained. Never thought I'd see the great Casanova Cortez off his game."

Lou groaned. "Why is everyone around here bitching and cackling about relationships like a bunch of…" He tapered off as he saw Del behind her father, tapping her foot while she waited for him to finish.

"Like a bunch of what, Lou?" she asked, her voice lethal.

The rest of the guys scattered, except for Liam.

"Old retired men," he improvised.

She grunted, but Liam looked pained.

"Sorry, she's meaner than you are."

Liam sighed. "True. Well, I'd best be getting back to Sophie anyway." He glanced at Lou. "Why don't you come to dinner soon? Sophie likes you."

"She has good taste."

Liam quirked a brow. "Yeah? So why did you tell her she could do better than me?"

"Because she can?" He chuckled and dodged the fist aimed at his shoulder. "Kidding. She just likes me because of that picture I sketched of you two."

Liam nodded. "You have some serious skills, boy. Damned if you don't. Think about dinner, okay?"

"I will." *Think about it, that is. With any luck, I'll soon be sharing a meal with Joey. Or eating Joey out. Either way works with me.*

Two hours later, after spending the rest of his time at the garage working on an Explorer's transmission with Johnny, Lou left for S&J Floral. He arrived at six, when he knew Joey would be there.

He saw her in the front chatting and laughing with some young guy who watched her a little too closely for Lou's peace of mind.

He entered the store and frowned at the familiar face, one he'd seen at Del's wedding. "Donnigan? Which one are you again?"

The boy grinned. "Hey, Lou. I remember you. You drew a picture of Cousin Mike's dog on a napkin for Colin. I'm Theo Donnigan. The good-looking, smart one in the family."

"Oh right." Lou smiled. Having met a lot of McCauley relations at Del's wedding, Lou had a difficult time keeping track of the many men in that family.

But Theo had been easy enough to impress and a nice kid to boot. "What are you doing here?"

Joey had yet to speak, but her cautious gaze gave him hope. Slightly nervous was workable. Downright panic, rage, or grief…no.

"I work here, man." Theo's eyes sparkled. "I'm part-timing, maybe getting ready to leave the coffee shop. Me and Maya are…" He cleared his throat. "Never mind. Pretty soon I'm joining the Marine Corps. Just waiting for the recruiter to get back to me. So I'm delivering flowers." Theo whipped some bills from his back pocket. "I made twenty bucks in tips today!"

Lou smiled. So did Joey, who said, "He's got a gift. The ladies love him."

"*All* the ladies?" Lou asked in a low voice, suggestive enough that Theo should get the hint.

Which he did, by the way his eyes widened. "Ah, I think I'm gonna go home now, Joey. Or did you want me to stay, you know? To fix that stuff in the back?"

A good kid, because the lie was obvious. He'd stay if Joey wanted him to, even knowing Lou could tear him apart should he feel like it.

Joey frowned at Lou. "I'm fine. I'll finish with Lou then lock up." She had another half an hour, so Lou figured to make the most of his time.

"Well, okay then. See you, Lou, Joey."

"Later." They both watched Theo leave, then waited until the chime of the back door sounded.

"Flowers for you?" Joey asked, all business, still staring at Theo's exit.

"Cut the shit." His bluntness caused her head to whip up. "What's the deal?"

"The deal?"

He blew out a breath. "You want to do this the hard way or the easy way? And don't even look like you're afraid of me. I'd rather wear a pink tutu and have my sisters talk about how much they love *Downton Abbey* than harm a hair on your head. Believe it."

"I—fine. I know that." She seemed exasperated. With him? "I'm not scared of you, Lou."

"Oh?" He waited.

"I'm scared of me," she blurted.

"Go on."

"I don't want to talk about it. Can't you just accept we're done?"

"Hmm. No."

"Well, good, I—No?"

"No. You and I are good together. You know it. I know it. But you got skittish and bolted. So I'm back to rein you in."

———

Like a horse? What was with the smirk he wore? Joey shook her head, determined to take the high road. His pride had been bruised, after all. "Lou, I don't want this to be a thing. I like you. You're a nice man."

He laughed. "No. I'm not."

"I don't know what you want."

He stopped laughing, his expression inscrutable. "Why don't you tell me what *you* want?"

"To be left alone. I have enough to do with work and at home. I don't need more complications."

"Complications. Huh." He didn't move around the counter, so she felt safe enough with it between them. But she could see his displeasure with the conversation.

Well, too bad. She had the right to reject him if she wanted.

"Are we done?"

He shook his head and walked around the counter, and instead of cornering her like the big bad wolf he tended to be, he moved back into the prep room. To the same table he'd previously bent her over.

"Such great memories." He sighed.

She felt her face heat. "I'd like you to go."

"First you tell me what happened at my place the other night. I was there. You were right with me. The kiss was fuckin' hot. Then you vanished."

"I didn't go anywhere."

"At first. Then you weren't with me—up here." He tapped his temple. "What happened?"

Since he sincerely seemed to be trying to understand, she owed it to him to put his mind at ease. Poor Lou had done nothing wrong. "We were having fun with cards," she said. "Then you turned it into something else."

He stared at her and slowly shook his head. "No. I gave you a simple kiss. *You* pulled me closer. *You* turned it into something else. Not that I would have objected, but I didn't invite you to my place to fuck you again."

She flinched.

"I wanted to spend time with you, to have fun with you." His scrutiny intense, his eyes penetrating, he added in a lower voice, "And for a while I did."

She started to panic, because he kept *looking* at her. As if he might understand her? Good luck when she didn't understand herself.

"Was all that crying and weirdness about what happened in here Friday night?" he continued.

She could work with that. Because no way in hell she wanted him to know she'd turned cold, turned off by sex because the thought of it with a nice guy did nothing for her. And that the idea of having sex at all, being such a disappointment to her parents, haunted her.

"You want to talk about it? Fine." She drew in a deep breath then let it out, fighting a hysterical laugh since it sounded like a rush of air escaping from a balloon. "When we were getting all hot and heavy in here, you were clearheaded enough to have a condom ready to go. You expected we'd have sex, maybe planned it," she accused.

He didn't break eye contact. "I always have a condom in my wallet. Because a good man is always prepared. But no, sadly, I hadn't planned it. I was just so happy you agreed to go out with me, and I had wanted to see you again. Trust me. I hadn't imagined the first time we made love to be in the back room of your flower shop."

Made love? She swallowed. "I still can't believe we did that."

His gaze roamed her figure. "I can. Touching you gets me hard. Hell, being around you gets me hard." He glanced down at his front.

She saw the shape of him as well. Suddenly she felt hot.

"I can't help it." Lou shrugged. "I don't try to. You and I, we click, physically. I think you'd agree to that at least?"

She'd come in seconds with him. Yeah, they had chemistry.

"But more than that, I like you, Joey. You don't know me that well, I get it. But the more time we spend together, the more you'll see I don't lie. I'm not the guy if you just want to scratch an itch. I like sex, hell yeah. But it's more than that with me. I'm not into casual hookups. I like to know my partner, you get me?"

"The thing is, I don't do casual hookups either." As if he'd believe that after Friday. "The last time I had sex was over a year ago, and he and I had been going out for months. I'm not a fast kind of girl. I know that seems unbelievable considering we barely knew each other before we—"

Lou held up a hand. "I understand. Look, I don't exactly come across as a guy who can keep it in his pants after Friday." He groaned. "It was amazing and embarrassing. I swear I can last longer than the two seconds it took me to come."

Man, she hated talking about this. Her face felt on fire. "Great. We both admit the sex was amazing. Okay. But then it wasn't. So what now?"

"Now we find out why we find each other so fascinating."

"Lou, I'm done. Remember? I just want to be friends."

"Please. Joey, it's me. Who wouldn't want more of this prime male specimen?" He did a pirouette, showing off his figure and ending with a wink.

She chuckled despite trying to get rid of him. He had confidence and a great sense of humor. And when he smiled like that, his eyes seemed to glow with a vibrant delight she wanted to snatch up and keep all to herself. Except she sucked at sex, and a man like Lou would only want more. No. Time to cut him loose.

"You're funny and sweet and sexy." She nodded. "And a bit too much for me. The other night at your place, I was overwhelmed."

His eyes narrowed. "By my petting you? Kissing you on the lips, no tongue? Hell, I kissed the top of your head. *That* was too much for you?"

"Does it matter? I'm telling you the truth."

"Hmm."

"What hmm? I'm not lying to you. I have no reason to. I just don't need any more drama in my life. So can we please stop this and get on with being friends?"

"On one condition."

"Fine."

"Kiss me."

Could he not take no for an answer? Was she that special he had to have her and no one else? And why, by all that was safe and orderly, did she let him pull her into his chaos? Let him make her want more than what she'd been getting by with for the past nine years?

Puzzled at why this man should make her want what so many others hadn't, she watched him, wondering. "Am I even your regular type?"

"I don't have a type."

"Everyone has a type." She shrugged. "You're not exactly mine."

"Oh?" His expression flattened.

"You're too good-looking. Too overwhelming. You walk into a place and all eyes swing your way."

"That's just because everyone's afraid the big bad Mexican's out to kick ass. And technically, I'm not totally Mexican. I think my great-grandfather came from Barcelona."

"Spain or Seattle, I think it's more like you have a chip on your shoulder and a mean attitude that scares people."

He blinked. "Me? Mean? Honey, I may not be the

nicest guy you'll ever meet, but I'm sincere. Pleasant. And, of course, handsome."

She snorted. "You're scary, and you like being scary."

"You're wrong. Was I scary at Del's wedding, twirling her around and helping Colin steal wedding cake?"

"Yes."

"Huh?"

She crossed her arms over her chest, easing into the discussion. "You kept following me around, looking at me like, ah…"

He pushed off the cutting counter and stalked her. "Like I'm looking at you right now, maybe?"

She swallowed. "Yes, as a matter of fact."

He walked right up to her and tilted her chin so she would meet his gaze. "Like I wanted to taste your mouth, to see if you're as sweet as you look?" He leaned down and kissed her, so brief, it was barely there. "To touch you and see if you're as soft all over?" He ran a hand over her cheek, then cupped the back of her neck and dragged her closer. "To bring you close and smell you, to know if that sultry perfume is you or the flowers around you?" He inhaled at the base of her throat and sighed. "No, that sweetness is all you."

He made her tremble, the large man with a romantic soul. But no. That gentle hold was supposed to turn her off, the way it had last time. Man, her body was so messed up. "You're good at this."

His fingers spanned her throat, and she grew damp. "This?"

"Seduction. Romance," she said, her voice hoarse. "The lines you spout to all the girls you want to drop their panties."

He smiled, but the heat in his gaze showed he was anything but amused. "I'm only as good as my inspiration. And you, Josephine Reeves, have been inspiring me for months."

"S-see? All that seduction stuff. It won't work with me, Lou. That time before, in here, was a freak chance. A one in a million. A—"

He kissed her, to shut her up, maybe. But the forceful heat and the hand at the back of her head, holding her in place, stole every thought she'd ever had. It confused her enough to get her out of her head, so that she once again let her body do the talking while her mind dwelled on Lou's taste, his touch, his strength.

The kiss ended, leaving them both winded.

"You're so damn fine, and you don't even know it." He sighed. "So tell me again why we couldn't do this at my place Saturday night."

She wished she knew.

He pulled his head back to stare down at her.

"I-I… Heck. I don't know," she groaned, half wishing he'd let her go so her brain would turn back on. "Sometimes I just get confused. My thoughts get jumbled, and it's all too much."

"Too much?" He chuckled. "Being with you, the words that come to mind are *not enough*." He pressed his hips tighter against hers. "You feel that? That's my dick wanting to get reacquainted."

She gasped. "Okay, that's not so romantic." Yet she was hooked on him and his dirty talk anyway.

"So what's different about today instead of my place? Is it the flower shop? Does doing it at work turn you on?" He didn't sound judgmental but curious.

She squirmed in his hold, but he refused to release her, so she glared up at him past her embarrassment. "No, I'm not an exhibitionist."

"Um, we're alone in here. Aren't we?" He gave an interested look around the room.

"Yes, we're alone. And no, I don't like being like this at work. All sexed up and stuff."

He bit his lip, and she knew he was working to hold onto a grin.

"Don't laugh at me."

"Wouldn't dream of it." He continued to hold her close, his hands somehow having found their way to her waist. "Let's reason this out. I'm hard for you all the time. We both know that."

She couldn't help feeling his excitement against her. And knowing he wanted her turned her on too much.

"But you get wrapped up in your head, you said. So last time in here, it hit us all of a sudden, right? And then we just went for it. Not thinking, little foreplay, then me bending you over the table and fucking you."

Her pulse raced, hearing him say it making her want to do it all over again.

"Yeah, there we go. I can see in your eyes you want some more." He kissed her thoroughly, leaving her panting. "Damn, *cariña*. You're addicting." He rubbed a thumb over her lower lip. "But the other night, I wasn't trying to seduce you. I was trying to court you."

She blinked. "Did you say 'court' me?" Had she lost a century in that kiss? "And oh my gosh, are you blushing?"

"Stop being a pain. You know what I mean. I was nice and respectful. Gentle. Not pawing at you like an animal." He cupped her breast, and her body sizzled under his firm hand. He pinched her nipple through her clothes, and she bit her lip to stifle a groan.

"See, I think your deal is you like a firmer hand."

"I do?" she rasped. That seemed a little too simple an answer. Not like she hadn't considered that herself. If she'd been able to figure out why she couldn't connect intimately with a partner, she'd have fixed herself long ago. But she had a feeling that the guilt from her first time had resulted in a lifetime of psychological problems when it came to relationships. God, she'd been single for nine long years. And on the rare times she did have sex, it was never any good.

Except that one time with Lou.

"Yeah. And by the way, that whole 'it's not you, it's me' line you tried is bullshit." His fierce tone startled her. "It's not all you, at least. A real man reads his woman, knows what she likes and doesn't like. So if you're not into it, I need to work with you to get you there."

This had to be the most awkward, arousing conversation she'd ever had. Discussing her dysfunctional sex life while pressed against a man with a steel bar in his pants. How could she still want him right now? When just a few days ago, they'd been alone, in the perfect space for some private time, and she'd bolted?

It *had* to be her. Lou was sex personified. "But it is me. I'm not trying to be patronizing, Lou. I have issues."

"You know, the first time we got so hot so fast, you didn't have time to think." His gaze narrowed. "You liked when I was in charge, didn't you?"

She blushed. "A little."

"Maybe a lot, huh?"

"Lou."

"*Joey.* You're not the only one with turnoffs. I like being in charge in bed. I really don't want a woman climbing over me and taking control unless I tell her to."

"But isn't letting her take control still you being in charge?"

"That's my point. Look, some guys are into breasts. Some are turned on by a nice, thick ass." He held her hips and ground against her belly. "I like a slender woman, one with dark-brown hair, a killer body, and a smile just like yours. See that? Your eyes got a little darker, your breath faster."

"I like you holding me close," she admitted. "A lot."

"You liked that first night, and you liked it Saturday night too. Until you started worrying too much, huh?" He suddenly let go of her hips and held her by the neck in a move so fast, he startled her. "Now what, *cariña*? What will you do? How will you get free if I don't wanna let you go?"

To her shock and shame, she felt a huge wave of desire. Like, a tsunami worth of want.

He didn't squeeze, but he held her tight. Controlling her. "You like that, don't you?"

"I don't know. Yes," she groaned. She wanted to feel worse about her sexual proclivities, but she couldn't focus past the angry curl of his lips. God, he was sexy when he was mean.

"You know…" He slid his hand up to grip her by the hair. Then he tightened his hold, and the bite of pain made it worse. Because she wanted him enough to drop her pants and spread her legs. *Right here, right now.* "Tell me, Joey. Tell me what you want." He pulled her hair, just a small tug.

And she moaned. "I don't understand, but I like this. It's…weird."

"It's not weird. It's fuckin' hot. I'm so hard right now. You know that? Because I get off on this. And so do you, it seems." He didn't give her a chance to argue. To tell him that good girls who followed the rules didn't like kinky, abnormal sex. Or that she should really be going home to her little boy and her disappointed parents and keep her legs closed for once.

Instead, she opened her mouth for him when he told her to, and she welcomed the kiss, the invading tongue, that stole her will and left nothing but pleasure.

After an eternity, Lou pulled back and must have liked what he saw. "Yeah, this is what we're going to do the next time we're together. You and me at my place. ¿Sí?"

She blinked, trying to gather her scattered thoughts. "What?"

"You tell me you can't want me, and then you lose yourself in our kiss." He kept his hand in her hair and gave a playful tug. "Focus on me when we're together. You let me be in charge, and I'll take care of you, sweetheart. Give us a chance, and you'll be crying out my name the next time I'm buried deep inside you." He let her go, his fingers sliding through her hair as he stepped back.

She couldn't help noticing the monstrous erection in his jeans.

"See? This is what bossing you around does to me." He grinned, then grimaced when he cupped himself. "I'm in pain because of you, woman. You have to say yes to this weekend. I might die if you don't." His hopeful leer made her laugh.

"I don't know how you can talk me into the things you do."

"What, coffee? A date? That's nothing. Wait until you're naked and I'm between those pretty thighs." He winked. "I know how to make you feel real good, Joey."

She exhaled, still hot and bothered and now no longer worried about losing her desire for Lou. "You're a smooth talker for sure."

"Yeah, but I can back it up." His thorough once-over had her wanting to squirm. And when she shifted, her legs slid all too easily, her own arousal more than obvious to her.

This connection she might never get again. And darn it, she *liked* Lou. How different to be with a man who put *her* needs first. "So, well, maybe we can get together Friday night. I have to see."

He didn't question her. Instead, he nodded. "Let me know. Same place, eight o'clock." He stepped back from her. "And as much as I want you, we can just hang, okay? No pressure." He stood, staring, as if unsure. Then he muttered under his breath, stepped close again, and kissed her.

With a lot of tongue and groping hands. When he moved away, he was swearing under his breath in Spanish. He visibly adjusted himself. "Sorry. But it's painful. You just don't know. Now do your closing, and I'll wait for you to lock up."

She hurried, and when she'd finished, he walked her out to her car. She got in and started it up, then rolled down her window to say goodbye.

He leaned down to meet her face-to-face. "Get some rest. You're going to need it for Friday."

"Oh?" She paused with the car running, her foot still on the brake.

"I've been practicing. Next time I'll be the one spanking you at gin." He chuckled. "And maybe spanking you for something else if I'm lucky. See you soon, *princesa*. Text me." He kissed her cheek, smiled, then walked away.

She wondered if her goofy smile matched his before she drove home to the little man in her life.

Chapter 10

FRIDAY EVENING CAME ALL TOO SOON. SENDING THAT text to Lou had been one of the more difficult things she'd done lately. But a conversation with Becky, then dealing with her parents again, had proved to her she had to start living for herself.

No, it wasn't exactly normal for her son to see a mother who never spent time with others outside the family. Grandma and Grandpa were all well and good, and for the most part, they dealt fairly with Brandon. Her mother did, at least. She loved the stuffing out of the boy.

Andrew could at times get preachy, but Brandon had found a way to ignore him while acting as if he paid attention. Joey would have admonished her son about it, but her father could get on her own last nerve. No doubt her boy had picked up the fake listening trait from her.

"So what do you two have planned for this weekend?" Amy asked as she dished some macaroni casserole onto Brandon's plate.

"I'm sleeping over at Colin's tonight."

"Colin? Didn't you just go to his birthday party last weekend?" Andrew asked.

"No, Grandpa. That was Todd. Colin was at the party, though. He's younger than we are, but he's super good at soccer, so Todd and me play with him sometimes at school. He's having a slumber party for his dog's birthday. Did you know dogs can celebrate birthdays?" Brandon shoved a huge helping of macaroni into his mouth and talked through his food.

Her father cringed while Joey shared a grin with her mom she quickly erased when her son looked her way.

"Brandon," Joey admonished. "Chew, swallow, *then* talk. Grandpa doesn't want to see your half-eaten food."

"Sure he does. Right, Grandpa?" Brandon talked with his mouth open, his words garbled. "Look at my cave full of Big Foot boogers."

Her father crossed his eyes. "That's just gross. Besides that, you're doing it wrong." Andrew took a big forkful of broccoli and chewed, then showed off green teeth and broccoli mush. "See? Slime from the planet Kazooma."

Brandon laughed. As much as her father could be such a downer at times, he had moments where he played and showed his love. He and Brandon continued to talk about dogs, soccer, and school.

"So, honey, what are you going to do while Brandon's at his friend's?" her mother asked in a quiet voice. "Got any big plans? Hanging out with Becky?" Amy paused. "Got a date?"

Hating to lie to her mother but in no way wanting a lecture about the perils of men in this day and age, she shrugged. "Nothing big planned. Becky mentioned maybe going out with some girlfriends. We'll see."

She noted her father half listening while pretending to be super engrossed in Brandon's play-by-play of his last soccer practice.

Amy frowned. "You know, I think it's time you started dating again. You're too young to be so alone."

Shocked that had come out of her mother's mouth minus a monologue on birth control, Joey stared.

"I mean, you've worked so hard raising Brandon, what with your job and going to school too. I just think you're missing the fun of being young and free."

A small frown appeared on Andrew's face before he pointedly looked from Brandon to Joey. "But she's not so free, is she?" Having said his piece, he turned back to his grandson and talked about the Sounders win over D.C. United—and the only reason Joey knew it was about soccer was because Brandon talked about no other sport lately.

Ignoring her father and mentally counting to ten before she said anything that could be construed as "defensive," Joey focused on her dinner. It now tasted like dust and went down as badly, but she managed to keep smiling, took another forkful, and replied, "Nah. I'm having all the fun I need, Mom. Managing the store has opened up some new opportunities for me." She hated that her father looked so satisfied. Did he never want his daughter to have a relationship outside the family? She forced herself to sound happier than she felt. "I might even have another wedding to do, and Stef is giving me the green light to run the whole thing. As in, it'll kind of be my own business. I think. Tied to the shop, of course. But we're talking about maybe making it a completely separate entity."

Her mother looked like she wanted to change the subject back to the forbidden—to men—but she refrained. "Good for you. You're naturally gifted when it comes to business. So smart." She beamed. "Just like me." They both laughed, and Joey relaxed a bit. "So other than work, what else are you doing this weekend? Your father and I are thinking of heading to Port Townsend, staying over Saturday night."

"For the craft show," Andrew chimed in. "No, Brandon. Like this." He made another face that sent her boy into gales of laughter.

"Did you want to come with us?" Amy asked.

"No. Brandon's sleepover tonight will make him crabby tomorrow. He has fun but never gets enough sleep at his friends'."

"You were the same way."

"Was I that independent at eight years old?"

"No. You wanted to move out at six!"

"And here I am." She sighed.

"And here you are," her father repeated. But this time he had a glint of humor in his gaze when he added, "The prettiest girl I know with the ugliest little boy. How did that happen, Amy?" He smiled at his wife. "Must be genes from your side of the family."

"Ha, ha." Amy rolled her eyes. "I know where he gets his goofy sense of humor from, that's for sure. And it's not me."

Grandson and grandfather both snorted with laughter, and Joey couldn't hold back her amusement. Better to laugh than cry, she told herself, cherishing the small moments with her father that never lasted.

An hour later, as she drove Brandon to Colin's house, something clicked. "Oh. This is Colin *McCauley*, isn't it?"

"Yeah, so?" Brandon fiddled with the radio stations, settling on some '80s throwback tunes.

"Nothing. Just curious." So she'd probably see Del then. Colin's stepmother.

Nervous at the prospect and not sure why, probably because it was one more connection to Lou, she tried to shrug off her nervousness. "Remember that wedding I worked? That was for Colin's new mom."

"Oh. Del. I like her." He leaned closer. "But sometimes she says bad words, and Colin's dad puts her in time-out."

She did her best not to smile. "Is that so?"

"Yeah. Colin's dad is really big. But he smiles a lot, and he's always giving Colin man-hugs."

"As opposed to regular hugs?"

Brandon nodded. "They're better because it shows how much Colin's dad loves him."

She swallowed around a lump in her throat. "That's nice."

They drove toward Queen Anne, and she wondered how that must feel, to have hugs from a man who loved you unconditionally.

"Mom?"

"Yes?"

"Is my dad still sick?"

She gripped the steering wheel. Hard. "Why do you ask?"

He shrugged and looked out the window. "I don't know. I just wonder about him sometimes."

Joey had never wanted to lie to her son, but telling Brandon his father hadn't wanted him was too cruel for anyone to hear, let alone a child. So she'd told a skewed sort of truth. "Yes, I think he is. He was very sick in his head and his heart when you were born, sweetie."

He plucked at his pants and sighed. "I know that, Mom. I just think it would be neat if I had a dad who could give me man-hugs. That's all." He glanced at her and smiled, her bright little boy with dark-brown eyes, a mirror image of her own. "But your mom-hugs are the best in the world. I told Colin that at soccer last week."

"Oh?"

"Yeah. His mom died when he was a baby, so now he's getting used to Del's hugs. And Del has strong arms." He laughed. "I think he's scared of her."

"*I'm* scared of her," she said drily. "She does have big muscles. And tattoos too."

Brandon blinked. "Really?"

"You've never seen them?"

"No. Cool. I'll ask her to show them to me."

And like that, mention of his father drifted to the far corner of his mind, his enthusiasm for another sleepover taking precedence.

Thank God. Though she'd been sorry things hadn't worked out between her and Felix, that he'd signed the release form had been a huge relief. She'd heard horror stories about angry exes and child custody nightmares. Granted, the money would have been nice to get, because babies were expensive. She hadn't been alone the night Brandon had been conceived, so why not split the cost of raising their child? Yet not having to deal with Felix and his rich, jerky parents at the expense of child support? She couldn't put a price tag on that.

Becky said he's back in town. Seattle had nearly seven hundred thousand people living in it at any given time. The odds of running into Felix were slim. Though she knew how the world worked, and with her luck, she'd end up running into him on a street corner.

She'd always known the possibility existed that

Brandon might someday see his father. So telling him his father had died, as her mother had wanted her to, didn't seem right. The sick theory had worked thus far, but she knew at some point she'd have to get more detailed as to why she and Felix hadn't worked out.

He'd been two years older than her when they'd separated. Which would make him twenty-six by now. And like the other times people had mentioned him in passing, she had only a vague curiosity about him. He belonged to her distant past, not her present or her future.

"There, Mom." Brandon pointed to a pretty blue house with pots of flowers outside and a black muscle car in front. Definitely Del McCauley's house. Joey parked behind Del's car and turned to Brandon.

"Honey, this is two weeks in a row. Are you sure you want to go?" She'd been asking him that since he'd made plans yesterday, feeling guilty because once again she had the perfect opportunity to see Lou. Thinking about having sex while her innocent son readied to play with his friends.

Ugh. She was going to hell, no two ways about it.

"Mom, seriously." He nodded. "I want to go. I can, right?"

"Sure, Brandon. I just wanted to make sure."

His wide grin told her she'd worried for nothing. "Good. Because his dog is awesome. And Del lets us have pizza and candy." He grabbed his bag and tore out of the car.

She sighed and followed him. Pizza, candy, and a dog. No way she could compete. She felt her guilt lessen, knowing her son would be having the time of his life while she fretted about what to do or not do with a man out of her league.

They rang the doorbell and waited. From within, Joey heard a deep male voice, barking, then feminine laughter. Del opened the door and smiled down at Brandon.

"Yo, champ. Hey, Joey. Come on in." She held the door open for them. "What's up, guys?"

Joey smiled. She liked Del. Pretty but with rough edges, Del McCauley could swear with the best of them. She had sleeves of tattoos on both arms, wore a loop through her eyebrow, and had a stud in her nose. Her ash-blond hair was typically done up in creative braids, as it was currently. Joey thought the woman's hair defied the laws of physics *and* the laws of beauty. Because despite all her badass, Del was a stunner.

"Mike, Brandon's here," Del yelled.

Another reason Joey liked her—she never felt low-class around Del, mostly because Del was a class all by herself. She yelled when she wanted to yell, swore when she wanted to swear, and laughed a lot. And she didn't tolerate fools, snobs, or idiots.

"I heard you, woman," Mike shouted back from somewhere in the house.

Joey grinned and glanced around. A lot of brown in the house, from the furniture to the carpet to the furnishings.

"I know. Don't say it. We like brown." Del shrugged. "It was like this when I moved in last year, and I'm not much into decorating. But man, it's work avoiding my sister-in-law, the interior designer, who can't seem to leave us alone about it. A major pain in my ass-*toundingly* tough hide," she said, recovering quickly as Colin, Brandon, and Todd stared at her.

"That's a dollar," Colin said with a crafty gleam.

"*Astounding* is not a swear word."

Colin frowned. "That's not what you were going to say."

"Oh?" Del's brow rose. "What was I going to say?"

Colin opened his mouth to answer when Brandon elbowed him in the arm and whispered, "If you say it, then *you* owe *her* a dollar."

Colin frowned. "That's sneaky." He grinned. "I'm going to try that with Ubie tomorrow."

Del ruffled his hair. "Go for it, kid. Now scram. I'm talking to a grown-up."

This time Brandon remembered to give Joey a kiss before dropping his bag and darting away with the boys. They nearly ran over Mike, Del's husband, in the hallway before disappearing into the house.

Mike McCauley. Like Joey, he was the image from which his own son had been imprinted. Same black hair, same blue eyes, same smirk. Man, was he good-looking and, by all accounts, a great dad.

Man-hugs. Nice.

Mike ambled over to Del and hugged *her*. "Hey, Joey."

She did an inward swoon and smiled back. "Hi, Mike. Geez, Del. Do you know any men who aren't more than six feet tall?"

Mike grinned, kissed his wife's cheek, then walked into his kitchen.

Del shrugged. "What can I say? My life is filled with testosterone."

"And pizza, candy, and a dog, so I hear."

Del laughed. "Yeah, in that order, though right now the dog's outside, thank God."

"We're also having salad," Mike announced. "And a side vegetable."

"Salad is a side vegetable." Del frowned at her

husband, who could be seen puttering around in the kitchen when he moved past the wide doorway. "We're getting a supreme pizza. It has veggies on it. We don't need more green at the table."

"Veggies," Mike growled, his voice pretty loud for being a room-length away, "are good for you. The kids need good carbs too."

"Hell, not this again. There's nothing wrong with boys eating pizza for dinner. *Just. Pizza*," Del said, her voice rising. But the wink she shot Joey told her Del was just screwing with the poor guy.

He roared, "I'm making broccoli."

"What?" Del roared back. "I don't think China heard you yelling!"

"Well, then." Joey swallowed. "I'll leave you two to your dinner discussion. Thanks again for inviting Brandon."

Del turned to her and spoke in a calm voice. "He's a great kid. He and Todd are pretty nice to Colin, which is cool considering they're two years older. It was tough for Colin being on the third-grade soccer team. But he was running rings around the kids his own age, so they made an exception." Del lowered her voice. "We try not to make too big a deal about it, but Colin is really good. And he's now obsessed with the sport. Christ, he's only seven, but he's totally into soccer." Del walked her to the door. "Swing by tomorrow at one to get him. That's if he's not mutated by all the vegetables he'll be forced to eat here." She grimaced. "Hell, he might call you tonight wanting to come home."

Joey grinned as she stepped outside with Del. "I doubt that. He had so much fun last weekend at Todd's sleepover, he was dying to go out again. I suddenly feel guilty for having so much free time."

Del chuckled. "Well, have fun tonight." She gave Joey a—there was no other word for it—"shit-eating" grin. "I have it on good authority your time might not be as free as you think it is."

"Huh?"

"Go on. You be good, but not too good. And if you need to let Lou down easily, don't. He could use a kick in the head. Too good-looking and suave, you ask me," she teased.

Joey didn't know how she felt about Del knowing her personal business.

"Sorry. Nothing stays secret at the garage. We're a small world filled with grease, swearing, and stinky men. But you know, I work with the absolute best mechanics in all of Seattle." She nodded, sincere. "Seriously. Every one of them is a stand-up guy. Good with tools and taking care of people they care about. Lou especially. You can trust him."

"Uh, okay."

"You're really red right now. Am I embarrassing you?" She shook her head. "Look, ignore me. I know nothing about you and Lou not dating or about you giving him a major brush-off that had him pissy for half the week. Not a thing." She paused. "All kidding aside, try not to break the guy's heart. He's big and strong and acts all tough. But Lou's a softie when it comes to the women in his life."

"Right. Well. I guess I should go now."

Del grabbed her by the arm, the woman's hand a lot bigger than Joey's. "Don't tell him I told you he was pissy. But I thought you should know. The guy really likes you." Del popped her in the arm, not hard, but it still stung. "And not to spread gossip or anything, but…"

The paused dragged on too long, and this time Joey tagged Del on her muscled arm. *Geez. All the people at Webster's had guns.* "Well? Come on. *But…?*"

"But Lou has a lot of women wanting to get back with him. He's a nice guy, he's hot as hell, and apparently he's a god in the sack…which you didn't know because your eyes are really wide. Hmm. But your cheeks are back to being scarlet red. So maybe you do know something—"

A crash, dog barking, and boy laughter sounded through past the door.

"*Damn it*," Mike yelled. "Jekyll, come back here with that!"

"Oh. I'd better go see what's happening." Del smiled. "Have fun tonight. And take a break for once. Your work ethic makes even me tired, and they all tell me I work too hard."

"You do. But so do I. Probably why we're friends."

"That and you didn't mind me being nuts for four months. So there's that." Del nodded. "Later, Joey. Give 'im hell." She slammed back into the house yelling for Mike.

Joey left the loud McCauleys behind and drove to Lou's, unsure, nervous, and excited all at once. Her palms were sweaty, her throat dry, and she wanted nothing more than to head home and soak in a hot bath until all her cares went away.

But memories of Lou holding her by the hair, of him bossing her around and her liking it, that thick rod in his pants all for her, had her speeding up instead. Time to see if she could get past her need to be a good girl and just live it up for once. And they didn't have to have sex either.

She thought about that the entire way to his house.

The hell they didn't.

Could the clock possibly move any slower? Maybe backward?

Lou paced in his living room, torn between adding more condoms to his back pocket and dumping them all together. He didn't want Joey to feel pressured into anything, even if he did fear dying of the worst case of blue balls known to man. Every time he remembered handling her in that damn flower shop, his dick grew to monumental proportions. Shit, he'd even impressed himself with how big he'd gotten.

How big he was getting now. Totally not the way to settle his nervous woman into trusting him to take care of her. That he had an opportunity to be with her again, to show her they could work, was way too important. He didn't know why Joey, of all the women he'd dated, got to him.

But he'd finally stopped questioning it. For five damn days he'd been wallowing in no man's land, not sure what he'd done to send her crying—fucking *crying*—from his home. But when he'd made things right Wednesday night, it had been like winning the lottery. Better than the dream of beating Johnny at darts or of having an art show where all the people in his life who'd said he'd never amount to anything would bow down and kiss his ass.

That kind of awesome.

Any minute now, and she'd be in his home again. The same home he'd dusted, scrubbed, and mopped until he feared stripping the varnish off the floor. He never had that much mess to begin with, but he wanted the place to be nice for Joey.

He looked out his front window and saw headlights in the drive.

Finally.

He waited until she rang the doorbell, then gave himself a minute before answering. No need to pounce on the poor woman and scare her away.

When he finally answered the door, he saw her nerves and realized they both needed to just chill. So he stood back and waved for her to enter.

She did, and his entire world felt right, grounded in a way he only ever felt when creating something from that well deep within.

"Hi." She turned to face him, standing with her hands in her coat pockets, her hair down, looking both guarded and so very young.

Something inside him softened. "Hi. Can I take your coat?"

She shrugged out of it, and he waited. He would have helped her out of it, but he didn't want to act pushy or too demanding. Or did he now seem impolite? *Fuck*. He kept second-guessing his moves before he made them, and it left him looking like a dithering moron. Case in point, she was staring at him in question while he debated whether to help or not.

"Lou?"

He took her coat and hung it in the closet, then made

a beeline for the kitchen. "I need a beer. You want any-thing to drink?"

"Um, I'll have a beer too. It's that kind of night."

"Tell me about it." He fetched them both something to drink, then stood in the kitchen with her, leaning back against the counter, doing his best to be casual. "So tell me."

"Yes?"

Was she as desperate to fill the sudden silence as he was? Because without something to distract him, he could think of nothing but that need for her that never went away when she stood near. "If you weren't here with me, what would you be doing tonight?"

She took a dainty sip of beer, and he worked not to smile. "Hmm. I think I might have gone out with my friend Becky. She's always on me to socialize, but I'm so busy, I never do."

He nodded. "The guys and I—my friends at Webster's—we used to go out a lot more before they all started hooking up with girlfriends. Ray's, a bar we hang at now and then, is usually how I spend my free time. That's if I want the noise and people. I like being by myself though."

"I do too. But for that, I'm called antisocial."

He knew how that went. "I hear that too. My mom, aunts, and sisters are on my case to find a nice girl and settle down. But I like my life the way it is. I'm indepen-dent, do what I want to do, and I'm not hurting anyone's feelings because I spend too much time drawing in my 'stupid sketchbook.'"

She studied him. "Did someone once accuse you of that? Of spending too much time *drawing*?"

"An ex of mine."

"Ex for a reason." She shook her head. "It's one thing if you're hitting the bars all the time or hanging with other girls, but drawing too much? That's a new one."

He grinned and drank, then put his beer down and crossed his arms. He liked the way she followed his movements, her gaze constantly darting to his biceps. He'd worn a plain blue T-shirt with jeans tonight. Nothing too dressy or too grungy. He liked the soft cotton of the shirt against his skin. And in a mood to indulge his senses, he'd worn his favorite tee.

"You have a tattoo. I kind of noticed before."

He followed her gaze to see his shirt had ridden up on his arm, so he rolled it up even more to show her the vines and thorns inked around his upper arm. "Yeah. Around my biceps and across my chest. Nothing too much, but I like the ink. It's tough though, because I'm picky about art, and especially what goes on my body."

"Oh. I hadn't thought about that. You could probably draw your own tattoos better than anyone else, huh?"

"I think so, but I'm biased." He made a decision he'd been toying with. His art was very personal to him. "Would you like to see my sketchbook?"

"Yes," she said right away, so he knew she'd been wondering.

"Hold on." He left and returned with his current book, having torn out the drawings of her. She might get creeped out by his many renditions of her profile, her face, her smokin'-hot body. Covered by clothing, but still.

He gestured her to the kitchen table, and they sat close so they could see his sketches. He let her page through them, commenting when she lingered so she'd know his process.

Most of the sketches were of cars, monsters, fantastical creatures, ideas for new custom jobs. But the occasional sketch of his friends or interesting characters he'd seen that wouldn't leave him until he put them to paper showed up as well.

She blinked. "Oh wow. That's Del. And another of the men at the garage. I remember him arguing with Del a few times. Brave guy."

Brave indeed. "That would be Foley."

"They look so real."

"Well, they are."

"Yes, but I mean, it almost looks like you took a photograph and blurred it a bit or something." She gaped at him. "Lou, you're an artist."

He frowned. "I told you that."

"No, I mean, you're an *amazing* artist. You do a lot more than just work on cars."

"Never thought I'd said I just work on cars." Not quite like that, at any rate.

"This is totally not coming out right." She blushed. "I thought…I don't know what I thought. I mean, I saw the snake on your car, and I had the impression you only did that kind of thing. Like, manly artwork on hot rods. And then you also work at Webster's changing oil and stuff."

"Changing oil?" He hoped his expression wasn't as pained as he felt. Seriously? Changing oil? Did the woman not understand what went into dealing with a blown motor or replacing a transmission? And don't get him started on repairing a head gasket. That was a whole different kind of art, making things run.

"I'm saying this wrong." She groaned. "I'm trying to tell you that I'm in awe of what you do."

"Oh. Well then." He winked at her, and it was then he realized how very close they sat. Their heads nearly touching.

She blew out a breath, and it washed over his lips.

He sat back and worked on maintaining an appearance of calm while his heart threatened to pound through his chest. "Yeah, so. Um. How about we watch a movie or something? Would that be okay?"

"No gin rummy?" Her eyes twinkled.

He did his best not to sigh like a lovesick fool. *No, lustsick. Just a bad case of infatuation with the previously unattainable flower chick. That's all*. Unfortunately, he knew it was so much more.

"Hey, what's this?" she asked, finding a portrait he'd done of her that he'd apparently missed, mashed between the back cover and the last few empty pages. He'd done it by memory and had given the project a soft, loving feel. Her eyes, tilted in laughter, her lips, full, quirked in a mystery smile as she'd laughed at something only she knew. Laughing at him and his pathetic crush, maybe.

Yep, he knew it was much more than infatuation.

And now, she did too.

Chapter 11

JOEY STARED FROM THE PICTURE TO LOU. HE SEEMED unsure about her reaction. But just…wow. Too tame a word to describe her feelings. The picture he'd drawn had captured her essence. In it, she saw the vulnerability behind a mocking smile, pretending she found everything else amusing when really she laughed at her own impossibilities. Yet… She looked closer.

"I don't look like that. Do I?"

"Like what?"

"Well." No other way to say it. "Beautiful."

He nodded, his focus on her palpable. "That's the way you look to me all the time." His accent thickened, his gaze lowered to her mouth, and he leaned back even further. "So let's see that movie, hmm?"

Lou left the table in a flash. And Joey wondered if he felt the same burning desire she'd felt since entering his house. Being near him caused a root of awareness to grow. Relief that she could and did feel something so warm for a man made her dizzy for a moment. But she knew it had to be the *right* man.

Knowing Lou felt the same way about her made all the difference.

She gave her picture a last look, seeing the mischief, the joy, the tension in the subtle lines at her mouth. Man, he must have thought her lips pretty sensual. Heck, the whole picture made her look like a woman eager for a man.

He really did capture me. So why had he darted away
from what could have been a kiss into the living room?
Lou Cortez, running from her? Joey chuckled at the
thought. Lou, trying to escape Joey's maniacal clutches?
Yeah, right.

She followed him into the living room, where he'd
already put on a movie. A comedy she recognized.

"My sisters like it, so I figured you would too."

She wondered where to sit, then saw him pat the spot
next to him on the couch. He had his ankles crossed, his
feet propped on the table in front of him. His arms lay
on either side of the pillows at his back, and she could
easily envision him the master in a harem house.

She joined him before she lost her nerve. After a
moment watching the show, he put his arm around her.

"Okay?" he leaned in to whisper, his lips touching
her ear.

She shivered. Because…*holy hell*. Her body seemed
to heat up at her ear, then send that shock wave straight
to her nipples and between her legs. Like an arrow of
desire that rushed through her blood cells to inflame her.

Everywhere.

She nodded, cleared her throat. "Great."

Too bad she sounded like she'd swallowed rocks.

He tugged her closer, and she scented a subtle
cologne, one that made her want to inhale him from
head to toe.

"Stella loves this part," he said, the weight of his arm
like a burning anvil. So much heat under a ton of power.
No wonder Lou was big. He had to be in order to cart all
that muscle around day after day.

Joey tried. She really did. But she couldn't follow the

movie at all, not with her senses attuned to every hitch in Lou's breathing, the smell of sandalwood and man, the muscular thigh brushing against hers. There seemed no part of him she'd consider soft.

A surreptitious glance at his crotch showed him affected by her there as well. *Oy. Was he.*

She shifted in her seat. Several times.

Until Lou put a hand on her leg to stop her. "This isn't working."

Should she play dumb? "What do you mean?"

He used the remote to mute the TV. "I mean I can't concentrate on the movie with all your squirming."

She flushed.

"And because that squirming has me so hard, I'm afraid I'll come in my pants." He leaned his head back on the couch and groaned. "I'm sorry, *cariña*. I've been trying to behave, but I can't stop thinking about how good you feel. How good you taste, smell. Damn, everything about you gets me going."

So glad it's not just me. "Lou, it's okay."

He opened his eyes. "It is?"

"I've thought about it a lot. About how you make me feel."

He sat up straight. "How's that?"

"Like my skin is on fire. Like if I don't kiss you, I might burn to a crisp."

"We can't have that, *princesa*. No dying on the couch at Lou's." He gave her a half smile. "Was that so hard to admit?"

She groaned. "Yes."

"Good. You said it anyway. Because you understand that you need what I can give you," he crooned, his voice having gone deep, thick. Filled with lust, she could only hope, because she needed to see tonight through. No matter what he said, she did want to be with him. Sexually. Connected together in the most intimate way possible.

Joey took a huge metaphorical leap. "So can we play? With you being in charge, I mean? Like you talked about?"

Lou sighed as he pulled her over his lap, forcing her knees on either side of his legs. "Honey, I think I might die if we don't."

He watched her while he stripped off her shirt, slowly fingering each button and sliding it free. He pushed her shirt apart and stared at her barely there breasts while she waited for him to tell her what next to do. "Man, I love your body." Then he tugged her shirt completely off.

Though she'd always felt too small up top, under his gaze, she felt beautiful. Lou wrapped his arms around her back, pressing his face against her chest, and unfastened her bra. He leaned back and slid the straps off her shoulders.

"Let it go." He tugged it down until the bra fell off her body. "So fucking hot," Lou whispered, his breath teasing her nipple before he took it between his lips. He nibbled and sucked his way to her lips, and she writhed on his lap, wanting more. When he gripped her hair to control her movements, she moaned into his mouth and couldn't stop herself from touching his cloth-covered chest, wishing she felt skin.

He pulled back, reading her mind. "Take if off me," he growled. "Then I want your mouth again."

She paused, taken aback at the demand in his tone. But his wink eased her, and she removed his shirt. He gripped her ass, then tugged at her zipper as he pulled her pants down, distracting her.

Somehow Lou had her naked and straddling his lap before she knew what he'd done.

She started to cover up when he grabbed her hands in one of his and stopped her.

"Oh, damn. You are just…" He pulled her close and drew her nipple back into his mouth. He sucked while he played with the curls between her legs, sliding through the arousal she couldn't stop.

When he shoved a finger inside her without warning, the intrusion was almost enough to make her come.

"You are so beautiful." Lou fucked her with his finger, watching her watch him, and she didn't know where to look. Or not to look. Should she close her eyes, to stop staring into his all-seeing gaze?

"Take me out," he said, still playing with her.

She reached between them and awkwardly unfastened his jeans. His erection poked stiffly through his underwear, and she saw a damp patch before he slid the material down, baring his shaft but not much else.

"Oh." She stared in awe at the size of him. Lou was big all over. A glance back at his chest showed the tattoo she'd started studying before he'd pulled her away with that kiss. He had vines and flowers across his chest, a skull in the center. And on his left bicep, thorny vines streaked with diamonds and hearts.

"Get me nice and ready for you," he rasped and fitted her hand around him. She squeezed, and he gasped, then he fucked her faster with his finger.

She pumped him, staring into his eyes as she took him closer to the fulfillment she could almost reach.

Lou groaned, then removed his finger. "Scoot back, then don't move."

She followed his orders, too enraptured to feel any kind of embarrassment, and watched while he fished a condom out of his pocket and put it on. Then he settled his hands on her hips and guided her over him.

"Hold me before you take me inside."

She licked her lips, grabbed the steely shaft, on fire to feel him again. "I-I thought you didn't like that."

"Christ. I love you on top of me—since *I'm* doing the driving," he said as he yanked her down over him.

Pleasure burst, and she cried out as the climax seized her while he pumped, harder and faster. Until he groaned and ceased all movement. He held her there, thick inside her while he trembled in release.

"Shit." Lou moaned. "So good. Oh fuck. Don't move. Stay right there."

Reality returned, and she blushed. She sat naked on top of Lou and felt both exposed and protected. Confusing, yet the pleasure refused to let her dwell too much. A warm lethargy overwhelmed her while she watched Lou still taking his pleasure.

She'd had another orgasm in mere seconds. That made three more with Lou than she'd ever had with any other man. No wonder women wanted him constantly around. He was like a pleasure magnet, sexy, powerful, and domineering. Yet kind when it counted.

He hugged her close, warming the parts of her starting to feel the cool evening air.

Lou lifted then nudged her off him. "Hand me a tissue, baby."

She grabbed one for him, and he tucked his spent

condom in it and tossed it to the floor. He tugged her back into his arms and leaned back on the couch, half-dressed, his jeans bunched under his ass, while she sat naked.

"That was… That was the best sex of my life…not counting doing you in the flower shop."

She buried her head against his chest and groaned while he laughed.

"Yeah, you're dysfunctional, all right. Can't orgasm with a man. Probably cold, frigid. A nightmare when it comes to sex." He kissed the top of her head. "A load of crap. There's nothing wrong with you, Joey. You just needed the right man to show you that. And Joey, that happens to be me."

She glanced up at him. "Yeah?"

"Oh yeah." He loomed, so big and strong. For once, Joey didn't have to worry about doing the wrong thing, picking the wrong choice. She could bask in the knowledge Lou would take care of her and make everything right. "You good with all this? I'm starting to understand what gets you off. You like it when I take charge." He paused. "Has this always been something you're into?"

She didn't want to own up to it, but he already knew. "I guess. I just thought I wasn't any good at sex, to be honest. But it's better when you, um, when you kind of do what you want and I follow along."

"Better?" He grunted. "If you were any better, I'd be dead." He stroked her back, her arms, then cupped her breasts. "Man, I love touching you. You fit so good right here." He hugged her, and she sighed with contentment, waiting to wake up at any moment. Because this could not possibly be real.

And it couldn't possibly last.

"I—"

"You're going to stay naked, for one," Lou inter-rupted. "And we're going to go snuggle up in my bed while I get my second wind to prove I'm not a one-second wonder. Christ. I'll really take care of you. I promise I'll last next time."

"Next time?" She blinked.

He laughed. "You didn't really think that orgasm was enough, did you?"

Having one in the first place had already tipped her scales. "I guess not?"

He smiled. "Right." Then his smile faded, and the menacing male sitting underneath her turned her to jelly.

"Lou?"

He palmed her ass, dragging her over his growing erection once more. "We might not need too long before I'm ready again. So let's get back to my bedroom now. Where I have more condoms."

———※———

A good move on his part, because Lou wanted her. Now. This time he wanted to take her while he was on top, staring into her eyes while he pounded inside her. Just thinking about it got him rock hard, and he followed her tight little ass into the back, toeing off his socks and dropping his jeans as he walked.

She darted to his bed and under the covers, as he'd assumed she would. The woman had a shyness com-pletely at odds with the sexual creature he'd just made love to on his couch. Damn, but he'd come hard. And fast. So embarrassing.

It normally took him a little longer to get in the mood,

to play with his partner and seduce her, and himself, into a long night of passion. But with Joey, he'd been too excited, too needy to wait. Thank God she'd been ready to go off, or he feared he might have left her behind. And that had douche-move written all over it.

He stood, arms akimbo, and studied her in the middle of his bed, clutching his sheets to her chest, her hair flowing over her shoulders and teasing her breasts. Man, she had a fine pair of tits. He wanted to suck on her pretty little nipples all over again, get her all hot and wet and begging.

Groaning, he felt himself now roaring to go once more.

Her big brown eyes widened, and she bit her lip.

"You think you can take me again, *princesa*?"

She nodded.

"Drop the sheets."

She turned pink but did as ordered. Sitting there, his sheets pooled around her trim waist, she looked exactly as he'd pictured she might. He slowly pushed his boxer briefs off, pleased when she followed the movement without blinking.

"See how hard you make me? I'm ready for you all over again."

She swallowed.

He could only hope they'd get to that one day, where she swallowed more than her nerves. He grinned and advanced. "Now let's show you what making love is all about, hmm?"

His cutie frowned. "I'm not a virgin, Lou."

"I'm sorry." He paused at the foot of the bed and forced a dark scowl. "Are you mouthing off to me?"

"I'm...huh?"

"I said"—he yanked the sheets down and away, leaving her naked and wary—"are you mouthing off to me? You need a spanking, *cariña*?"

She gaped. "You want to spank me?"

He sighed, gave her glorious body a once-over, and couldn't help a naughty grin. "Want? No. But obviously you need it." He tugged her by the foot down the bed while she gave an undignified squeal and turned over onto her belly.

Her protest only made him harder.

"Joey, Joey." He tsked, realigned his hand, and tightened his grip on her ankle. "Stop moving."

She immediately stilled.

"That's better." He sat on the bed next to her, staring at her toned back and thighs. Cupping her taut ass, he started rubbing, not surprised when she gave a small groan and buried her head in her hands on the bed. "You're a little tense, hmm?"

She didn't answer.

"Maybe because you're being a little stubborn." Lou gave her a light swat that shocked her into rolling onto her side to stare at him.

"Back on your belly," he ordered, though it pained him to deny himself her beauty.

She stared, comprehension dawning as she realized he was playing with her. She quickly rolled back over.

"Hands together, under your chin."

She put her hands where he told her, and then he started stroking her. Because he had to. She had the softest, prettiest skin.

"You're a beautiful woman. Responsive. Silky." He heard her breath catch as he caressed the inside of her calf, her knee, then her thigh. He nudged her legs wider and continued to stroke upward. But before he reached her slick sex, he slid his hands to the sides of her body, around her thighs and over her ass. She had dimples there, and he leaned down to kiss them both.

She gasped, and he chuckled. "Look, Joey. I'm already kissing your ass."

"Lou." The half groan/half chuckle came out muffled against the bed.

He kneaded her, wanting badly to spread her wider and take her from behind, on top, shoving deep inside. Touching her aroused him anew, because learning her showed him how much she belonged with him. Right now, she was his, to touch, to please, to love into a mass of writhing desire. So first he'd relax her, and then he'd drive her wild.

Lou continued to treasure her, loving the feel of such soft woman over hard muscle. She might be small, but Joey worked for a living. He could feel it in the tender strength of her frame. Moving up the small of her back, he shifted to straddle her for better position.

And knew he'd have to concentrate to last. Leaning over her for a side dresser, he fished out a condom and put it on. Then he returned to Joey, more than ready to satisfy his lover.

He didn't put his full weight on her; rather he balanced on his knees. But the urge to lower himself, to rub over her, increased. Instead, he dug his fingers into the taut area between her shoulder blades.

"You're too tight." He heard her groan and smiled. "Need to loosen you up." He rubbed at the knot until it softened. She seemed to melt under him, and he had to taste her again. So he leaned close and kissed her shoulder blades, then continued up her spine, pushing her hair aside so he could kiss his way up her neck to her cheek.

She turned her head before he could ask and met his mouth, ravenous to feel his lips on hers, apparently.

He indulged her a moment, then whispered in her ear, "How about you turn over so I can do your front?" He nipped her earlobe, and her breathing grew erratic.

Lou leaned back and moved off her, waiting for her to turn.

She did, slowly, and he was treated to her blushing breasts, tight nipples, and slender belly. So fucking ripe, so feminine and pleasing. God, he wanted her.

Watching him with dark eyes full of trust and need, she twisted that desire inside him into a fuller, richer sense of emotion. Lou straddled her again, settling on his haunches and resting his balls on her belly, his dick so hard that just a few rubs and he'd go off.

"You're big," she said, breathy.

"You make me that way," he growled. "Now be quiet and lie back. I'm not done with you."

Her small grin turned his heart inside out, but he steeled himself to hold back. Lou kissed her cheeks, her neck, her throat. He palmed her breasts and ran his mouth down her throat to her chest, taking his time with her.

So sensitive at her breasts, she arched and pleaded with him to give her some respite. But he wouldn't be rushed. Not after waiting for her for what felt like forever. He finally had her all to himself, sequestered in his big bed. And the fantasy of having her didn't come close to the reality.

She had a sweetness, an innate sense of purity that no amount of mussing would corrupt. He threaded his fingers through hers, keeping her hands occupied while he continued down her body, licking a trail down her taut belly to her sultry sex.

Lou sighed, nuzzled her there, the downy hair that covered her core, that thin strip of dark brown that hid her secrets. Then he let go of her hands to spread her wider and stared at the essence of Joey.

"Fuck me," he whispered, not at all poetic, and finally did what he'd been dreaming of. He set his mouth at the juncture of her thighs and ferreted the sweet, sharp taste of her. Lou moaned and lapped her up. With his tongue and teeth, he drove her wild, exciting himself in the process.

She curled her fingers in his hair, moaning his name.

There, with him. She called for Lou, not some faceless partner in her bed.

"Yes, please. Lou, in me," she begged.

And he knew he'd found heaven in the golden taste of Josephine Reeves. He thrust a finger inside her and worked her clit, teething the hard nub while he filled her with one, then two digits.

"Yes, yes. Oh God," she cried out and seized, climaxing so prettily.

Lou kissed her through it, then couldn't wait any longer. While she continued to tremble, he rose over her, nudged her thighs wide, then pushed inside. The tremors and tight glove of her pussy had him shoving hard, fast, and deep.

She continued to come, and he plunged in and out, staring into her slumberous eyes while he crested his own fulfilment. Joey's tiny nails dug into his hips, then his ass as she held him while he poured into her on a roar, the shock of his climax obliterating.

What felt like a long time later, Lou came back to himself and worried he was crushing her.

"No, stay." She stroked his arms, tracing the tats across his chest.

"Damn, baby. If I was a cat, I'd be purring," he said, hoarse and still trying to catch his breath. She felt so snug around him, and despite the fact he'd recently climaxed, he felt thick, locked in her body's embrace.

Lou swore and shifted, pulling out only to shove himself back into her warmth. "Joey." He leaned down to kiss her, taken with the gentle kiss he received in return.

She nibbled at his lips, stroking with those small hands.

"You're really good at sex," she murmured.

He laughed, feeling sleepy. "Almost as good as you, huh?"

"No, not me. I have problems with it."

They both laughed at what they'd proved a fallacy and snuggled together.

After some time, Lou felt sleepy, so he withdrew from Joey's fine body and left for the bathroom. "Be right back."

He returned cleaned up, the condom disposed of.

Then it was her turn for a pit stop. He pulled the covers over him while she was gone.

She came back and slid into his arms again.

He sighed and kissed her forehead while he held her tight. "You fit, Joey."

"Hmm. My own personal electric blanket."

"You say the sweetest things," Lou teased. "But baby, I know I'm hot."

She chuckled. "True. And so humble."

He smiled. "I'm too sated to be humble. Gotta get some rest so I can fuck you again." He heard himself slurring but didn't care. "You're so good. So sweet."

"Not that sweet, because here I am." She stroked his chest. "I should go."

He automatically tightened his arms around her. "Not yet. Stay longer."

"Just a little."

He yawned. "Give me five…" and drifted into sleep.

But some part of his subconscious knew he held a once-in-a-lifetime opportunity in his arms, and he woke up later in the dark of morning and had her again. And again.

When he finally woke to the sun shining through his window, she was gone. But the floral scent of her remained.

He stretched. "Joey?"

Nothing.

Damn.

He rose, hit the john, then found a note on the kitchen counter for him.

> *See you again soon, I hope. Thanks, Lou.*
> *Joey*

And hearts. A lot of hand-drawn hearts.

Lou smiled. "Oh baby. I'll be seeing you soon for sure. You can take that to the bank."

Chapter 12

JOEY YAWNED AGAIN, UNABLE TO STOP HERSELF.

"That's fourteen yawns, Mom." Brandon huffed. "Come on. We're missing the balloon animals."

"Of course we are." She followed her son, eager to get back home where she could take a much-needed nap.

One on Saturday had come much sooner than expected. Falling asleep in Lou's arms had been a huge mistake. Because he'd felt so incredibly good. So sexy. Despite their rough beginning, they'd muddled along way too easily. With sex and more sex.

She'd been desperate to get out in one piece, but before she could simply take off and leave a note, he'd nearly done her in. After a brief few hours of sleep, her sex machine—lover?—had woken her for more. He especially liked being on top, doing her beneath him. On her belly or her back didn't matter with Lou "doing the driving." And God, she had no problem riding in the passenger seat.

She'd been pinned, overwhelmed, and so turned on, she couldn't function in her race to climax. Lou had continued to wear a condom without being asked. She tingled, remembering how good he'd felt inside her. And that mouth. Sinful. She sighed. Then she yawned again.

"Fifteen," Brandon growled.

"Yes, dear." She quirked a grin, only half-awake. She

and Brandon spent the afternoon in Seattle Center at one of the many excuses Seattle had to celebrate a festival. This one had plenty of carnival food, gluten-free offerings, prize booths, and energy-efficient storyboarding as they walked around. Oh good, and there, a walking penis talking about safe sex.

"Mom, what's that? A giant hot dog?"

She shrugged. As good a description as any. "Yep." She turned him. "Come on, I see funnel cake."

Nothing like sugaring her son up and enjoying his hyped rush while she followed him around like a zombie.

She still couldn't get over the fact that she'd spent the night. Joey *never* did that. But she'd fallen asleep with Lou, not bothered by his body heat or closeness. So odd. Except after that blissful wake-up with more sex, Joey hadn't been able to fall back to sleep, her brain buzzing along with her body.

"Oh, look, Mom. Kittens!"

She groaned and followed Brandon, doing her best to put Lou out of her thoughts. For a few minutes, at least.

They petted a few stray kittens needing good homes, and for once, Brandon didn't bug her to adopt an animal. His attention had been lured away by wooden swords at a toy concession in the next booth.

She opened her mouth to tease him when she spotted the unthinkable. She blinked her eyes to be sure, but the apparition staring back at her—at them—didn't fade. Across the grassy field, the man responsible for an event that had totally changed her life, the father of her child, stood staring at them. Felix Rogers.

Even Brandon could feel the weight of his stare. Brandon frowned. "Mom, who's that?"

"What? I don't know. Come on, honey. Let's go home. Your mom needs a nap. Now tell me about your sleepover." Home, where she could try to recover from hardly any sleep and sore inner thighs and pretend her world wasn't about to change for the worse.

While Brandon told her all about Jekyll the dog's exploits and Colin and Todd, Joey kept a subtle eye out for Felix. She saw him watching them, but he did nothing to come closer. It was all she could do to walk normally with her son when she had an urge to protect him, to keep him away from…his father.

Not his dad, because Felix had done nothing to parent or support her child. And he didn't have to, legally.

Joey didn't understand him. No amount of paper signed could negate the fact Felix had a son. Adoption for her had never been an option, not when she had two hands, a strong back used to the burden of hard work, and a brain. That and a need to raise and love her boy.

On the drive home, she realized that, from a distance, Felix looked exactly the same. Oh, he had a bit more maturity, but he still looked like the most popular kid on campus. Same light-blond hair, cut short and styled to within an inch of its life. No doubt the same blue eyes and killer grin. She'd been too far away to see his face clearly but close enough to know he was Felix.

Hadn't she said with her luck she'd run into him on the street one day? Only she hadn't counted on having Brandon by her side when it happened.

Too tired to deal with the worry that would no doubt hit her harder later, she yawned and finished the drive home. Once there, she told Brandon she was going to take a nap on Grandma's couch, leaving him to play in her parents' house or watch TV. His choice.

Two hours later, waking from a sound sleep, she saw her phone on the coffee table and the television on low. Brandon must have been watching cartoons, but she didn't see him.

He walked out of the kitchen carrying a monstrous bowl of ice cream. When he saw her, he froze.

She gave a defeated laugh. "Bring another spoon."

He brightened and returned with a second spoon, then sat next to her. As they watched *The Amazing World of Gumball* and ate vanilla ice cream smothered in chocolate sauce, the world seemed to right itself.

"I'm glad you had fun last night."

"Yeah. Mr. Mike is really nice, and Del is too."

"Not Ms. Del?"

"Well, I tried calling them Mr. and Mrs. McCauley, but Del kept asking why I wanted to talk to Colin's grandparents. Then Mike said I could call him Mr. Mike. Del laughed at that a lot. But when I called her Ms. Del, she didn't think it was so funny. Mr. Mike did though."

"I see."

"It was so fun, Mom. We played games and got popcorn. The pizza was really good, and we had to eat salad too, which I liked. But Colin made faces and did a fake throw-up. It was so good! He even spilled out chewed-up food to make it look real! We practiced it later in his room. And mine came in second place."

"Oh, er, interesting. So did he fool his parents?"

"Del, but not Mr. Mike. He just rolled his eyes and made Colin more salad."

"Nice."

Brandon chuckled. "He's pretty patient." Her eight-year-old-going-on-forty often displayed the maturity of a boy twice his age. "Colin has a lot of energy."

"I know Colin's only seven, but it seems like you and Todd had a good time. Would you like to go over again sometime if he asks?" She would like to have had her son ask Colin over for a reciprocal sleepover, but where would they stay? In their living room above the garage? In the shared bedroom she and Brandon used?

Just one more reason to find a new place to live.

"Hey, Brandon, can you go get me my laptop?"

"Sure."

He returned soon after. She shoved the rest of the ice cream his way. He gobbled it down and watched more cartoons while she went online searching for afford-able housing. Something in a decent-enough area near Brandon's school but not so expensive it would break her.

Her raise only went so far, but having to pay rent for years had taught her how to budget and live frugally. Andrew had had a point, she granted. Because of him and his strict rules, she had a head on her shoulders when it came to managing her money.

After finding a few apartments that might prove promising, nothing huge but with potential, she did laundry and some house chores and figured out what she and Brandon would have for dinner. It was nice to cook in a real kitchen with a stove, not just a tiny microwave and cooktop burner. But Joey used her own food, not soaking off Mom and Dad.

Her mother and father had been so strict after Brandon's birth. Not the happier, mellowed-out grand-parents they were today. A lot of blame, disappointment, and continued reminders that she'd better not depend on them to get her out of the mess she'd gotten herself into.

God, she'd had sex *one time*. She'd have thought the world ended. But for Andrew and Amy Reeves, it had. Their only child, the daughter they doted on and used as a yardstick to measure their own successes, apparently, had failed them.

After years of her working herself into an exhausted sleep every day, her parents had finally eased off. Her mother now adored Brandon. Her father loved him as well, though there were always conditions attached to that affection—as she well knew.

Brandon was well-behaved, polite, and kind. Because she'd raised him that way. And yes, it galled her that she'd had to rely on her parents for financial support with the basic necessities—food and clothes and a house—but for God's sake, she'd been all of fifteen when she'd gotten pregnant.

No stranger to diligence, she'd done her best. Five years ago, Joey had mostly become independent. She still used her mother to babysit, and she still paid a small amount in rent, living in her parents' rental unit, but she bought her own groceries and paid her own bills otherwise.

She'd had lean years to get to where she was now. The reason she never went out? She didn't have many trendy clothes, only what she had for work. And she never had the money to spend on frivolities, saving each penny in hopes of one day escaping this place.

"You make the best hot dogs, Mom." Brandon munched with enthusiasm.

"That's me, the hot dog queen," she said drily. Hot

dogs, macaroni and cheese, and baked beans. The meal of champions. It would be good for a few days, and she could add salad or other veggies to it throughout the week to keep the meal fresh. One thing she'd taught her son—*thou shalt not waste*.

After they ate, she locked up the house and took Brandon back up to their unit. She tucked him in and read him a story, pleased he still let her. Then she closed the bedroom door and went back to the laptop, searching for a new place to live. But as she looked online, she couldn't help thinking about Lou and his charming home in Rainier Valley.

About his charming bed in that charming home. About his wide smile, big hands, and charming kisses...

Joey sighed, felt the goofy grin stretching her mouth, and didn't care. For once she'd taken care of herself, and it felt wonderful. She and Lou hadn't promised each other anything but a good time. They'd been responsible, hurting no one.

I want to do it again.

Sex with a man she liked? A man she'd easily call a friend?

She texted Becky, arranging for a favor in the form of a sitter for later in the week, and then texted Lou, who'd been surprisingly quiet. She had a moment to reconsider after she'd sent him the text, but he answered right away.

Yes! Thursday night. My place. First, gin rummy. Second, dinner. Third, you, me, and a blindfold.

She laughed, texted back a few enthusiastic emojis, then went back to house hunting. All the rest of her worries could wait. She had a hot date with an even hotter man, her son was happy, and life was good. She'd take what she could get before the wind changed.

———∿∿∿———

Lou spent a pleasant week at work. The guys at Webster's razzed him for being so cheerful and smiling. Though he normally enjoyed work, he knew he had Joey to thank for putting a big-ass grin on his face. He hadn't even been bothered when Del laughed at him, proclaiming him a man in love, or when Foley stuck him with Blue Altima's evil cousin, Demon-Red F-150.

He just worked with a smile, singing along to the radio.

"I know you're normally a decent guy to work with, but this is taking it too far," Johnny said Wednesday morning, standing over Lou, a line wrench in hand. "Lara told me she saw you and Heller at Ray's the other night hanging out and laughing together. Laughing with *Heller?*"

"I was laughing at him, actually. Because Rena still won't give him the time of day. And you know, he's not a bad guy. He just looks tough." Johnny just stared at him. "Okay, he can be an asshole, and he has hands like bricks. I wouldn't want to get into a fight with the guy. But he runs a decent shop and treats his people right."

"Rena dogging the guy? Oh, that's okay then." Johnny nodded, having heard what he needed, apparently. "So you and the flower chick, huh?"

Lou groaned. "Why is it a guy is in a good mood, and everyone associates that with whoever he's dating?"

"Maybe because you're normally a prick with a smart mouth who likes to insult us in *two* languages," Foley answered, the ass, "and lately you're all smiles and shit."

Sam dragged himself out from under a Nissan and raised a greased brow. "Yeah, and you gave me tons of crap about Ivy. You get what you give, man. It's called karma."

"One can only hope. I live a clean life." Lou had been working out at the gym on those nights he hadn't spent at Heller's shop sanding down the Vette. He ate a balanced diet, not touching sugars and bad carbs. And he treated his family right. He figured he was owed a woman like Joey Reeves.

Man, she'd been fine. If he was a little bothered they couldn't see more of each other right away due to her insane schedule—and his, truth be told—he knew it to be a good thing. The chemistry between them had him half-convinced he was falling for her. His appetite suffered, forcing him to consume energy bars to make up the needed calories. And he got jittery at a simple text from the woman. All signs he needed to proceed with caution, so good for her for not rushing things.

Except he wanted to be with her all the fucking time. Like, right now.

"What's with the frown, Cortez?" Foley asked, a little too innocently. "Afraid she's gonna dump you already?" He glanced at Lou's phone vibrating on his workbench.

Lou swore under his breath, ignored the guys, and noted a message from his mother. "For your information, Foley, Mama wants to know what I want for dinner tonight."

Activity in the garage ceased, all eyes on Lou.

"She wants to know if she should make enough for the guys at the garage. I wonder if she means Heller or you clowns?"

Sam shrugged. "Remember, I was being nice. Honest."

"Nice?"

Even Foley blinked at that.

Sam sighed. "Well, for me. I didn't grind you about her. Tell your mom to make those corn cake thingies."

"Her sweet corn cakes?" Johnny looked hopeful. "Oh, hey, Lou." He gave a fake laugh. "You know I was just kidding, right?"

"You guys are so easy." Lou snorted. "And you," he said, pointing at Foley. "No extra tamales for you."

"That's just mean."

"Hey, you got a hot girlfriend. Suck up to her and see if she'll make you something good."

Foley frowned. "Yeah, but Cyn can't do tamales. That takes authentic work, man." He glanced around. "Don't tell her I said that. Ever."

Johnny gave an evil laugh. "What's it worth to you? Maybe some pizzelles for the gang the next time she makes them? Like tonight?"

Not a bad choice. Lou loved the anise-flavored Italian cookies.

"Blackmail, Johnny?" Foley cringed.

"You know it."

Foley sighed. "My own fault for forgetting who I'm with."

"Who's that?" Sam asked.

"Satan's minions. And look, our whip-wielding tor-menter herself."

Del paused in step, having just come back from a coffee run. She sipped her drink, frowned, and said, "What?"

"Cracccckkk," Johnny whispered, and the guys laughed.

She glared, dragged a jagged fingernail across her

throat, and barked, "Back to work." Then she darted into her office.

"Aye, aye, captain," Foley muttered. "I swear, if she had an eye patch and a parrot, she could be Blackbeard's evil sister."

"Say it a little louder, Foley. I don't think Captain Death heard you," Sam encouraged, and they all looked to Del's open office doorway.

No one spoke.

Lou, content with his world at present, got back to work, singing along with Clapton, much to the annoyance of his peers. *Ah, life is good.*

He made a quick stop at Heller's after leaving the garage. He noted the metallic-green paint job on a Mazda that had been yellow last week. Nicely done. He checked on the pieces in his bay, realizing the power buffer had done its work. A few more touch-ups, some fine sanding to the driver's side door, and he'd probably be ready to paint in a few days. Mateo had helped out because the Corvette now needed to be done early. The owner was paying through the nose to have it ready for a car show in California he'd added to his to-do list.

Lou nodded, pleased at the progress. He waved to Smith, leaving through the back, then went to check the main office. He planned to say hi to Heller if the guy was in, which of course he was. Heller had no life. When not working at the shop, he went home or, more recently, could be found tutoring the guys at darts at Ray's. Poor Foley actually thought he might be able to beat Johnny someday. The sap.

"Yo, you heading home soon?" he asked, frowning when he saw Heller with his head in his hands, staring at his uncluttered desktop. "Heller?" After a pause. "Axel, you okay?"

When Heller glanced up, Lou saw tears in his eyes.

"Shit, man, you okay? What's wrong?"

Heller blinked, but the glassy shine remained. "You should go home. The car is where it needs to be."

"Hey, it's me. What's up?" Lou asked, his voice quiet.

Heller stared at him, the raw emotion making his dark-blue eyes nearly black. "My mother. She's gone."

Lou prayed he was wrong in his assumption. "Gone as in left your father, finally?" he asked, daring to hope.

Heller shook his head. "The cancer. It took the rest of her."

"Damn. I'm so sorry." He hadn't known she had cancer. Lou had only met Heller's mom once, and she'd been a hell of a woman. Loud, brash, and loving toward her only son. Unlike the guy's father, Heller's mom had been a genuinely nice person. "I had no idea she was sick."

"None of us did." Heller sighed, wiped his eyes, and stood. "I'm going home."

"Want some company?" Lou asked, knowing he'd miss Joey, but Heller needed a friend.

"*Nein*. I have things to do. Plans to make. The funeral…"

"You need anything, I'm here for you, man."

Heller moved around the desk and grabbed Lou by the shoulders. Then he pulled him in for a bone-crushing hug. "*Danke*, Lou. *Danke*."

"You're welcome. Look, take some time. Okay? You need anything, call me. Need me to handle the shop for you? No problem. I mean it."

Heller gave a watery smile, then shoved Lou toward the door. "Leave so I can lock up."

"Okay. Man, I'm so sorry."

Heller nodded. Lou left, his step a lot heavier than when he'd arrived. As he drove to his mom's for a midweek meal, he thought about how he'd feel if she passed away. As much as he'd had some real problems with her growing up, he loved the hell out of Renata Cortez. She was by no means perfect, but she was his mom. No matter how many bad choices she made in men or how many siblings she ended up giving him—and, God willing, Rosie was the last—he had a soft spot for the beautiful, naive, too-giving woman who'd raised him.

At fifty-five, his mother should be thinking about retirement, not more children. At least his aunts had tapered off on the kids, mostly. Except for Tía Chavela, who wanted a boy after two girls. Crazy woman. Didn't she have enough proof that the Cortez family only made girls? He and Javier were anomalies, the only boys in a family of a bazillion women.

Sadly, not one of his aunts had found a lasting love. Two had husbands they'd loved who had died. Three, counting Mama, because she'd loved Rosie's daddy, and he'd been a decent guy. The rest of her sisters had grown up with Abuela in Cuernavaca, outside of Mexico City. Moving to the States thirty years ago, they'd forged new lives for themselves. But he could count on one hand the number of stand-up men in their lives since his grandfather had died.

Hell, Lou had been his own role model growing up. After that small stint in a juvenile correctional facility and an even more interminable sentence passed by the women in his family, he'd found the straight and narrow.

Now he spent his time caring for his sisters, trying to make sure they found happiness and stability. Carla and Maria were the most centered. Both had educations and happy social lives. Stella needed help, so he kept an eye on her. Lucia, she remained a mystery. But she liked it that way. Of all his sisters, he worried about her the least. Then Rosie, the youngest, his baby girl. The closest thing he'd ever get to a daughter.

Lou had spent his lifetime raising children. He wanted freedom from that responsibility. Time for romance, no one woman but a bevy of monogamous lovers. Lou liked his women one at a time, focusing his attention on just one.

Like Joey.

He parked along the street in front of his mother's house and sat there.

Joey. What to do about her? Unlike all the others, and Lou admitted there had been many women in his life who weren't family, Joey Reeves absorbed all his attention. She had his dick in a knot for sure, but she tampered with his emotions without meaning to.

They'd texted back and forth throughout the week, little things about their days or something that struck them as funny. Yet for all their communication, there remained a wall between them. Normally Lou encouraged such distance, wanting fun and not much else by way of a one-to-one sexual commitment. But with Joey, he wanted more.

He'd actually thought about inviting her tonight, to a family meal. Lou didn't do that. His sisters occasionally met a girlfriend if they all went out, and that had happened maybe half a dozen times. Ever. But he never brought anyone home to Abuela or Mama. And sure as shit not to Rosie.

He'd grown up watching a carousel of men swing past his door while they romanced his pretty mom. No way. No how. Family was life, and he would do nothing to fuck that up. Not when he'd spent his childhood, adolescence, and every waking moment patching up the holes left by a loving, if at times thoughtless, mother.

With a sigh, he left the car and joined everyone in the house. As usual, he left money on the fridge. Tonight, everyone had gathered upstairs, not in the basement. He saw his sisters, Javier and Javier's mom, Tía Guadalupe, and her two girls as well. "Hey, Abuela." He gave his frail grandma a kiss, and she smacked him. "Ow. What's that for?"

As they went to sit in the dining room around his mother's giant table, she answered in Spanish, and he switched channels in his brain automatically, realizing the entire household had gone off-English. "What?"

Abuela moved down the table to sit by her daughters while the others brought in tostadas, *mole*, refried beans, and more homemade goodness and set them in the center of the table. The youngest, Rosie and Stella, set places and handed out silverware. Then everyone sat to eat.

He was still rubbing his arm when his grandmother asked, "Where is this flower girl? I want to meet her."

Well, shit.

Chapter 13

LOU BLINKED. "WHAT?" DESPITE HAVING MENTIONED Joey the last time everyone had gathered, he'd thought they would have forgotten her by now. Lou had lots of girlfriends. No biggie.

"Stella." His grandma pointed to his smirking sister, drinking lemonade next to Lucia farther down the table. "She tells us all about how you are sick in the heart for this woman."

Lou glared at his sneaky sister. "No, Abuela. Joey is nice, but—"

"Are you embarrassed of us? Is that it?"

He shook his head. "Of course not, I just—"

"So why isn't she here? We should be looking her over, seeing if she is good enough to go out with my handsome grandson." She handed a bowl of chilaquiles to Guadalupe, then everyone followed, passing the food around.

Lucia cupped her hands around her mouth like a megaphone. "And good enough for my wonderful brother," she said loudly. Like he couldn't hear her from where he sat. Jesus, what a pain.

"*My* Guapo," Maria said, batting her eyelashes at him. "Whom I love *sooo* much."

"Laying it on a bit thick, eh?" he grumbled.

"And *my* lovely nephew," Tía Guadalupe had to say. She nudged Javier. "Right, Son?"

Lou smirked at his cousin, the poor kid. "Yeah, J. Listen to Tía Guadalupe."

J. grimaced and gave Lou a pained shrug. "Ah, sure, Mama. Whatever you say."

Lou drew on his patience as he scooped beans and rice onto his plate before passing the bowls. "Look, if I bring her here, you'll scare her away. Besides, we're new. Sure, everything now is fun and exciting. But that stuff fades. You know how it is. We'll go our separate ways in a while. We'll probably stay friends, but that's it."

What he couldn't say was that she'd been different from the beginning. And friendship had never been the end-all he wanted from her. What he did want he couldn't quantify, not yet.

"Bring her to meet me then," his mother said. "Just me. I won't scare her off."

"Well, I'll see," was all he'd commit to, though he had no intention of bringing Joey to meet anyone. Or did he?

To his chagrin, the thought of having his family close, and Joey closer, tempted him. She would fit in with a Wednesday night Cortez meal. She had a sweetness to her that would call to his mother's, grandmother's, and aunts' protective instincts. Plus, Joey was kind. Rosie would take to her right off, he knew. And Rosie could be particular when it came to friendships.

And why the hell am I trying to fit Joey into my family? He wanted to pull his hair out, especially when they stared at him pushing the food around on his plate. At his grandmother's raised brow, he lied. "I ate earlier." He hadn't eaten since the banana Del had forced on him midmorning.

"Hmm." Abuela grinned at him. She whispered something to Guadalupe that had the older woman laughing her head off, which got his mother involved, then Lucia. The group talked about him in low whispers, as if he couldn't see them pointing, staring, and laughing at him.

"I'm right here," he growled.

Rosie giggled.

Near enough to hear them, J. grimaced and said to Lou, "You don't want to know."

Lou sighed. "Why me?"

Dinner passed swiftly enough, mostly with the ladies making fun of him and teasing Javier about a new girl at school. Feeling for the boy, he took the fourteen-year-old aside after dinner, and they went out to look at Guadalupe's car.

"The engine keeps pinging, and Mama's filling up the tank too much. I think maybe the timing is off," J. said.

"Could be." Not bad for the little mechanic-in-training. "Want to come down to the garage with me next week to work on it?"

J. lit up. "Yeah, man. That'd be cool, *primo*."

"Not *guapo*? Just *primo*?" Frankly, Lou preferred *handsome* over the pedestrian *cousin*.

J. gagged. "You ain't that pretty to me."

Lou grinned. "You trying to talk smack, J.? Man, ain't you cute."

"Shit. You might be big, but me and my boys could tear you up if we wanted to. Not that I'd let them, since you're family and all," J. teased.

At mention of his "boys," Lou knew the time had come for a little talk. He stared J. down.

J. flushed. "Kidding, man. Geez, Lou. Take a joke, why don't you."

"Yeah? I think you're funny. Until I hear you're hanging with some bad-news guys." He'd had a quick discussion with Guadalupe earlier when she'd cornered him on his way out of the bathroom. "Stay away from Paul Lasko and Diego Suarez."

J. blinked. "How do you know about them?" He groaned. "Mama told you."

"You think those punks own your high school?" Lou snorted. "Try again. They work for Toto."

"That's what they said, but I doubt it."

"Don't. Toto has a hand in a lot of schools. And I know for a fact anyone who associates or talks about associating with him is in for a world of hurt. Right now, the Righteous are ready to move on his house."

"No way." A white-power gang had it in for the Mexican stronghold on drugs in the city schools around their area. "Dang."

"So if your friends think they can run shit for Toto and talk big about it? Those two are headed for trouble. Especially because word has it the feds are soon going to be up Toto's ass right after they put the Righteous away. You don't want to be near any of it when it goes down."

J. frowned. "How do you know all this?" He gasped. "You a narc?"

"Please." Lou laughed at the thought of ever cooperating with the cops. Not that he didn't respect the law, but you only lived so long as people trusted you. And in his line of work—completely legal *now*, of course—a lot of his customers tended to have strained relationships with the law. "I have a lot of friends, and I work on a lot of cars, the kind with rich owners. Not all of them got rich from stock options on Wall Street. These business-men, they hear things. You get me?"

J. nodded, looking relieved.

"So keep your distance from Lasko and Suarez."

"I hear you." J. was a smart kid. He'd do the right thing.

Or Lou would hand him his balls one by one, yank him out of that school, and straight-up send him to the military academy his aunt had been thinking about.

J. kicked a rock around. "I'll stay away, but… They might not like it."

"You have any problems at all, you mention my name. Then you tell them anyone who fucks with you fucks with the guy working on Mantego's wheels. And that unlucky guy is gonna have to answer to me first, Mantego second."

J. swallowed. "No problem."

Mantego ran the streets in many parts of Seattle. He'd been rumored to have been involved in the House, where Sam used to do his illegal fights before the place had been shut down. Mantego owned a bunch of clubs around town, and he policed his own. Even the cops gave the gunrunner a wide berth. Personally, Lou had no problem with the guy. He was funny and had a head for numbers. Lou liked him.

Lou grabbed J. close and shook him. "You mess around with those assholes, and I'll be forced to take action. The kind that gets you jail time. Think about this: I go, who takes care of all our women? You?"

J. paled.

"That's right. We have responsibilities to our family. Family is first. Family is everything. Not some punk drug-dealer wannabes. Keep your nose clean, and the only thing we have to talk about are the car and your new girlfriend. What's her name again?"

J. flushed. "Angela. But she's not my girlfriend yet."

Lou studied his cousin, seeing the same good looks that kept his entire family in trouble with the opposite sex. And in his cousin Salome's case, the same sex. "Nah, you got this. Remember to be charming, not just good-looking, and you'll do fine."

"I'm a stud." J. laughed. "So hard being so sexy, eh, Guapo?"

"Shut it, little man." He shoved the kid in a playful way, satisfied Javier would be okay.

"Hey, at least I'm honest. You think you're seriously hiding anything from the family? They all know about the flower chick and—"

"Her name is Joey."

"—that you're in love with her. Stella told them." J. burst into gales of laughter as Lou tickled and mock-wrestled him before dragging him back to the house in a headlock. "Help, Mama," J. said, half laughing, half semistrangling on Lou's biceps. "Primo is being mean to me."

Guadalupe and Lou's mother ignored him. His grandmother rolled her eyes. "Eh. Boys."

Stella sighed. "Poor J. We should help him."

"I'm not dealing with all that," Carla said and stepped back, munching on chips.

Rosie barreled into them and dragged J. away. "I'll save you, Guapo."

"There's my favorite sister." He shot his other sisters dirty looks.

J. stared at her. "Save *him*? I'm the one getting beaten up."

"Yeah, but if you hurt Guapo, the flower lady might not come over, and I really want to meet her. Lou's in love."

J. laughed at Lou's expression. So did the others.

Lou glared. "Stella…"

"Hey, I'm single and pinning all my hopes on you. I need to see a real relationship succeed before I'm scarred for life." She sounded way too smug to be sad, to his way of thinking. "Besides, I like her. I told everyone about her."

Lou groaned.

"Yep, everyone." She held up her phone. "Even Sam, while you were outside with Javier."

"J.," the boy corrected.

Stella ignored him. "Sam and I are friends, and I thought he'd want to know how to help you if you suddenly blew it with Joey. He thanked me for being concerned."

Lou covered his eyes and wished for the ground to swallow him. "Hell."

―⁓―

"My life is not in a good place right now," Lou admitted to Joey Thursday night after she settled on his couch and made herself comfortable.

"Oh? What's wrong?"

"The guys are giving me a lot of grief about you. The flower chick."

"The flower chick? I have a title?"

"Yeah. If you hadn't spent so much time blowing me off for months before Del's wedding, I wouldn't be in this predicament and… Are you laughing at me?"

Joey's wide grin reflected the mirth in her big brown

eyes. She didn't even try to hide it. Such a different person than the shy, contained woman who'd hidden behind the flower counter two and a half weeks ago. "Sorry. That's terrible."

He sat next to her and grabbed a deck of cards from the coffee table. "You sound distinctly insincere."

She laughed. His heart did somersaults. The sight of those bright-white teeth and those full lips curled in a smile hitting him harder than a right hook to the jaw.

"Poor Lou."

"You know, the more smack talk before the game, the harder I trounce you after." He saw her pulse jump in her throat and knew a sense of satisfaction that he wasn't the only one affected by being together.

"You be nice, Lou Cortez," she warned and took the cards from him, shuffling like a professional dealer. "I'm just a poor flower girl trying to get by. And that's not easy dealing with your type." She pointed right at him. "You have no idea how difficult it was for me to walk into the garage and deal with Del for her wedding. And having to go by you guys was scary."

"So you've said before." He smiled.

"Don't look so smug."

"Well, you deserve it. You had me doubting myself, and one thing I'm good at it is being me. Lou Cortez, The Man." He pounded his chest.

"You're so deluded."

"You're so fuckin' sexy," he said right back and leaned close to steal a kiss. The warmth the kiss generated drove him crazy, because the sparks trailed from his mouth, down his chest, and centered in his cock. "Man, I always just want you closer. Under me."

She blushed. "Lou." Yet the hand that pressed against his chest curled to keep him close. "I thought we were going to play gin, then dinner, *then* fun?"

"Well, there's no real order to it. We can do whatever we want." And right now, he wanted her spread open while he sampled from his own perfect appetizer. "You have to be in at eight tomorrow, right?"

She sucked in a breath when he trailed a finger over her collarbone. "Um, nine. But I can't stay too late. I need to be back home by eleven."

He frowned. "Eleven? Why?" She stiffened, so he relented. His questions could keep for now. "Fine, fine. Relax. I'll let you go by ten-thirty. That's another three hours away though. Time for us to reschedule a few things." He felt uncomfortably hard. "You hungry?"

As if she'd read his mind, she glanced down and stared at his groin. "For what, exactly?"

He groaned. "I think we need to talk."

—∿∿—

Joey's gaze flashed back up to Lou's face, and she felt her cheeks heat. "Oh my gosh. I can't believe I hinted…*that*."

He grinned. Oh wow, he was too handsome for words. His eyes seemed almost to glow when he looked at her. Such a strong jaw, those lips, those darkly lashed eyes. He was like a model, complete with a bodybuilder's frame. So what was he doing with her again?

She couldn't help glancing back at his prominent erection, remembering how big he could get. Goodness, but she felt way too hot sitting so close to the man.

"Oh yeah. Definitely past time we had The Talk."

"The Talk?"

He nodded. "The one we should have had at the very beginning of all this. So here it is. I haven't been with a woman in months. I always practice safe sex, and my last doctor's visit, back in February, was good to go. A clean bill of health. I want to be with you again, and I'm fine wearing condoms. Now you."

He waited, and she wondered that in all her years, she'd never had such a frank conversation about sex before. Or that, for once, she hadn't had to instigate the embarrassing discussion. Yet it bothered her that she hadn't brought it up before now. What was wrong with her? One look into Lou's big brown eyes and she lost her sense?

He cleared his throat.

"Oh. Right. The Talk." She blew out a breath. "Well, I also practice safe sex." *No question about that—now.* "I haven't had a boyfriend in over a year, and my last physical checked out okay."

Lou frowned. "A *year?*"

She shrugged, uncomfortable that she probably now appeared as pathetic as she'd felt for so long. Lou had made her forget for a while that she wasn't exactly a diamond in the rough. More like a shiny pebble in a fast-moving stream, brushing by and over her. "I've been really busy with work and trying to get enough funds to move out of my house. It takes a lot of time and money. And I paid for myself to go through school, you know."

He watched her, his eyes wide.

"What?"

"Well, one, we can take shy off the table. Because you're no longer shy with me, more like confrontational—and I love it." He grinned. "And two, I wasn't aware I was dealing with a self-made woman. You don't talk about yourself much."

"Oh. Not much to tell, really."

"I disagree." Lou looked her over and smiled. "Beautiful, intelligent, and ambitious. So you put yourself through school?"

"Yes. I had to balance work and family and a full-time job. It wasn't easy." Especially when said family had been undergoing potty training at the same time. "I did it on my own with a little help from my parents. But not much."

That first year, her parents had done their best to distance themselves, forcing her to do everything on her own. Except her mother would sneak in to her room to handle the baby. More for her grandson than to help Joey. A not-so-subtle form of punishment Joey would never forget. Sure, her parents had been there to help her, but on their terms and without much sympathy for a young girl who'd made a mistake. She would never treat Brandon that way. Not ever.

"Hey, you okay?" Lou asked and reached for her hand. "You looked pretty sad there, *cariña*. What's the matter?"

She shook off feelings that didn't belong here. Lou had never treated her like she didn't matter or know her own mind. "Just family stuff. Sometimes I can't help thinking about it."

He rubbed his fingers over her knuckles. "I know what you mean." He paused. "Can I ask you something?"

"Sure."

"Your parents. They helped you, but not a lot, you said?"

"No, they helped a lot, I guess. But on their terms. I know I should be grateful they never kicked me out onto the street." Yet she still felt so much anger when it came to them. "It sounds like you're pretty close to your family." At his nod, she continued. "We were a tight group when I was growing up. Or rather, my mom and I were. Dad was always working. Still is, to be honest. But he loves me." *I think.* "Then, well, some stuff happened. I did something I shouldn't have, but it all worked out in the end." She loved Brandon. Period. "But for a long time, they never let me forget it. Punishing me for something that, yeah, was my fault. But I was so young when it happened."

He snorted. "You're young now, so I can't imagine how old you were when you messed up. How old are you, anyway?"

"Twenty-four. Almost twenty-five."

He blinked. "Yeah? I mean, you look it. But you seem so much older."

"How old are you?" She'd put him at late twenties.

"Thirty-five."

She stared. "Seriously? You're an old man."

He grimaced, and she laughed, feeling lighter having unburdened herself. She hadn't told him about Brandon yet. Her baby boy belonged to her and her alone. Though she liked Lou, a lot, she didn't know if she could trust him with her most precious joy.

"I feel old sometimes," he admitted, still holding her hand. She'd scooted closer so he wasn't stretching her arm so much. When he grinned, she realized he'd intended to get her nearer.

"Nice move."

"I've got more." He waggled his brows but didn't let her go. The connection felt more than physical as he spoke, as if by holding her and sharing himself, he was entwining a ribbon of trust around them. "I pretty much grew up taking care of my sisters. And my mama kept adding to the family, not always with the same man." He sighed. "I love her, my mama. She's a beautiful woman. Just like all my sisters."

"Just like you."

To her delight, a tinge of red lit his cheeks. "Yeah, well, we're a handsome family. Makes it a real pain in the ass to keep everyone together and out of the hands of men who should know better. My mama, she's got such a big heart, so much kindness inside." He looked at Joey. "Not to be all weird about it, but you remind me of her in a lot of ways."

"That's nice."

He shrugged. "It's true. But my mama, she's *too* nice. She has five girls by three men. My father was an asshole. Good for nothing but taking advantage of a sweet woman." He shook his head. "Mama is pretty, and men like her. A little flattery, and she'd give them whatever they wanted."

Joey wanted to duck her head. She had a lot more in common with Lou's mom than he might think. *But I learned from it*, she told herself.

"I don't want you to think my mom's bad or anything, she's just too kind-hearted. Which explains why a lot of the discipline in our family comes from me. I was five when Lucia was born. Carla came three years after that, Maria a year later. Then Stella and Rosie. Rosie's eight." He groaned. "If my mama would just go gray and start wrinkling up, lose some teeth, get a walker, I'd be spared more stress."

She laughed with him. "So all girls. Didn't you have any male relatives to help out?"

"I learned a lot from my *abuelo,* my grandfather. But he died when I was little, and my uncles were never that much interested in our family. They had too much to take care of with their own. So I pretty much helped raise all my sisters. I love them, but they're a handful."

"I'll bet." She could see Lou as a family man, a decent soul overcoming heartache, doling out love and a sense of home. "You'll be a great father someday." A man like that would understand her having a son. She saw the empathy, the care, and wanted to trust him. He'd offered himself, opening up like that. She wanted to do the same. Yet something held her back.

"Yeah, well, I don't plan to have any kids. I'm done raising them," he said bluntly, his hold on her hand tight before he realized he'd gripped her too hard. He let her go. "I just want to be the happy uncle with a great ride, a woman by my side, and fun in the future. Nothing heavy, nothing too serious."

The way he looked at her told her he meant the warning for her.

She chuckled to ease the hurt. And why should she feel any pain because of what he said? Not like she'd imagined them as a couple or anything long-term. *Just friends who make each other feel good, right?*

"Don't worry about me," she said. "I'm not into hearts and flowers—well, flowers maybe." He grinned with her. "I like being independent. And I have too much to do with my life to settle down now."

So why did her confession feel like a fat big lie? Why had she rested even the tiniest hope that she and

Lou might blossom into something fuller? Because he respected family, cared for those needing help, and had been the first man ever to see to her pleasure before his own? Yes, she'd allowed their sexual intimacy to create a false sense of emotional intimacy. That had to be it.

"Man, that brain is going and going. I can tell." He tugged her closer. "So why do you have to leave at eleven?"

The question came out of nowhere, no segue or anything. She just blinked at him, having no other excuse than a need to get her little boy from Becky, her sitter for the night.

Lou frowned. "Joey, is there someone else?"

Not like you mean. "No."

He clearly didn't buy her denial, but he didn't say anything. Instead, he cupped her face and kissed her.

The kiss cleared all the cobwebs from her mind and stirred the fires she'd barely banked. Desire rose swift and sure, and she found herself clinging to his broad shoulders as he drew her into his arms. So much larger than her, Lou surrounded her with muscle and with a firmness growing solidly larger under her as they kissed.

He muttered words she didn't understand, gripped her hair, and held her in place while he kissed the sense out of her. His lips, his tongue and teeth, he used every part of his mouth to force her body to surrender. And she loved it.

With one kiss, he'd turned her into a shivery mass of need.

"Tell me what you want, *amor*," he murmured against her throat. "Are you hungry, baby? You want something to eat right now? I got dinner waiting for you.

Something sweet for dessert too." He ground her against him and groaned. "Or did you want something else?"

She wanted to explore her carnality, the desire to make him feel what she had the last time they'd been together. She'd fantasized about it, because she'd heard and seen the act but had never actually done it. It seemed to give the woman power, pleasing her man.

Lou pulled back and stared into her eyes, his dark and full of need.

"I'm hungry, Lou." She ran a finger over his lips. "For something special. Something only you can give me."

The flare of desire made his eyes darker, and she knew what she wanted.

"I want to kiss you the way you kissed me before."

"Where?" he growled. "Tell me."

Instead she showed him by reaching between them and grazing the bulge between his legs. "Here. I want to kiss you here."

Chapter 14

SHE DIDN'T THINK SHE'D EVER SEEN LOU MOVE SO fast. One minute she'd been on his lap, the next he had her hurrying toward his back bedroom. He slammed the door shut and locked it. "Sorry, habit."

Before she could ask what that meant, he had his shirt off and his pants unzipped.

"Take me out."

She shook her head, surprising herself at her temerity. "I want to… Can you take off all your clothes?"

His slow smile answered for him. He stripped, completely bare. "Now you." But before she could take off her clothes, Lou was there doing it for her.

"First, the shirt." He dragged it up and off her, then tossed it to a chair in his bedroom. She'd only been back here the one time before, and it had been mostly dark then. Now she made out a thick leather chair in the corner, a large king-size bed in the center, and an armoire to the side. Nothing else in the room save the nightstands on either side of the bed.

Where he kept his condoms.

She tingled, especially when Lou watched her as he unfastened her bra and tugged it off her. He had a thing for her breasts, because he spent a lot of time touching and kissing them. She'd never realized how much she liked it. He was about to show her again.

He picked her up as if she weighed nothing and

sucked her nipple into his mouth. He groaned as he tongued and teethed, then treated the other side to the same attention. Panting with lust, she could barely think as he set her down. Then his clever hands had her pants unfastened, her jeans pushed down to her ankles.

Lou bent down to remove the rest of her clothes, then stood and studied her. "I need to draw you. To paint you." He licked his lips. "You are so beautiful, Joey."

She blushed with pleasure. "So are you." She loved the chance to see those tattoos, the subtle artwork crossing his broad chest, tracing the cut of muscle on his darker skin and trailing it downward, to the long, thick cock made hard because of her.

It thrilled her to know she could get a man like Lou, older and sexier, to want her so much.

"You still hungry, baby?" He gripped himself, holding himself out to her. "I'll show you what I like. Stand here. Spread your legs."

"What?"

He was on his knees in front of her in seconds, his mouth plastered to her sex as he licked and stroked her nearly to orgasm. Had he not stopped when he did, she'd have come.

"You see? Hunger. I want to taste that cream you make for me. So soft, silky." He slid a finger inside her, holding her still by the hip when she jerked.

"Lou," she moaned. "I was going to—"

"After. You suck me down *after* I taste you. So fuckin' good." He kissed her again, toying with her clit while he moved his thick finger in and out, rubbing against her in all the places that mattered. She held tightly to his shoulders, her body spiraling out of control.

"Lou, I'm going to… I need to…"

He sucked her harder and continued to thrust in and out of her. Then he stroked a finger between her buttocks, rubbing her cleft while he drew on her clit with a love bite.

Joey couldn't stop the rush of ecstasy as she came over his tongue, moaning while pleasure became her world. Dimly aware of Lou petting her through it, she found herself in his arms being hugged and kissed and tasted herself on his lips.

When he pulled back, she gazed at him in wonder. "I taste me."

He nodded, his intensity so focused, she trembled in the face of it. She felt his erection against her belly, so hard for her still. "You taste like cream. So soft, so sweet. I could eat you for days." He continued to murmur things even as he wrapped her hand around his cock and let her pump him before he groaned and made her let go.

"On your knees for me." He spread his stance wider, his hand on her shoulder. And the dominant pose only added to the fantasy she'd had of them doing this.

She had to stand on her knees to reach him, and he frowned. "Don't move." He fetched a pillow from his bed, then returned and had her kneel on that. "Better?"

She nodded, unable to look away from him.

"You good with this?" he asked, stroking her hair. "I told you I was clean, but you have to trust me on that."

She glanced away from his impressive size to see his sober expression. And right then, she knew. Against all odds, having just come to know the man, really, she did. "I trust you, Lou. You'd never hurt me like that."

"I'd never hurt you at all," he whispered. "Unless you asked me to." He winked.

She sighed, so caught up in the man, she would do anything to see him feel what she just had. Without asking, without looking away from his face, she leaned close, rested a hand on his hip, and felt him tense. Then she stuck out her tongue and licked the tip of him.

Lou looked so tense she feared he'd break. His muscles all bunched, and the veins on his forearms stood in relief.

"Again," he barked, his grip on her hair tightening.

Knowing he liked it, she did it again, lapping at him like a kitten to milk.

The flow of Spanish and the rocking of his hips told her she'd done well. But after that, she had no real idea of what to do next. Sucking on him seemed the answer, and she'd seen women do that in the movies, so it had to be right. But Lou was thick, and her jaw didn't stretch that wide, she didn't think.

Joey held him by the root to keep him still, then put her mouth over him.

"*Madre de Dios*, yes. Fucking blow me, baby. Oh yeah," he moaned as she took more of him inside. She hadn't gone a third of the way down when her jaw started to ache. How did women do this?

"Easy. Let me help," he rasped. He held her by the hair and withdrew, then pushed in again. Slowly, he started moving in and out of her mouth, telling her how to lick, to stroke. He had her cup his balls, which he seemed to love, because he jolted and thrust deeper in response.

"*Lo siento*," he apologized, hoarse, and immediately pulled back. "Damn, but I'm not going to last." He groaned.

She rubbed him, held the weight of his balls in her hand, and stroked the hard globes covered in such soft skin. He had hair there, but not much. Like the rest of his body, Lou had a smoothness, a sleekness to him. Even the hair around his cock had been trimmed, which made him look huge.

Not that he tried to look that way. He *was* huge.

She wanted to take more of him. So while cupping him, she leaned closer, and his hands in her hair slackened. She bobbed over him, taking more, learning the feel of him. Her jaw still ached, but she felt more used to the size of him. His girth, at least. She still couldn't completely take all of him in her mouth without gagging.

"More, more," he chanted. "Gonna come, baby. So hard. You don't want it down your throat, pull away and I'll come on your tits." He was talking so dirty, so lost in her, and she loved it. No tender care, no treating her like a fragile princess. He was a man with needs she was taking care of. No fumbling teenager, Lou took her like a man possessed.

"Coming," he warned, and she bore down, sucking him even deeper into her mouth while he moaned her name.

He held her head steady as warmth filled her mouth. She swallowed as he emptied, wanting all of Lou. Not that watching him release wouldn't be erotic, but knowing she'd made him lose himself in her gave her a sense of accomplishment. Of being a real woman, one who grew aroused feeling him orgasm.

He had a lot to give, and she swallowed him down until he finally withdrew.

He yanked her to her feet and tossed her on the bed. She yelped as she bounced on the mattress. But then Lou was there, on top of her, kissing her until she once again lost herself in him.

He stroked her, petting her breasts, her belly, then her sex, sliding his fingers between her legs while he came down off his euphoric high.

"Jesus. You blew me away." He chuckled and kissed her throat. "So good, baby. God, I'll never forget the sight of you licking my cock." He shivered. "You have no idea how many times I imagined that. And it was never so good as you doing it." He shoved her back and leaned over her, not yet ready to take her again, unfortunately.

Joey was ready to go, but Lou seemed soft against her.

"Got you wet blowing me, didn't it?" He smiled.

"Yes." She sighed. "I was already relaxed from when you, um, blew me."

"You were so sweet." He seemed smug. "You like me kissing that pretty pussy, don't you?"

She blushed.

"Yeah, you like me eating you out. Going down on you. But baby, it's nothing on watching my dick in your mouth. Me fucking those lips." He rubbed himself against her. "I want to fuck you again. Right now. But I need some time. You sucked me dry." He laughed at her blush. "Come on. You like when I talk like this, no?" He leaned close, his hot breath over her ear, and whispered, "That pussy hungry for me? Those tits ready for some biting? You know how hard you make me, all the time?"

She groaned. "Shouldn't I be too tired to want you again?"

"Nah. You're a young, sexy woman with drive. I just need a few minutes, and I'll be ready to take you. And *princesa*, I'll give it to you so good. Only thing better

would be no condom. Because jetting into your mouth…
Fuck me, best thing I ever felt."

"Really?"

"Really. The condom is good for protection, but I can't feel like I can when it's just you and me. But I'll wear it, no problem."

She wanted to tell him to take it off, to feel him inside her. But worries about making babies persisted. "No. I think you should wear it. Not because I don't trust you, but…"

"I know. Babies. Got to think about that." He palmed her belly and got a strange look on his face. "And much as I'd love to be in you, the pullout method ain't the best."

"No." Not that she'd ever tried that one. Her mistake had been trusting that Felix had known what he was talking about when he'd calculated and said it was the right time to make love and not worry about conception. As if the boy had known about her cycle. She couldn't believe she'd ever been that naive.

Lou rolled them over so she lay on top of him this time. He petted her back, lulling her to do anything he wanted. God, he felt good.

She sighed and stroked him, tracing the vines to the skull with a heart in the center of his chest.

"Joey, can I ask you something?"

"Sure." She sat up, astride him, and stared, the sight of him going straight to her head.

"Have you done that before? Blown a guy, I mean?"

She tensed. "Why? Did I do something wrong?"

His smile seemed so gentle. "No, baby. Any more perfect, and I'd have had a heart attack."

She relaxed.

"But you were a little tentative. That's okay, especially because you and I are new. I just wondered. Not complaining at all," he reassured her.

"Oh. No. I mean, I wanted to try it once, but the guy I was with was too nervous, so we didn't."

Lou groaned. "Your first blow job. You should have told me. I'd have been less rough."

"I liked it."

Lou relaxed. "Yeah, you did. You like it a little rough. Good."

She cleared her throat, not wanting to ask but asking anyway. "You sure it was okay?"

He rolled her over so fast, she saw stars. "Uh-uh. You don't get to second-guess yourself. It was so good, all I can think of is a way to get hard so we can do it again. Maybe a sixty-nine." His eyes narrowed. "Ever tried that?"

She blushed. "No."

He seemed intrigued, not put off. "Tell me. What exactly have you tried? I get the feeling you're not that experienced when it comes to sex."

"I'm not. Sadly."

He laughed. "I can fix that."

"I, well, this is embarrassing."

"No, Joey. Don't feel bad about anything. Not with me." He radiated sincerity, so she couldn't help but agree.

"I've had regular sex when I've had it. Um, *missionary*, I think, is the word. And once from behind, before you. But I didn't like it, and the guy came and left before I realized it was over. Mostly sex has been not so great. I didn't think I liked it or was good at it until you."

He shook his head. "I get the impression the guys you

were with didn't care about making it good for you. Just so they got theirs."

"Pretty much."

He said something in Spanish that sounded like a swear. "Those losers didn't deserve you. A good lover sees to his woman. You first, me second. Watching you come gets me hard, gets me off, you want the truth. I love going down on you. Love sucking those pretty nipples." He palmed one as he spoke. "Your body is a miracle. So soft yet strong. When I'm in you"—he paused, staring straight into her eyes—"it's perfection. And no, before you ask, I don't say this to every woman. Just you, Joey. Just you."

He kissed her before she could say anything, and then she lost herself in Lou. And, surprise, surprise, he didn't need as much time as he'd thought to get ready for her again. But this time he let her put the condom on, and she learned something else new. That preparing for safe sex could be just as much fun as having it…if the guy telling her how to get ready happened to be Lou.

—⁓—

By the time they'd finished pleasuring each other, it was time for Joey to go.

"Man, time flies when you're making love," Lou teased and hugged her tight, standing with her in the living room. They'd both dressed, unfortunately, and she kept putting off leaving.

"I have to go." She brushed his hair off his forehead, and he leaned down so she could kiss him. "Wish I could stay longer."

"Me too."

His stare unnerved her.

"What?"

In a quiet voice, he asked, "Joey, you aren't seeing someone else, are you?"

"No. Why?"

He looked relieved as he let her step back. A good thing, because she needed the distance. "It's just, I can sense you're holding things back."

Brandon. "I know." She wiped a hand over her face. "I can't... I'm not trying to lie, but I... My life is complicated. I'm not dating anyone else. I don't have a boyfriend, husband, or lover. Well, except you."

His serious expression turned into a warm smile. "I love when you turn pink. You do it a lot, you know?"

"I know." She wished she could turn off her emotions sometimes.

"But you're adorable."

She glared. "Cute?"

"I meant sexy. Fine. Motherfuckin' hot as hell. Better?"

She tried not to laugh. "A little."

Lou watched her gather her things as she readied to leave. "Hey, you didn't get anything to eat." He glanced down at himself. "Well, besides me."

"Lou."

He chuckled. "Seriously. Take the pie. I made it for you."

"You did?" She stared.

"Well, no. Actually I bought it from NCB. They have a new place they get some of their baked goods from. It's peach cobbler."

"Oh. I could take a slice."

"You'll take the whole thing. I don't do sugar."

"So why the pie?"

He handed the box to her. "Because you like sweets. Sweets for my sweet." He grinned. "Clichéd, right?"

"A little. But still…sweet." She laughed and kissed his cheek. Until he turned his face and met her mouth with a hungry one of his own.

Breathless and once again ready to have sex—make love—with the beautiful man, she forced herself to step back. "I—I—" She shook her head. "Stop kissing me. I can't think when you do that."

"Good to know," he said in a smoky voice.

"Lou." She laughed. "I have to leave."

"I know." He made a sad face and walked her to the door. "So when do I see you again?"

"I'm not sure." Brandon had soccer on Wednesday. Maybe she could drop him off for practice? Get a ride home for him with someone else? "Wednesday might work." She should tell him about Brandon. Get it out in the open.

And then he might not want to see her again, thinking she was looking for a new baby daddy. And there was Brandon to consider. As much as she was coming to care for Lou, she had her son to protect.

No, not yet.

"Joey?" Lou watched her.

"I'll call or text you. Okay?"

He nodded, kissed her again, then walked her outside to her car wearing nothing but jeans.

"Aren't you cold?"

"With you by my side? *Princesa,* I'm burning up."

She shook her head. "Typical man. I can see you're freezing." She leaned closer. "Your nipples are like little pebbles."

He grinned. "That's from you, not the cold. Like when I suck on yours, and they get so firm and wet. And then I slip my hand down your belly to—"

She slapped a hand over his mouth. "*Shush*."

His laughing eyes made her reconsider the idea of deepening their relationship, wanting more with this man. Who the heck was she fooling? She *liked* Lou? Of course she did. She just feared she was coming to *like* him a lot more than she should. On a downward slope toward that other l-word for sure.

"I have to go."

"So go." He took her hand and kissed it. "I *will* see you this week."

"Yes," she said on a sigh. Then she got into her car and left, not looking back, because if she did, she would call Becky and ask for another hour. And that she couldn't afford if she wanted to go into work not walking funny in the morning.

———※———

Lou watched her leave, then turned around, headed back inside, and, after locking up, sought his bed. He dropped onto it like a sack of used-up man.

He groaned and stared up at the ceiling, his entire body one huge mass of relief. *Fuck.* He'd come so hard so many times. He hadn't planned to make their evening just about sex. But Joey wanted to do so much. It was like she'd been locked away for years and now finally had the sexual freedom to live a little.

Part of him felt bad for her, that she hadn't experienced an orgasm with a man until him, a sad tidbit she'd shared after their last coming together. The other part was ecstatic. He'd been her first blow job. Her first sixty-nine. God. The first one to give her an *orgasm*.

With that came a sense of responsibility. A need to make things right so—

Bullshit.

He hated lying to himself, and he refused to start now.

He didn't feel responsible for the woman. He liked her. He liked her a lot. In fact, he thought he might… love her.

And how did he know that? Because he flat-out recognized that woman was lying to him about someone else being in her life. Yet he'd made love to her anyway. Like a sickness, she'd invaded his mind, his blood. Being with her, touching her, seeing her smile made the world go away so that nothing existed but Joey.

So young yet so old. He hadn't been bothered by their age difference, and he knew why. Because she had a maturity to her that typical twenty-four-year-olds didn't have. Unlike Stella, just a year younger than Joey, Joey didn't have tunnel vision. She had her sights set on the future.

He'd worried that he might be growing too attached, so he'd given her the no-kids speech up front. And while his lips had been flapping, he'd been envisioning kids with Joey. Actual children who would grow up with her as a mom, him as a dad.

Totally wacked-out bullshit. And then he'd confessed wanting to come inside her, had put his hand on her belly and could easily imagine new life there, a seed he'd planted.

Total craziness. He knew it. But that didn't stop some part of him from wanting more from her. That she hadn't argued or tried to reason him into wanting children had annoyed him. Why shouldn't she want him to commit more to her? Because she didn't plan on committing more to him?

He rubbed his eyes, tired and sated and confused.

What did he want from the woman? She'd fucking *swallowed*. And he'd nearly had a transcendental moment during his orgasm. A moment in time where everything was perfect, including the woman at his feet.

Maybe his favorite new position—Joey on her knees, loving him. He'd seen her pleasure and knew she hadn't been making it up to get him off. She'd genuinely loved making him feel good. Because Joey was like that. Giving, sweet, kind, and a closet sexual submissive begging for dominance.

Lou didn't live the lifestyle or anything. He just liked bossing a woman in bed. And Joey loved being bossed. She could handle his tenderness if he showed her she mattered on another level. Her inexperience in bed baffled him. A woman as beautiful as Joey should have had a lot of boyfriends, at least a few lovers to show her what to do with a man.

But when he let her take charge, even a little bit, she seemed unsure, hesitant. Her mouth over his cock had been heaven, no lie, but her strokes had been learning. Not practiced.

And yeah, he was a prick because even that got him off about her, that she had little experience until she'd been with him.

He groaned. "Why me?"

No one answered him, and why should they? The powers that be had given him love all his life. Granted, a high-maintenance, all-encompassing feminine love, but a love all the same. He'd always known he mattered to his family. And not just because they took care of him. His *abuela* loved him no matter what. She'd been his rock through most of his life. His mama cared for him as best she could, loving unconditionally. And his sisters might complain about him, but they knew he'd move mountains to help them, the same as they'd do for him.

Poor Joey didn't seem to come from the same supportive family. He was dying to know more about her, but she kept herself closed off. Why?

What the hell was she hiding?

Lou didn't do married women or women with boyfriends. Might not be a ring on her finger, but he respected a close relationship. He never wanted to be the "other guy," especially having seen his mother in the role of the "other woman" a few times in her life.

Yet for Joey, he'd pushed all that to the side, anything to have her in his arms again.

He exhaled on a moan. Scared because he thought he might love her. He didn't know why, didn't know how it had happened, and so soon. But it had.

Now what to do about it and how to make her trust him with more than her body but with her heart and secrets as well?

Chapter 15

JOEY STOOD WITH HER PARENTS AT BRANDON'S SOCCER game Saturday afternoon. Near them, she saw Del and her family. Big Mike and his parents. Had to be his father because the man was a carbon copy of Mike and little Colin. And then Del's father and her brother, J.T. A nice guy, handsome and again big, like the rest of the men in Del's life.

Joey looked at her father, a small man. A professional, even in repose. Her father looked old to her, his brown hair slightly gray, his loafers, khaki pants and rolled up blue oxford sleeves screaming *white collar* even at a kid's soccer game.

In fact, many of the attendees at the game reminded her of her dad. He talked to a few friends they saw regularly and laughed at something one of the other grandfathers said. Dressed in high-end outdoor clothing and cheering politely for their grandchildren, they looked like ads for an L.L.Bean spring collection.

Unlike Del and her family, rooting loudly, being reminded not to swear, and wearing jeans and sneakers and sweatshirts.

A lot like Joey.

"Excuse me. I'm going to go say hi to some friends," she said to her mom.

Amy blinked, looked over at Del, and smiled. "Oh sure, sweetie. Tell Colin's mom and dad I said hi."

Joey nodded. She walked over to Del and saw the other woman smile.

"Hey, Joey. Did you see that assist Brandon made? Nice." She held up a hand, and Joey slapped it. Then she started talking plays and strategies, which her husband and brother kept interrupting.

Lively, fun, and real. Being with this group of people and away from the picture-perfect-yet-anything-but family she called her own, she found herself wishing Lou could have been there to share in the moment. He'd have laughed, said stuff in Spanish she couldn't understand. They'd stand arm in arm, like Mike and Del, and he'd cheer when Brandon—

"Earth to Joey. You in there?" J.T. asked, grinning. The hot man who was Del's brother always put her at ease despite the fact he had a habit of looking her over like she was a prime filet.

"Sorry. Woolgathering." She glanced at her parents. "It's boring over there. I like it over here much better."

"Well, shit. That was a foul!" Colin's grandfather roared.

Next to him, his girlfriend Sophie, a pretty woman with white hair, yanked him by the arm. "Liam, language." She nodded at the small children nearby watching him with wide eyes.

Liam flushed. "Sorry. I mean, shoot! Call the foul!"

Sophie rolled her eyes.

J.T. chuckled. "Dad really gets into the games. You should have seen me playing football as a kid. Man, he was brutal."

"I can see you playing football." She eyed his wide shoulders, big hands, and thick thighs. "Why is every guy who knows Del a giant with huge arms?"

J.T. shrugged. "Except for Mike, you mean?"

Mike glanced over, gave J.T. a subtle finger, then turned back to the game.

Joey couldn't help laughing.

"No idea. My sister is badass with a capital B." J.T. leaned closer and murmured, "I'd call her a badass bitch, with love, you know, but she'd probably rip off my arm and beat me to death with it. She's the mean one in our family."

Joey nodded. "I can believe it. She scared me during the wedding planning. Man, when she changes her mind about irises, she means it."

Del narrowed her eyes at the pair, and Joey pasted on a bright smile and waved. J.T. did the same and chuckled when Del pointed to her eyes, then to him as if to say, *I'm watching you.*

"So, Joey," J.T. drawled. "What's this I hear about you and Lou being a thing?"

She'd known the topic would come up at some point. Her worlds colliding. Brandon on the soccer field, Lou working with the people on the sidelines. Joey sighed. Not like she was hiding Brandon, exactly. Sort of. Maybe a little.

"We're kind of dating. Just casually."

"Liar." J.T. grinned when her eyes widened. "Dude is into you. We all know it. The Casanova of the garage had his heart handed to him by a—"

"If you say 'flower chick,' I might belt you."

"Petite, feminine flower. How's that?"

She groaned.

He laughed. "Anyway, the guy is gone for you. So why isn't he here? He blow you off or something?"

The word *blow* conjured images from the last time she'd seen Lou, so she focused her gaze on the field and her son, hoping J.T. wouldn't notice her heated cheeks. "We aren't joined at the hip, J.T."

"I'm pretty sure he'd like to be. Has he met Brandon yet?"

"Are you this chatty with all the people you don't know that well?" she snapped, nerves making her obnoxious.

But J.T. only grinned. "That's a no then. You afraid he'll bolt if he knows you have a kid?"

"This is your business why?"

He laughed. "I like you, Joey. But I like Lou too. He's into you pretty hard."

She didn't know about that, and she sure didn't think Lou would like his buddy telling her about his feelings. "He and I are friends. But Brandon is my *son*. I don't introduce him to every man I date. It's no one's business but mine that I have a child." True, yet… "And it's not like I'm hiding him. He plays with Colin. He's here in plain view of—" *Oh. My. God*. More stress she didn't need.

"What?"

"N-never mind. The point is my relationship with Lou is just fine. When and if we talk about my son has nothing to do with you."

"Put in my place. Damn, girl. You're a lot tougher than you look." He seemed approving, not put off at all. Men. Such a puzzle. His phone jingled. "Sorry, gotta take this." He stepped away and talked to someone about a tattoo.

Which gave her time to process the fact that she'd seen Felix standing in the parking lot, watching the soccer game. He stared at her when they locked gazes, but he didn't leave. His presence here, now, meant that conversation with him she'd hoped to avoid would have to happen.

But unlike in the past, Joey wouldn't let anyone badger her into anything. Not sex, not a warm welcome, and not a free pass to the son he'd signed away his rights to. Joey had a young boy to protect, and she wouldn't let anything—or anyone—stand in her way. She walked from the crowded game toward the lot, saw Felix straighten, and hurried her step. Time to get this one issue out of the way for good.

———

J.T. watched Joey Reeves hightail it off the field toward the parking lot. Must have forgotten something in her car. He turned back to the field in time to watch Colin dribble around some boy and nail a pass to his teammate waiting in front of the goal. "Nice one."

"Hey, asswipe, I'm talking to you," Lou growled over the phone.

"Sorry. Colin just made a beautiful pass."

"Oh. You at the game?"

"Yeah."

"So why are you talking to me then? Enjoy your nephew's soccer game."

"I am. I can still talk business." J.T. wanted badly to mention Joey, but he didn't want to do anything to ruin Lou's shot at love. Because he knew the guy, and in all the years they'd been friends, Lou had dated. A lot. But never had he acted lovesick about any of the women he'd been with. Never worn that stupid grin, been mooning about a woman and daydreaming at work. Or been so focused on a chick for this long. For months the guy had been beside himself trying to get Joey's notice. Yet now that he was dating her, had most likely already had sex with her, Lou seemed in no rush to cut her loose.

"So I'm thinking I'm ready to tattoo my right arm. Same as the left, but with the drawing I made to accompany the vines."

"Uh-huh." J.T. glanced at the lot. No sign of Joey. She'd better hurry or she'd miss halftime, when the second-grade tumbling team gave a brief show. "So this tattoo wouldn't be a picture of a certain flower chick, would it? Or her name or anything?"

Lou laughed. "Hell no. That's the kiss of death. A woman's name on your arm practically guarantees she dumps you soon after." Fortunately, Lou hadn't completely lost his mind. "But I am thinking about getting a flower. To go with the rose on my chest. But not a rose, something different."

"A flower?" J.T. shook his head.

"This has nothing to do with Joey, damn it." Lou sighed. "Don't be a pain in the ass."

"Bring me the sketch. I'll do it if I approve."

"Fuck you."

J.T. laughed. "Kidding, man. Chill." He watched as the other team scored. That had to hurt. Colin looked furious. "So what's up with you and Joey anyway? You seem kind of serious about her."

"I am." Lou sounded weirded out. "She's so sweet. Gentle." J.T. didn't know about that. "Different from the women I'm used to. She fits me, man."

Oh boy. "But you're a lone wolf. *El lobo* single-o."

"You're so sad. First of all, 'lone' is *solitario*. But
we don't use 'lone wolf' in Spanish. You'd say *un
soltero. Gringo*."

"Yeah, that. Somehow I see Joey with a passel of
kids." At least one of them a boy. "Think she'd be
happy being Lou's woman, no kids, no attachments?"

"Hey. I'm attached to my family. You've met them.
All twenty-five of us," he muttered.

"Twenty-six. You always forget Chavela's youngest." J.T. grinned. He loved Lou's family. So many
pretty ladies, and they all thought him finer than fine.

"Yeah, well, Tía Chavela's youngest is twenty-one,
player. Keep it in your pants."

"Lou, you wound me." He laughed at the fast-and-
furious swear words coming his way. "Just something to
think about with Joey. She's cool, man. We all like her."

"So do I." Lou paused. "Not to change the subject,
but did you talk to Heller lately?"

"No, why?"

Lou told him about Heller's mom dying.

"Shit. That's so sad. I'll call him."

"Good. I was going to stop by the shop later today,
because knowing him, he's working."

"Sounds about right. I'll stop in too. Around three."

"Good. See you then." Lou disconnected before J.T.
could razz him more about Joey.

Poor Heller. J.T. liked the guy a lot. Heller had always
been close to his mom, a giant of a woman with a heart
as big. So nice, and she kept her husband Carl in line.
Probably the reason Heller hadn't killed the guy yet.
Such an asshole. J.T. wondered if Heller had had to deal
with his old man yet about arrangements for the funeral.

Hell. He tried calling Heller and got his voicemail. Halftime started, distracting him, and he watched a bunch of little kids rolling over the ground and each other, much to their parents' enthusiastic laughter and applause.

Being around all this family crap gave J.T. the warm and fuzzies. Seeing his sister so happy was the best thing ever. Yeah, he could handle the McCauleys. A great family who treated Del like she belonged. To his surprise, they treated him the same way. None of them seemed to care that his dead mom had been black, that he owned a tattoo parlor, or that he and his family were a lot less well-off than the McCauleys.

Nonjudgmental and nice as shit. Just what his sister needed. His father too. He glanced at Liam, who fairly glowed with contentment next to Sophie Ayers.

J.T. had a huge mom-crush on Sophie. She'd never had kids and now treated him like a son. He had a feeling his dad might be gearing up to propose to the woman, but Liam was no doubt afraid she wouldn't have him.

J.T. snorted. Liam was turning into a real pussy. Time to handle his business before a fine woman like Sophie left his ass for someone who'd pop the question.

He joined his dad and Sophie and wrapped an arm around her slender shoulders. "Hey, Miss Sophie. When are you going to drop my dad and consider a younger, sexier man?" He waggled his brows.

She blushed. "Stop it, J.T."

"Don't be an ass," Liam growled, but his father had a sparkle in his eye. "My Sophie is plenty happy with me. She knows I worship the ground she walks on."

Sophie smiled. "That's true."

Over her head, J.T. mouthed, "What about a ring?" and lifted his arm, pointing at his ring finger.

His dad turned red.

"Liam?"

Liam gently extricated Sophie from under J.T.'s arm and tugged her closer to him, putting a proprietary arm around her. "Ignore him, Sophie. All those paint fumes going to his head."

"Paint fumes? I paint people, not cars."

Sophie frowned. "Ignore what about him? He's just teasing, Liam. I highly doubt J.T. plans to get you out of the way so we can date. He's not my type anyway."

J.T. saw her fighting a smile and acted offended. "Oh? What? I'm too handsome for you?"

"Yes. I like my men rougher around the edges."

Liam preened. Only his father would take that as a compliment. "Yeah. I'm rough. No pretty boy like my son."

J.T. rolled his eyes. "Get a room, you two."

They laughed, as did the older McCauleys, who'd apparently been paying attention to the pair. Beth waved J.T. over, then whispered, "Do you think he might propose?"

J.T. might have made a slight error in judgment, teasing his dad about a ring. Then again, he liked Sophie. His father loved her, and the old man wasn't getting any younger. Time for him to find happiness again. "I don't know. But I'm all for it. Sophie's great."

Beth beamed. "My baby sister, married."

"Well, now, let's not jinx it, honey," James, her husband, cautioned. "If Liam's anything like me, he'll need to go at his own pace." Then he glanced at J.T. and smirked. "But nothing says we can't help get him there before the next century."

J.T. grinned. He noticed Del and Mike arguing over a call, the boys taking the field again, but no Joey. Hmm. Now where had she gotten off to?

———

Joey's pulse raced as she stared at the face that'd meant so much to her so long ago, and now…nothing. "Felix."

Still blond and blue eyed, still oh so easy on the eyes. He had filled out in the nine years since she'd seen him last. Now twenty-six, a grown man, no longer a scared teenager. She wondered if he still did everything his mother said. Not making the Rogers name look bad had been all Gina Rogers had cared about back then. A congressman's wife who'd had her eye set on a Senate seat. And now that her husband had it, she'd apparently been right to keep her son from his own child.

"Joey." He smiled, his gaze warm. "It's great to see you again."

"What do you want, Felix?" Polite but firm and uninviting. Just the tone she'd been hoping for.

His smile left him, and he swallowed. He seemed… nervous? Very unlike the captain of the football team, prom king, and student council president of long ago.

"It must be a shock to see me again."

She said nothing, knowing she was missing her son's soccer game. Wanting this to be over so she could go back to her life.

"I'm back in the city now. For good."

"And?"

He sighed. "And I wanted to talk to you. About…
Brandon."

She hated hearing her son's name on his lips. "What
about him? You signed your rights away a long time
ago. Remember? Right before we broke up and you pretended I'd never existed." She wanted to punch him, the
old hurt swimming back despite the dam she'd made to
keep the past in the past.

"I'm so sorry." He took a deep breath and let it out,
running a nervous hand through this hair. The familiar gesture upset her, because she still knew that much
about him. "So much that happened back then was a
mistake. Not you or Brandon," he said quickly. "I meant
letting my mother muddle my thinking. Letting her and
my father tell me what to do."

"It's over with. You're back. Okay. Are you done?"

He frowned. "No. I'm not. I want to meet him."

"Who?" She knew damn well who. Her palms were
sweating. None of this should be happening. He'd said he'd
stay away. He'd signed official documents to that effect.

"This isn't the time or place. I just wanted to see him
again. But I should have called you, set up a time for us
to talk without him around." He looked over her shoulder,
and she knew he was watching *her*—not *their*—son play.
"Can we meet and talk later? Maybe tonight?" He handed
her a card. "Here's my number."

She crushed the card in her fist. "I'm busy tonight."
Spending time with my son.

"Then later this week?" He looked determined.
"Putting me off won't make me go away. I need to talk
to you, to explain things."

"I thought you explained them just fine when you

agreed I was a whore who'd tried to trap you with a baby. Remember?"

He flushed. God, why was she saying all these things? She thought she'd gotten past it all.

"Please, Joey," he said quietly. "This isn't about you and me. It's about Brandon. Our son."

Rage filled her. All the sacrifices she'd made while he'd partied and gone off to school, getting his dream job, his dream wedding. Everything she'd had to endure as a female of "loose morals and standing" while the boy who'd browbeaten her into giving up her virginity had come out the hero. What a crock of shit.

"You know what? I want to be mature about this," she said, her voice even, doing her best to keep it together. "I want to be a good mother. Do you know what I told *my* son about his father when he asked?"

Felix looked pained as he shook his head.

"I told him his father was sick. Because only a very sick person could deny his child. You didn't want him back then." She pointed at him, dying to sink her finger into his chest, his skull. "You threw him away." Her eyes blurred. "You hurt me, and I could have gotten over that. But you threw him away too. None of it was his fault. So you took your moneyed, entitled ass away to school and didn't give 'your' son a second thought. *I* bathed him. *I* changed him. *I* fed him. I paid for it all and never got a moment's peace because my family was always there to remind me of what a mistake I'd made. But I have a precious little boy because of it. Me, not you. You signed away your rights years ago. And you got off scot-free. No money, no responsibility." She did poke him then; she couldn't help it.

"That's the way you wanted it. I played it your way a long time ago."

She poked him again. And it felt *so* good. "Felix?"

"Yes?"

"*Fuck off.* He's my son. Not yours."

He looked shocked at the end, but she felt too scared and elated to care.

Except as she walked away, she heard him loud and clear and knew it wasn't over.

"Not the way I wanted it, Joey. Not at all."

She hurried back onto the field, praying he'd leave. She was shaking, and she hated that she'd let him get to her. Felix Rogers, golden athlete, Mr. Popular. She'd been right there with him through his senior year. Then she'd quietly dropped out of school to have and raise his baby while he'd pretended nothing had happened. The student body still treated him like a god while she'd been designated the school whore.

Hell. The only reason she'd slept with the boy she'd thought she'd loved was because he'd kept pressuring her. She'd wanted to wait, but Felix had wanted more. And truth be told, their kissing and heavy petting had been exciting.

She watched Brandon, now playing on defense, deflect a shot at goal with a nice kick back to his offensive line. He turned to wave at her, to make sure she'd seen, and she waved back, her thoughts a tangled mess.

That blond hair. Just like his fath—like Felix.

In her defense, she hadn't been a complete idiot to date Felix. Back in the day, Felix had been a real keeper. He'd been polite to her parents, gorgeous, so nice and fun to be around. Everyone liked him, and it hadn't hurt that his father was on the rise in politics or that they came from money. Not that she'd cared one iota about his family's finances. But it had been interesting to note an unspoiled, caring rich kid for once. Until he'd knocked her up and reverted to type.

For six months they'd dated. She'd been a sopho-more, he a senior. She'd been in love. He'd been so great to be with, and she'd thought he'd loved her too. He'd been her first, but the sex had been lacking. At least for her. Felix must have known he'd been a dud, because he'd been skittish about having sex again after that. They'd continued being boyfriend and girlfriend, and he'd treated her like gold.

Until she'd missed her period. The pregnancy test proved positive. He was scared, wanted her to have an abortion. But she couldn't do it. She'd loved Felix, and though it was much earlier than she'd hoped to have a child, she wanted the baby. Then before she knew it, he was out of her life, she was out of his and out of school not two months later.

It being high school, everyone knew her business and started taking sides about who had done what. She'd tried to trap him with a baby. She was a whore. Half the football team had done her. Through it all, Felix remained tight-lipped. Never saying a bad word about her, but not saying a good word either. She'd tried talk-ing to him until his mother had point-blank told her to go away and never come back.

She couldn't remember whose idea it had been to sign away Felix's rights to the baby, but in any case, he'd signed the paperwork. Refused to look her in the eye and broke her heart all over again. Not wanting her?

Crushing. Not wanting his own child? A true blow to her already-fragile heart.

And now he thought he could just come walking back into her life, into her son's life? Fuck him.

The f-word blazed like a torch. Her parents, J.T., even Del asked her what was the matter, but she just smiled through her teeth and lied about an unhappy customer she had to deal with. There was time enough to factor Felix into the equation. But she needed to make sure she protected Brandon first and foremost.

After his game, she took him out for ice cream, alone, having promised her parents they'd join them soon enough. In the ice-cream parlor, she constantly looked around to make sure Felix wasn't near.

"Mom?" Brandon eyed her with puzzlement. "Are you okay?"

She laughed, forcing herself to act normally. "I'm fine, sweetie. Just got word of an unhappy customer from Tonya at work."

"Oh. Here." He pushed the cup of rainbow sherbet at her. "Have some of this. You'll feel much better."

She looked from his smiling face to the sherbet and felt the tears form. "I love you so much, you know that?"

He flushed. "Aw, Mom. Stop being mushy. You can have it all if you want."

"No. Just a taste." She took a bite from his spoon, then handed him back the treat.

And as she sat waiting for him to finish, she wished she had Lou to lean on. His powerful presence seemed like a shield against all things bad. After all, she'd felt nothing but good around him since accepting him into her bed, into her body.

And into her heart?

Oh God. Not now. She could barely handle dealing with Felix.

Yeah. Fuck you. So clever. She groaned. All the F-you's in the world wouldn't keep the senator's son from her door. She should know better. Despite her poor taste in ex-boyfriends, she had a head on her shoulders.

If she wanted to deal with Felix, she needed to take control. Figure out what he really wanted, talk to him like a mature adult, and handle this. Before he took it upon himself to intrude on Brandon's life. She put her hand in her pocket, fingering his crumpled business card.

Of course he'd become a successful lawyer. Money, looks, charm, and he wanted his son.

But if he could give Brandon the male support—not financial but emotional—of a father Brandon lacked, wasn't that more important than hurt feelings? So long as Felix didn't treat Brandon like dirt or change his mind about wanting him after meeting him. Then she could and would kick him so hard, he'd never sit down again without regretting his treatment of her boy. And she'd laugh about it.

Right. Okay, that was what a good mom would do.

She nodded, her mind made up. "Brandon, time to go. I have a few things to do. And I think you and Grandma need some bonding time."

He grinned. "She's going to take me bowling. If I win, I get five dollars."

"A sucker's bet. You know Grandma is in a league." She shook her head.

He started crying, right there in the shop, and she gaped. "Brandon?"

The tears dried up, and he laughed. "Ha! See? Colin taught me that. Now when she wins, I'll just cry, and she'll buy me pizza. Maybe even beer."

Joey couldn't help but laugh. "Okay, con man. You try that. Let me know how it turns out for you." Because even her real tears hadn't been enough to get her mother to forgive her, not for a very long time.

"I'm so sad. Forever crying and crying… Oh no…" Brandon sputtered and tried to cry again. But his tears had dried up.

She snorted. "Come on, Brando. Time to go home."

"Who?"

The Xbox generation. She sighed. "Never mind. Grab your coat."

Chapter 16

BECKY SHOOK HER HEAD. "I TOLD YOU HE WAS BACK IN town." They sat across from each other at Becky's kitchen table Saturday evening, munching on a tray of decadent cookies Becky had picked up from NCB. Lou was right. Their new baker was fabulous.

"I know." Joey sighed as she ate another cookie, no longer feeling guilty for leaving Brandon with her mother. Considering her mother had all but thrown her out of the house to have special grandma time, she didn't know why she bothered with regrets anyway. "Has anyone ever told you that you have too much junk food around the house?"

"What can I say? I only eat like this when my love life sucks." Becky wolfed down a chocolate chip cookie. "But at least my ex-baby daddy isn't in town to shake me down for my kid."

"Thanks so much for putting that into words I can understand," Joey said drily.

"I aim to please." Becky washed down the cookie with a glass of milk. "Ah. Well, what do you plan to do now that you've finally told Felix to fuck off?" Becky started laughing. "I'm sorry. I feel for you. But I have to know. What was the face he made when you said that?"

Joey mimicked the shock he'd worn, and Becky snorted milk from her nose, which Joey found hilarious. The laughter eased some of the nerves making her head swim.

"God." Joey started on a snickerdoodle, stress eating and trying to give a crap. "I can't believe this is happening."

"Whoa. Before you get all melodramatic and the-world-is-ending on me, why not see what he wants? Yeah, okay, he totally deserved the fuck off. I agree. He walked away smelling like roses, while you got big as a house and were painted the town whore. Sorry, high school whore."

"I'd feel a lot better if the word *whore* stopped being thrown around. I had sex *one* time and got pregnant. Not like I was rolling around with everyone."

"I know. I just think it's funny to call you a ho. You're about as buttoned up as a girl can get."

She had to say it. "That's not what Lou thinks."

"Go, Team Joey." Becky high-fived her. "So you and the mechanic have been bumping uglies. And you're loving it."

She nodded, her face hot, but she needed to talk about it with someone.

"Does he know about Brandon yet?"

"No, and I'm thinking maybe I should tell him."

"Because it's more than bumping uglies. Now you want to stare at that ugliness all the time? Talk to it? Laugh at it?"

"I'm confused. When did I ever say he's ugly?" Joey frowned. "Lou is seriously good-looking. Like, makes-you-stop-in-your-tracks hotness."

Becky groaned. "No one ever gets my analogies. Not the fourth graders, the first graders, and not my twenty-five-year-old best friend."

"Twenty-four."

"Whatever. My point is you are falling for this guy,

and can I just say…*I knew it*. You don't do casual sex, Joey. You never have."

"So?"

"Don't get defensive. That's not a bad thing. It's who you are. You commit. You're into more than just loving and leaving them. Unlike me. A sexual Mata Hari."

Joey shook her head. "Sorry, again not getting the comparison. You're saying you're a sexual spy?"

"I was going for sexual assassin. Like, I kill because I'm so dang good in the sack. Yes? No? Never mind. Just realize it's okay to be you, Joey. You spend so much time trying to make your parents happy, Brandon happy, Stef happy, then you forget about making you happy."

"Not always. I mean, I did what you said. I enjoyed myself with Lou." *A lot*. She fanned herself.

"And there's nothing wrong with that. Just like there's nothing wrong with wanting to date the guy you're banging. Or not banging," she grumbled.

"Oh, Trent still away?"

"No, he came back. But I learned he's mega religious and a prude too. All that sexiness wasted on a priest."

Joey choked on her sip of milk. "*What?*"

"I saw him 'in uniform' the other day. Man, talk about throwing me for a loop. I've been avoiding him since. I don't know. Seducing a priest just feels wrong."

Joey tried not to laugh at her friend's misery.

"It's awful, because I really liked him. Like, we have stuff in common. He's a terrific person."

"Wait. He lives here. Not at a church. Are you sure he's a priest?"

"I think it's some kind of nondenominational thing. That's why he's normally dressed in jeans and sweatshirts.

Teasing the female population, letting us think we might be able to get lucky. God. And no pun intended there."

Joey stifled a laugh.

"Yep. Mr. Sweatshirt and Jeans, hence me confusing him for a guy who can have sex." She growled. "What a tease!"

"Ah, okay. Though pastors can have families, you know, and—"

"That whole helping-his-grandmother bit, him acting like he wanted to see me when he got back. What's up with that?"

"Maybe he can have a relationship. As I was saying before you rudely interrupted, some religions let their pastors marry, you know."

"I don't care. I just can't. I was raised Roman Catholic. A priest is a priest. Gah. I mean, come on. If we ever did get together, I'd be thinking anal beads, he'd be thinking rosary beads. It would never work."

Joey started laughing and couldn't stop.

"You laugh at my misfortune. You *are* a whore. A sympathy whore."

Joey caught her breath, still smiling despite her crappy situation. "Okay, that analogy I understood."

"Well, gee, I'm one for three tonight." Becky studied her as they looked at the remaining cookies on the tray. She chose a sugared soccer ball. "In honor of Brandon, I'll take this one." She bit into it and groaned. "So worth the five extra pounds I'll have tomorrow. So tell me this. You and Lou. Do you have stuff in common?"

"I think so. He loves his family. He's loyal. He's a hard worker."

"And he likes having sex with you, obviously."

Joey sighed. "But he doesn't want children."

"Oh, wow. You had a talk about kids already?"

Joey explained how Lou had told her. "Like he was warning me or something. I think he knows I'm really into him. I didn't mean to be. I just can't turn off my feelings while we're together. And today, after seeing Felix, I kind of wanted Lou there. I just had a feeling he'd make everything better. He has this sense of strength and stability about him."

"But he doesn't want kids."

Joey groaned and put her head in her hands on the tabletop. "I know."

"Well, maybe you guys can date and not have a permanent ending. I mean, just because he knows you have a child doesn't mean you're angling for a new daddy for Brandon. Are you?"

"No." Definitely not.

"And then you still have Felix to deal with."

"Yeah." She sighed. "I don't want to lose Lou. He seems to really appreciate me for me. I kind of need that support right now."

"So don't tell him about Brandon."

"But now it would feel like I'm lying." So confusing. "Before, I didn't know Lou that well. And we were just, I don't know—"

"Horizontal barn dancing? Hitting skins? Shaking the sheets? Waxing some ass? Bonking the—"

"I get it! We were just having sex, okay?"

"Oh, sorry. Just didn't want any confusion there."

She glared at Becky, who wasn't trying too hard not to laugh. She sputtered with her own amusement. "Stop making this funny. I'm stressed."

"But now you're smiling. Okay, continue."

Freakin' Becky. Joey chuckled, then cleared her throat. "When Lou and I were new and casual friends, him not knowing about Brandon made sense. Now it feels like we're more, and I want him to know me. All of me."

"So tell him." Becky could not seem to make up her mind.

"But what if he leaves?" Hearing herself say that, Joey cringed. "Oh man. I'm not thinking about protecting Brandon anymore. I'm thinking about protecting me. How did that happen?"

"Um, it's called being normal? You're too good a mom to ever let a man get between you and your son. Not Lou, not Felix, not anyone. I say tell Lou the truth about why you have to leave early or skip Saturday quickies." At Joey's look, she amended, "I mean, Saturday 'luncheons.' Then meet with Felix and find out exactly what he wants and why he's back. After you hear him out, then you might have reason to panic. And hey, you want me there with you when you meet him, let me know. I'd love to tell him to fuck off too. He totally did you wrong."

"I know. Thanks, Becky." She moved around the table to hug her best friend. Unfortunately, that left her far enough away from the remaining molasses cookie. They both eyed it before Becky grabbed it and stuffed it into her mouth.

"Mine," Becky said around the giant cookie, looking like a squirrel storing acorns in her cheeks.

"Ugh. You can have it."

Becky removed the crumbled mess and licked the one piece she could have shared. "You sure?"

Joey grimaced. "Um, yeah." Inspired by a bit of humor herself, she added, "And this is why you're in dating hell with the priest. Not sharing cookies."

Becky looked at the empty tray with horror. "I think you're right."

Joey laughed. "Well, if it's any consolation, you're sacrificing the size of your thighs and butt for mine. So thanks."

Becky shoved the mess of cookie away from her and crossed her fingers at it. "Back, vile sugar!"

"And that's my cue to go. I have someone to talk to."

Lou finished cleaning up his garage, having fixed the faulty gas valve on the mower. With spring edging closer to summer, he knew he needed to be more vigilant about lawn care. It was a guy thing. A green lawn was the equivalent of having a big dick. And if Old Man Lentz thought he could rule the neighborhood with that manicured lawn he *paid for*, he could think again.

"Hiring a landscaper is cheating." Lou would stick to his guns. Especially because he didn't want to waste his money on a lawn guy when he could just as easily get J. to mow the lawn for a Coke, a pack of gum, and a break from his mom.

He finished up, running behind and hoping Joey wouldn't arrive until he'd had a chance to clean up and throw on a T-shirt and pair of clean jeans. He'd taken off his shirt, now covered with grease, and tried wiping the rest of the grease off with a rag. He was cleaning his hands when Joey pulled up in his drive. Crap.

She parked and walked up the driveway, less spring

in her step than usual. She looked cute in a pair of pink shorts and an athletic T-shirt. Such toned thighs and calves on a woman of her stature. Like a mini Amazon. He would have teased her, but she looked frazzled.

"Hey, Joey, what's up?"

She blinked and saw him standing just inside the garage. Her eyes grew bigger as she stared.

"Sorry," he apologized. "I meant to clean up, but the mower's been a bitch." He motioned her closer so he could close the garage. Once it closed, he turned to the back door, but she stopped him. "*Princesa*, what—"

Her attack took him completely by surprise. She shoved him back against the wall and pulled him down by the neck for a kiss. He opened his mouth to ask what the hell had happened when she thrust her tongue inside his mouth.

Hell yeah.

Had he said he liked his women nonaggressive? He must have been out of his fucking mind because he couldn't think past the huge bar growing in his pants.

As quickly as she'd instigated it, she backed off. "Sorry, but I had to." She gave him a smile. "Wow. I've never done that before. It felt good. Thanks for taking my mind off my problems."

He just stared at her, nonplussed. "Sorry?"

She blushed. "I had an awful day. I didn't want to wait to see you. I was feeling really down, but then here you are. No shirt, all sexy and manly." She sighed. "So I had to kiss you."

"Hell no."

She bit her lip, looking dismayed. "I'm sorry, I—"

"Shut up." He dragged her with him into the house,

back to his bathroom. There he stripped down to nothing. "You too. Clothes off."

She slowly disrobed, looking confused. "I hope I didn't—"

"Yeah, you did. I'm hard, I'm horny, and all I want is you. Get in the shower."

"But I'm not dirty." A half smile played at her mouth.

"You will be."

He grabbed a condom and set it on the sink counter, then joined her in the shower. She tried to keep her hair out of it, he could tell, but Lou didn't want her slinking off after, acting as if she hadn't been with him. He wanted whomever—wherever—she went to when she wasn't with him to know she'd been a dirty girl who needed to be clean.

"I actually came to talk to you," she said.

"Later." He didn't give her another chance to speak. He kissed her, ravenous and out of control.

And she lapped it up. Moaning, melting under him while he took charge. He tugged her by the hair to her knees, and she went willingly enough. He didn't even have to tell her to open her mouth. While he stood with his back to the rushing water, she leaned forward and took him between her lips, then started blowing him with an eagerness that had him close to spilling his load.

"Not yet," he rasped. He yanked her to her feet and turned her around. Then, before he could second-guess his need to take her bareback, Lou gritted his teeth and reached for the condom. He rolled the condom on, shoved her ankles wider as he yanked her hips back, then thrust home in one solid push through her tight, wet sex.

She moaned his name as he banged her in the shower. And it was incredible. Nothing soft or loving about the act. This was pure possession, aggressive fucking. He owned her orgasm as she came screaming his name while he continued to push for more.

Grinding, thrusting. Getting as deep as he could and knowing it wasn't enough.

"*Coming*." He swore in Spanish as he shot hard, gripping her hips like a lifeline. He saw stars for a moment, light-headed and so incredibly replete, he never wanted to let her go.

He gradually felt the hot water pelting his side, felt her trembling beneath him, pressed against the shower wall. "Hell. Sorry, *cariña*." He moved back to give her space.

She turned in his arms and hugged him. Her smaller body so warm and soft against his.

"Whoa. You okay, honey?"

She nodded against his chest. "I missed you."

Damn, but that made him feel *so* good. "I missed you too." Bad to admit? He didn't care.

She stood there, so close. Not moving, just still in the circle of his arms. He moved back to look at her and saw the worry she couldn't hide.

"What's wrong?"

She sniffed. *Oh no*. No tears.

He hugged her again, pressing her face to his chest. "No crying. You just stand right here and let me make everything better. Okay?" Panicked at the thought of her sadness, he held her.

And she sighed into his arms, snuggled tight. Against his chest, he heard a muffled, "You need soap."

He pulled back, saw a smudge of grease on her cheeks, and smiled. "You too."

He refused to let her do anything but stand in the hot water and relax. Lou washed himself free of dirt, then her, taking his time, showing her the affection he felt but couldn't admit out loud. Not yet. Unable to help himself, he bent to kiss each breast. Then her chin, her cheeks. Her lips.

He sighed into her mouth, so gone on this woman.

"Lou." She cupped his cheeks, and he lost it. Fuck, he loved the shit out of Josephine Reeves. She must have seen something of it in his eyes, because she blushed and glanced down. "Oh, again?"

He chuckled, his cock having a mind of its own. "Sorry. You get me hard."

"Thanks, I think."

He laughed again. "Come on. Let's dry off, then you can tell me why you assaulted me in the garage."

"I'm sorry."

"No. *That* you can't ever be sorry about. I changed my mind about aggressive women. Jump me anytime."

They dried off amid teasing. She dressed in her clothes, and he threw on sweats and a T-shirt. Once in his kitchen sipping lemonade, he waited for her to speak, pleased to see her wet hair, evidence of their time together.

She leaned against the counter next to him, a bundle of nerves. "I've had a bad day."

"Oh, sweetheart. I'm sorry." And she wanted to come to him to feel better? He felt like he'd just been handed free rein to showcase his work in the Louvre.

"Someone, a man I used to know, is back in the city. And, well, he's part of that mistake I made a long time ago."

Lou said nothing, seeing the pleading look in her eyes.

"I'm afraid he's going to make life hard for me."

The hell he was. "'Nuff said. Want me to make him go away?" He didn't add the *permanently*. He'd wait for her answer first, then offer it if she seemed game. Lou knew people… Not that he'd bury any bodies or anything. He'd just make the jackass prefer death instead of bothering Joey ever again.

She gaped. "What? Oh, no. No, no." She gave a nervous laugh. "I didn't mean he'll be abusive or nasty. At least, I don't think he'll be mean. I'm having a hard time letting go of all my anger toward him. He wants something from me, but I don't know what yet."

"Anger is good." Lust, passion, attraction—not so good.

"Lou, I…" She swallowed nervously.

"What's wrong?"

In a quiet voice, she admitted, "I didn't let him tell me what he wanted. I told him…I said for him to fuck off."

Lou blinked. "You told him to fuck off?" Somehow, he hadn't seen that coming. He started laughing. The image of cute little Joey Reeves telling some guy to fuck off being absurdly funny.

"Hey."

He kept laughing.

She looked annoyed, then grudgingly laughed with him. "It wasn't that funny."

"It's hilarious. Sorry, baby. But you look so sweet and innocent. You and the word *fuck* don't come into play, unless we're talking about me and you doing it. Then, yeah." He winked. She blushed, and they were good once more. "So the guy left you alone after you told him to fuck off, right?"

"Yes. But that doesn't solve my problem of why he's back. The smart, mature thing would have been to deal with him and not be so emotional. But I have anger I still haven't dealt with, I guess."

"Seems like." He straightened, took a swig of lemonade, and asked the question. "So what's the history with this guy?"

She stared him straight in the eye, and he knew it was serious. "Well, he was my first." She blew out a breath. "He took my virginity. Then he dumped me, and everyone at school knew."

"What an asshole." Feeling for the shy, lovely girl she must have been, he wanted to pound the dick. "Can I hit him? Not once, but a couple of times?"

Tears filled her gorgeous brown eyes. "Where were you nine years ago?"

"Ah, let's see. Keeping Lucia from getting knocked up by her immature boyfriend. Oh, and Carla and Maria from joining a gang. My mother had just started dating Rosie's dad, and for once, we liked the guy. Oh, and—"

She put two fingers over his lips, and the motion surprised him into complete quiet. "There's something else. You see, Felix—"

Pounding at the door startled them both. They looked at each other.

"You expecting someone?" she asked him.

"No. Hold on." He walked to the front, conscious of keeping his woman behind him, protected. He didn't know when he'd come to identify Joey as "his woman," but it fit. And though he had nothing to protect her from, it was instinctive to need to try.

He peeked out the front window and swore.

"Lou?"

"It's bad, Joey." He opened the door. "My sisters have come calling."

"And Mama," his mother piped in from behind Stella, Lucia, and Rosie.

"Fuck."

"Luis!" His mother stood next to him and stopped, spotting Joey.

He knew what she saw. Joey and her wet hair. Lou looking way too casual for going out, his own hair still damp, curling to his cheeks.

His mother smiled.

"Why is your hair wet, Guapo?" Rosie asked. "Oh, and your friend's hair is wet too. Did it rain or something?"

Her innocent question turned Joey's cheeks bright red. Lucia and Stella didn't even try not to laugh. His mother raised a brow. "I'm sure it's a coincidence. Hello, Joey. You are Joey, yes?"

Joey nodded. His mother pushed him aside and took Joey's hand in her own. "It's so nice to meet you. I'm Renata"—she nodded at Lou—"this one's mother."

"And mine too," Stella added. "Hi, Joey. Fancy seeing you here."

Lucia grinned. "I'm Lucia. This is Rosie, our sister. Delivered any flowers lately?"

Before Joey could bolt, Lou's mother put an arm around her shoulders and dragged her back into the kitchen. It was then he noticed the bags his sisters held. "What's all this?"

"Dinner," Rosie said and skipped around him to join his mother and Joey.

"Why are you here?" he asked Stella and Lucia. How

the hell had they known Joey would be here now? Her visit had been impromptu.

"Oh, my friend told me," Stella confessed. "I told Mr. Lentz if he ever saw a pretty, short brunette with a gray Toyota to give me a call. That bowl of chicken-and-corn chilaquiles is for him."

"I'll take it to him." Lucia glided out the front door.

Freakin' Lentz. Another thing Lou would have to take care of after trouncing the old man in the turf war. Getting the old fart to mind his own damn business.

"So Joey looks pretty with wet hair." Stella rubbed his head before he could dodge her. "Hmm. You too? Conserving water while you clean up together, *hermano*?"

"No one likes a nosy little sister."

"Almost as annoying as a bossy older brother, I'll bet." She gave him a wide smile, then walked around him to join the others in the kitchen.

Lou said a few quick prayers. At least they'd left his grandmother at home. He'd count his small blessings.

To his shock, the dinner turned out to be friendly, funny, and perfect. As he'd suspected, Joey fit in with his family as if made to be a Cortez—a thought that haunted him throughout the meal. She answered his mother's interrogation with grace and humor. Avoided his sisters' direct questions about her relationship with Lou with a deftness he had to admire. And she treated Rosie like another person, not a little kid who didn't matter.

"You're so cute. I bet the boys like you too much," Joey said to Rosie. "Like the rest of your whole family, you're too pretty for your own good." She gave him a look he couldn't misunderstand. His girl loved his looks. He preened…and saw his mother, Lucia, and Stella exchanging glances.

"We're the charismatic Cortez family. That's what my teacher calls us. She likes Lou a lot."

"I'll bet," Joey muttered.

He liked her jealousy too. Hell. He liked everything about her.

"So are you Guapo's girlfriend? Are you the flower chick? Are you gonna get married and give me a little brother so Mama doesn't have to?"

"Rosie," Renata exclaimed. "Manners, *m'ija*."

"But Mama, you said—"

"That you should behave," Lucia cut in. Good timing. Joey looked ready to dart for the door and not look back. To Lou, Lucia added, "Be glad. Stella wanted Abuela to come."

"Abuela?" Joey looked back and forth from his sisters to him.

"My grandmother," he explained. "I love her, but she thinks she's an ace detective. She might be right. Nothing gets past her."

Joey smiled. "I miss my grandmother. She lives on a farm in Montana, so we don't see her much."

"We?" Renata asked. "Do you have siblings, Joey?"

"Just my parents and me. I'm an only child."

Yet something in Joey's tone was off. A subtle reminder that she'd been about to tell him something when his mother and the instigators had shown up. He should have been more upset with them, but seeing his girl and his family together only reinforced the notion she belonged with him, by his side.

Now how to get her to open up, trust him, and figure

out what role she'd play in his future. Because he kept having weird feelings about seeing her pregnant with his kid. And while having sex, Lou typically didn't fantasize about impregnating his lover. Jesus, he needed help!

Fortunately, Mama had brought flan. His one great weakness and comfort food.

"Oh, flan." Joey smiled. "My favorite."

He was doomed.

Chapter 17

LOU HAD PLANNED TO TALK TO HELLER AT THE GARAGE Saturday at three, but with Heller not answering his cell and not at the garage when Lou had shown up, there had been no need for conversation. And, well, then Joey had come over.

Sunday afternoon, he sat with J.T. at Ray's, nursing a beer and talking about Heller. He and J.T. were playing darts. Any practice Lou could get in without letting Johnny know was a win. Cocky mother had never been beaten by any of them except Heller. J.T. wasn't great either, but he gave Lou enough of a challenge to make it interesting.

Lou lined up to take a shot.

"Poor bastard." J.T. shook his head and glanced at his phone. "Oh, not you. I meant Heller."

Lou flipped him off, but oblivious J.T. didn't notice.

"He just texted me. He's heading back to Germany for a few weeks. He left Mateo in charge."

"Good choice."

"You and I are supposed to help Mateo if he needs it. But otherwise you stay on your jobs."

"Why are *you* telling me this?" Lou asked as he sized up his throw. Did Heller expect him to take orders from J.T.? Yeah, right.

"Because Heller's low on battery and was answering a text I'd sent when he thought he should mention Mateo. Dude is scrambling. I can't blame him."

"Yeah." Lou considered his friend. "Your mom died when you were a kid, right?"

J.T. nodded. "About killed my dad. He mourned her for decades, man." J.T. watched as Lou nailed a bull's-eye. "Damn. Nice throw."

"Thanks." Lou sat and watched J.T. step up. "Relationships can be brutal. And love seems to fuck up guys as much as it makes them happy. That blond you were eyeing at the wedding. What was her name?" He smiled to himself as J.T. tensed.

J.T. totally flubbed his throw. The dart glanced off the metal rim and hit the ground. "Shit." He glared at Lou. "Asshole."

"Hey, not my fault you're still not getting any." Lou kicked back in his chair and sighed. "My flower chick is so nice to me."

"Yeah, yeah." J.T. mumbled under his breath. "And now you're in love like the rest of the losers at the garage. Hell, that place is like Cupid on crack. Step away from the love juice, man. Just step away."

They both chuckled.

"Dude, I wish I could." Lou sighed. "I am straight-up drinking the Kool-Aid. I can't explain it, and I hate to get all talky-talky, especially since the guys have started that shit at the garage."

J.T. winced. "I feel for you. But go ahead, lay it on me. Us artistic types are allowed to be emotional dick-heads. Comes with the temperament."

"Thanks so much, J.T."

J.T. held up a glass in mock toast. "Here for you, man."

"It's just, Joey is different. She's real. I really, really dig her." Lou stared morosely at his half-empty glass. "I think I could see a lot of tomorrows with her. And I know she's lying to me."

———

After choking on his beer, J.T. wiped his mouth and blinked. "Ah, what?"

Cool, J.T. Play it cool.

He waited for Lou to reason it out. Unless Lou was thinking Joey lied about something other than having a son. A man on the side, maybe?

No. No way. Del's flower chick buddy, Lou's new flame, didn't have that feel. She wasn't a player, was a damn good mom, according to Del, and blushed if he so much as looked at her funny. The woman was sweet for sure, but not too nice or Lou wouldn't be able to deal with her. She had to have a little nasty in there to satisfy the garage's legendary ar-teest.

Lou looked confused, kind of sappy, and downright pathetic. J.T. shook his head. "Christ. I hope I never get like this. Being single is a blessing, I'm thinking."

"You know it." Lou downed the rest of his beer. "What makes it all worse? My family loves her."

J.T. gaped, knowing how much Lou treasured his family. The guy never took his ladies to meet his mom. "You took her home to the family?"

"No way. My mom and sisters surprised us yesterday. An uninvited pop-in with dinner."

"Oh, dinner." J.T. loved Renata's cooking. Lou, that bastard, had no idea how good he had it. Del, his dad, and his cousin, Rena, all sucked at cooking. Meaning J.T. had grown up with no one to make him good food or even cookies unless his aunt was in the mood. And that damn woman was usually too busy getting her *tele-novela* love life in check to bother with feeding her poor, starving nephew.

Lou was shaking his head. "They just showed up at the door."

"Oh man, that could have been some seriously bad timing." J.T. chuckled.

"Seriously." Lou grinned, then sighed. The guy had a bad case of love asthma. "My mom likes her."

"Your mom likes everybody."

Lou grunted. "Stella likes her too."

"Well, now, that changes things. Stella?" The cutie snarled at everyone she didn't deem worthy of her time. Of course she liked J.T., but come on. Everyone did.

"Yeah. And Joey was great with Rosie. I can totally see her with kids someday."

J.T. choked on the sip of beer he'd been taking. Lou pounded him on the back.

"That's twice. Slow down, lightweight, before you drown yourself."

"Thanks." He cleared his throat. "So is this thing between you guys real? Like, a relationship leading to the m-word?"

He waited for Lou to tell him no. Hell no. What the fuck, no.

Except the big man just sat and started peeling the label off his bottle. J.T. worried for his friend. "That's great, man."

"No, it's not."

"Why not?"

"Didn't you hear me earlier? I said she's lying to me."

"How do you know?"

"I just know." Lou got up and hit two more bull's-eyes. *Damn.* "She can't spend the night with me. She never has me to her place. I mean, I know we're new to going out and shit, but not once are we going to her house, meeting her friends, her family."

"It's pretty soon for that."

"It should be." Lou agreed. "But it's not. I know she lives with her parents and has been saving up to move out. I also know some dickhead who screwed with her a long time ago is back in town, messing with her head. I want to be there for her, but she holds back."

"Force a confrontation."

"I don't want to hurt her."

"I don't mean pound on her. Dude, she's a girl."

Lou shot him a look. "I know that, jackass. I just meant I don't want her to feel bad. She was close to crying because of that old boyfriend yesterday and freaked me out. I hate tears."

"You see them all the time."

"From my sisters, yeah, but—"

"Oh, right. Your sisters. I meant from your clients when they see your crappy artwork." J.T. laughed, then yelped when Lou slugged him in the arm. "Kidding, geez. Easy on my guns, man. I have to use these arms to hold up God's gifts to the art world." J.T. held up his hands like a surgeon awaiting plastic gloves.

"Gimme a break."

He could see Lou trying to stifle a smile.

"Look, Lou. All I'm saying is if you really like this girl, and you do, you can't be afraid to argue or disagree. Sure, you want her smiling and happy with life all the time, but if she's holding back, you need to know. I'd want to know."

"Yeah."

Apparently not anything the guy hadn't already thought about. "So if we're done with the—what did you call it?"

"Talky-talky. You know, emotional bullshit where we discuss feelings ad nauseam."

J.T. cringed. "Ah, right. We're done with that, right?"

"I hope to hell so. Bad enough I have to hear all this from my sisters on a daily basis. I'm done bitching about it. In fact, we never had this conversation, *comprendes*?"

"Then can we get back to the game? I'm closing in on you."

"I have twenty more points before I'm out. Dream on."

Unfortunately, Lou apparently played better when in an emotional quandary.

J.T. groaned and ordered them some hot wings. And, being the loser, he paid.

Rena arrived half an hour later when their waitress went on break. "Hey guys. How's it going? Need anything?"

"Nah, we're good." Lou smiled. "I'm trouncing your cousin. Life is awesome."

"Shut up." J.T. waited for Rena to say something snippy. Instead, she casually glanced around the bar. He smirked. "Looking for someone?"

She narrowed her eyes. "As a matter of fact, I am."

"Oh, did you tell her?" Lou asked him.

She said, "I'm looking for Earl" at the same time J.T. said, "Heller's mom died,"

She gasped. "Oh my gosh. Axel's mom is dead? That's awful. What happened?"

"Cancer," Lou answered quietly. "He's gone back to Germany to settle things. Won't be back for weeks."

"Poor Axel." She shook her head and wandered away.

"Just goes to show you," J.T. said. "Life is short. You like Joey? Figure it out before it's figured out for you."

"Amen to that."

They drank a toast to Heller. And J.T. secretly added well wishes for Lou. He hoped the guy sorted out his relationship with Joey, because it was only a matter of time before Lou learned that not only was Joey a kid person but that she had a special one all her own.

"Rena," he yelled to his cousin across the bar. "Another beer." He glanced at his introspective friend. "Actually, make it a pitcher."

Joey would much rather have spent her afternoon with Lou, but she had an ex-boyfriend to handle. Referring to him as that and not as Brandon's father helped her deal with Felix's reappearance in her life.

She sat at a coffee shop in Green Lake, far from home and Brandon and her mother. Another grandma day, and her mother was tickled to have Brandon all to herself once more. Andrew loved it, because he didn't have to take his wife to the coffee gathering with her book club friends. Instead, she'd dragged Brandon with her to show him off.

Joey sighed. At least someone would be having fun today. She sipped from her decaf hazelnut latte, not needing any more stimulants in her day. Her knee bobbed, she kept tapping on the table, and the urge to bite her nails felt impossible to ignore.

"Hey, sweetheart, you doing okay?" The handsome guy from behind the counter came to sit with her for a moment.

Startled, she just stared. Were the people who worked here supposed to just sit down with the customers?

"You look upset."

"I do?" She patted her hair and straightened her shoulders, not wanting to look less than amazing when dealing with Felix.

"Better." He smiled and held out a hand. She didn't get the impression he was hitting on her. Just being friendly. "I'm Elliot."

"Joey." She shook his hand before clutching her coffee cup once more.

"Mind if I ask why you're here? And yes, it's nosy beyond belief to be all up in your biz-ness." He grinned. "But that's how I roll."

She couldn't help grinning with him. Elliot had dark hair and deep-green eyes, a killer smile, and a body that didn't quit. Not as large or muscular as Lou, but he was handsome and charming and closer to her own age. And he didn't feel threatening.

"I'm meeting an ex-boyfriend for a talk I'd rather not have." She sighed. Her knee bobbed again.

Elliot took her hand and squeezed. "Well, you're beautiful, sweet, and will look perfect as soon as you switch seats." He nodded to the one next to her. Puzzled, she nonetheless moved to it, and he nodded. "There you go. Now when he comes in, he'll be in the sun. Let's raise the blind, shall we?" He went behind her, pulled up the shades, and let a beam of sunlight hit the chair she'd recently vacated. "Oh, new customers. Gotta go. Give him hell, Joey."

She felt more at ease and smiled. "Thanks, Elliot. I will."

Felix walked through the door.

Elliot glanced from her to the newcomer, whistled, then hurried to the counter to charm the people lining up to order.

Joey didn't stand when Felix appeared by her side. She waited for him to join her.

"I'm going to get a coffee if that's all right." At her nod, he said, "Be right back."

She waited, watching, and gathered her composure. She would run this little meeting, not him. Brandon was her son, not his. Well, technically yes, but legally, she had papers. She kept clinging to that notion, not wanting to imagine the rich and connected Rogers family ganging up on her to take her son.

Think positive. You own this. Stop worrying! "Easier said than done," she mumbled to herself. Yet as she watched Felix, she started to see his edges fraying.

Had she not known better, she'd have thought Felix perfectly calm. But she saw the tells he tried to hide, the way he subtly wiped his hand on his pants and pulled at his sleeves. After he got his coffee and walked away from the counter, Elliot made a face at his back, and she had to work not to laugh.

She was definitely coming back to Sofa's in the future. If for no other reason than the funny barista.

Felix sat and rolled up his sleeves. The warmer June weekend had taken a turn for the cool, so she wasn't surprised to see him in jeans and a long-sleeved button-down. No ratty jean jacket or Seahawks sweatshirt for a Rogers.

She hated that he still looked so handsome and clean-cut.

"Well?" she barked, totally ruining her attempt to appear unfazed by their meeting.

He blew out a breath. "Look, I deserved that big 'fuck you' yesterday. Weird hearing you say it, but I get it."

"Thanks so much." Man, sarcastic Joey really wanted her say. Where had her goal to be mature and sensible gone? Not two seconds into the conversation, and she couldn't just let it happen and get it over with?

"I know you're not happy to see me. In your place, I wouldn't be either. I'm not here to make trouble or try to take Brandon away. Not at all. I swear."

She relaxed a fraction. "Then what do you want?"

He shrugged. "Closure? Forgiveness? A way to feel not so much a failure?"

Okay, all things she hadn't for the life of her expected. "Go on."

He gave a ghost of a smile. "I never knew how good I had it when I was with you. I know we were young, but that's no excuse for how I behaved. After."

She sipped her coffee, not sure to believe anything he said. The school's golden boy didn't seem so golden. She saw sadness in those big blue eyes.

"Man, back then, everything was there for the taking. I had the prettiest girl in school. My folks had prestige, my dad was running a Senate campaign. Mom was involved in every PTA and charity event for miles. Dan, you remember Dan." His older brother. She nodded. "He'd just gotten accepted to Harvard Law."

Was there a point to all his greatness?

"But you. You didn't care about the campaigning, my mother's largesse, Dan's impressive resume." Trust Felix to use a word like *largesse* in casual conversation.

"You just liked being around me for me." He sighed, ignoring the coffee that would soon be going cold in his hands. "I loved being with you, Joey. You were so sweet, and we had so much fun. Then all the guys were pressuring me about making out with you, going all the way. God, it's so stupid now. But I felt like I had to put a check in that box to get my official man card."

He gave a wry smile she returned. Hard not to laugh with a man laughing at himself.

"I know it wasn't any good for you. Jesus, I remember it to this day."

She fought a blush. Goodness, but Felix really wanted a run down memory lane. She'd thought he wanted to discuss Brandon, but not *the actual conception* of Brandon.

"My first time was magical. But I rushed you, then I freaked out because I knew we shouldn't have done anything. I knew the possibility was there you'd get pregnant." He scowled at himself. "But no. I had to have you. And you went along because you cared about me."

"I loved you."

He nodded, regret clear on his face. "And I didn't deserve it. I think I knew that deep down. But I took your affection anyway. Then, when you told me you were pregnant, I freaked. I immediately told Dan. Huge mistake, because he ratted me out to Mom. And then, well, you remember my mom."

Unfortunately. "Yes."

"She was going to make it all go away. I thought I could handle it, but when you wouldn't have that abortion, I got mad." He had the grace to look ashamed. "I wish I could take back the things I said."

"And didn't say," she had to add. "When everyone was making things up about me, you said nothing."

"At the advice of my counsel—Mom." He snorted. "I swear. That woman has done more to control me and ruin my life than anyone. She wanted me to dump you. I dumped you. She wanted me to leave all the rumors alone, to say nothing. I didn't say a thing. She wanted me to go to Harvard, like Dan. And I married the woman she picked out for me. Christ, I was a puppet, and she had her hand right up my ass."

Joey cringed.

"Too much? Sadly, true." He finally took a sip of his coffee. "But you know, through all of my mother's manipulations, I couldn't stop thinking about the child we'd created. A little boy." The wonder on his face touched her. Deeply. And she wished it hadn't. "I never hated you or thought you'd done anything to hurt me, Joey. That was all my mom's talk. I loved you." A quiet pause, and she wondered what he felt now, because the look he gave her worried her. "I knew you'd probably never forgive me for bailing on you like I did. I had one moment where I almost changed my mind. But your father talked to me, told me to do the best thing for you and just go away. So I did.

"I signed your papers. I left you alone, married, divorced, finally told my mother to kiss my ass. But my biggest regret was walking away from you. Walking away from our son."

Chapter 18

"YOU TALKED TO MY DAD?" JOEY HADN'T KNOWN about that.

Felix nodded. "I was seventeen. Not as young as you, but not yet an adult. I was a stupid kid who believed his own hype. And when it mattered, I feel like the adults in my life let me down. My mother only wanted what looked best for the family. Not what I needed." He just looked at her. "She told me she'd never recognize Brandon as my son. And if I pursued this, she wouldn't see me either."

Joey didn't know what to say.

"But I couldn't live with myself anymore." He groaned. "I went to school, got my fancy law degree, handled big-name divorce cases, 'cause, yeah, I finally did something I wanted. Family, not corporate, law. And I saw so many kids in a bad situation because of their parents. Rich assholes who fought about money, never about what really mattered."

"Wow. You sound like the boy I once knew."

He gave her a sad smile. "Took me a long time to grow a pair."

"You said it." She smirked.

He laughed, and a sense of camaraderie enveloped them. Until Joey reminded herself that this was about more than Felix apologizing.

He must have seen her wariness because he hurried

to continue. "I'm sorry. I'm so sorry for everything I put you through." He hesitated. "I brought you a check. Not to pay you off or insult you or to insinuate that money could ever make up for what I did to you. I brought the check to support my son. The child support you should have had all those years ago. But I'm afraid if I hand it to you, you might slap me or tell me to fuck off again."

"I might." She didn't know about the money, but that he'd finally acknowledged he'd been wrong alleviated the buried anger she'd had for so long.

Felix sighed. "Was it really bad, Joey? I know the kids were cruel, but your parents were smart to take you out of school. Were they supportive? You mentioned they gave you a hard time. What was it like?"

He seemed sincerely to want to know, so she told him. "Dad was furious. Mom was disappointed. I swear she looked like she wanted to cry for the entire nine months I carried Brandon. Even after he was born, my parents treated me like a leper. Oh, Mom would sneak in and cuddle him, but other than that, I was on my own. At first I just stayed at home, working toward my GED, taking care of the baby. Always aware I needed to be independent and 'take care of my own messes.'" She sighed. "They were so mad and disappointed. It really hurt. But I had food, shelter, clothes. Brandon didn't need for anything, and he has a great pediatrician—still."

"Good, for Brandon, I mean. I'm sorry about the rest."

She shrugged. "I was partly responsible for it all. I'm not that naive. I could have said no, but I didn't. Anyway, it took a while, years, but my parents settled down. Mom's over it all and so in love with Brandon, he's like her personal mini-me. She dotes on him, and he loves her. Dad is still judgmental, still makes me feel like a fifteen-year-old who should have said no. But he loves me in his own way." *Probably*. "I managed to get a bachelor's degree in business. Put myself through school while working and taking care of Brandon. I just got a promotion to manager, and I'm thinking about starting an offshoot of the floral business with my boss's okay."

Felix smiled. "That's awesome. Amazing. You're so much better than me, Joey. You had no one to help—well, your parents, but we both know that wasn't easy. And you still managed to come out on top. I'm proud of you. It might not mean much coming from me, but I know our son will be a much better person for having been raised by you and not me." He shook his head. "I might have a fancy law degree and some money to go with the stupid name, but I'm just me."

"Odd, you never seemed so down on yourself when we were together."

"I hid it from everyone. My mother and father pretty much let me know they loved Dan more than me. I was the second son in case he didn't work out," he said drily. "Dan does the family proud, so they can ignore me for being the black sheep of the family."

"Black sheep?"

"My GPA was lower than Dan's. I'm also a divorced man in his midtwenties with an illegitimate child. I might as well be stricken from the family Bible."

"Ouch." She felt for him, but part of her held back from showing open compassion. Was all his woe-is-me stuff just a ploy to make her relax so he could steal Brandon away? Hell, he was a high-priced lawyer. He could probably find a way to wrestle her son away from her. Wasn't he more successful, could give Brandon more than she could?

"Why are you looking at me like that?"

She didn't want to play games. "I'm sorry for all you went through. I'm glad you apologized, because I deserved it. But I won't let you take Brandon from me."

He sighed. "I knew it wouldn't be easy to get you to trust me." He reached into his back pocket and withdrew his wallet. Then he pulled out a check and handed it to her. "I know this isn't much, not for all the years that have gone by, but I'd be thankful if you'd take it."

She stared at the check and blinked, not sure about all the zeroes. "Felix," she hissed. "What the heck? This is for thirty thousand dollars."

He flushed. "I know, not much considering, if you do the math, I'm still in arrears by, like, forty grand. But I want you to have it. I have savings, more for him."

Panicked, because that was a lot of freaking money that no doubt had strings attached, she pushed the check back to him. "You can't buy your way into our lives. You can't have him."

He put his hand over hers, and the shock of his touch froze her. "Joey, stop." His voice was low, calm, and the warmth of his palm over hers felt…good. Not smothering, as she would have expected. "This is for Brandon. And you, I'll be honest. Call it what it is. Guilt money. I'm not trying to buy my way into Brandon's goodwill. I'm trying to atone for being a complete waste for most of my life."

She stared into his eyes, wanting but afraid to believe him.

"Go see your lawyer. Take the custody paperwork,

my check, and tell him or her everything. Hell, rip up the check. I'll write you another one. Aside from the money, though, can you just think about letting me see him? I won't interfere, won't swing by your work or home to harass you. I just want to meet him." He swallowed, his eyes looking shiny. "To get to know him. He's the one good thing I've done with my life, Joey. You have to know I don't want to mess him up." He laughed and rubbed his eyes. "Shit. I'm not crying. Had something in my eye."

She stared, so completely turned around she didn't know what to feel.

"I'm going to go." He pushed the check and another business card her way. "In case you tore up the card I gave you yesterday," he teased. "Think about letting me get to know him and him getting to know me. Without my parents or yours involved. Just you and me and him. I promise you I only want to get to know him. Nothing nefarious."

And with that, the man who spoke as if he'd swallowed a dictionary left.

She stared after him, still in awe that they'd had the conversation they had. Never in a million years would she have expected an apology and *thirty thousand dollars*. To hell with a conscience or denying she needed the money. Heck yeah, she could use it. And she would, but only if a lawyer gave her the okay.

Now to find someone she could trust to tell her the truth. Someone not connected to her parents or her past.

As she left, with a wave to Elliot, still busy at the counter, she wanted badly to tell someone what had happened. To her bemusement, the person she wanted to talk to wasn't Becky. It was Lou. What would he make of all this? Would he tell her to trust Felix or to run the other way? As much as he loved his family and protected them, would he encourage Brandon's father to make amends? Or would he say to protect her son at all costs?

"And he has no idea I have a son." Joey swore under her breath as she got into the car and sat, clutching the steering wheel. How the heck did she tell Lou she had a son? Now that they'd been going out...well, heck. Only a few weeks? It felt like she'd known him forever. But a few weeks didn't mean she'd been keeping secrets, just looking out for her boy. Yet she had a feeling Lou wouldn't take her admission well. Because he'd asked her if there was someone else. Had given her opportunities to disclose the fact that her son existed. She hadn't.

He also didn't want children. And she had one she planned on keeping.

She drove home, needing to think. To plan. And to find a way to make everything work for her and Brandon. *Daddy's not so sick anymore, sweetie. And I think...I'd like you to meet him.*

Tuesday afternoon, while Lou made up his time at Webster's working on Blue Altima's second cousin, Green Shitty Santa Fe, he joked with the guys. After his talk with J.T. on Sunday, Lou knew the time had come to have a sit-down with Joey, to explain he'd come to care for her—without saying the l-word and scaring her off.

He'd gently coax the truth from her. Or not. He sighed.

If she wouldn't tell him about whatever was bothering her, he'd simply wait. God, he hated himself being such a love-struck pussy, but he was a serious douche in love.

The thought of Joey leaving made him ill.

"Hey, Cortez, what's with the lemon face?" Johnny asked, palming a screwdriver. "Did Joey finally dump your sorry ass?" He snickered, clearly knowing the opposite to be true. Johnny could be a pain, but he would never deliberately hurt a friend's feelings if said friend were down and out.

But Lou still hadn't come close to beating the punk-ass's darts scores Sunday. "Sorry. Was thinking of the last time Lara asked me out and how sad she was when I turned her down. It's just…I mean, she's your woman. Keep her happy, man, and she won't come to me."

"Yeah, right."

"Wasn't that on Sunday?" Foley asked Sam.

Sam, straight-faced, nodded. "Yep. I heard from Rena that J.T. was there too. Saw the whole sad thing. I wasn't going to say anything to him until later. You know, in private."

Johnny stared, wide-eyed, then glared. "You ass-holes aren't funny. Lara was with her nieces Sunday." He gripped the screwdriver tightly. "Lou, you're a dick. You know that?" He flipped off Sam and Foley. "So are you assholes."

"Oh, my bad. Must have been a different Lara I was thinking of," Lou said as he buried his face under the car's hood once more. "Lemon face this, motherfucker."

He ignored Johnny's muttering and Foley and Sam's self-congratulations and once again thought about how best to talk to Joey about his feelings. She cared for him—a lot. He knew it. Could feel it when they were together. Despite them being new, he understood the difference between fucking and making love, between affection and deeper feelings. Joey wasn't the type to give herself so completely to just any guy. The fact that she hadn't been with anyone for a year before Lou said as much.

Man, that kind of commitment blew his mind.

Unless she'd been lying?

A niggle of doubt remained, because he wanted to know what she was hiding.

"Oh, wow. This is awesome. Can I use the drill, Mom? Can I?" Colin McCauley's enthusiasm made him smile.

Lou straightened from the car and turned to see Colin holding Del's hand, skipping next to her and dragging her deeper into the garage.

He raised a brow. "Skipping school? Del, you're such a bad influence."

She grinned. "Can it, Lou. Colin had a dental appointment. I just thought I'd swing by here to pick up some paperwork before I took him back."

"And I wanted to miss math." Colin made a face.

"Shh. That's our secret. I'm here for pa-per-work. Remember?" Del reminded him.

He grinned. "Oh, right. We're here for paperwork, Lou."

Foley chuckled. "Good job, Del. So slick. I'm sure McCauley will never realize you're teaching the kid to lie."

Del frowned.

The nice thing about Del marrying into the McCauley clan—they'd gotten a lot of extra business because of it. The McCauleys knew everyone in Seattle, or at least it seemed that way. And now they had even more clients out the ass, because they were the best auto shop in town and because of all Del's new relatives. *Family*. He chuckled.

"What are you laughing about, Lou?" Colin asked him and tugged free from Del.

Lou nodded to her. "I'll watch him. Well, Colin, I'm laughing because you McCauleys seem to know everybody. And now we have so much business, your mom keeps us chained here overnight working on cars. She whips us, won't let us eat or drink—"

Del thumbed at the break room. "Hello? New coffee machine in there."

"Yeah," Foley cut in on the action. "She even forced me and Sam to work so much for so long, our girlfriends almost broke up with us."

"Really?" Colin's eyes grew wide.

"Yep." Sam nodded and crossed to them. "She's so *mean*."

"Oh for fu—fudge's sake," Del snarled. "They got in trouble with their girlfriends for spending too much time at Ray's. So a little bird told me over drinks this past weekend."

"That was no little bird," Johnny said with a smirk. "That was Cyn."

"A big bird." Colin nodded, having met the towering Cyn. "Not Big Bird. I mean, a tall, pretty red bird."

Foley grinned. "Yeah, she'd like that. Not a cardinal or anything. More like a hawk."

"Who digests entrails," Johnny said.

"Bloody guts and little boys," Sam added with a scary smile.

Lou couldn't stop laughing.

"And who eats micey men for breakfast." Del shook her head. "I'm so telling her you said that."

Colin was laughing as well. Lou knew for a fact the kid was as sly and clever as Johnny. "What have you been up to besides the dentist, Colin? I hear you're good at soccer."

"I am," he boasted while Del tried not to smile. "I scored three goals on Saturday. Brandon and Todd assisted. It was awesome."

"So you have little assistants now? You going pro on us, keeping your minions tight so they can keep you scoring in the millions?" Foley asked, deliberately sounding confused. "I mean, you're a McCauley. I shouldn't be surprised."

"Ha, ha, Foley." Colin did an unconscious impression of his dad, fisting his hands on his hips as he turned to confront the goliath. "They aren't my minions. They're my friends. Todd Bennett and Brandon Reeves. That's who helped me."

Del's sudden tension penetrated at the same time as the name Reeves did.

Lou blinked. "Reeves?"

Del shrugged, but he could see her pretending not to be so uncomfortable. "Yeah. You know Joey Reeves? My friend and your, ah, friend? She's Brandon's mom."

He blinked. "*What?*"

The rest of the guys suddenly grew super busy as they darted back to their respective projects.

"Um, Lou. Could you come with me for a minute?" Del asked. "Colin, you—"

"He can help Sam organize his tools," Foley offered. "God knows he needs the help."

Sam glared at him but motioned to Colin. "Yeah.

I'm a mess. Can you help me out?" In an overloud loud whisper, he added, "And play with the lift a little."

Colin whooped and raced over to Sam.

Lou had a hard time processing Joey's big secret. "A kid?"

"Come on, Lou." Del marched over and dragged him with her into her office.

Once inside, she shut the door. "So I gather she didn't tell you about Brandon yet."

"Yet?" She'd been going to tell him something the other night before his mother and sisters had interrupted. Had she been about to explain about her son? A son. A boy. A child.

Man, that put a whole new spin on *everything*.

"Sit down." Del's gentle voice.

He whipped his gaze to hers. "You knew?"

"Dude, I'm Colin's mom. He plays soccer every day. And Joey's my friend. Yeah, I knew."

"You never said anything." He felt betrayed and couldn't have said why. Joey had never told him she *didn't* have a child. But… He never dated single moms. Ever. Because they reminded him of his mother and her inability to care for her children when dating.

He never wanted to be that guy who came between a mother and son. Had he been without knowing?

"Wasn't my place to say anything." Del leaned back against her desk. "I knew you had a thing for her. But you two weren't dating. Then you were, and you seemed so happy. Who cares if she has a son? She's not looking for a baby daddy."

"How do you know?"

She sighed. "If she was, she'd have told you by now.

You're hot, you got money. And you're clearly into the girl. Has she tried to get you to buy her anything for the kid? Legos, toys, a college fund, maybe?"

"Don't be ridiculous." He snorted. A college fund?

"Yeah, well, don't *you* be ridiculous. She didn't tell you about the boy. So what? She's not hiding him or anything. Jesus, the whole McCauley clan was there Saturday. J.T. too. We all know who Brandon belongs to. Joey was there, cheering for him."

"Wait. J.T. was there on Saturday?" And hadn't said a goddamn thing on Sunday when Lou had poured his heart out to the guy. J.T. knew Lou's stance on women with children. Damn it.

"Yeah. So was my dad. Joey's parents, hell, anyone with a kid in the greater Seattle area seemed to be slumming around the soccer field." Del groaned. "Lou, don't do this."

"Don't do what?" No wonder Joey had been so good with Rosie. She'd had a lot of practice.

"Don't fuck this up. You've been happier the past weeks with Joey than you ever have. Of all the guys in the garage, you're the most normal." At his raised brow, she snapped, "You know what I mean. The most stable. You have a great family life, you respect women, and you're the most talented paint guy I know. And no, I am not comparing you to J.T., so don't go there. He does people, you do cars. No comparison."

Actually, there was. But Lou knew she couldn't in good conscience choose him over her brother. "Your point?"

"I can see the wheels turning in your tiny brain. Telling you that Joey being a mom is a BFD." A big fuckin' deal.

"You think it isn't? Del, you married Mike *and* Colin. You know what I'm talking about."

"Duh. I know that. I just meant you need to not over-think it and go with the flow. She's a sweetheart and a hell of a mom. And she's young. Like, I did the math. She must have had Brandon when she was still in high school. Can't have been easy, but her kid is one of the nicest boys I've met. And I've met a ton of kids since getting shackled with Colin." Her big grin made her so much more than a pretty woman with tats and piercings. Del was beautiful in her love for her family.

"I want to paint you like that."

"What?" She blinked.

"All in love and shit. You glow, you know that?"

She turned bright red. "Shut up and get out of my office. And remember what I said. Be the normal, non-freak of the garage when it comes to your girlfriend."

"Sure, sure. Still glowing." He slowly rose, inwardly feeling like an old man and still reeling from the news about Joey.

"*Out.*"

He left and returned to work.

"You good, man?" Sam asked.

"Fine. Just surprised is all." *Understatement of the year.*

"Okay. If you need to talk, Mr. Emotional is by the Accord."

"Hey," Johnny yelled, buried under said Accord. "But he's right. I'm here for you, Lou. A man of experi-ence, wisdom, and emotional drivel."

"More talky-talky. Great," Lou muttered and lost himself in work. But he knew the time had come for a major sit-down with Joey, one he didn't welcome because he didn't know how it would end.

Chapter 19

WEDNESDAY AFTERNOON, WAITING FOR HER PARENTS to join her for lunch in their kitchen, Joey couldn't contain her nerves. She'd talked to a lawyer. He had looked over her documents, listened to her story, and told her what she'd prayed to hear. She could accept the money without repercussion. Felix had legally signed over his rights to the child years ago. Though he didn't owe any child support, if he *chose* to give her the money, it would be construed as a gift. Period. According to the law, Felix had no legal standing when it came to Brandon.

She'd been so relieved to hear it, she'd cried. Becky had called her a wuss and shoved a cookie in her face. So now Joey had to sacrifice *her* ass and thighs in repayment for Becky's referral.

Joey had thirty grand sitting in her savings account, and she kept having to squash her guilt for having accepted it. Why? Felix had sure the heck been there when Brandon had been made. Yet she'd borne the financial burden to raise her son all these years. With that money in savings, she could confidently find a new place for her and Brandon to live. One where he could invite a friend to sleep over. One where *she* could invite a handsome man over for dinner.

Her nerves made her mouth dry.

Lou. She'd been thinking about him nonstop since meeting with Felix. Comparing the two men, thinking

how different they were. She had to tell him about
Brandon. She wanted to see where she and Lou might go
next. As much as she wanted to think they had a future,
one where they'd hold hands at Brandon's soccer games
and play family together, she knew she was dreaming.

They might never be a family, but she had a sexy
male friend, one who treated her like she mattered and
gave her orgasms. What wasn't to love?

Brandon didn't need Lou in his life. He had her. And
maybe, just maybe, he'd have a new "friend" in Felix.

She still didn't know about introducing Felix to
Brandon as his father. It felt too iffy, and she didn't
want to do anything to damage her son psychologically
should Felix prove squirrelly. She'd half expected his
check to bounce. It hadn't. So he had money. That didn't
mean he would be good for her son.

Heck, Becky had agreed with her. The guidance
counselor with a background in child psychology
thought she should gradually familiarize Brandon with
Felix. For two main reasons. One, it showed the boy
that his mother could have male friends, so when she
did finally get a boyfriend, Brandon wouldn't freak out
about it.

And two, if Felix turned out to be "not such an
asshole"—Becky's words—then it would be that much
easier to forge a connection between father and son.

That Becky had agreed with her instincts to introduce the pair confirmed her decision.

Her parents came through the door at the same
time. Odd.

"Mom? Dad?"

Her mother laughed. "Met him on the way in. I was

just coming back from picking up a few things at the grocery store." Since her mother did medical transcription from home, that explained her being gone. Amy put the milk and eggs away, then tossed a bag of pretzels into the pantry.

"I only have an hour," her father announced. "I'm taking an extended lunch to be home, so whatever this is about, make it quick."

Wouldn't want to inconvenience you. Joey never asked her father for anything, mostly for this reason. Her entire existence seemed to be one big awkward mess for her beleaguered parents.

She resolved to be firm, matter-of-fact, and not annoyed and waited while her parents took a seat at the kitchen island across from her. Andrew looked bored, Amy vaguely interested. But as Becky had guessed, Joey's parents would likely have a fit over her news. Oh well. It was Joey's life, after all, not theirs.

"Mom, Dad, I have some news to share."

"Oh God. Please don't tell me you're pregnant again," her father deadpanned.

"That's not funny, Dad," Joey snapped. "And totally uncalled for."

He looked taken aback. "I was just kidding."

"You're always 'just kidding.' Yeah, I had sex for the first time at fifteen and got pregnant. For nine years, you've never let me forget it. Been there, done that. Let's get past it, okay?"

Andrew blinked and slowly nodded, as if seeing his daughter for the first time.

Amy agreed, "Yes, let's. So what is it you have to tell us, honey?"

Joey took a deep breath, then let it out. "I saw Felix Rogers the other day."

Her parents stared.

"He was at Brandon's soccer game, actually. We chatted briefly. Well, mostly I told him to kiss off. Then I saw him yesterday, and we talked again."

Andrew recovered first. "I hope you told him to go to hell."

"I used a word starting with F, but yeah. That was my first response."

"Good." Her dad grunted.

"First response?" Her mother's eyes narrowed. "What was the second?"

"To talk to Felix, find out what he wanted, and deal with it."

"And?" her father asked.

"He wants to meet Brandon."

"Hell no." Her father glared, as if she'd been the one to suggest it.

"No way. Not my grandson," Amy said, vehement, angry.

Joey sighed. "Again, my first response." She shared with them the whole of her discussion with Felix, leaving out exactly how much he'd given her and the more intimate details of Brandon's conception.

Her mother was incensed. "So he thinks he can just buy his way back into your good graces?"

"He ditched his parents? That'll be the day." Andrew snorted. "Boy has always been tied to his mother's purse strings. But he could cause problems." He and Amy shared a look. "I'll contact George, an attorney friend. He helped one of our doctors in his last divorce, and—"

"Dad, no."

"Oh, good." Amy nodded, ignoring her daughter. "We'll have to get a restraining order. I can tell—"

"*No*." Joey stood to be seen, heard. "I have this handled. *I'm* Brandon's mother, and I am fully capable of dealing with Felix. I just wanted you two to be aware Felix is in town and asking about Brandon."

Her parents just watched her, like an animal at the zoo.

"Well? What are you going to do?" her mother asked.

Her father crossed his arms and leaned back in his chair. "I can't wait to hear this."

Joey was really trying to hold onto her temper, but he didn't make it easy. "I cashed his check for one. And before you two start going apeshit"—their mouths fell open at her language—"I consulted a lawyer. Felix has no legal rights to Brandon at all. None. No matter how much money he has or doesn't have, he has no rights over my son."

Her father slowly nodded. "Good."

"However," she added, "he's Brandon's father. So I'm going to allow them to meet."

"No." Her mother glared at her. "You will not take my grandson to meet *that man*."

"No, you won't." Her father agreed with Amy. Big surprise.

"Yes, I will." Joey centered herself, confident, positive. "Brandon is my son. I would like him to get to know his father, even though I won't tell Brandon who Felix is until *I* determine it's okay to do so. Felix agreed with me."

"He would. Can't you see he's no good for you?" Her father leaned closer. "Or did he snap his fingers and bring you to heel once more?"

"Andrew." Amy looked at him in shock.

"That's right, Dad. Let it all out," Joey said, her voice rising. "Just say what you've always thought. That your daughter is a whore who spreads her legs for anyone!"

He turned red. "I never said that."

"Sure you have. Plenty of times. Damn, Dad. I made a mistake. I was just a kid. I learned from it. Can't you see that?"

"How can I when you're making the same mistake all over again?"

She huffed. "Please. You think I'm stupid. You always have. No matter how good my grades were or how hard I worked, I've never been good enough to be your fucking daughter. Well, guess what? I'm the only one you've got."

"Don't remind me." Oh, his words cut. "And watch your mouth. I don't know why you're talking to us like that."

"Andrew, Josephine. Stop." Amy had tears in her eyes. "He doesn't mean it, honey. We're just shocked you could fall right back in with Felix after what he did to you."

"Did to me? Or did to *you*?" she shot back. "You've both treated me like dirt since the moment I got pregnant."

"That's not true," Amy argued.

"We gave you a home! Food, clothes. We paid your medical bills. Everything you needed," her father said. The medical coverage had been a no-brainer, part of his benefits package when working for the clinic for so many years. Not that she didn't appreciate it, but he hadn't gone into hock so she could have a baby.

"Yeah, and you never let me forget that I lived here only because you *let* me. That I owed you everything for it." Angry, she wanted to lash out, to finally have the say she'd held in for nine long years. "I know I ruined your dreams of a scholarship for me. But they were never *my* dreams to begin with. I love working at S&J. I love that I got my degree with my own hard-earned money. Everything with you two is about owing you something because you took care of me—when I was *fifteen years old*. Guess what? I'm family! Brandon is family! You should take care of those you love without keeping a score book."

"That's not fair," her mother said hotly. "We love you. We're looking out for you."

"Because you can't look out for yourself," Andrew retorted.

"I can too!" *Great comeback, Joey. Why not add a yuh-huh to his nuh-uh?*

"Really? You're twenty-four and living above *my* garage," he roared back. "You worked for seven damn years for a promotion." He laughed. "In a flower shop. Selling *flowers*. Christ, I got promoted after six months at my very first job. I now run the clinic, honey. You can barely snip roses without asking your boss if you have permission to wipe your own ass."

Amy looked askance at her husband. Even Joey was taken aback by his vitriol.

"You think getting your GED and a degree from a community college makes you special? It makes you average. So very, very average." Her father shook his head. "We raised you to be special. Read to you as a baby, instilled discipline. Taught you right from wrong. I just don't understand how you could throw it all away on Felix Rogers."

"I. Made. A. Mistake," she hissed. "One you never let me forget."

"How can I? He sleeps right near you every night."

"So now Brandon is a mistake?" she shouted.

Her father paused. "No. I didn't mean that. I meant—"

"That's *exactly* what you meant. And don't you say anything, Mom. You love Brandon now, because he's so cute and polite and you can show him off like a damn toy poodle. Well, guess what? I don't need this."

Her mother hit back with, "You sure seem to need a babysitter well enough though. I don't hear you complaining about that."

Andrew nodded. "Or about your cheap rent. Why don't we hear you complaining then? When we're giving you what you 'need'?"

"You know what? You're right." She smiled through her teeth. "Brandon and I will be moving out. Congrats, Dad. You can have your rental unit back and make some real money. And Mom, you don't need to worry about having to slave over your grandson anymore." How *dare she* shove babysitting in Joey's face? Half the time Joey let her mother watch Brandon because Amy asked to, even when Joey had other plans. "I lived with your disappointment and shame for years, because I wasn't smart enough to"—she said more to her father—"keep my legs closed. I never date. I never have sex. And I'm always mindful to put my best foot forward because I sure don't want to upset Mom and Dad again.

"But nothing I do will be good enough for you, Dad. And you, Mom, will judge me forever, apparently. Brandon is a little joy, and I'm just the stupid girl who got lucky with such a great son. Really? Who the hell do you think taught him manners? Taught him to respect his parents and grandparents? To get good grades? Not you two, who are so busy using him to show how great *you* are that you forget how great *he* is." Okay, not exactly fair, and she really was talking more about her than Brandon, but fuck it.

"None of that's true," Amy said, sounding shocked.

Joey had had enough. "I'm done with you two. You're nasty, hurtful people. And you can just... *Oh*." She couldn't get herself to tell them to eff off or kiss her ass. Her parents, after all, were her parents. But she sure didn't like them very much. She stood, ignored their demands to sit back down and listen to them, and stormed out of the house. She hurried upstairs, grabbed a large trash bag from under the sink, and started stuffing her clothes into it.

She heard heavy footsteps and knew her father had come. "You wait one minute, Josephine," he said as he slammed into the unit.

"No." She continued packing until he grabbed the bag from her and threw it across the room.

"Yes. You are my daughter, by God, and I'll—"

She started laughing. "Seriously? I'm your daughter? Does that make me as smart as you? Or a disappointment because I'm nowhere near as amazing as the incredible Andrew Reeves? No matter what I do, it's not good enough."

"That's not true." He was shaking in his anger.

And she didn't care. "I'm done trying to please you. Done trying to get you to even *like* me."

"What are you talking about?"

"Dad, I have spent every second of my life, it seems,

trying to get you to like me. You never spent time with me growing up. You were always too busy or too tired to handle a yappy little girl. So I would be quiet. Then Mom would tell me you didn't want to spend time with a mopey little girl. So I'd be super happy. Still didn't take you away from your day job."

"The one I worked my ass off in? That one? You know, to give you what I never had?"

"What? All this?" She waved a hand around. "I'm so happy you have the rental property you always wanted."

"I meant food on the table, smart-ass. Sorry I didn't hug you enough between my job and overtime. You know how I spent my early years? Hoarding breakfast so I could have one meal at school with friends, because my father never made enough money to support us," he growled. "Why the hell do you think I worked so damn hard?"

"I wouldn't know. You don't talk to me. You talk *at* me. Mom talks down to me. What the hell would I know about anything? I'm just a stupid little girl who got fucked by a rich kid and still can't keep her legs cl—"

He slapped her.

The action stunned them both. In all the years of dismissal and disappointment, she'd never once been hit by either parent.

She put a hand to her stinging cheek, staring at him in shock.

He stared back at her in horror. "Joey, I'm so—"

She tore out of the apartment and down the steps and ran smack into her mother.

"You're not leaving," her mother ordered. "Go back upstairs and… What happened to your face?"

"I'll get my things later. Or you can throw them on

the front lawn. I really don't give a crap." Joey wiped her tears and hurried to her car, glad she'd left her purse inside. She peeled out of the driveway and didn't look back.

Lou stared at a very quiet Joey, not sure what to make of this saddened woman. On the one hand, he wanted to kiss her and make it all better. She'd called him, not anyone else, but Lou, needing a shoulder to cry on. So shit yeah, he'd taken off work early. Johnny could cover Lou's ass for once.

So on the one hand, he was her go-to. And that made him feel ten feet tall. On the other, he wanted to shake her, find out why she didn't trust him enough to tell him she had *a son*. After all they'd been to each other, did she really only see him as someone to fuck and no more?

"Thanks for letting me come over," she said, her voice hollow.

He frowned. She didn't look good. "You okay?"

"I've been better." She sat on the edge of his couch, as if poised to flee at any moment.

Then she glanced at him, her eyes pools of sorrow.

He couldn't stand it. "Well, fuck." Before she could blink, he dragged her into his arms and hugged her, sitting her in his lap. "Come on. You need it."

She tucked her head under his chin, and he swore he felt tears soaking his shirt. His heart dropped, her pain affecting him, making it difficult to talk. "Oh, Joey. *Amor*, it'll be okay. *Háblame*, sweetheart. Talk to me. I'm here."

She sniffed. "I'm sorry. I'm such a mess."

"A beautiful mess. Even with that snot sticking to

my shirt." That got a hiccup of laughter out of her. He stroked her soft hair. "You want something to drink to replace all those tears soaking my shirt? I have lemonade or water but no milk, sorry. Rosie drained the last of it yesterday."

She sighed. "You are such a good man, Lou."

His pulse hammered.

"I shouldn't be here, but I wanted to see you. To have you make it all better." Her breath hitched. "Maybe I am a sorry excuse for a woman. Weak."

"Bullshit." He tugged her back by the shoulders so he could look into her beautiful brown eyes. "Everyone needs someone to lean on now and then. You're one of the strongest women I know." Especially now that he understood she'd had a son at fifteen. "Lean on me. I got you."

She stared into his eyes, cupped his cheeks, and kissed him. So light, so heartfelt. So incredibly powerful. He felt her taking care of him, of reaching into him and pulling out his best parts.

"Lou, you're beautiful to me. Strong. Kind." She sighed and kissed him again. "Sexy."

Yet the affection she doled was so much more than physical. As she petted him, his body responded, but so did his heart. She was gentle with him, loving, real. He responded, kissing her back. Then he lifted her higher, placing his head on her chest, so close to her heart, he could hear it race.

"With you, I'm so much more than they think I am," she whispered as she stroked his hair and sniffed again.

"*Amor*, you're killing me with the tears." He wanted to pound the shit out of whomever had made her feel bad. But he wanted her smiling more.

"Dry my tears, Lou. Make me stop crying. Kiss me again."

He lowered her for a kiss, and she took the tenderness he offered and turned it into something else. Something hot, wet. Punishing.

He groaned, wanting to offer comfort.

She wouldn't let him.

"Right here. Now. In me." She reached between them and found him hard. No surprise there. She left him to hurriedly undress, but when she returned, she didn't wait for him to do more than pull off his shirt before she unbuttoned his jeans and tugged him free.

Then she wriggled to her knees and was blowing him, her mouth around him. She found a rhythm he liked all too well. Jesus, she was wild, and he could barely think. His climax neared in a sudden storm. Too fast. Too much pleasure.

"*No*." He lifted her to sit astride him. Before he could reach for the condom in his back pocket, she stopped him by grabbing his cock and easing over him.

Skin to skin. No rubber.

His eyes nearly crossed. So fucking tight... He groaned. "Joey."

"*No*. I want this. You in me. I'm on birth control, Lou. And I trust you." Her eyes glinted with angry tears. "Only you."

He didn't like seeing her despair, and soon he found it hard to think as she continued to take him inside her, until he was fully seated, her body like a warm glove.

"Fuck me," she whispered and kissed him. "In me. *Amor*."

My love. He swore and lost all control. Needing this

woman like he needed to breathe. Joey was like a fey thing, raw and needy and sexy as sin. He gripped her hips, forcing her to a harder pace while they kissed. Touched. She ran her fingernails down his chest. He palmed her breasts, pinched her nipples.

She ground harder, moaning, her breathy little rasps so hot. And he'd never been so hard, the overwhelming sensation of her pussy holding him tight almost unbearable.

So close, so fucking close to coming inside my woman.

"Lean back and show me your tits," he growled, loving how she obeyed him without having to ask twice. She did, and he grabbed her, lifting her almost off his dick while he sucked one nipple, then turned to bite the other.

"Lou, please. I need you."

Yo también, sí. Sí. Lou released her nipple with a decadent lick, and she slammed back over him. So hard she came—and forced him into coming with her.

She cried out, her body clamping him tight while Lou poured into her, hugging and grinding her over him, emptying completely into the woman turning him inside out.

He said what he felt, unable to keep the words inside for one second more. He shuddered as he finished coming, his orgasm explosive.

Life-changing.

As they sat entangled, lost in each other, Lou realized he well and truly loved Joey Reeves. A woman who had a child he wanted no part of, and a future that couldn't be his.

If she ignored her child for him, he would never respect her. Wouldn't recognize her as the woman he'd fallen in love with.

And if she chose her child over him, as surely she would, he'd lose her before he'd had a chance to have her.

Chapter 20

JOEY SAT ON LOU'S LAP, LOU STILL INSIDE HER. A MAN'S seed in her for the first time in nine years. The panic she should have felt refused to come. Because it was Lou, and it was right.

She sighed and wrapped her arms around his thick neck, feeling the harried rise and fall of his chest as they both regained their breath.

Amazing. Incandescent. Overwhelming.

Lou was so much more than a friend or even a lover. He gave and he gave, asking nothing in return. She blinked away tears, these not sad but filled with too much emotion. Her parents might reject her, might always find her lacking. But Lou... He made her feel worthy, like a real woman who had a brain in her head. And he inspired so much feeling. God, he continued to make sure she was protected. He'd been the one to want a condom, to offer her a hug and let her know he cared.

She loved him.

That should have scared her. She knew it would...after. For now, she'd let herself bask in his arms and affection.

So they sat, joined, even as he softened inside her. Neither moved, and she wanted to think he desired the connection to last, like she did.

Her cheek pressed to his shoulder, her head under his chin, she opened her mouth, and it all came tumbling out. "Lou? I have a son."

He tensed.

Her brain continued to have no say over her heart taking charge, spilling everything. "I wanted to tell you before. But Brandon comes first. He's eight, nearly nine, I should say. He's the love of my life." She let out a watery sigh. "I had him was I was very young, a baby having a baby." She sighed, stroking Lou's arm. "Everything revolves around my boy. My decisions, my actions. But with you, I wanted… I just wanted something for me."

His arms tightened around her, but still he said nothing.

"I didn't tell you about him because I'm protective. I mean, in the all the years since I had him, the few times, and I mean *few* times, I dated, he never came up in conversation. I don't talk about my son with strangers. Then you and I grew closer. And I wanted to tell you. I almost did that evening your mom and sisters showed up." She rubbed her cheek against him. He sighed and stroked her hair, and she felt more cared for, naked in his arms, than she ever had anywhere else. "I have a son. And I know you said you don't want to have children. You raised your sisters your whole life, and you want a break. I get it. I really do." She had to see his face.

She leaned back, still holding onto him, and was lost in the gorgeous eyes regarding her with so much intensity.

"Joey, I—"

She put a finger over his lips, not wanting to hear him reject her. Not today, after her parents had. "I'm trying to explain. I don't want you because I need a father figure for my son. I'm his world, all he needs. He has a father, even if that man isn't what I'd hoped he might be. But you, I'd like you to be just mine. Not for Brandon.

Heck, you guys never even have to meet. But I'd like to keep seeing you, Lou. You make me feel good." She swallowed, took his palm to her heart, and splayed his fingers. "In here."

He looked from her eyes to his hand and back. "You are fucking lethal, you know that?" His accent was thick, his frown fierce. But never scary. Not to her. "I feel for you. A lot. And your son... I didn't expect that. Hell, you barely look out of your teens." He grimaced. "Okay, that came out as pervy considering how we're sitting."

She smiled.

"But you know what I mean. I feel for you, *cariña*. And I'm sorry you had such a bad day." He paused. "You want to tell me about it?"

She waited, but that's all he said. "That's it? No big surprise about my son?" She narrowed her eyes. "You knew."

He stroked her back. "I found out yesterday when Colin came to visit Del. Shocked the hell out of me."

"Oh. I'm sorry." She kissed his chest. "I didn't mean to lie. But he's not someone I share with a man I'm, um, you know."

He nodded.

"And I don't bring men home to meet my son. I never have."

"Good. That's how it should be." He looked sad for a moment, and her heart skipped. "I want you too much to let you go. I don't want to be anyone else's father, Joey. I'm not lying about that."

"I know." They were doomed before they could begin. But like Lou, she didn't want to let go either.

"But why can't we keep seeing each other? Just you

and me on date nights? While it works, let's keep it going. Eh?"

She nodded, relieved to still have Lou. "Good. But maybe we can start doing date night at my place."

"At your parents'?" He looked skeptical.

"Ah, no." She explained her earlier altercation, not mentioning the slap her dad had given her. The smack hadn't done more than shock her, as much as it had shocked Andrew Reeves. But the anger and intent behind it, to belittle her, make her feel less, that wound still festered.

"Well, hell. That sucks." He shook his head. "Your parents don't get you, do they? So busy making judgments, they're missing out on a wonderful daughter."

"That's why I keep you around. Well, and this." She wriggled, then wished she hadn't when he spilled out of her.

"Uh-oh. That's a mess."

She rushed to his bathroom and ran back with a hand towel. But Lou was already cleaning up and laughing at her.

If he was laughing, he couldn't be too upset with her. Could he?

"You're fast, Joey. And I sure do like to watch you leave."

"Easy for you to say." She blushed to her roots. "You're half-dressed. I'm…not."

"Yeah. We need to remedy that." He dropped his pants and underwear, then walked pretty as you please up to her. He lifted her in his arms with ease, and she sighed into his hold. He kissed her as he walked them down the hallway to his room. "So we're gonna do that again, right? You and me? No condom?" He settled her on the bed and blanketed her with his body. "You okay with that?"

"Yeah." She sighed. "And no. Having Brandon the way I did freaked me out about sex, as you know from me being weird before."

"Not so weird anymore though, are you?"

She stared up at him in surprise. "No. I'm not."

He gave a look of satisfaction. "That's because on some level you trust me."

"I trust you on all levels, Lou," she said quietly. "I've never talked to anyone the way I talk to you. Well, aside from Becky, but she doesn't count."

He lay over her, leaning up on his elbows while his lower body made contact with hers. Yet he just watched her, stroking back her hair, caressing with his gaze. "What about your first guy? The one who's Brandon's father?"

"Felix? No. He was sweet and just a boy. My first love, but not a lasting love."

"Yeah," he growled. "He was a dick who deserted you. I'd never do that."

"Not even if you were seventeen and scared?"

He shook his head. "Nope. I'm stubborn. Would have stuck by you even while your mom swatted me with a broom."

She paused. "A broom?"

He grimaced. "Something Abuela was fond of doing when I was just a kid."

"I want to meet her."

"I want you to meet her," he said, surprising them both. "She'd like you." He didn't say any more, and she didn't either, not wanting to ruin the sharing moment with reminders about their close—but not-too-close—relationship.

Joey threaded her fingers through his hair, watched his eyes close, his lashes fanning his cheeks, his full lips curling into a smile, and stupidly fell deeper into love.

Then Lou kissed her, and she lost herself in his embrace.

—∿∿—

The one bright spot in her fight with her parents had been finding her independence.

Joey and Brandon bunked down with Becky for two nights on a "stay-cation," which Brandon found thrilling, while Joey took some emergency time off, with Stef's blessing, to hunt down housing. She'd found an apartment recently vacated, something Lou happened to mention. It was perfect. A two-bedroom unit right across the street from Seward Park. The entire place was six hundred fifty square feet, and the bedrooms had probably just been one room before a savvy homeowner had divided it, but it worked for her and her budget. Even better—Brandon would have his own space.

The apartment belonged in a fourplex, one large ranch house divided into smaller units. She was in a middle unit, with one tenant to her left. The places had soundproofed insulation and were clean and in a decent neighborhood. It would be more of a drive to get to work and Brandon's school, but for the price, she'd make the trek without complaint.

Excited to be in her own place, she rode with Brandon in Becky's car to the new apartment Friday evening. She planned to start moving them in the following day, just as soon as she picked up the rest of her things in the morning. Joey coughed, not pleased to find her throat scratchy. What with the changing weather, from cool to hot to freakin' cold, stress, and her continued nonspeaking terms with her parents, she wasn't surprised by her sickness.

"You sure you can get your stuff tomorrow alone? I can help," Becky said under her breath as they pulled behind the building into the tiny parking lot.

Joey stifled a cough. "No. You're doing plenty helping me watch Brandon."

"I'm dropping him off at your friend Del's for the weekend." Becky raised a brow. "How exactly is that doing plenty?"

"You let us stay with you. That's a ton, trust me."

She glanced over her shoulder while Becky turned off the car. Brandon waved. "Hi, Mom! I like Ms. Becky's car."

"Yeah. Freedom 420 has character." Becky had named her pot-green car some time ago. In the years before she and Joey had reconnected, during Becky's experimental years, apparently.

Joey chuckled, which turned into a cough.

"Ew. Stay back, Brandon." Becky cupped her hand over her nose and mouth. "Your mom is infected. I think she's turning into a…zombie."

Brandon gave an ear-piercing shriek, then darted out of the car and ran around and around in circles before flopping in the nearby grass.

"Yeah, that vanilla milk shake at the drive-through. Great idea, Becky."

Becky grinned. "Hey, he's hyper. Not sick."

They all walked to the new apartment, waiting with

anticipation as Joey dug out her new keys. The process had been surprisingly simple. Since Lou had mentioned her by name and since he knew someone who knew the landlord, the application had been approved in no time. An oddity, but she didn't question it. Joey needed all the luck she could get.

She opened the door and flicked on the light, and they walked into the darkening living area. A neutral gray, with laminate wood floors and a teeny kitchen, it still boasted more than she was used to. *Two* small bedrooms, a bathroom, a living/dining area, and a small kitchen complete with a sink, microwave, refrigerator, and full-size stove.

"Mom! You can make cookies."

"I know. So exciting." She muffled more coughing, ignored her scratchy throat, and ran around pretending to be a plane with her son and best friend. Only one thing was missing to mar the perfection of the moment—Lou.

━━━

Lou spent his Saturday morning doing chores. His laundry, the lawn, some grocery shopping. He got enough to feed company. Like his family...or Joey, if she had time for him this weekend.

As he scrubbed down his already-clean counters, determined never to live like Sam, the garage's number one slob, he wondered what she might be up to. They'd texted back and forth since Wednesday afternoon. He knew she'd moved into her new place or, at least, had begun the process. He'd started and stopped messaging her half a dozen times since, offering to help move her in. Then canceling before he hit send.

Her son would be there, and he didn't want to send the wrong message. She'd said she had her girlfriend helping. Becky. A woman he knew he would like, because she sounded as sarcastic as most of Lou's family. Speaking of which, Rosie kept asking when she'd get to talk to Joey again. She seemed fascinated that someone as pretty and feminine as Joey should have a boy's name.

Then again, Joey worked with flowers, and Rosie loved anything floral. So perhaps the appeal lay in Joey's work with petals.

He frowned, realizing he'd been thinking about the woman nonstop. Since admitting to himself how much he loved her, he couldn't stop being miserable without her. And just why the hell had she been so eager to keep them dating but not sharing their lives? At the least, he'd expected her to beg him to reconsider, to give her kid a chance. But she'd wanted to keep Brandon apart from him. Because he'd told her he didn't want to deal with kids, or because she didn't feel as deeply for him as he did for her?

The constant second-guessing himself annoyed the shit out of him. He scrubbed harder, making those counters shine. As usual, Joey had impressed him. She'd put her son first, as it should be. She'd told him about standing up to her parents. And she'd even told him about Fuckhead Felix, the boy who'd done her wrong. The man who happened to be back in town wanting closure.

He would have been more bothered by the guy, except she'd barely given him a mention before going down on Lou Wednesday, before she left. Man, that woman could suck. She used her whole mouth, her tongue, lips, a hint of teeth.

He groaned, trying to will away his erection as he cleaned his oven burners.

His phone rang, distracting him, thank God. Sam's number, but he'd pick up anyway. "Yo."

"Hello." The voice on the other end surprised, then delighted him.

"Ivy?" Sam's girl.

"Hi, Lou." Her sweet voice matched the pretty blond who'd stolen his friend's heart. "I just wanted to let you know that my new neighbor is moving in." She chuckled at something Sam must have said. Lou caught a deep voice but not much else. "She's super nice—I remember her from Del's wedding. And so pretty! Your new girlfriend, hmm?"

"Kind of." He waited for her to add more, and when she didn't, he had to pry details out of her. "So is she alone or what?"

Ivy laughed. "Sam was right. You're not so smooth about Joey. She's alone. She told me her son was at a soccer game, then going to stay with friends while she moved them in. She wants to surprise him with it all being done. And she doesn't have much furniture, so it'll probably be a quick move."

"No furniture?" He frowned.

"Well, I saw sleeping bags, bags with clothes, and a few boxes. But that's it. She said something about her furniture coming later. I don't know."

Lou didn't like that. At all. But with her son gone, it wouldn't hurt to pop in and see if she was okay. "Thanks, Ivy. I've gotta go."

"Sure thing. Sam said not to be a slacker and—Sam, I can't tell him that. Bye, Lou." She disconnected, and Lou grinned, imagining what Sam might have said.

He jumped in his car, pleased to hear it purr, and drove over to Ivy's, or rather, Joey's place. A cute rancher converted into four apartments, the place had a surprising view of Lake Washington. He'd used Ivy to help Joey get the place, but he hadn't realized how nice it was. Wow, she'd lucked out. A cute park across the street, close to a high school—hmm, maybe not so lucky after all.

He parked in front of the fourplex and walked to the unit right next to Ivy's. He knocked and was surprised when the door opened right away.

Joey looked like crap. A stuffy nose, watery eyes, and frazzled hair. She wore sweats that looked a size too large for her. Then she sneezed. "Lou?"

"Oh man. You look awful." He picked her up, holding her at a distance, and stepped inside. After putting her down and ignoring her sputtering, he closed the door behind him. He'd been to Ivy's once, when Sam had been busting at the seams, proud of having a girlfriend who could cook. The pair had invited him to dinner, but it had been dark, and he hadn't seen much of the outside. The unit was tiny but homey, and he'd had more fun teasing Sam and watching Ivy blush than should have been allowed.

"I like the place." Mostly empty, with a few small boxes, plastic trash bags overflowing with clothing, and not much else. He walked around her into the small hallway, saw a single bathroom, a small bedroom for her, and a smaller one for the boy, he'd imagine. He thought she could maybe get a queen-size bed in her room if she had no other furniture but a nightstand. And no way more than a single bed would fit in the kid's room.

Tight but cozy. Knowing Joey, she'd make it a home. But a neat home?

He turned and nearly tripped over her. "Oh, hey."

"What are you doing here?" came out nasally due to her stuffed-up nose. He tried, he really tried, not to smile, but she was adorable, even sick and tired.

"I came to welcome you to the neighborhood."

She frowned. "You don't live here."

"But Ivy does."

"You know Ivy?" She didn't look pleased.

He wanted to smile with glee. "Don't be jealous, baby. That's Sam's girl."

She coughed. "I knew that." Then she scowled. "Stop smiling."

"Uh-huh." He looked around, seeing no furniture. "So. Where you going to sleep, *princesa*?"

"I have a sleeping bag. Brandon thinks it's awesome. We're camping in our new home." She smiled, her joy apparent. "This is my first place away from my parents, Lou. I feel so grown up." She laughed, hoarse but happy.

He hugged her tight, unable to stay away. "I'm glad for you. But you need furniture."

"I'll get it. I just need to go shopping for it." She started coughing again.

"Yeah. No."

"What?"

"I hear Brandon has plans today. Yes?"

"He's staying with Del this weekend, actually. She's doing me a favor while I get my place together."

"Sure thing. You and that death rattle of a cough sound really busy."

"What?"

"Exactly. What kind of friend would I be if I left you sick and hacking, all alone, in this place?"

"Wait. Lou. Where are we going?" she asked as he dragged her by the hand toward the front door.

"Keys?"

She reached in her pocket and showed them to him, then took them back. "Speak, *señor*."

"*Muy bien, mi corazón.*"

She frowned. "Isn't that the word for heart?"

"Yep. You've stolen my heart with those baggy sweats and red-rimmed eyes. Your beauty knows no bounds."

She flushed. "Ass."

He laughed and wrestled the keys out of her hands. "Come on. Let me help you get better. You don't want to get Brandon sick, do you?"

Sneaky, because she caved without much prodding after that. He drove her back to his house, then ran her a bath. And he found he liked caring for her.

"I don't have any clothes to change into but my dirty sweats," she complained. Which he'd thought about while hustling her out of her place.

"You can wear something of mine." *Yes, that's perfect. My woman, my house, my clothing on her hot little body.*

Hours later, he realized he hadn't been exaggerating about her hot little body. Poor Joey had a fever.

"I should go home," she muttered, then sneezed. "I don't want to get you sick too."

He stared at her, all bundled up in his bed, and

wondered how he'd manage to let her go. Because eventually, he'd have to.

Lou brushed her hair back from her sweaty forehead. "Just sleep. I'll take care of you, *amor*."

She blinked up at him and smiled. "You are so hot when you speak Spanish. Have I ever told you that?"

"No. Tell me again."

She laughed. "Did you know Brandon's learning Spanish in school? I told him my friend speaks it, so he's going to teach me a few words."

Lou didn't know how he felt about her talking to her son about him. Bridging them all closer while Lou stubbornly resisted the idea of more kids. Yet Joey's son was already a part of her. Her son had made her who she was today: a sweet, responsible, beautiful woman, inside and out.

"Come on, Lou. Say something else in Spanish," she murmured, half-asleep.

So he did. "What am I going to do with you, sweetheart? You have my heart, my body, and I'm afraid my soul. So how do we make this work? Maybe I start bending a little, not so stiff to break when you have so much love to give, eh?"

"So pretty. I love how you talk."

"*Y te amo mucho*." He sighed. *And I love you*.

Chapter 21

SUNDAY AFTERNOON, JOEY'S PHONE RANG. SINCE she'd been sleeping most of the weekend thanks to illness and sleep-inducing medicine, Lou answered for her, half hoping her parents called. He knew he shouldn't butt in, but he couldn't help it. No one fucked with his girl and got away with it.

"Yeah?" he growled.

"Um, Joey?"

He frowned. "Is this Del?"

"Yo. Hey, sorry to interrupt. Is Joey coming to get the kid or what? We're happy to keep him longer, but at some point, she'll probably want him back."

"Shit. Sorry. I meant to call you for her. She's been sick all weekend. She thinks it's flu, but I think it's just a really bad cold." On top of the stress she'd been dealing with.

"Bummer. Hey, I'll have Mike swing him back later if you want. We can keep him for dinner."

He frowned. Joey would need to go home. With Brandon. But they had no beds. Nothing to eat, and she was still in a bad way. He could call her friend Becky for help. Or hell, he could ask Del. She'd step in for the kid. But a real friend, a true friend, would help no matter how uncomfortable it made him. A man who loved her would want to take care of her.

"If you can keep him for dinner, I can swing by and pick him up. But his mom is staying here with me.

So maybe if you make the introductions, he won't be screaming stranger danger the whole way to my place."

She chuckled. "No problem. So I'll tell him his mom's… Fill in the blank, Lou. His mom's boyfriend, lover, wall-banger, what?"

"Del." He gave an exasperated sigh. "Friend."

"*Friend* is helping out while she's sick. Sure thing. Come get him at seven, okay?"

He thanked her before hanging up. Now to get things situated…

Hours later, he arrived at Del's at seven on the dot. Mike opened the door, sized him up, grunted, and turned around.

"Thanks for the warm welcome, McCauley," Lou said loudly.

"Mike." Del glared at her husband. "Be nice."

Mike gave him the evil eye. "He flirts too much."

Lou acted wounded. "I can't help it she wants me. I try to tone it down, man. But I'm only human."

"So not funny, Lou," Mike grumbled, then stalked down the hallway yelling for Brandon.

Jekyll appeared out of nowhere, and Lou caught the dog as it made a jump for his face.

"Nice discipline, Del."

She flushed. "Sorry." She grabbed Jekyll by the collar, and the dog turned a loving tongue her way. He'd licked her throat and cheek and nearly had her eyeball before Colin raced in to grab his dog.

"Oh, hi, Lou." Colin left the dog to run up and high-five Lou, while Del wrestled with the overlarge canine.

Then a small boy with a shock of spiky blond hair and Joey's features cautiously entered the living area.

Lou's heart rocked, seeing that tentative smile, the same dark-brown eyes tilting in pleasure. Oh man, Joey's kid was so cute. A chip off her block.

He cleared his throat, oddly nervous to meet Joey Jr. "Hi. I'm—"

"This is Lou," Colin interrupted. "He's the best drawer in all Seattle. He works with Mom at the garage. Lou, this is Brandon. He's on my soccer team. And he's almost nine. And his mom is Joey. She sells flowers. And he's on a vacation, and he just moved, and—"

"Great intro, Colin." Del grabbed him by the collar and tugged him away from Lou. Kid in one hand, dog in the other. "Brandon, your mom isn't feeling too good so her friend Lou here has been helping her. It's okay if you go home with Lou. He'll take you to your mom."

Colin nodded. "Yeah, he's nice. And Jekyll likes him. Watch." Colin wrangled out of Del's hold and grabbed the dog. Then he pointed at Lou. "Lick 'em, Jekyll. Go!" The dog leapt for Lou again.

"Jesus. Colin, cut it out," Lou said, laughing as the dog tried to lick him over and over again. "Great trick."

Mike watched smugly from the hallway.

Del shook her head. "Please tell me you didn't teach him that."

"Well, it sure wasn't Brody. He can't even control his own dog." Mike turned to Jekyll. "Jekyll, heel. Sit."

In a snap, the dog stopped jumping, then sat.

Brandon whistled. Or at least he tried to. "That was awesome, Mr. Mike."

Mike shot Lou a look, as if daring him to make something of the name. Lou pursed his lips, turned to Brandon, and said, "Hey, Brandon. I'm Lou. Not Mr.

Lou. Just Lou." He saw Del try to hide a smile as she gave Mike a teasing look. "Your mom is pretty sick and coughing all over. It's pretty gross, but I'm holding up okay. She's at my house recovering since you guys don't have towels or beds yet. She needs a good place to sleep to get better."

Brandon listened, was quiet for a moment, then nodded and stuck out his hand. "Hi, Lou. I'm Brandon Reeves. Nice to meet you."

Lou shook the tiny guy's hand, realizing how much bigger he was than the kid, understanding how intimidating it might be to leave with a big, male stranger. "I was going to take you to your mama. She's a good friend of mine. But you don't know me that well, so if you want, we can call her friend Becky to—"

"Are you my mom's friend who speaks Spanish?" Brandon studied him, then smiled. "You have big muscles and big brown eyes. And Colin said you're a drawer."

Lou blinked, surprised at the all-over warmth he felt from Brandon's acceptance. "Yep. That's me."

"*Hola. My llama es Brandon.*" My llama is Brandon?

Lou chuckled. "*Me llamo Brandon*, I think you mean. Because a llama is a pack animal."

"Oh, yeah." Brandon, Del, and Colin chuckled. Even Mike cracked a smile. "Well, let's go get Mom, Lou." Then the little guy put his hand in Lou's and tugged him toward the door. "Bye, Del, Mr. Mike. See you, Colin. Thanks for having me." He dragged his backpack until Lou picked it up.

As they left, he heard Del saying to Mike, "Most polite kid I've ever met. See that, Colin? Take a note."

"Aw, Mom." Then he laughed.

Lou walked with Brandon toward his car, pleased when the kid's eyes lit up. "Wow. Is this your car?"

"Yep."

He held the door open for Brandon and waited for him to scurry into the back, where he tossed the boy's bag. "Buckle up."

"I will. It's the law." Oh man, totally a mini-Joey.

Lou laughed to himself and got in.

"I like your car a lot. I like the snake too!"

"Thanks. I painted him myself."

"Wow." Brandon's eyes were huge, Lou saw as he checked the rearview mirror.

The ride back to his house proved enjoyable. Brandon had a terrific personality. A little boy but mature enough to converse with an adult and not cross too many boundaries. The boy was far from the smart-ass Lou had been growing up. He used *please* and *thank you* when appropriate and seemed super impressed with Lou.

"I like snakes too. And purple." The boy's reflection in the rearview showed a smile.

"Yeah? What grade are you in, Brandon?"

"Third. I'm a year and ten months older than Colin, but he's my friend. He's a really good soccer player. Do you like soccer, Lou?"

"As a matter of fact, I do."

The discussion turned to FIFA and world *fútbol* clubs. The real word for soccer. Pleased to have a rational discussion about his favorite sport without having to explain his love for the real and true game of *fútbol*, Lou expressed his love for Guadalajara, better known as Chivas. His favorite team.

"I like the Sounders," Brandon said.

They were nothing compared to Chivas, but no way would Lou crush the kid. "They're a fun team to watch."

Brandon leaned forward in the car just as Lou parked. "You've been to a game? For real?"

Lou laughed and left the car, waiting with the door open for Brandon. "Yep. You should see one."

"Oh. I'll have to ask Mom."

Before he could think the better of it, Lou said, "It would be fun. I could take you and your mom sometime if she likes soccer."

"No, she thinks it's boring unless I'm playing. But you could take me." Brandon beamed.

And this is why a child and a woman don't mix with you, moron. Because now Lou was making suggestions he had no right making, and if he didn't follow through, the kid would be disappointed. Like Lou had been by so many of his mother's boyfriends.

He forced a smile. "That sounds like fun." Surely one game would be okay. "But let's go see if your mom's better now."

"I hope she's not too sick." Brandon started to sound worried. "My dad got sick and left me."

Lou started. "What?"

Brandon nodded. "Mom told me dad was sick in the head and the heart and had to go away. So I don't have a dad now. But I have Grandpa." Brandon bit his lip, so like Joey that he melted Lou's reserve. "Grandpa's kind of mean sometimes."

Lou treaded on unstable ground. "He hits you?"

"Oh, no. Never hit me. But he's not so nice about Mom. Sometimes he says things I don't like."

Lou nodded, escorting the boy inside his home.

"Wow. This place is neat." Brandon immediately went to the drawings on the wall. The many cars and fantastical beasts. "I bet you did those."

Lou nodded, impressed with the boy's eye for detail. "I did." He showed Brandon around before asking, "So what does your grandpa say about your mom?"

"That she's too smart for what she's doing. That she's so pretty and nice and ruining her life." Brandon frowned. "I think she's smart and nice too. But she's happy, not ruined."

"I agree." Lou wanted to knock some sense into Andrew Reeves. "Want to see if your mom's up?"

Brandon nodded. They walked down the hallway before the boy grabbed him by the hand. Lou looked down, only to see Brandon worried.

The boy bit his lip before asking, "She never even gets a cough. You sure she's not too sick? She won't go away or die, right?"

"Ah, no." Lou felt for the boy. He grabbed Brandon's hand. "Buddy, your mama, she's beautiful. Sweet, kind. And she loves you more than anything in the world. You are her *corazón*. Her heart." He put a hand over Brandon's chest. "She can't live without you."

The boy gave a tremulous smile. "Her *corazón*. Okay."

They pushed open Lou's bedroom door to see Joey sleeping like an angel. Brandon made an exaggerated tiptoe Lou did his best not to laugh at. Then the boy kissed his mother on the forehead and patted her on the shoulder.

"Come on," Lou whispered and motioned to the door.

Once out in the hallway, they stared at each other, Lou wondering what to do with the kid now and the boy just staring up at him.

"When are we going to my new home?" he asked.

Lou nodded for the boy to follow him. Once in the kitchen, he grabbed a box of ice-cream sandwiches from the freezer he kept on hand for Rosie.

Brandon's eyes widened.

"You want one?"

"Yes, please."

Again with the manners. Nice kid. "Here you go." While Brandon neatly removed the wrapper, Lou put the rest of the bars away, then explained the situation. "Okay, Brandon. Here's the deal. Until your mom gets your furniture in, you guys are gonna stay with me. Okay?"

Brandon looked a little unsure, though he nodded and nibbled at his ice cream.

So innocent and small. He called to all of Lou's protective instincts. "It's okay. I have a guest room all made up for you. I even packed you some clothes from your new place. It's pretty neat, your new house. Do you like it?"

Brandon gave a shy smile. "I have my own room now."

"You're lucky. I had to share a room with my sisters until I was fifteen."

"You have sisters?"

"Five of them. My youngest sister is near your age. Rosie's eight."

Brandon stared at Lou. "Really?"

Lou smiled. "Really. My mom loves babies."

"Do you have any?"

"Um, no." *Not yet* was on the tip of his tongue. Which made little sense.

"My mom loves babies too. She loves me a lot."

"I know. She told me."

Brandon nodded. "It's good she has friends now. For a long time, she had old-people friends. Like Grandma and Grandpa. And Stef and Tonya. They work with her. Well, and Ms. Becky. Now you. That's it."

Lou blinked. "How about Del?"

"Oh yeah. Her too. And some guy named Felix. I'm going to meet him this week. She thinks I might like him." Brandon leaned closer and whispered, "Don't tell, but I heard her tell Ms. Becky she likes you a lot. Maybe like-like. Kissy-like." Brandon grinned.

"I see." He totally didn't and needed to talk to Joey. She was talking to Felix? Did she still have a thing for the guy? Or was it all about Brandon? And why, when Lou had been adamant about not dealing with kids who weren't his own, did he suddenly feel the need to watch over Brandon?

"I'm done." Brandon held his ice cream wrapper. "Where can I throw this away?"

"You clean up after yourself too? Are you real?"

Brandon chuckled. "That's what my grandma says."

Lou pointed to the trash can and watched the boy throw the wrapper away. "Come on, kid. Let me show you your room. It's getting late, and I think you have a bedtime, right?"

"Maybe. Sometimes I don't. I think tonight I can stay up a long time, in fact."

Thank God. The kid was human after all.

After Lou showed Brandon the spare room, complete with the kiddie night-light Rosie always used and some spare stuffed animals she'd left behind, he said, "I'll be sleeping on the couch if you need me."

"Not with Mom?"

Lou almost choked on his answer. "Ah, no. Why? Do her friends usually sleep in her bed?"

"Oh, no. Mom never has sleepovers. But I slept in Colin's room. Todd's too."

"Well, if your mom wasn't sick, you could sleep in her room with her."

Brandon made a face. "Nah. I love Mom. But we always share the same room. I want my own room from now on." He paused. "But it has that little light, right?"

Lou nodded. She'd shared a room with her son? No wonder the woman never had sleepovers.

An hour later, he had Brandon in bed, confounded when told he needed to read the boy a story. So he found one of Rosie's old Barbie books and proceeded to replace all the girlie parts with things that blew up or raced on two wheels.

By the end, Brandon looked pleased but sleepy, hugging Rosie's second-favorite stuffed owl.

"You take care of Owlie, okay?" Lou said to Brandon, who hugged the ratty thing tighter.

"I will."

Lou leaned down and kissed the boy's forehead before thinking the better of it. Something he always did with Rosie.

"G'night, Lou."

Pride, affection, and warmth stole through him as he looked at the blond head snuggling into the pillow. Just like his mother down the hall. "*Buenas noches*, Brandon."

Brandon smiled, yawned, and closed his eyes.

And Lou spent one uncomfortable night on the couch, but it was nothing next to the chaos that became his morning.

———

"So then what?" Becky asked, slurping her coffee and staring at Joey.

They sat together at the park drinking coffee Thursday evening while Brandon and Felix walked around, talking.

"So I woke up in the middle of the night, not sure what the heck was going on. I find Brandon all tucked in bed in Lou's spare room, hugging a stuffed animal not his own."

Becky goggled. "Lou's?"

"Probably his little sister's. Then I find Lou on the couch looking uncomfortable. Becky, he took care of me all weekend. He picked up my son, for God's sake. And he tried to act like it was no big deal the next day. I'm freaking out because we're late and we don't have what we need for school or work. He just takes charge, showing Brandon how to work the shower, handing him clothes he'd picked up. Then he took me aside, looked me over, and slapped me on the ass. Proclaimed me all better and showed me how to work his shower, gave me *my* clothes, and made us breakfast. It was surreal."

And an experience she wanted to replay for the rest of her days. She'd felt so normal and domestic. Mom and dad and boy getting ready for their Monday morning.

Lou had looked especially handsome in his jeans and tee, a hint of his tattoo showing. Brandon already thought him the most awesome man in the world. Not only did Lou have an awesome car, speak Spanish, and draw, he also loved soccer.

And so Tuesday and Wednesday morning followed

the same pattern. Brandon went to an after-school program she could now afford. She picked him up after work, drove them to their new apartment, where they continued to settle in, then Lou would show up with dinner and help her put together the IKEA furniture she'd purchased, and they'd all go back to Lou's to sleep.

"I feel like we're growing closer. All of us."

"But no sex since you were sick?" Becky asked.

That bothered her. Still did, in fact. "No. We transitioned from lovers to domestic partners with no problem. Brandon loves Lou. I mean, I thought he might have a little problem adapting to a man in my life. Even if he is just 'a friend.' But Brandon doesn't want to go back home and leave Lou. He told me that today."

Becky laughed. "Nice. Lou has won over the boy without trying." She paused. "Still no word from your parents?"

"My mother left me a voice mail. She apologized, and she sounds sincere. I guess. No word from Dad."

"No news is good news." Becky shrugged. "And Felix? How's that going?"

She watched father and son walking together, pointing at things on the ground and in the trees. "Felix and I have come to an understanding. He wants to get to know Brandon, to be a friend first, a father second. He made a few hints about seeing where he and I might be today. But I shut that down quick."

"Oh?"

"I told him I had a man in my life and was happy. And he left it at that."

"Simple enough. If you believe it."

"What does he have to gain? To try to get back with me to get Brandon? I doubt that."

"So you're really buying his born-again misery crap?"

"What?"

"Well, not religious born-again. More like he realized what an asshole he was, and he's now reborn. Kind of."

Joey shook her head at her friend. "Kind of."

They watched Brandon and Felix. "So what are you going to do about loving Lou?"

Joey groaned. "I don't know. What should I do?"

"Maybe have an honest conversation with the guy? I mean, you are living with him."

"Not really. We're putting Brandon's bed together tonight."

"Oh, we're up to beds." Becky rubbed her hands together.

Joey sighed. "I wish."

"You need to talk to him. Don't be one of those TSTL heroines in a bad novel."

"Too Stupid To Live?"

"To Stupid To Love." Becky nodded. "Just because my love happened to turn to God doesn't mean yours will."

"I still don't see how you know this guy is a priest."

"Um, he wore a priest thingie? That white collar block at his throat? That?"

"Maybe he was going to a costume party."

"Nah, he's always nice." She sighed. "He found God. I'm so screwed."

Joey tried not to laugh.

Later that evening, after she and Lou had put Brandon's bed together and Brandon had talked and talked about his time with Felix, they drove back to Lou's house in silence, the radio their only companion.

Brandon soon went to bed, and the new routine consisted of Joey kissing him good night followed by Lou coming in to ruffle his hair, then add a kiss to Brandon's forehead. Each time she saw it, her heart gave a leap. And she fell that much more in love with Lou.

Half an hour later, after watching some television on Lou's current bed—the couch—she turned to him. "We need to talk."

He nodded. "I agree."

Nervous but willing to put herself out there, she started. "Me first."

"Fine."

He didn't look happy, and she wasn't sure she should go through with it. But then she knew she had to. "Lou, I can't thank you enough for all you've done to help."

He shrugged. "No biggie."

"No, it *is* a big deal. You helped me. You helped my son." She moved closer to hug him. But to her dismay, he didn't hug her back. "Lou?"

"I've been thinking."

"The three words a woman never wants to hear," she teased, thinking Becky would love that line.

Lou didn't smile back. "I think it would be best if you and Brandon moved back home tomorrow."

She wanted to cry. "I know you said you didn't want children in your life. I respect that, but I—" His pained look stopped her, and she was glad, because she didn't know what else she might have said.

"It's not him. Well, partly it is." Lou ran his hand through his hair. "The boy is awesome. He's sweet, polite, so cute, and a helluva soccer player." Lou swallowed. "Hell, Joey. I want to keep being around to see him, but I'm not his father."

"I never said you were."

"No. Felix is. And he's trying to bond with Brandon. Me being in the way isn't helping."

Joey frowned. "I know my son and what's best for him. Being friends with you doesn't detract from what he can have with Felix."

"You're too close to the situation. You don't understand. The boy needs his father."

"Excuse me?" Was he saying she wasn't caring for her son? "He's been just fine without a father for nearly nine long years, Lou."

"That came out wrong." He swore in Spanish. "Joey, I lo—" He started coughing. "Sorry. I like you. A lot. But you have a son to think about. And, well, I have a life to get back to."

Joey was hurt. "Don't you care about me?"

"Of course I do."

"Then why can't we try to be together? All of us?" She'd seen his affection for her son. She knew it wasn't her pushing for a relationship that wasn't there. "Or is this because you think I'd have you raising him? I hate it, but I understand if you don't want this responsibility. It's mine, and I'm fine with it being mine."

"But it's not. It's Felix's too. And you guys need to work that out. Don't put me in the middle of it."

"I'm not." She stared. "I'm confused. Are you saying you don't want to be with me? You don't"—she put it all on the line—"love me?"

He blew out a breath. "See. This shouldn't be about you and me. It's about Brandon. He should come first, Joey."

"Okay, that came out exactly the way you meant it to, didn't it?"

"Yeah." He crossed his massive arms over his chest.

"It did. I'm sorry if it sounds judgy, but it's true. Woman gets interested in a man, and her kids fall to the wayside. I've seen it too many times, even in good women."

"Lou?" she said sweetly, enraged that he could possibly find fault in her parenting. Hell, everything she'd ever done with her life had been for Brandon's sake. Everything except Lou. And he meant to punish her for it?

"I'm sorry, but that's the way I feel."

She stared at him, so disappointed, she wanted to cry. After she slapped him in the head. "You don't know me at all." Then she turned on her heel and went back to his bedroom. She gathered her clothes and took them and herself to sleep with Brandon. She wouldn't spend one more night in Lou's big bed, alone, hoping for him to return. Not when he obviously considered her a piss-poor mother who put sex ahead of her baby boy.

No. She and Brandon were leaving tomorrow. And Lou Cortez would rue the day he'd sat in judgment of her. Because he'd ruined the best thing he could have had. Joey and her son.

She wiped her tears and joined Brandon in the small bed.

Time to stop dreaming and start living again.

Chapter 22

STELLA HAD HAD IT UP TO HERE WITH HER MOPEY brother. Why he let some stupid woman break his heart, stomped all to pieces… She had been warned by everyone, Abuela too, to leave well enough alone. Well, screw that.

The Cortez family had been stepped on one too many times. *Man*. Joey had a son? An ex-baby daddy floating around? She hated that Joey had fucked Lou over. Her brother might not show it, but he had a heart of gold. He cared for all of them. Hell, he'd taken care of Joey's kid without having been asked. She'd heard all about it from her mama, after Mama had heard about it from Del after dropping off some cookies at the shop. God forbid Lou tell them anything.

He just walked around, not eating, pale, losing weight, like he'd caught the goddamn love plague. For two weeks he'd been the walking wounded, and she'd had enough.

She parked her car near Joey's address and waited across the street near the park. That's when she saw them. Joey sitting away from the man and boy walking together.

The kid had to be hers. He had her face stamped on his, but with blond hair, like the guy's. And yeah, a bit of the guy on the boy's face too.

Stella left the car and angled toward the woods, on the trail, out of sight of Joey but close enough to over-hear the conversation between the man and the boy.

"...so she's sad?" the man asked, his voice deep.

"Yeah. I can't help her either. She hides the crying." The boy sounded on the verge of tears, pulling Stella's heartstrings. It helped to know Joey was miserable.

"I'm so sorry, Brandon. I wish I could help."

"Be her friend, Felix. Tell her to talk to Lou. I bet he'd talk to her if she'd call him." Brandon paused, kicked a rock. "He said he'd take me to a Sounders game someday."

"Yeah? That's nice." Felix walked with the boy. They neared Stella, so she kept her attention on the water, subtly turning her back to the pair. "Hey, you want me to talk to him?"

"Yes, please. That would be really great." Brandon sniffed. "What if Mom gets so sad she gets heartsick? And she might leave me? My dad did. He got sick of me."

Felix paused. She felt for him, because that had to be a real kick in the nuts, hearing your kid tell you he knew you'd abandoned him.

"You know what I think, Brandon? I think your dad was a confused kid when you were born. A real idiot, if you don't mind me saying. But your mom is so strong. She could never get sick of you or because of you. She would probably be sick if you went away though."

"Oh. I should stay around then."

"Yes. Definitely." She saw Felix pat him on the shoulder. And she noticed how very attractive the man was. Wow. Like, all-American, Caucasian hotness.

"And something else," he was saying as he knelt to look into the boy's eyes. "There has never, *ever*, been anything wrong with you or your mom. Anyone who says there is has something wrong with them."

"Like Grandpa?"

"Why do you say that?"

"He said mean things to Mom, and now they're taking a time-out from each other. Grandma was nasty too, but she apologized. So Mom said she has to be gracious and accept Grandma's apologies. Because when you're wrong, you say you're sorry. And if you mean it, you get forgiven. That's grace."

Stella eyed Joey sitting apart, alone, small, and feeling dejected from her parents. And Stella's brother? If she was into Lou, why had Joey dumped him? It made no sense. Sure, Felix was sexy, but Joey didn't sound like she was into him anymore.

Felix continued. "So if I did something wrong, say, to you. I should apologize with my whole heart, and you'd forgive me?" he asked, his voice thick.

"Yes." Brandon nodded and put hand on his Felix's shoulder. "I'd forgive you. Dad."

Felix blinked at his son, and as the moment settled, Stella felt tears prick her eyes.

"Damn. I mean, darn. You're too smart for me." Felix laughed and wiped his eyes.

"I am smart. Super smart." Brandon nodded. "Besides, we have the same hair."

"I guess we do." Felix sighed. "I'm so sorry I left you guys. It was the biggest mistake I ever made in my life. And I haven't been whole without you, Brandon. If you'll let me, I'd like to be your friend."

"That would be good. Do you think you could like soccer?"

"For you, I could."

"And Mom? Could you like her too?"

"I already do. She's my friend. But probably *only* my friend. I don't think we're going to be the kind of friends who get married. Is that okay?"

"Are you sure?"

Felix nodded. "Another thing I learned. You can't go back and relive the past. You have to make your own future."

"Sounds deep."

Felix laughed. "It is." He stood and gripped his son's shoulder. "Go on back to your mom. She's had a rough time, so go easy on her. And remember, she'll never be heartsick unless she doesn't have you."

"Okay. Bye, Felix." Brandon ran back to his mother. Joey took him with her, waved to Felix, then went across the street to their housing complex.

"All right, lady. Want to tell me why you're so interested in that young man's conversation?"

She blinked and found herself under scrutiny from the bluest eyes she'd ever seen. She stammered a "H-huh?" and felt like the biggest moron on the planet.

"Well, hel-lo, Ms. Nosy." Felix smiled, and wow, did he have straight, white teeth. "Now tell me why such a pretty lady is wasting time on an eight—sorry, Brandon—almost nine-year-old when she'd do much better with a man more her own age."

Staring at that smile, she nearly swallowed her own tongue. "You know what, Mr. Handsome? I think you and I have some things to talk about."

His grin grew wider. Then she mentioned her brother.

He lost all trace of happiness. "You're right. Let's go grab a drink. And talk."

Lou had a headache. Between Mateo being clueless, Heller still being gone, and Foley bitching about a transmission job gone wrong—that Lou had had nothing the fuck to do with—he wanted to go to bed and never wake up. The day had gone on forever, ending only after Del had yelled at everyone to get the hell gone.

He clomped into his house and made his way to the kitchen to grab a cold and much-deserved beer.

And was met by his sisters and some douche in a suit.

"What the hell is this?" Lou asked, not even trying to be polite.

He heard scuffling down the hallway but got distracted by Lucia moving forward to poke him in the chest. "Why are you not defending your woman? You love Joey, yet you leave her to this?" She pointed to Suit Guy.

Hell. To Felix.

"What the fuck do you want?" he growled at the guy. "Didn't you already do enough damage?"

Felix sneered. "Didn't you?"

Before Lou thought about it, he felt himself moving, launching a fist, and making contact with Felix's jaw.

His sisters Lucia and Stella gasped. Felix went flying and slammed into the fridge.

Felix, the guy who'd gotten Joey pregnant, then ditched her. The same schmuck who'd never been there when she was alone and lonely and dealing with her asshole parents. "Hold on, motherfucker." Lou gave him a mean smile. "I'm not done."

Except Stella inserted herself between Felix's pretty face and Lou's fist.

"You hit me, I'll hit you back," she snarled.

Felix's eyes widened. "He'll hit you?"

"No. I meant to add *if*. *If* he hits me."

"I'd never hit my sister. Jesus." Lou backed away in disgust. "Why are you here? All of you," he added to the person, no doubt his mother or Carla, hiding in the hallway.

"Why did you hit me?" Felix asked.

"Because you're a prick who took advantage of a young girl and left her to fend for herself. Why else?"

"What do you care? You handed her off just like I did. Except she had her parents to go to when I left. You dumped her, and she has no one."

"Bullshit. I didn't dump her. I was trying to do the right thing."

"Which is what?" Stella interrupted. "Making her decisions for her? She says she likes you, why don't you believe her?"

"She needs to do what's right for Brandon."

"She is." Felix straightened and tugged at his cuffs. "She's a better mother than the one I had. Than the one she has. I trust in her judgment. Why don't you?"

"First of all, I don't trust you, so I could give a rat's ass about you," Lou scoffed. "Second, Lucia, Stella, *why are you here?*"

Lucia answered, "Because I want to hear my brother tell me, looking me in the eye, that he's just a scared coward."

"*What?*"

"Yeah. You heard me." Only Lucia would be brave enough to get in his face after the day he'd had. Then she poked him. Fucking *poked* him. "Look. You love

Joey. We all know it. Abuela called it after dinner at
Mama's. Then you take her and her son in. You care
for them. You help them. And you dump them? What is
that? Why you running scared?"

"I'm not scared. And you." He pointed at Felix. "Get
the hell out of my house."

—∿∿—

Stella and Felix exchanged a wary glance. This had
seemed like a great plan at the time. Enrage her brother
into confessing his love while Joey hid in the hallway,
overhearing it all. Except Lucia had gone off script. Lou
had punched Felix, and if she wasn't mistaken, by the
sounds of the scuffle in the hallway, it was taking Carla
and Maria to hold Joey in place. The woman wanted to
leave and not look at their brother again. Oy.

No, wait. There she was, standing in the kitchen with
Carla and Maria looking sorry. *Fuck*.

Her hands on her hips, Joey taunted, "Yeah, Lou.
Why are you running scared?"

—∿∿—

Joey wanted to know. She missed Lou like crazy. Every
minute without him felt like forever. She'd thought she
could get over him easily enough. But she loved him and
she missed him. She'd put on a brave face for Brandon,
but he hadn't bought it. Proof he hadn't believed her had
come when Felix and Lou's sisters had arrived to kidnap
her while Becky and Brandon shook hands and placed
bets on who would apologize first. Not cool, Becky.

And since when did Felix get to involve himself in her
life? He'd blown his wad, literally, nearly a decade ago.

Then again, what did she have left to lose? "Yeah, Lou. Why are you running scared?" she'd asked, and she wanted an answer.

He started, seeing her there. She wondered if he realized how lost and confused and hungry he looked. Hungry for her.

Behind him, Stella rolled her finger, as if to signal "keep going."

"I've missed you, Lou. Why did you throw me away?" She hadn't meant to add that last part, and it came out with a few tears.

He softened perceptibly. "Aw, *cariña*. I'm sorry. It's just—"

"He thinks you're going to be like our mom," Lucia answered. "Because when we were little, Mama, bless her giving soul, had a lot of boyfriends. *A lot*. We didn't have money for sitters, hell, for food. And she'd be out laughing, wining and dining her flavor of the week. So Lou took care of us. He watched us, changed diapers, somehow scrounged food for us. Abuela would find out, scold Mama, and come help out to get us back on our feet. All would be well. Then she'd find a new man and ignore us all over again."

Stella looked sad. "And poor Lou thinks you'll do that. That any woman with a kid is capable of it if she's single. So he doesn't date single moms."

"And he doesn't want kids of his own," Carla added. "Oh, Lou. You're so wonderful. Why would you not want to share that with your own child?"

Lou looked more than uncomfortable. "Can we talk about this later? In private?" he asked his sisters, glancing at Joey, then Felix.

"No." Joey gave what she wanted him to hear. "I love you, Lou Cortez. Do you love me or not?"

He looked irritated. "Yes, damn it. You happy?" He shocked the entire room when he slammed his fist down on the kitchen island. The bang made Joey jump. "I can't eat. I can't sleep. I miss you all the time. *Fuck*. What do you want from me?"

"A chance, you big idiot," Stella answered before Joey could.

Felix bit back a grin and tugged Stella with him toward the front room. Out of the corner of her eye, Joey saw Carla, Maria, and Lucia join them, edging out the front door.

Leaving Joey and Lou alone. Together.

"You promised my son a Sounders game," she said.

He grimaced. "I didn't mean to. He's just so damn cute and likeable."

"You said you cared for me. You just admitted you love me."

"You're damn cute and likeable too," he growled.

"But I'm not your mother. I don't care how sexy you are, Lou. My son comes first. He always has. He always will. You need to trust me enough to know that."

"I do. I think." He rounded the counter and took her in his arms, searing her with a kiss that made her needy in seconds. "God. I want you so much. I need you back. But I'm... If I ever made Brandon feel like I did when I was young, I'd never forgive myself. Joey, I love my mother. But when I was a kid, and she was dating this guy or that one, sometimes I hated her," he ended in a whisper.

"Yeah? Well, I love and hate my parents all the time.

They judge me, they misunderstand me, and they insult me. How? By not acknowledging *I have my own mind*." She punctuated that last by poking him in the chest.

"Ow. Cut it out!"

"No." She punched him in the arm. And damn, but it felt good. "I love you, Lou. And it scares me to death. I've taken care of myself my whole life. I don't need anyone but Brandon. And you." She refused to cry again. "You showed me how to trust. How to open myself to a man and experience real love." She yanked him closer and took him by the chin, staring up into his eyes. "I know you'll always be there for me, because that's who you are. The kind of man who watches his girlfriend's apartment. Cares for her son and is always there for his family.

"Let me be part of that family. Let me help take care of you for a change."

"Joey."

"I want a real answer. Take a chance on me, Lou. Say yes and be there for kid soccer games. Taco Tuesday. Awkward dinners with the in-laws." Seeing him look ready to bolt at mention of "in-laws," she smiled. "A figure of speech. How about, the parents of your girl-friend instead? I tried, but I can't scrub you out of my mind. Or my heart. I love you. And I don't know what to do without you."

"Joey, I'm scared, *amor*. Of making you cry again. I hate hurting you." He pulled her in for a hug.

"Then how about you stop treating me like I'm frag-ile and make love to me again? I know I was an ugly sick person, but come on. You wouldn't touch me after you moved us in. Why?"

He flushed. "Because the boy was here."

"You're going to have to get over that. I want a man I can make love to. Not a tease."

"Stop." He dragged her closer and put her hand over his crotch. "You make me hard by breathing, *cariña*. You want me to prove it? We can go into the back and—"

"No. Stop!" His mother and grandmother appeared in the kitchen, his *abuela* with her hands over her ears.

Lou angled Joey in front of him, swearing under his breath.

"*M'ijo*, I'm so sorry." Renata sobbed. "It's all my fault. Oh, Luis, I'm sorry." Renata hugged her son to her with a desperation Joey would have called overly dramatic, except she felt it, being crushed between the pair. Apparently Abuela and Lou thought so too, because they sighed and rolled their eyes.

"See?" Lou said to her over his mother's head. "This is what you get if you come to live with me."

"Live with you?" Joey swallowed. "Brandon too?"

"Yeah. I owe him a Sounders game." Lou smiled, seeming finally to drop the tension and worry he'd been carrying. "I love you, baby. I'm sorry. I'll try to do better. But if it doesn't work, I'll—"

"Make it work," Abuela said in English, plain as day.

Lou gaped at his grandma. So did his mother.

Joey frowned. Hadn't he said his grandma didn't speak English? That sounded plain enough for her to understand. "What? Your grandma makes sense. No giving up or going back. Together, right...*Guapo*?" She laughed.

Lou gently nudged his mom aside. "Excuse me,

Mama, Abuela. Sorry, but I need to take my woman in hand. Can you get everyone outside to go home? I need privacy for me and my...*novia*."

Abuela and Renata clapped and yelled, then hustled out the door.

"Finally." Lou dragged Joey to the bedroom. "I promise. We'll move you guys in."

"Wait. *Novia*?"

"Sweetheart. The permanent kind."

"Oh, that's fine. But the moving in? That's a little soon for me, but—"

"No buts. Well, not those kind." He waggled his brows, and she blushed. "Strip, woman. We'll talk after. But right now I'm about to explode if I'm not inside you in the next forty-five seconds."

"Forty-five? Kind of specific, aren't you?"

"Forty-four, forty-three, forty-two..." he counted down as he stripped.

True to his word, he caused a major explosion when he got to one. Joey lost her mind, and her heart, to the second-most important man in her life. Her flower guy.

Chapter 23

A WEEK LATER, LOU THOUGHT IT A CRYING SHAME Joey continued to tease him about losing weight and getting crabby. So he'd missed her. So what? But no. Now she teased him about being sensitive. And J.T., that bastard, didn't deny it.

"Oh yeah. He was nearly in tears, missing you," the jerk was confiding as Joey shook with laughter while watching Brandon's soccer team race around the field on a sunny Saturday afternoon.

"Come on, Colin. Get the lead out," Del yelled as they watched her son run in pursuit of a goal.

"Go, Brandon," Lou boomed, turning several heads. "Sorry, too loud?"

"No, no." Liam smiled. "You're fine, Lou. Just fine."

J.T. chuckled. "Dad's just glad someone other than him is getting ogled by the SMA."

Joey frowned. "SMA?"

J.T. grinned. "Soccer Mom Association."

Joey and Del glared at him, and Joey said, "I'm a soccer mom, J.T."

"So am I," Del growled.

"In his defense, I wouldn't say ogled so much as frowned at," Liam added to be helpful.

Both Del and Joey glared him into silence.

"Anyway." Lou put his arm around Joey and led her a step away from J.T. "Are the new accommodations to your liking?" He'd officially moved her and Brandon into the house the previous night. Brandon had his own room, Joey and he had christened his bed the right way, and they had plans to see her parents at dinner. At her parents' home. Tonight. *Shoot me now.*

"I love the house." Joey pulled his face close. "I love you." She kissed him on the lips.

"Hurray!" From the field, Brandon cheered and pointed at them. Then got hit in the head with the ball because he hadn't been paying attention to the game.

"Ouch." Lou felt for the kid, who just smiled, all goofy, and went after the ball. Lou turned to Joey, only to see her staring at something in the parking lot. He followed her gaze. "What the... Is that Felix? With *Stella?*"

She smiled. "I thought I sensed something there. Don't worry. Felix isn't the boy he once was."

"But...*Stella?*"

"Look at it this way. He's a lawyer, and he's got a successful job. He's not a rocker, married, or in the mob."

Lou would talk to his little sister later. Felix...well, hell. He actually liked the guy. More because Felix had finally done right by Joey and Brandon. And because he didn't care for Joey's parents either. They had that solidarity going for them.

After a moment, Joey leaned back against his chest and wrapped his arm around her middle. "This, Lou. This is what I've always wanted."

"Yeah, me too," he whispered. "I love you."

"Now about us making Brandon that soccer team he wanted." She rubbed his hand over her belly. "Any thoughts about that?"

"One play at a time, Joey. Let's get through the wedding first."

"Soon as you're ready to propose, I'll think about saying I do."

He grinned. "I can do that. Just as soon as you come to Ray's with me to meet the guys, all proper-like."

"Oh boy. Is this some kind of rite of passage?"

J.T. must have overhead, because he snickered.

"What?" Lou asked.

"Even with her there, you won't beat him."

Joey tugged on his hand. "Explain."

"You're my good-luck charm. I need you with me to beat Johnny at darts. I do, *princesa*."

"Princess, hmm? So if I'm your princess, what does that make you?"

"Court jester?" J.T. offered.

"Your knight in shining armor," Lou corrected, sparing a glare for Del's troublemaking brother. "I'll be nice to your parents tonight. My best behavior."

"Done." She smiled then turned to J.T. "Now, J.T., when you get that date with a certain blond you've been *hoping* for, maybe we can double—hey, where are you going?" They watched him make an excuse and leave. To Lou, she said, "Too much?"

"Not enough. Damn, girl. Where have you been all my life?"

She smiled and kissed his hand. "Waiting for you."

About the Author

Caffeine addict, boy referee, and romance aficionado, *New York Times* and *USA Today* bestselling author Marie Harte is a confessed bibliophile and devotee of action movies. Whether hiking in Central Oregon, biking around town, or hanging at the local tea shop, she's constantly plotting to give everyone a happily ever after. Visit marieharte.com and fall in love.

ALL I WANT
FOR HALLOWEEN

Tonight, she plans to let go.

Dressed up and anonymous, Sadie Liberato feels powerful, sexy, and free. Where better to lose herself than a costume party?

Gear Blackstone's cheating ex and scheming best friend have managed to spin his life into a serious downward spiral. At least with a mask on he can cut loose for one night. And cut loose he does—with the sexiest, snarkiest woman he's ever met.

After a scorching-hot encounter, Sadie and Gear are desperate to find each other in real life. But can the heat last when the masks come off?

"Readers will swoon at the romantic gestures and fan themselves during the steamy love scenes."

—RT Book Reviews for Roadside Assistance

For more Marie Harte, visit:
www.sourcebooks.com

Also by Marie Harte

THE MCCAULEY BROTHERS
The Troublemaker Next Door
How to Handle a Heartbreaker
Ruining Mr. Perfect
What to Do with a Bad Boy

BODY SHOP BAD BOYS
Test Drive
Roadside Assistance
Zero to Sixty
Collision Course

THE DONNIGANS
A Sure Thing
Just the Thing

All I Want for Halloween